This is Not a House

Brandon Kitchen

Plotted Twists Publishing—Akron OH
ISBN: 979-8-218-33617-2
eBook ISBN: 979-8-8691-5978-6
Library of Congress Control Number: 2023924110
Title: *This is Not a House*
Author: Brandon Kitchen
Digital distribution | 2024
Paperback | 2024

Published in the United States by New Book Authors Publishing

Dedication

For all the houses that creak and moan in the night.

Ashwood. Before.

Ten-year-old Beatrice woke in her daybed to the sound of screaming from somewhere in the sleeping house. The powder blue comforter was draped over her tiny body, shielding her from whatever evil lurked in another room. Sitting up, she blinked in the darkness of her bedroom. Shadows from the jagged tree branches outside the turret window swayed against the walls and the floor, beckoning her to wake up. Her crocheted elephant lay next to her, its button eyes unfazed by the noises.

The screaming hadn't stopped, and Beatrice realized that it was coming from downstairs. Her thin eyebrows pulled together in confusion. *Why on earth would someone be screaming that loudly this late in the night?* Beatrice thought to herself, angling her body to look out the window at the full moon in the starry sky. Ashwood was suffocated in strange noises, but nothing was quite as terrifying as the scream from downstairs.

The white wooden door to the bedroom burst open and Beatrice's mother, Lena, barreled through in a hurry. She wore a plain white t-shirt and high-waisted jeans, her forehead covered in sweat. Her wavy brown hair was in a loose ponytail down her back, and she was flinging herself toward Beatrice with so much force Beatrice thought she was being thrown.

"Beatrice sweetie, we're leaving," her mother told her, grabbing her hard by the wrist and yanking her out of the bed. The tug was so hard that Beatrice yelped in pain and she wondered if her shoulder had dislocated.

"Where are we going?" Beatrice wondered, able to snatch up her elephant by the ear at the last second.

The ancient floor beneath them creaked under their weight. Beatrice struggled to find her balance. Lena snatched her daughter's coat off the back of the door, bundling her up inside it as fast as possible. Her actions were fleeting and twitchy, uncoordinated, and full of a fear that Beatrice had never seen in her mother before. Her eyes kept flickering right then left and then above, as though something was going to come exploding out of the walls. All of the adults in Beatrice's life seemed like they were fearless. Living in Ashwood should have that quality on a person. But her mom, this terrified, was something Beatrice never thought she would see. It forced a fear so significant to swell inside of her, that a ball the size of her fist formed quickly in her throat. Tears flooded her eyes and a single one streamed down her cheek.

"You are going to listen to what I say, okay, honey?" Her mother squatted down to be at eye level with her daughter. Her huge, chocolate brown eyes were pretty much the only quality that Beatrice's parents shared, all three of them having the same pair—according to Lena.

Beatrice nodded her head, ignoring her heart fluttering around in her rib cage, like a lost little hummingbird, desperate for an escape.

"We're going to run as fast as we can out the front door, okay?" she asked, cupping Beatrice's face in her ice-cold hands. Her words trembled out of her mouth and a few strands of her hair stuck to her forehead. "No matter what we hear or see, we're going to run really, really fast into the hall, down the stairs, and then out the door. Do you understand?"

Beatrice felt the ball in her throat grow larger, going from a fist size to what seemed like the size of her very own head. Tears tried coming to her eyes but Beatrice held them back as best as she could. Her mother never liked seeing her cry though, so she simply nodded so she wouldn't have to speak.

"Do you understand?" Lena demanded in a sterner voice this time, shaking Beatrice's head in her hands.

"Y-yes," she stammered. "Yes, I understand."

"Let's go." Her mother held onto her hand so hard that Beatrice wondered if *she* was more afraid than Beatrice was.

As her mother dragged Beatrice into the hallway, she could feel the bone in her hand *click*. The screaming had stopped but there was a rumbling noise from downstairs. Beatrice wasn't sure what the noise was, but it reminded her of a growling stomach. It was almost like the entire house was shifting against the earth, stirring in its sleep. Or like something inside of it was bubbling with life, preying on whatever was in sight.

Beatrice listened to her mother's heavy breathing on their way down the hall and then down the stairs. The front door was right at the bottom and the two of them dashed out of it so fast, Beatrice couldn't even glance behind her to the kitchen. Where was everyone else? If this was some big emergency, shouldn't Aunt Edie and Aunt Marley be following them out? Shouldn't they wait for them?

The front lawn was cold with dew by the time Beatrice and her mother approached it. The moon hung low and fat in the sky, the twinkling stars around it oblivious to whatever was happening all the way down here on Earth. The carved jack-o-lanterns lit up the night with candles inside of their mouths, their faces menacing and beginning to rot.

"Keep running, baby," her mom told Beatrice halfway across the round, cobblestone driveway. "I'll catch up with you."

"Where are you going?" Beatrice asked her, stopping to wait.

Her mom was already trotting back toward the house, the moon shining down on her like a spotlight. "Bea, I said go! *Now!*"

And that was the last time Beatrice saw her. Her figure faded away into the darkness of the night, darkness that had no leverage over what Ashwood was carrying.

· ══◇══ ·

Chapter 1

“I don't know what to say,” Beatrice Millstone says, stifling a laugh as she awkwardly fingers the doorknob to her apartment.

"Well, aren't you going to invite me in?" Kevin-something asks, looming over her with a douchey grin playing across his douchey lips. They're standing under the dim wall lights in the hallway, making them both look equally unflattering but unequally drunk. Beatrice is all for her red wine, but this guy was downing his glass at dinner like beer at a frat party.

Beatrice doesn't usually do dating apps. When she does, she typically doesn't go out on a whim and takes someone's offer. Tonight's was to buy her a colorful drink at a not-very-colorful bar or a fancy dinner at a restaurant with menu items she doesn't even know how to pronounce. And she sure as hell tries to dodge those awkward coffee dates where it might end in a strange goodbye hug or a kiss that tastes too much like bad coffee. She's had her fair share. Or, rather, *unfair* share.

Kevin falls under the category of every other guy Beatrice has found on dumb dating apps she only downloads when she's bored... or when she remembers that she's not getting any younger and finding someone to love might not be a bad thing after all. Kevin doesn't make the cut. His privilege is a turnoff, and he has this arrogance about him that a lot of the guys here in New York tend to carry on their broad, hairless backs. They're all the same. They spend the summers in the Hamptons on boats owned by their fathers. Some of them live on trust funds and most of them have past college scandals that have been covered up with stacks of money.

"I don't think that's a good idea," she responds, fiddling with her keys in her hand, wishing her neighbor, Ralph, would come out of his apartment to scare him off. Ralph is the only good thing about this building. An older gentleman, he's made friends with most of the younger females to fend off predators if he deems it necessary. Ralph's husband died years ago and instead of remarrying, he spends his days driving away the Kevins of the world. "It's late, I'm tired, you're

1

probably tired…."

"Oh, come on." Kevin leans in some more, his breath smelling of mashed potatoes and the showy, costly, buttery steak from dinner. *Ew.* "I can sleep over. We can make a night of it. I'll even let you cook me breakfast."

Beatrice scoffs. He will *let* her cook? She smiles sweetly with a dash of thinly veiled sarcasm in it. Tess had taught her well. "First off, the fact that you think I need your permission to do anything, speaks volumes. Secondly, I don't cook. Especially for guys like you. Good night."

"Fine." Kevin grunts, his face distorting into that of a pouty child, one who has never been told 'no.' "You're not my type anyway."

"Funny how quickly things change, huh?" Beatrice shuts the door to her apartment behind her. She moves to drop her keys into the bowl on the table to her left. Then she remembers that there is no bowl anymore because there is no table.

The furniture in the apartment is scarce of the sturdy chairs and odds and ends which used to make Beatrice feel like she finally made it. After all of these years of being lost in the world, she thought that when she made it to the city, she really *made* it into adulthood. To Beatrice, one of the best things to do as an adult was spending money on furniture and décor for a place she could finally call her own. Together, she and Tess decked the whole place out in creative, Japanese art and high-back chairs and Parisian chaise lounges from the antique store where Beatrice works. Tess even brought home some Mexican-inspired pillows and curtains to make Bea feel like she was more at "home"—even though her dad's side of the family is Hispanic and he didn't raise her and she wasn't even born in Mexico.

Now, standing here alone, staring at the almost empty apartment, Beatrice is not only sad but also insanely stressed. Her landlord gave her an eviction notice last week with a perky smile and a, *"Sorry you're not rich enough to live in the city!"* tone of voice. It took everything in Beatrice not to smack the powdery makeup off her doughy cheeks. Instead, she wasted no time logging into her unused Facebook account to list almost everything in her apartment on the marketplace. From the unused pizza oven to the Japanese rug under the coffee table, her life was online, on display for all to judge its worth. Everything had to leave before it was her turn. She wasn't sure where she was going or how she would get there, but she couldn't do it without any money. She keeps telling herself it'll be an adventure, that she'll be one of those edgy girls who just go with the flow of things, free from worry about what's to follow. Frustratingly, Beatrice knows she can't lie to herself *that* well.

She was unprepared for this upheaval; her now ex-bestie and roommate went MIA, off to follow her drug-addicted boyfriend, without warning. When Beatrice called to inform her about how she's been having to pay full price for rent, Tess laughed it off and said it was no big deal. Bitch. Two months later, the eviction notice came, and Beatrice has been scrambling ever since.

And yeah, she's been on a date or two since then. If anyone else was in her position, they would do the same thing. They would try meeting an eligible bachelor and if he has all the right qualities for a boyfriend, they could easily move in together in no time. She wouldn't have any worries. New York City dating moves just as fast as the bustling traffic. Needless to say, that isn't the route working for her, so with exactly $823.79 to her name, she's way too broke to live on her own in New York… unless she moves "in" with the homeless crew in front of the church around the corner.

Beatrice jumps at the sound of her ringing phone. She takes it out of the pocket of her brown leather satchel slung on her shoulder. Clara's name is across the screen, and a photo of them smiling on Beatrice's fourteenth birthday.

"Before you even ask, it didn't go well." Beatrice puts the phone to her ear, making her way into the living room and plopping down on the bamboo chair, her last available spot to sit.

"Why not?" Clara whines on the other end, sounding like a teenage girl instead of the 40-something-year-old woman she is. "I told you to show off some cleavage, didn't I? That was the problem, wasn't it? You weren't showing enough boob."

Beatrice rolls her eyes. "I shouldn't have to show off boobs to get a guy to like me."

"What era are you living in, sweetie?" Clara jokes.

Beatrice sighs heavily, grinning anyway. She picks up her stuffed elephant from under her thigh and stares at the green buttons on the face. "Maybe I'll become an elephant lady."

"An elephant lady?"

"Instead of a cat lady. I'll move to Africa and just own a bunch of elephants. You know they're the only animal to think humans are cute?"

"Cats are a lot easier to take care of."

"Yeah, but being a cat lady is too cliché," Beatrice responds casually, tossing the plushie onto the bamboo stool in front of her.

"Well, dammit," Clara says. "I poured myself a glass of red wine, all eager to hear about your date. I really thought he was going to be your prince charming."

"Ew, please don't ever think I'm going to have a prince charming," Beatrice barks, reaching down to untie her boots. "Besides, I don't have time to find a guy to take me in right away anymore. I have to be out of this place by like, yesterday."

Of course, Beatrice has considered asking Clara if she could move in with her. After her mother's death, instead of going into the foster system like an orphan, Clara, her mom's best friend, scooped her up and signed the adoption papers without any hesitation. She had no kids of her own at the time and did everything in her power to be what had been taken from Beatrice: a loving, supportive, wonderful mother. No one would ever be Lena. But if there was anyone in the world that came damn close, it was Clara.

On the way home from the police station *that* night, Clara and Beatrice stopped at a Walmart and bought an air mattress for Beatrice to sleep on for the night in Clara's constricted downtown apartment. When they got to Beatrice's new home, they made a fort with every pillow and blanket they could find in the apartment and slept together on the lumpy air mattress that popped the very next day. Beatrice quietly sobbed herself to sleep again that night, replaying what happened with her mother at Ashwood over and over again in her head, concluding that she may never know the truth.

Clara now has a wife and two sons. Even though she never *asked* Clara to take her in when she was ten, and never asked for anything from her, for that matter, she still doesn't want to disrupt the pretty little family Clara has built for herself. That isn't fair. Sure, Clara is the one who fought for custody after the whole debacle, but Beatrice doesn't want to take away from her life now. She's done enough already. Inserting herself into her home with her kids and wife is something she can't bring herself to do. Of course, Clara has offered repeatedly to take her in until she finds a new place but Beatrice vowed to her that she would figure things out on her own, still forcing herself to believe she's more grown-up than she is.

"We still have the couch available over here," Clara tells her, bringing her back to reality. "It's a pullout with squeaky springs that are just *screaming* your name."

"Sounds tempting." Beatrice traces her fingers over a wine stand in the bamboo chair cushion.

"I'm serious, Beatrice," she tells her. "You know that Mandy and I would have no problem making room for you here. I hate to see you struggle."

"I'm fine," Beatrice promises. "Really. I'll figure something out. If worse comes to worse, I'll take you up on your squeaky pull-out sofa bed."

Clara smiles through the phone. "If you say so. Just call or text if you need anything. Even if it's food."

"Will do."

Beatrice stays seated for a few minutes, drumming her fingers against her knee, her eyes glued to her phone. She's been considering phoning Aunt Edie for quite some time, but it's a consideration she's never spoken aloud to anyone yet. She and Aunt Edie are the last two living branches of the Millstone family tree. Aunt Edie never offered to care for Beatrice after that final night at Ashwood. She would make her routine calls every Christmas and birthday, but they were usually clipped conversations over the phone, both of them in a hurry to get on with their days instead of doing the whole small talk thing. Beatrice once asked Clara why a member of her own family didn't take her after that night.

Clara considered Beatrice's question for a moment before answering. "Your Aunt Edie is pretty old, kiddo. It's probably best if I just keep you for now."

At the time, the response made Beatrice feel like a piece of furniture passed from person to person, a piece delicate and rare, something most find unsuitable for the "everyday." A piece that clashed with the rest of the design. That emotion didn't last long, though. Clara was the best.

As much as she doesn't *want* to call her aunt, Beatrice is running out of options… there's also a small part of her that is curious about facing her childhood. A very slim part that Beatrice has ignored for years. The last she checked, Aunt Edie was still living at Ashwood, renting rooms out to college students who work for her to be maids and housekeepers. Surely Aunt Edie would immediately let Beatrice in, wouldn't she? Wouldn't she give a shit or two about a family member in need? After all, it's the least she could do, considering she didn't even budge when Beatrice required a new guardian.

Beatrice makes her way into the kitchen, her mind buzzing with thoughts and predictions on what Aunt Edie could answer with. Maybe she's changed after all these years. Maybe she'd say no and claim that her house is already being rented by a student or two and there is no room for her there. Or, maybe, she'll say yes and the two of them will reconnect like nothing has changed. Beatrice stands on her tiptoes to reach for the jumbo bag of Chex-Mix off the top of her fridge. She highly doubts the two of them will bond with each other the way they did back when Beatrice was a resident at Ashwood. That train has been long gone, frozen in the past and only movable in memories.

She plops down on the kitchen floor, opens the bag, and stuffs her hand inside. This is what her life has become: sitting on her kitchen floor because she doesn't have furniture and eating Chex-Mix for dinner because she doesn't have food in the fridge and she had Kevin buy her a lame salad earlier. She is going to swallow whatever awkward pride she has been carrying around after all these years and call up her last living relative to ask for a very simple favor. Hell, she could even get some work done there. Beatrice's boss, Declan, loves it when his employees bring in fresh furniture for the store. The Ashwood attic was stuffed with old furniture not being used the last time Beatrice was there.

Beatrice's heart drums loudly within her chest as she scrolls through her contact list in search of her aunt's name. She isn't quite sure why she's so nervous. She doesn't want to be. She knows this is the last resort. If this doesn't work out, she might as well take that bamboo chair from the living room and attach a mailbox to it because she's sure to be stuffed under that in the streets in no time. Pulling up Aunt Edie's contact, Beatrice holds her breath as she clicks on the little phone icon, her screen switching into call mode. She holds her breath during the four rings it takes before there's a *click*.

"Beatrice?" Aunt Edie asks on the other end, concern bleeding through her tone of voice. "Are you all right?"

"Yes, I'm fine," Beatrice lies. There is nothing fine about what is happening right now. It's truly pathetic, but she doesn't want to worry Aunt Edie right off the bat. She'll ease into the conversation. Like slowly dipping into a pool, maybe even convincing her that returning home for a bit is her idea and that she's not being forced to. "Why wouldn't I be?"

"Oh, well, I don't know," she says in her usual breathy voice that had always reminded Beatrice of old Hollywood actresses who wore glamorous ball gowns and dripped in pearls. That's Edie in a nutshell.

"Usually we don't call each other unless it's on an important day." There's rustling on her end. "It's October eighteenth."

"I know, and I hate to call so late, but I kind of have a small, little, tiny favor to ask you." Beatrice winces at her attempt at trying to make the fact she's going to ask her to move in sound like the smallest favor in the world. But comparing this to the favor of becoming her legal guardian is a pretty big difference.

"Of course," Aunt Edie quickly agrees. Concern is no longer leaking through the phone's speaker. Instead, it's guilt. Guilt that she didn't buck up years ago and take Beatrice under her wing after her mother died. That is what family is supposed to do, especially a family as close as theirs. "Anything, darling."

Beatrice swallows a chunk of pretzel and clears her throat. "So, I was hoping to come by Ashwood soon. The antique store I work at has been doing super well and my boss is worried that we're going to run out of all our big pieces of furniture by the end of the month. So, he's been encouraging us to find anything we can anywhere. And then I remembered the attic and how there was a lot of unused stuff up there that you and Ma were trying to get rid of at one point, right?"

"Oh yes, there's quite a load up there," she confirms, sounding a little annoyed at the admission. "You can take what you want. The more of that old shit that gets out of here, the better."

Beatrice raises her eyebrows at how quickly she agrees. She and Aunt Edie aren't exactly as close as they used to be, but she surely didn't expect her to agree to this so fast. "Really?"

"Of course," Aunt Edie tells her smoothly. "In fact, I'm going to need all that junk cleared out anyway. I've been toying with the idea of putting the house on the market."

The statement makes Beatrice's blood run cold, but she has no idea why. She hasn't stepped foot in Ashwood in over fifteen years. Why should it matter that Aunt Edie wants to sell it? Beatrice thinks on it a little longer, remembering the hell that took place in that house. All of the strange happenings that no one could explain. She was a resident there for ten years. Even though she can't remember every single thing that happened, the big stuff still rings alarms inside of her mind. That last night can still play through her head like a movie she sat down and watched just minutes ago. A horrible, terrifying, life-changing movie.

So now, Aunt Edie wants to put it up for sale for some new people to buy it? Why? So they can experience what their family had to experience? To prove that the Millstone Curse has nothing to do with the house but only the family members inside of it? Honestly, if Aunt Edie was even close to being smart, she wouldn't sell it to just anyone. She could put it on the market for one of those tourist places people take their picture in front of, posting on social media that they were in *the* Ashwood house. Then, they could make up lies about feeling a brush of cold air against their arm or hearing walking around upstairs. It *must* be a ghost.

Or, instead of either of those things, she could always burn the damn thing down. It might help save a lot of people.

"You're selling the house?" Beatrice finally brings herself to say, wandering back to their conversation.

"It's nothing set in stone yet," she promises, catching Beatrice's attention again. "But this house is fairly big for little old me. And even though I'm not getting as old as one might think I am, it might be time to find something a little cozier."

If there's one thing that Beatrice hasn't forgotten about Aunt Edie, it's her age denial.

"Don't you rent out a room to people?"

"That has slowed down significantly." She sighs heavily, crackling coming through the phone. "They come and go so fast that I spend more time looking for tenants than I do with them living here. Can you believe that?"

Yes. Yes I can, Beatrice wants to say but she bites her tongue. Perhaps this isn't a good idea. Maybe Beatrice is scrambling a little *too* much for a new home. Does she really want to go back there? Does she really want to put herself in a position to experience what she experienced in that house as a kid? There's probably a reason why none of the people she recruits stick around. That house is screwed up in ways their sheltered little minds could never fathom. But Beatrice grew up around those happenings. It was almost normal in her childhood, but that doesn't mean she's fully prepared to go back.

When she moved in with Clara and was given a therapist and even went to public school full-time, she realized that her childhood was far from normal. She learned that other kids lived in suburban neighborhoods with houses right next door. She learned that when doors slammed shut by themselves in their homes, it was something out of the ordinary. Or that sleepwalking and night terrors aren't things that are supposed to happen every couple of days with multiple people in the house. Everything Beatrice grew up around was tilted on its axis and was no longer something normal. It became a strange thing to look back on, scary, even. So why in the hell is she calling up Aunt Edie asking for her old room back?

"Maybe this was a bad idea," Beatrice finds herself saying into the phone, clearing her voice. Her cousins were taken from that yard. Uncle Eli, Grandpa Hugh, and Aunt Marley all died in that house. Beatrice's mother saved her daughter before going back inside just to join them in death. All of those things just go to prove that moving back to Ashwood is more like a death wish than a last resort.

"What are you talking about?" Aunt Edie scolds, the way she used to do when she caught the kids running too fast inside. "I think it sounds magnificent. And, I know how expensive city living can be, especially when you don't crap dollar bills if you know what I mean. If you help me fix up the house a bit, I can pay you."

Beatrice perks up. "Like, a job?"

"Yes, that's right," she replies. "You can fix up the house and get paid for it while you get a handle on all that old furniture upstairs. It's a win-win. You get a pretty little penny, and I can get out of here faster than I thought."

Beatrice wonders how on earth Aunt Edie could stay in that house after all these years in the first place. But it doesn't take her long to remember that even though Beatrice began realizing how unusual Ashwood was, being with Clara and living in Brooklyn made her start to miss it. She would regret not cherishing the woods behind the house where she and the twins would play with Xander, making crowns and thrones out of logs and sticks. She would spend nights wishing she was in her own bed, listening to the creaks and moans of the house, bracing itself against the gusts of wind outside. She would miss the smell of old books in the cluttered study on the second floor and how her mother and Aunt Marley tried their hand at gardening but their flowers never fully bloomed. She missed the smell of Grandma Astrid's cinnamon cookies, a smell that never really went away. She missed the brick fireplace in the mud room off the kitchen and how they would all gather around it during the winter instead of turning on the furnace. She remembers waddling around Ashwood bundled up in clothes her mother put her in, rolling from room to room. Despite that house being a series of unfortunate events, it's still Aunt Edie's home. And whether Beatrice liked it or not, it was her home, too.

"I miss you," Aunt Edie says after a moment of silence.

Beatrice runs her tongue over her teeth, wondering what she should say back to that. Regular people would probably respond with an, *I miss you too.* But Beatrice doesn't miss her and she doesn't miss that house. Her eyes flicker up at the 80's-movie-of-the-month calendar tacked to the wall across from the fridge. She needs to be out of here by the day after tomorrow. She has run out of options. She rubs her nails against the side of her thigh, trying to conjure up her mom to tell her what she should do. It'll just be for a few short nights. She doesn't even have to spend every waking minute inside. She will get there, do some work for her aunt, collect the furniture from upstairs, and see how things go after that. Maybe that weird stuff doesn't even happen anymore. Maybe now, after all these years, things will be different, and Beatrice can walk away from it this time with a little more money in her pocket.

"You're sure I won't be a burden?" Beatrice asks warily, kind of hoping Aunt Edie will return to being her overly blunt self and agree with her. "I don't want to be in your way."

"Nonsense, my dear," Aunt Edie scolds with a *tsk* sound. "The house misses you."

After hanging up, Beatrice tosses the rest of the Chex-Mix bag into the trash, the little crumbs at the bottom falling out. She makes her way into her bedroom, where her mattress waits on the floor. She collapses onto it, mentally exhausted from the day's events. Her phone is at 8% battery, a little pop-up slides down the top of her screen to suggest plugging it in. She deletes Tinder, Kevin probably unmatching with her before he even reached his car on the curb outside. Another one bites the dust, apparently.

She plugs her phone into the outlet next to her mattress and tosses it to the side. She curls up under the blanket and thinks about what it will be like to return to Ashwood as she pulls her nameless elephant close to her chest. This is something she can't tell Clara about. She will be on the first cab to Massachusetts, determined to drag her away from the house without a minute's thought. Beatrice can't entirely blame her. She'd do the same thing.

Beatrice has never believed in hauntings or ghosts or any of that paranormal bullshit that other people have tried forcing down her throat her entire life. But there is something in Ashwood, something that lingers in the night. Something that wasn't a ghost, but most certainly wasn't human, either.

Chapter 2

The following day, Beatrice wakes up bright and early to start packing. By bright and early, it's actually going on noon, but she had a rough day yesterday so cut her some slack.

She starts with her clothes in the closet. Yanking her shirts off hangers, she stuffs them into the last two suitcases Tess left behind before she departed. She claimed that she was only going to use one of the suitcases for her trip with her boyfriend but she pretty much took them all. Beatrice begins making a pile of clothes to sell, next. She has the entire day. She could meet up with a few more people off Facebook and sell more of her shit before leaving for Massachusetts. Even if a shirt costs seven dollars, that is money that is making her seven whole dollars richer. She'll take what she can get, at this point—even if she spots twinkling pennies in parking lots.

Beatrice bundles up her jeans and shorts—though she won't need the shorts since it's the middle of October. She squeezes them into the two suitcases she has, tossing more than half of them into the sell pile. This is going to be an eventful day. She will finally be rid of this shitty apartment that is way too expensive and she will no longer be drowning her bank account with payments she can't afford. When things go wrong with her boyfriend, Tess will come back to an empty place and have nowhere to go. By that time, Beatrice will be set with a few large funds in her account and she will be back here in the city in no time. She can feel it.

There's a knock at the front door and Beatrice tosses a few camisoles into her suitcase before heading into the living room to open it.

The landlord, Becky, stands in the poorly lit hallway with a pinched smile across her pale pink lips. She has shiny blond hair that curls at the end, apparently going for a Carol Brady-type look that makes Beatrice want to reach out and flat iron it every time she sees her.

"Sandra, hi," Becky greets her in that high-pitched voice that would make you want to claw at your ears until they fall off. "Just the gal I wanted to see."

"Well, I am the only one that lives here," Beatrice utters as Becky makes her way into the apartment, an assaulting cloud of Chanel No. 5 perfume lingering over her. "And my name is Beatrice, by the way."

"Oh, I'm sorry, what did I say?" Becky puts a hand to her chest, giggling like a schoolgirl. She wears a tweed pink jacket and matching short skirt, her kitten pumps something straight out of the 1950s. "So, listen, today is your last day in the building and I really need you to be out of here faster than you were hoping."

Beatrice blinks. "You said I had until tomorrow to be out."

"Now, now, now, missy." Becky wags her finger in front of her. "No need to get tight with me. I am still your landlord, you know."

"Not if I need to be out ASAP," Beatrice shoots at her. "What do you mean, sooner than I expected?"

"Well, I have a potential tenant who wants to check the place out," Becky explains before looking around in disgust. "And no offense, but it's going to take a bit of time to scrub the grime off the floors and walls. I would like them to picture what this place has to offer. The negative energy that you lug around just won't do it."

Beatrice sets her jaw back as she marches into her bedroom to finish up her packing. She ignores the comment about the negativity she lugs around. Not everyone can be rainbows and sunshine like pretty little Becky. "Well, if I would've known this sooner, I could've been out of your hair already."

"I tried calling the landline but since you haven't paid your electric bill, it didn't go through." Becky follows her into the bedroom, that bitchy little smirk on her face and the annoying clacking of her kitten heels following after.

No wonder Beatrice woke up with an uncharged phone and no night light—damn electric bill.

"Well, that information is loud and clear," Beatrice says to her, throwing the last of her clothes into the pathetic suitcases waiting to be stuffed on her bed. "I'll be out in no time."

"Do you have a new place to go?" Becky's tone is thick with fake sympathy, a question she doesn't care to know the answer to but is taking the opportunity to milk this moment for what it is.

Beatrice squints, yanking her charger out of the wall. "What's it to you?"

"Now, now, Belinda, no need to get all defensive," Becky singsongs, putting her lace-gloved hands on her rounded hips. "I'm your friend. Excuse me for being concerned if you have a roof over your head and food to eat. I mean, anything would beat what you've made in this apartment. Trust me, I've smelled a thing or two from the hallway and my appetite was lost so fast—"

"Last I checked, the only thing you were concerned with is getting your rent check on time," Beatrice fires back. Part of her wants to get out of here as fast as possible so she won't have to deal with Becky's bullshit any longer. But the other part of her doesn't want to leave without a little something. "Also, that eviction notice you gave me didn't say anything about my stay here being cut short under any circumstances. So, unless you want me to sue your ass, I suggest you buy some of the things that I can't haul out of here in time for your new precious tenant. And before they get here, I'll make sure all types of grime are on these floors from those God-awful meals I used to make."

Becky's smile is no longer pinched. It's nonexistent. She's flaring her nostrils the way ladies do at retail stores before asking for a manager. She digs into the pocket of her skirt for her lime green coin purse. "What needs to be purchased?"

There was no way Beatrice was going to sue Becky. She would have to have money for a lawyer for that to happen. But lucky for her, Becky doesn't know how broke she is. So, after selling her bamboo chair and her clothes, Beatrice is walking away with a hundred more dollars than she was originally going to leave with. Did someone say cha-ching?

She checks the time on her way down the sidewalk with her suitcase. It's going on two. She called Aunt Edie before leaving the apartment, asking if it was okay if she got there a little earlier than expected but Edie said 5:00 worked better for her so Beatrice has an hour to stop by the shop to tell Declan her big news—probably the only person that will know where she is. As much as she wants to tell Clara about her leaving, it will have to wait until she comes up with a reasonable lie about where she's going and for how long.

After taking a cab to the other side of Brooklyn, Beatrice lugs her suitcases into Trinkets and Treasures behind her, the rusty bell above the door announcing her arrival, as it did the first day she started work here. Beatrice found her job here soon after telling Clara that she wouldn't be attending college and she was welcomed into the Trinkets and Treasure family with open arms. The team consists of Beatrice, her boss Declan, and a girl named Jewel with bright pink hair and a resting bitch face. Beatrice and Jewel get along well. They're the only two who run the store so they're constantly working together. But it's not one of those friendships where they force hanging out with each other outside of work. They simply talk each other's ear off behind the counter and then go their separate ways when they clock out. It's just the way Beatrice likes it and it seems like Jewel prefers it that way, too.

Trinkets and Treasures is located in an old red brick building with noisy wooden floors and ocean-blue walls that sort of make you feel like you're drowning. Chandeliers and similar lights for sale hang from the ceiling, casting different shades of glow onto various pieces of furniture collected over a couple of decades. The entire place is cluttered with junk to some, treasure to others.

"Hey," Beatrice greets Jewel at the counter on the right side of the main floor, careful to not run her luggage into anything fragile.

"Moving in?" Jewel raises a pierced eyebrow as she observes Beatrice's suitcase. She's leaning over the counter with a thick book in front of her, the title in a language Beatrice isn't familiar with.

"Actually, moving out. Of the city." Beatrice holds her chin in the air, as though the news is something she couldn't wait to announce. Usually, people are proud to say that they're moving *to* the city. They're not always that excited when they have to move out because money is stupid and being broke pretty much means death in today's day and age.

Jewel's eyebrow stays inched up her forehead and she curiously closes her book. "No, you're not."

"What does this look like?" Beatrice gestures to her suitcase.

"Looks pretty sad if all of your belongings are actually in there," Jewel says back, studying her closely. She leans forward a little, her breath smelling like caramel and coffee. "Oh my god, please tell me you're on the run from the police. That would make you so much more interesting."

"Shut up." Beatrice grins and then heaves a breath. "No, I'm not on the lam. I'm taking a trip to Massachusetts to do some work."

"For here?"

Beatrice nods. "If it's all right with Declan."

"If what's all right with Declan?" Declan himself comes sweeping into the main floor from the basement door—where a lot of vintage children's stuff is. He's carrying a set of teacups in his hands, gently setting them down on the counter. He's forty-something and tall, with smooth dark skin and a bald head. Veins are almost always popping out of his arms and face and Jewel and Beatrice joke that he constantly looks constipated.

"I was hoping that you'd let me have some time off to do some work in Massachusetts," Beatrice explains, talking fast before he can tell her that it's a terrible idea. "There's a house there that has some nice pieces, stuff we've never seen before. I thought I'd swing by, take some notes, do some research, send pictures… that sort of thing."

It's not uncommon for the three of them to venture off to find new things for the shop. When Jewel was visiting her family in Vietnam, she brought back a bunch of old dolls and ceramics, anything she could bring back on the plane with her. And when Declan's parents died, he wiped their house clean with anything that could be used in the shop, showing no emotional attachment to a single thing.

Declan's upturned nose wrinkles. "What house?"

Jewel squints when Beatrice doesn't answer right away. Beatrice mentioned stuff from her past here and there in conversations with the two of them, but she never dove into the deep end with all of Ashwood's baggage. The two of them never realized how much of a shit show her childhood home has been painted to be in the media because they never once gushed about all the rumors *they* heard online. That could only mean they don't know a single thing about Ashwood and Beatrice would like to keep it that way.

"I have a relative—an aunt—she's getting rid of some stuff before she sells her house," Beatrice answers honestly. "She needs some help with housework before putting it on the market and I'm the only one she has."

Jewel looks excited, her eyes flickering over to their boss. "Does this mean I get overtime?" She looks back at Beatrice. "No offense to you, you'll be missed and all, but I'm like, broker than broke."

Trust me, you're not, Beatrice wants to say.

Declan thinks about it. "How long do you think you'll be out?"

Beatrice shrugs her shoulders because she honestly doesn't know yet. "Depends on what needs to be done, how much there is. But I promise I will keep in contact as much as I can."

"Okay," Declan agrees. "I don't see why not. My niece is looking for a part-time job so maybe she can fill in for the time being."

Beatrice feels like a weight has been lifted. She smiles. "Perfect."

After saying goodbye to Jewel and Declan, Beatrice soon finds herself in a Starbucks sandwiched between a pizza joint and a pub. She plugs her phone and her laptop into the outlet under her table, charging up for the ride. She turns her laptop on, impatiently waiting for it to boot up and flicker to her home screen. Her wallpaper is a photo of her and

Clara, arms around each other at her high school graduation. After the picture was taken, Clara burst into tears about how fast Beatrice was growing up and how proud she was of her, even though Beatrice told her she wasn't going to college the night before. After a long conversation about it, Clara finally agreed and said she would be supportive of her no matter what she does.

She pulls up Google on her laptop, her fingers hovering over the patient keyboard. When she had access to technology after moving in with Clara, Beatrice found herself diving into the deep corners of the internet, pockets of the online world where most people didn't bother venturing into. She would read article after article and theory after theory about Ashwood. People all over the country post on forums and gossip pages about the Millstone family, determined to solve the case of this huge curse that has plagued them all. Even though Beatrice no longer lived at Ashwood, doesn't mean she unplugged it from her life. Every now and again, she'd load a site or two dedicated to her family and read about sightings of her mother and what Jax and Juniper would look like today. She shakes the thought from her mind, the twins spilling out of her thoughts like dropped pieces of candy.

Ashwood, Silver Creek, Massachusetts Beatrice types into the bar stretching across the screen. Silver Creek is a small town about two hours away from Boston. Its rivers run like veins under its large bridges and through patches of wood. The town is layered with houses on hills and little shops through cobblestone streets. The homes are mostly all old Victorian structures that have since been renovated into modern homes that residents change after moving in. Nothing has ever been adjusted when it comes to Ashwood, as far as Beatrice knows. It has stayed the same since it was built. That's how the Millstones liked it.

The first few results are the usual articles with the usual headlines:

Is Ashwood Cursed?

Whatever happened to Twins Jax and Juniper Millstone? We Break Down the Case.

Will the Mysteries of Ashwood Get its Own Show on Netflix?

Are Any Members of the Millstone Family Alive?

Ashwood: Cursed From Within.

Beatrice scrolls down the page, hunting for the site she used to select that was run by everyday people, not hungry journalists posting for click-bait. And then she finds it under an article saying Aunt Edie refuses to do interviews about the house. It's a site called *Inside Ashwood,* as though the creators have lived inside of it themselves.

Beatrice clicks on the link anyway and a pixelated site loads onto the screen, a black and white image of Ashwood displayed behind the homepage as though it's some ancient, haunted house that will soon be the star of its own Hollywood film—not some Netflix original. Beatrice leans in closer to read the introduction paragraph in the hard-to-read white script:

Greetings from Ashwood! This website is dedicated to all things Ashwood House: the mysterious home belonging to the Millstone family that took more than half of its members inside. Please feel free to share any information regarding the house and the mysterious deaths and disappearances of the family. If you have any serious info that is FACTS, please call the Silver Creek police IMMEDIATELY. There are two children still missing. Any information that is placed in the wrong hands can be detrimental to them and the family. The users of this site take this very seriously. Those who make asses of themselves will be BLOCKED. Happy sharing!

Beatrice clicks on the tab labeled *Forums*. Nothing about the site has changed since she last checked it a few years back. The next screen displays a very long column of message boards and topics people post when they have nothing else better to do with their lives.

Jax & Juniper Disappearance.
Millstone Family Sightings.
Ashwood Interior (ONLY PICTURES).
Ashwood Exterior (ONLY PICTURES).
Theories.
Ashwood Experiences.
Millstone Family Experiences.
The Paranormal of Ashwood.
What Does the Family NOT Want Us to Know?

Beatrice selects the one about the family sightings. She doesn't believe that any of her missing family members are alive, but it's always a little interesting how fast people will believe they see her mother walking about in town. Or how someone in their history class looks *exactly* like one of the twins. Some people out there don't believe the members of Beatrice's family are all even dead—even though Aunt Marley's body was found in the kitchen that night Beatrice fled. The same with her mother. The only two that have never been found are Beatrice's cousins, Jax and Juniper.

The first response to the topic is a grainy photo of a woman with strawberry blond hair pumping gas outside of a Circle K. The caption reads, *OMG. Does this not look like Marley Millstone?!*

Someone responded with, *Marley was found dead the night her sister tried leaving and wound up dead, too. Idiot.*

Someone else replied: *It does sort of look like her…*

Another person with the username foxGirl22 commented, *Dude, you can't even see her face. Stop posting dumb shit.*

Beatrice scrolls down for another picture taken by the same person, their username is LilScarecrow41. He or she or they posted a picture a few months ago. A woman with brown hair walking with grocery bags slung onto her elbows, strutting through a parking lot. Her face is masked with a large pair of sunglasses and the large sweatshirt she's wearing hides her body shape.

LilScarecrow41: *Anyone else thinks this looks exactly like Beatrice's mom or is it just me?*

Maria_gal898: *Sorry but if Lena was on the lam, the last thing she'd be doing is buying groceries LOL.*

Byron_the_Trex00: *Missing people have to eat 2!!*

ClaudetteLovesHippos1234: *LENA ISN'T MISSING. SHE'S DEAD.*

Beatrice winces at the aggression with the capital letters and scrolls through a few more blurry pictures of people that are being mistaken for a Millstone. Even a few girls that look like her pop up in places Beatrice has never been, the users commenting about how these girls *must* be Beatrice with thick curly brown hair and dark honey skin, and huge brown eyes. She comes across one that actually *is* her in New York City. It's blurry, but Beatrice can make out her penny coat and her patched jeans.

YOOOOOO I think I just spotted Beatrice fucking Millstone!!!! the caption screams.

That's not Beatrice… Someone responded the following day.

A username with more numbers than letters in the title responds: *Yeah, I agree. That chick is way too ugly to be Beatrice Millstone. Nice try, tho.*

Beatrice half-grins at herself, almost relieved that these people truly don't know the truth when it's right in front of them. She sifts through the rest of the site, roaming the forums and topics and reading about people's theories on what kind of ghost is stuck in Ashwood, sharing their thoughts on if it's a poltergeist or some lost spirit. People have even posted stuff about what their priests and ministers believe needs to happen, as though some sort of exorcism needs to take place by the power of a crucifix and a splash of holy water. But aren't any of these people smart enough to know that what is inside of those walls is not some sort of ghost in a TV? It's not some demon stuck in a doll's body. It's not a dark shadow gliding through the halls at night, the cause of strange noises and windows creaking back open. All of these people claiming to be Ashwood fanatics should know enough by now that what takes place on the grounds isn't what they think. It isn't what *anyone* thinks.

And no, Beatrice herself doesn't know what lurks in the walls of her childhood home. But she will never forget the conversation she once had with Grammy Astrid in the kitchen one glossy spring afternoon. Beatrice was around five years old and she had just come in from playing in the garden with Aunt Marley and the twins. Aunt Marley gathered Jax and Juniper up for a bath while Grandma Astrid ushered Beatrice into the kitchen for pre-supper cookies. She used to call them appetizers.

"Grammy, I heard noises last night," Beatrice told her as she sat at the breakfast bar with a round plate of three cookies in front of her. Her hair was pulled into a long braid down her back and her oversized flannel shirt was so big she could swim in it.

"Noises?" Grammy padded around the kitchen, her dark grey curls framing her wrinkly sagging face. "What kind of noises?"

Beatrice shrugged, biting into a cookie. "Weird ones. Like something was walking around down here. It came up the stairs and stopped outside my room."

Grandma Astrid glanced at her on her way to the sink, gently placing all the kitchen utensils she used inside. "I'm sure it was your mother up for a drink of water. She was probably just stopping to check in on you."

Beatrice shook her head. "It didn't sound like a person. Was it a ghost?"

Grammy smiled at her the way she did whenever she was impressed that a girl as young as Beatrice was so curious and aware of her surroundings.

"There are no ghosts in this house, little one," Grammy told her, making her way over to the other side of the breakfast bar. She braided her fingers together, her long red nails newly painted. She stared at Beatrice for a long, pregnant pause before speaking again. "What you hear isn't what you believe."

Beatrice tilted her head, thoughtfully chewing her cookie. It sounded so insightful but she had no clue what it meant. Grammy Astrid often spoke this way, like she was reading out of a book she wrote herself.

"What's that mean?"

"It means that ghosts do not exist in this house."

"Then what do I hear at night?"

"Those are just the House Things, sweetheart."

And from that day on, every time nails would scratch across the walls or a growl would come from another room, everyone would just blame it on one of the House Things—whatever they were. Beatrice lived the next five years, comfortable with living in a place where a House Thing exists. And it wasn't until she attempted friends at her school that she realized not every little girl and boy grew up with House Things. She was in a grade behind the other kids, given the lack of homeschooling she had growing up, so she was already at a disadvantage. Her upbringing made it even more difficult for her to socialize.

Once she grows tired of reading the bullshit online, Beatrice shuts her laptop, realizing she's late to catch the bus. She stuffs her laptop between two sweatshirts inside of her suitcase with its charger and then rises from the chair. She's now paranoid, wondering if any of the people here in Starbucks are some of the cult members on that site. She glances around as she slides her arms into the denim jacket she took off when she got here. There's a burnout in the corner with Bob Marley on his shirt and headphones in. A businesswoman is chattering into her cell phone as she impatiently waits for her pumpkin spice latte. A group of high school kids in uniforms laugh together over something on one of their phones.

Beatrice lets out a little sigh. *Stop being paranoid*, she tells herself, and then steps out onto the sidewalk.

Chapter 3

The drive away from New York is bittersweet. The bitter part is she's grown to love the city. She could be Beatrice Millstone: a former resident of Ashwood, without worrying about standing out. In a city that big and bustling, she could hide wherever and whenever she needed to. She could be in plain sight, tricking the eyes of people who believe her to be on the news or in the papers or on ancient sites claiming she's some sort of final girl straight out of a horror movie, surviving whatever curse lingered in that house.

The sweet part is that she has somewhere to go. Aunt Edie helping her out after all this time is truly a blessing and she isn't sure what she would do without it. The other bitter part is returning to Ashwood and facing the House Things once more as though she's never left. She ignores that part, though, determined to start over as an adult. This is life. This isn't some novel or made-for-TV movie. There is some reasonable explanation as to why Aunt Marley, Grammy Astrid, Grandpa Hugh, her mother, Uncle Eli, and everyone before them met mysterious and untimely deaths inside. Juniper and Jax, Marley's kids, were kidnapped right from their backyard. None of it makes sense, yet Beatrice chalks it up to coincidence because that's the only thing she's able to do. It's her way of trying to gain an ounce of control over her past.

Beatrice rides the bus to stop after stop, staring out the window at the blur of red and orange leaves passing her by, all of them tangled together in beautiful canopies that is the season of autumn. Fall in Silver Creek is something special and looks like it's jumped right out of a postcard. With giant trees made up of golden leaves reflecting off the many rivers, it's pretty idyllic. The town square goes all out this time of year. With hay bales outside of business doors, Halloween activities for the kids, a pumpkin patch, and a hayride running every day of the week, this time of year can't be beaten. It's what Beatrice misses about it the most. She can't exactly do any of it in New York. The closest thing she has are the trees in Central Park.

Even though Beatrice and the rest of her family wouldn't always take advantage of this kind of stuff, she's almost excited to partake in a thing or two now that she's here. If there's one thing she can count on from the residents of Silver Creek, it's that they won't look at her like she's a rabbit just pulled from a magician's hat. In fact, Beatrice once asked Aunt Edie over the phone if anyone ever asks about what happened.

"They don't care to know," Aunt Edie had told her, way back when. "They understand that things happen."

Beatrice didn't know what that meant at the time. But now she wonders if it's a territorial thing. So many people probably come into town to hunt for the infamous Millstone house. The residents are probably so over it at this point that they stopped caring when it became a tourist attraction and not their hometown. They roll their eyes when people ask directions to Ashwood or get defensive when they hear gossip from tourists about the Millstones—even though they all probably once dished it at one point or another.

Once she reaches Silver Creek, Beatrice calls a cab instead of an Uber because she's still tight on money. She would rather be squished in the back of a car with stained seats than pay out the ass for the same service. When the cab picks her up at the station, she lets the driver stuff her suitcase into the trunk, grunting as he heaves it up into the car. Beatrice gives him the house address instead of simply saying *Ashwood*, treating it like it's an actual house and not a national landmark. It's not uncommon for Victorian houses to have names like people. That's what separates them from modern homes. They have history, personality, charm. Whereas today's houses all look the same: modern, sleek, boring.

Beatrice doesn't formally suffer from anxiety but if there was ever a time she was convinced she does, it's now. She chews on her pinkie nail in the backseat of the cab, Silver Creek spilling out before her. The doughnut shop looks completely new, and the ice cream stand on the corner of Rex Hill and South Main Street is missing. The grocery store has been renamed from I.D.A to Ruehler's. Everything looks so different, yet so much the same that Beatrice looks away from the window and pretends to respond to messages on her phone. Every single one of her inboxes is empty but she can't bear to look outside for another minute. It puts her back at ten years old, sitting in the back of the squad car as she was brought to the police station once everything went down at home.

Instead of being daytime back then, it was Halloween night. She remembers watching lit jack-o-lanterns winking at her from porch railings. She remembers passing a house throwing a party where a slutty Peter Pan was making out with a sluttier Snow White. Late trick-or-treaters were still wandering the streets in costumes with pillowcases full of candy. She recalls the night being so dark and lonely, thrown into a state of stupefaction when nothing was real but at the same time, everything was *too* real. The smell of the chilly autumn night, a dog barking in the distance, the way the traffic lights blinked from green to yellow to red.

As the cab pulls up to the round driveway in front of Ashwood, the familiar sight sends chills down Beatrice's back—and not in a good way. The pale-yellow siding, the red brick chimney crawling up the side, the wraparound porch. Everything looks exactly how Beatrice had left it all those years ago. Even the ivy slithering around the porch banister like a long snake made directly from the earth hasn't changed. She doesn't move. Not yet. She keeps her eyes glued to the front of the Victorian house that has stood with pride since the late 1800s. With a big red oak door, a rounded turret on the corner, and porch spindles that look like legs of furniture, it is as though it's smiling at Beatrice, saying *Welcome home.*

"This is your home?" the heavyset cab driver asks in a thick, New York accent. His baseball cap covers his bald head and he's staring at Ashwood like it's on fire...eyes bulging out of his head and his mouth gaped open.

Beatrice nods, even though he isn't looking at her, and she hands him a floppy twenty-dollar bill. Twenty dollars poorer. "Thanks for the ride."

"Here, let me get your bags," he says, reaching to unbuckle himself.

Beatrice holds her hand out. "No, I got it."

The last thing she wants is to spend more time with someone that might ask her the usual list of questions when they find out she once lived here:

Are the rumors true?

Does your family actually have a curse on them?

Your mom isn't a witch, is she? Because if so, does that make you one?

Hey, whatever happened to Juniper and Jax?

So like, what really *happened in that house? Trust me, it's not like I'm going to tell* anyone…

Beatrice shakes the questions out of her groggy mind. She refuses to torture herself with the same pain she's dealt with since leaving. She rounds the taxi and drags her suitcase out of the trunk, patting the door twice with her palm to tell the driver she's finished. Beatrice glares down at the bruised luggage now sitting in front of her. Her entire life crammed into luggage so small should be illegal.

"There she is!" a familiar voice calls out from the porch.

Great Aunt Edie, as glorious as ever, comes prancing down the creaky porch steps, her arms open wide as she trots across the cobblestone driveway, her bony ankles nearly twisting in her heels. She's wearing an obnoxious sunhat and a long silk dress that Beatrice mistakes for a nightgown. Her lips are painted with ruby red lipstick and she's wearing a hint of smoky eye shadow that she once taught Beatrice how to wear. Her sandy blond hair is kept in a tight bun at the nape of her neck and smile wrinkles form on either side of her mouth as her face lights up like Christmas at the sight of her niece.

"Hi, Aunt Edie," Beatrice greets her awkwardly, wiping her nose before returning Aunt Edie's hug: something they haven't done in years. She smells like expensive perfume, the same kind she wore when Beatrice was a kid. She remembers the perfume coming in lavender bottles from somewhere in France.

Aunt Edie is Beatrice's mother's aunt, Grandpa Hugh's and Uncle Eli's sister. Lachlan was the oldest of the three, then Edie, then Hugh. Aunt Edie isn't old and crotchety like most great aunts. She can still get around just fine, she doesn't have any signs of arthritis or any disease for that matter, and she still goes dancing every weekend, according to a phone call they had last Christmas.

"Ugh, you've gotten so big," Aunt Edie says, looking her up and down in awe. "In a good way, of course. It's not like you're looking to audition for *Precious 2* or anything."

Beatrice winces because that is what people say when they haven't seen a child in a long time...that they look *so big*. But Beatrice is not a child, she's 25. She hasn't heard anyone comment on her height or size for a very long time. Perhaps it's because she hasn't seen a family member in over a decade.

"Here, grab your luggage," Aunt Edie instructs, gesturing for them to start up to the house, which is looming over them as though it's begging to be part of the conversation. "I just put some hot chocolate on the stove for you. I even added the little marshmallows you always liked—and that says a lot because I usually don't do that kind of stuff for people, you know."

Beatrice blinks, not sure what she's talking about. But then she remembers those cold winters here at Ashwood; where she and her cousins would gather around the kitchen table with mugs of steaming hot chocolate after spending hours playing out in the snow. Beatrice is more of a tea person nowadays, but she isn't going to tell Aunt Edie that. She can be sensitively dramatic at times. Beatrice's mom would always roll her eyes at her and make Beatrice promise to never grow up being that theatrical. Beatrice pinkie swore every single time. She likes to think she's kept up her end of the bargain.

She follows her up the crooked cobblestone path lined by uncared-for shrubs. This is all so trippy. It's like she's stepping back into a time warp or something and is going to find the inside lit up with life and voices and even the lingering smell of Grandma Astrid's cinnamon cookies. Two uncarved pumpkins sit side by side on the porch banister and the sight makes Beatrice frown. When she was a kid, they would decorate the front of the house and yard with every decoration they found in the attic. Beatrice's mom would even go out and buy more decorations every year— as though they had the room for it. Seeing two sad little pumpkins as the only décor is depressing in more ways than one.

"I didn't have time to clean up too well," Aunt Edie warns, opening the front door and letting her inside first. "But I suppose that's why you're here, right? To clean and fix this place up and all that good stuff?"

Beatrice steps into the foyer, must assaulting her nostrils like it always did. The sitting room is to the left, through a rounded doorway, the sunlight bouncing off tan couch cushions and lamps with thick lampshades. The stairs are directly to the right of the front door, that ugly rooster painting still strung up on the wall over the landing, even after all this time of Aunt Edie saying she hated the damn thing. Yet, there it hangs. Up ahead is a wide hall leading to a mud room and the kitchen and dining area. Edie is right: this place isn't spotless, but it looks normal for a home. A pair of heels is tossed against the wall and a few tote bags and a jacket are slung on the back of the wooden chair at the desk. A thin layer of dust layers the bulky bookshelf in the hall, and the large, oriental rugs look like they could use a good sweep.

"Seeing you here feels like you never even left." Aunt Edie is smiling at her, wrinkles creasing through her milky white skin. She looks like one of those old Hollywood movie stars that flaunt furry boas and laugh at men who bow down at her feet. Aunt Edie has always been glamorous, too glamorous for a place like Silver Creek. "I'm really glad you're here, Bea."

Beatrice hasn't been called *Bea* since her mother passed away over ten years ago. It was her family nickname. Hearing it within these walls stuns her too much for her to even answer.

"I will show you to your room," Aunt Edie says, as though Beatrice is a guest and forgot where her bedroom is. Does it still count as her room if she hasn't slept in it since her childhood? Aunt Edie leads the way up the stairs, pausing on the landing. "You are okay with your old bedroom, right?"

Beatrice nods her head. "Yeah, of course."

The second floor of Ashwood includes a very narrow hallway at the top of the stairs, the walls lined with artwork and portraits of dead family members. The wallpaper is the same as the kind downstairs: a creamy white with ugly yellow round diamond shapes covering the whole thing. After a while, the shapes start to look like screaming ghosts, all of them with their mouths wide open and their eyes huge from fear.

The door to Beatrice's old bedroom groans when Aunt Edie leads the way inside. "Here we are."

The view almost takes Beatrice's breath away. She can't find herself to step foot across the threshold. The room looks like it hasn't been touched for over a decade—which makes sense, in some ways. Beatrice always figured that Aunt Edie would do *something* with the room. But even when the twins disappeared, their room was locked up and never to be stepped foot in again, so why would Beatrice's be any different? Everyone's rooms in Ashwood had been sealed up shortly after their deaths or disappearances, as though the house longed for their returns.

The daybed sits against the wall, the former fluffy comforters are now matted down from not being used, and the pillows lack any form of imperfection or wrinkles. The cracked mirror above the white dresser is still decorated with stickers, and the rounded window seat in the corner still holds stiff plush pillows that are simply for design and not for comfort. The wooden floorboards creak under Beatrice's weight as she makes her way inside, the round rug in the center of the room covered in dust and dead insects.

"If you want, you can sleep downstairs for tonight, until we're able to clean it up a little," Aunt Edie offers, twisting a giant silver ring around and around her thumb. "You came on such short notice, that I didn't entirely have the heads up to clean your room."

"No, it's not your fault," she assures, dragging her suitcase to the dresser. "This is fine. Just needs a little T.L.C. And I can go into town tomorrow for new bedsheets and whatnot."

"Okay." Aunt Edie smiles again, relieved that she doesn't have to do any of the work. Typical. "Well, why don't I fix you something to eat? You must've spent so much time traveling today, right?"

Honestly, food sounds nice. The last full meal Beatrice ate was with Kevin and she couldn't even enjoy the meal through his arrogance.

"That sounds good," Beatrice agrees, setting her purse down at the foot of her bed.

"Why don't you sweep the room while I throw something together downstairs?" she suggests, looking like a child about to have her first play-date. It makes Beatrice wonder how lonely she is living on this hill all by herself. Aunt Edie rarely helped out around the house when Beatrice was a kid, but maybe being forced to care for herself made her learn a chore or two.

Beatrice nods again. "Sounds like a plan."

Aunt Edie goes back into the hallway and Beatrice runs her hands up and down her face, trying to gather herself. She needs to stop looking at this like it's something terrible, like being back here is like stepping into a lion's den or Hell itself. Being here, having a place to live, food to eat, *rent-free* is more than she could have wished for. Yes, Ashwood isn't the most perfect place in the world but Beatrice doesn't need perfect. She just needs money and time, which are forever interchangeably locked together.

Beatrice finds the sweeper in its usual place in the hall closet under shelves full of bedsheets and extra towels. She quickly sweeps the room, all of the dead things and dirt sucked up so fast it's like they were never there in the first place. She does a little bit of dusting around her old dresser, taking a few minutes to find the trinkets that were important to her back then. An old clown figure stands nice and tall in the corner of the surface, chunky dust in the corners of his eyes. A jewelry box that plays to the tune Uncle Eli told her was called "Come Out and Play" sits in front of it. Beatrice reaches for it, gently opening the lid. The twinkly music begins to play, filling the room with sound it hasn't heard since Beatrice left it. A little ballerina twirls around and around with her porcelain arms at perfect angles, her pointed feet vertical. Inside the box sits a tangled web of necklaces and bracelets, forgotten about. Under the box is a glossy piece of folded paper Beatrice doesn't bother looking at again.

Beatrice looks at the other contents of the dresser. There's a photo of her and her mom on Christmas morning, sitting together in front of the lit-up tree. A ceramic bunny Beatrice once painted sits next to it, the color drained off its face after sitting for so long in the sunlight streaming in through the windows. A hairbrush still containing strands of hair is near the edge, and play makeup is scattered over other random tiny toys she used to play with when she was a kid.

"Looks like we're back," Beatrice says to her plush elephant, who watches her from the bed, propped up against the pillows.

"Beatrice!" she calls from downstairs. "Food is done!"

Aunt Edie has chicken cordon bleu and mashed potatoes waiting for her on a plate when she reaches the kitchen. It's the same as it has always been, but a little tidier than the rest of the house. With an island in the middle and a breakfast bar separating it from the mud room, the kitchen is made up of a bunch of fork and spoon designs. The handles on all of the cupboards are in the shapes of forks. The spice rack on the wall is in the shape of a spoon, and there is a pair of wooden utensils hanging on the wall leading into the dining room.

"What do the French people say?" Aunt Edie sets her own plate down across from Beatrice's seat. "Bon Appetit?"

"Wow, that was fast." Beatrice sits down at the table and picks up her fork, diving right into the chicken to split it in half.

"The mashed potatoes are leftovers," Aunt Edie admits, chowing down, too. Beatrice wonders when the last time *she* ate was. "And the chicken is just from the freezer."

The two of them sit in silence, neither of them sure what to say and more unsure of how to figure it out. Beatrice swallows a chunk of food, glancing up from her plate to her aunt, who doesn't look bothered by the silence. How could she? She's probably spent every day for the last fifteen years eating alone without any noise. This is no different. But it's different for Beatrice and silence makes her uncomfortable. She often finds herself waiting to hear a noise or feel a gust of cold air if she sits in the quiet for too long. Growing up in Ashwood does that sort of thing.

"I can't even explain to you how thankful I am that you're letting me stay here," Beatrice explains to her, nearly catching Aunt Edie off guard with her voice. "Really. You're saving me a lot of trouble."

"Nonsense." She flaps her hand in her direction, her heavy rings glinting in the little chandelier light hanging over them. "You're saving *me*. Do you know how much easier it'll be for you to make this place look nice versus people marching through here with other intentions?"

Beatrice studies her. She has to be talking about the rumor mill surrounding the house and the family members inside it. Aunt Edie can't be a stranger to what people say about them and this place online or even in person. So, she's right. Beatrice coming in here to do the job is far better than strangers waltzing through the doors just to get a real peek at the guts of Ashwood.

"Are people around here still weird about it?" Beatrice asks her, curiosity eating away at her.

Aunt Edie shakes her head, chewing. "Not entirely. I mean, there are a few kids around here that think this is some folklore house or whatever they're calling it nowadays. They sneak up here around Halloween and dare each other to ring the doorbell. Dumb shit like that. But most of the adults I've become rather close to aren't bothered by a thing. I let them inside without another thought."

Beatrice raises her eyebrows a little. She remembers being a kid and not having anyone over. Sure, she and the twins didn't have many friends, except for Xander, who lived down the street, closer to civilization. But even the adults of the house, when they would make friends with people, would very rarely invite them inside. It's like they were fearful that the House Things would swallow them whole or they'd melt into a puddle one foot past the front door.

"You let people in?" Beatrice scoops up some potato onto her fork. "Like, inside and everything?"

Aunt Edie nods in confirmation. "Me and a few other women have a garden club."

Beatrice almost chokes. For an old lady who loves using the word *nonsense*, that sure is bullshit. Growing up, Aunt Edie barely lifted a finger to help out around the house. She would lounge with her feet up and the back of her hand draped across her forehead as she'd threaten to faint if she did too much housework. She would never be caught dead getting dirt under her fingernails or wearing shoes that don't have a heel to them. This is a newly improved Aunt Edie that Beatrice isn't even sure she likes yet.

"A garden club," Beatrice echoes her. "That sounds like fun."

"It truly is," she responds, proudly. She stabs at a piece of ham sliding out of her chicken. "You'll have to meet them sometime. I'm sure they'll all love you, really."

Beatrice nods, unsure how to respond. She apparently doesn't need to because Aunt Edie speaks again.

"What about you, sweetie?" Aunt Edie asks. "How's Clara? Do you two still keep in touch? When she was friends with your mother in college, they were always off and on. Girl drama and all that other bull crap."

"Of course we do," Beatrice snaps a little more bitchier than she intends. *She was the only one who offered to take me in after shit hit the fan, remember?* She bites her tongue, knowing that getting started on the wrong foot would make her stay here shorter than she needs it to. "We talk every day."

"Good, that's good." A pause, the sound of their forks and knives filling the void. "And how is the store going? Time and Tokens, or something?"

"Trinkets and Treasures," she corrects her. "But close."

"Ah yes, I'm sorry." Aunt Edie reaches for her wine glass, slipping her slender fingers around the stem. "All of those short-lived small businesses all sound the same to me."

"It's going well," Beatrice says honestly and loudly and maybe a little defensively. "You'd be surprised how many people are antique hunting these days. My boss says that vintage is coming back in style. Are you sure it's okay for me to take some of that stuff to the attic back to New York? I already talked to Declan about it and he's excited—"

"Declan, huh?" Her voice changes to something a little more girly like they're two high school girls cooing about the prom king. It's the tone she always used to carry whenever she talked about anything back then. It's typical Aunt Edie. Beatrice kind of missed it. "Is he a romantic interest of yours?"

"What? No," Beatrice sputters. "Of course not. He's my boss."

"Don't say that like it's such a bad thing." Aunt Edie laughs, shaking her head as she pokes around at her food. "When you get to my age, you're going to wish you had more sexual relationships. And with a name like Declan, it sounds like he has a fairly large—"

"Please stop talking," Beatrice quickly interjects, forcing a laugh to keep the mood light. "He's just my boss and I think he's gay."

"Aren't they all, these days?" She sighs as though she has personal experience and it kind of makes Beatrice wonder how. "So, I take it that you aren't dating around? Slutting it up?"

Beatrice almost chokes again and she takes a huge gulp of her iced water. "I can't believe you just asked me that."

"What?" Aunt Edie asks casually. "You're young and free. You should treat your vagina the same."

They spend the rest of the dinner making small talk about residents in town that Beatrice doesn't remember and answering questions about the shop that Beatrice knows doesn't interest Aunt Edie in the slightest. She helps clear the table and they quickly wash dishes together, Aunt Edie drying while Beatrice washes. They talk a little more about what kind of renovations Aunt Edie wants with the house before it sells and how Beatrice can stay for as long as she needs—which was more than a good thing to hear.

"All right, you rest well, now," Aunt Edie tells her when she flips the kitchen light off. "I'm sure you're exhausted."

"That's a little bit of an understatement." Beatrice can feel her eyes half-shut already. "But yeah, I should be turning in."

"Me too." Aunt Edie grabs hold of Beatrice's hand when she tries making her way up the stairs. "I really do mean it when I say I'm glad you're here, Bea."

Beatrice genuinely smiles back at her. Even though she knows this house has its fair share of unfortunate things surrounding it, being back here sure does feel like being home. Seeing Aunt Edie again, despite the grudge Beatrice holds against her, is like a breath of fresh air—which is odd and random but still a little comforting.

Aunt Edie's smile broadens. "The house really did miss you."

Chapter 4

That night, Beatrice lies awake in her childhood bed, staring up at the popcorn ceiling, tossing and turning as she attempts to get more comfortable in a bed she hasn't slept in since she was ten.

The memory of her last night here swims through her mind on a loop, reminding her of the entire downfall that became her life. Lying in this bed, watching those shadows outside the window, her stuffed elephant— which has stayed with her after all this time—lying next to her, aware of their new—yet old—environment. Everything about being back here is far too familiar for comfort. Silver Creek itself is like an old sweater forgotten about in the back of a closet, only to be found years later just how it was left: itchy and no longer fits.

The house really did miss you.

Aunt Edie's words make her toss some more. Beatrice even tries putting a pillow over her head as though her aunt's words are echoing throughout the room. Her uncle Eli, Edie's husband, died when Beatrice was around four, so she doesn't have too many memories of him except for the home movies tucked into an armoire somewhere in the house. She has one faint memory of herself wandering around the front lawn, where her mother was going to have a picnic with her. Lena had run back inside to fetch some napkins and Beatrice was plucking blades of grass. Uncle Eli was standing on the side of the house, staring up at the structure.

His head was balding and his face was a web of wrinkles. He wore a sad expression as he stared at the siding and Beatrice curiously watched him, wondering why he wore such a frown.

"What's wrong, Uncle Eli?" Beatrice called out to him innocently.

Uncle Eli jumped at the sound of her voice and he snatched his arm away from the house. He blinked at her in surprise, bathed in the shadow of the house. "What's that, honey?"

"What's wrong?" Beatrice asked again. "You look sad."

"I'm not sad," he responded. "The house is."

Beatrice laughed at the time but now, she knows that it's not that funny. Sure, Uncle Eli was apparently not all right in the head. According to Aunt Marley, he had a few screws loose, which was why he did the things that he did. He made the attic windows in triangle shapes and he replaced all the drawers on his dresser with old locker doors that came out of nowhere. Even though Beatrice doesn't remember much about him other than that odd memory of him on the side of the house, she does recall him muttering things under his breath almost constantly, talking to things that weren't there. And of course, she vividly remembers the last day he was alive.

When the slanted fall sunlight cuts through the window on the other side of the room, Beatrice's eyes flutter open. She feels like she only got three hours of sleep. On any other day, she would be upset. But, today is the start of a new day. She has food downstairs and a roof over her head. She can stay here as long as Aunt Edie will let her, giving her as much time as she needs to collect some money before figuring out what to do next.

She climbs out of the bed, her back as stiff as a board from the mattress. She makes a mental note to try and find a new mattress while she's out in town today getting other supplies. There's no way she'll be able to sleep on that bed the full time she's here.

Beatrice plops down on the floor of the room, shoving the last of her clothes into the dresser and bureau to empty her suitcase. Maybe she'll do a thing or two about the contents of this room, too. She can pack up her old stuff and put it upstairs or something. Her mother would kill her if she sold any of it and Beatrice can't entirely say she wouldn't do the same. She throws on a navy blue turtleneck and jeans, stuffing her feet into her only pair of shoes, and then marches out of the room.

Back then, she would walk out of her room to the smell of eggs or bacon or French toast and pancakes but today, all she smells is old house. She isn't complaining, though. In fact, *she* should be the one making Aunt Edie breakfast, given she's letting her live here rent-free despite the fact they've pretty much been strangers for the last fifteen years. She ventures down the creaky old stairs into the foyer after brushing her teeth and skipping breakfast, stopping when she can just make out Aunt Edie lounging on the vintage couch in the sitting room, her ankle draped over the arm and her eyes shut. With the sunlight pouring in through the windows behind the couch, she looks like something out of an old Renaissance painting, like one of those painted ladies in dramatic poses with their boobs flopping out of their tops. Luckily for Beatrice, her aunt's breasts are tucked away.

Beatrice slowly approaches the doorway, wondering if she still has trouble sleepwalking. A galaxy of dust floats in the air in front of her, like tiny little diamonds forgetting to land. Beatrice bites the inside of her cheek, her hands behind her back, and she suddenly feels like a child again, afraid to wake her sleeping aunt. Just as she opens her mouth to wake her, Aunt Edie startles herself into consciousness, gasping so loud it makes Beatrice jump.

Aunt Edie grips the wooden back of the couch with her fingers, her knuckles beaming white as she sits up further, blinking rapidly. Beatrice stares at her with wide eyes, unsure if she should wait to speak until she's calmed down or if she should ask if she's all right.

"Beatrice." Aunt Edie stares at her, panting for breath, as though she forgot she was here. Her eyes slide around the room and slowly, her face begins to morph into reality. Her eyes, on the other hand, still look confused. Like Beatrice just tried smothering her with a pillow or something. "What are you doing? It's the middle of the night."

Beatrice blinks, uncomfortable. She glances out the window just to make sure that she's not the crazy one. You can never be sure in a house like this one. "No, Aunt Edie. It's not. It's going on 9:30."

Aunt Edie mirrors her blink, her red lipstick smeared, and the bun at the nape of her neck nearly undone. Her sunhat sits on the glass coffee table in front of the velvet couch between two identical naked men sculptures. She breathes in through her nose and sniffles, wiping thin strands of hair away from her face. "I must have lost track of time."

"Do you need me to get you anything?" Beatrice offers awkwardly. "Water? Tea?"

She shakes her head, rising to her feet, her silk dress spilling down her skinny frame, jagged wrinkles decorating the material. "No, that's all right. I just need to take a B12."

Beatrice steps out of her way and she starts into the foyer, rubbing the back of her neck with a crinkled hand. Beatrice follows. "Well, do you need anything from the store? I'm going into town today to grab some bathroom stuff and maybe hunt down a new mattress."

"No, that's all right, sweetheart." Aunt Edie is already halfway up the stairs, her voice aimed in the complete other direction as the stairs loudly creak under her weight. "You can take my car, the keys are by the door."

Just like how they hung all those years ago, sets of keys hang on little wooden hooks by the front door. One leads to the storm cellar door, the other leads to the shed out back, another is one for the main house, and the last set is for Aunt Edie's car. Beatrice plucks it off the hook and considers calling out a goodbye but she decides against it.

Aunt Edie's Volkswagen Beatle from the '60s is parked in the round driveway, shiny under the early morning sun. It's wet from overnight dew but patiently waits to be flaunted around town the way Aunt Edie always used to back when Beatrice was growing up.

"When you have nice things, dear, you need to make other people feel bad about not having them," Aunt Edie once told her with a proud smile on her mouth as they drove through town on a hot summer day. Aunt Edie sported a thin white scarf that was wrapped over her head, the knot just under her chin. With a pair of expensive sunglasses, Beatrice wondered at the time if Aunt Edie was trying to be in disguise.

Beatrice climbs into the front seat, plugging the keys into the ignition and feeling the car come to life. She remembers Jax swearing up and down that he will have this car when he's old enough to drive. The memory makes Beatrice frown.

"Cars like this won't even be alive at that time!" Juniper told him, plopping down on the hood of the car.

"This one will be," Jax argued back.

Sadly, any chance of him driving this, or any other car for that matter, vanished right along with him.

The car lurches out of the driveway and down the hill lined by maple trees. Something loudly hums under the car's floor but Beatrice chooses to ignore it. If Aunt Edie has driven it for this long and has done just fine, she can too. She passes Xander's old house at the end of the street just before reaching town. Xander used to walk up the street to their house when they were kids and play with her and the twins. He wasn't over all the time but when he would show up, he'd be with them the whole day, the four of them wandering the grounds of Ashwood and making up games as the day came and went. Beatrice wasn't too sure that the adults of Ashwood were fans of Xander. She used to think that they didn't like how he ate their food or that he would track mud through their house or press his nose up against the screen windows, but he was never told that he wasn't allowed to play with the others. He was kind of just glanced upon and that was it.

Beatrice parks in the tiny lot of Ruehler's and hops out, slinging her satchel purse onto her shoulder. The front display of the grocery store consists of huge boxes of pumpkins, hay bales on sale, and smiley scarecrows to put outside front doors. She glances at a woman pushing a car out the automatic doors. The lady stares back at her and Beatrice quickly ducks her head, hiding behind a curtain of thick brown hair.

The last thing she wants to do is get recognized by someone. She doesn't want them chasing after her on the sidewalk calling out, *Hey, I know you! You're a Millstone!*

Beatrice grabs a cart inside and wanders through the produce section. She picks up packaged caramel apples, debating on whether she should bring them home for Aunt Edie. Perhaps they can chow down on fall foods and watch a movie together. They can try growing the bond they had back to the way it was. She returns them to the shelf, convinced that all the caramel apples in the world wouldn't help repair what has been done.

She sifts through bananas, looking for a good enough bunch before setting them in the cart. She grabs some canned foods and meat, going through her mind about what she can make for dinner to show Aunt Edie that she doesn't expect her to do all the cooking. Beatrice never really did any of that kind of stuff when she lived with Tess. The thing she loved most about living with the girl was that Tess was so good at doing everything Beatrice was too impatient to do. Tess would whisk up some new recipe she found on a Facebook page and they would end up having it until they got sick of it. Tess never told Beatrice she had to do her part for their living arrangement to work out. She only became a bitch after she left.

Beatrice drops a few more things into the cart before hunting down the beauty section. She grabs some shampoo and conditioner and a new loofah, realizing she pretty much forgot all of her bathroom shit back at her apartment.

"Oh. My. God," a voice says from further down the aisle at the medicine section.

Beatrice looks over to see an older lady gaping at her. She has white hair in huge curls surrounding her face and stopping just below her pierced ears. Pearls hang around her neck and she's wearing a crisp white business suit, square-shaped heels to match. She glows with money and luxury but Beatrice doesn't recognize her. Shit. She's already been found out. It's only a matter of time before this hits those weird online blogs and people come waiting outside of Ashwood for a glimpse of her. They're all pretty much tired of seeing Aunt Edie.

"Little Beatrice Millstone," the lady goes on, folding her arms over her chest as she takes a few steps closer. A plastic shopping basket hangs from her elbow, lightly filled with vitamins and bottles of seltzer water. "You are all grown up."

Beatrice studies her. "I'm sorry, do I know you?"

"Uh, I would hope you'd remember me." She scoffs, putting a hand to her chest as though she's offended. "It's me, Marilyn. Marilyn Vance."

Beatrice waits for the name to ring a bell but her mind remains blank. She bites the inside of her cheek, not meaning to offend the woman but aren't older people not supposed to be very good with names?

"I'm your aunt Edie's friend?" she proceeds as though it will help. "I used to stop by now and again? We used to play poker."

"O-oh, right," Beatrice stutters, lying through her teeth. She still has no clue who this lady is but it's better to lie and pretend she does to save them both from feeling more uncomfortable. "Sorry, I spaced. It's been a while."

"No, it's all right." Marilyn flaps her long slender hand in her direction, a ring glimmering in the dull grocery store lights. "I suppose you were so young at the time, anyway. You and your cousins were always already put to sleep when I was there. How are you *doing*? Does Edie know you're here?"

"I'm staying with her," Beatrice informs, pretending to look intrigued with the label on a deodorant stick. "I'm helping her with some home renovations and I'm doing a couple of things for work while I'm here."

"What do you do?"

"I work at an antique shop in New York," she answers, deciding she's looked at the label for too long so she drops it into her cart despite it being for menopausal women.

"Oh, how retro," Marilyn says, as though she's a young girl ogling over vintage fashion instead of being a woman who *grew up* in that fashion. Seems like she and Aunt Edie have a lot in common. "It's so nice seeing you. I can't remember the last time you were here in town."

Beatrice thinks about this. Obviously, the last time she was here was when her mother and her Aunt Marley died the same night. Everyone in Silver Creek should already know that. Everyone should know the story like the back of their hands. Hell, there are people here who probably still have the newspaper from the following morning, the headline screaming those words forever etched into Beatrice's brain: *Horror at Ashwood: Sisters Found Dead.* But perhaps Marilyn telling her that she doesn't remember the last time she was here means that other people don't, either. Maybe the real world isn't anything like what she has seen online where people obsess over her family like they're characters in a show versus real-life people with real-life feelings.

"It's been a long time," Beatrice responds finally, sliding her hands back and forth across the bar of the cart. "But I'm glad to be back here. It's a little comforting knowing that some things never change."

"You don't have to tell me that twice," Marilyn says. "When you get to my age, that becomes more and more of a blessing every day."

Beatrice finishes up her shopping after departing from Marilyn, avoiding her throughout the entire rest of the store so they wouldn't have to make even more awkward conversation. Beatrice has never been a good people person. She isn't sure what it is about her, but when people speak, she tends to just say whatever first comes to her mind without thinking about it. It seems right in the minute and then after the conversation has ended, she finds herself pinching her arm for sounding like such an idiot. Whatever. Marilyn seems nice enough that she didn't think anything of it.

Beatrice pays for the groceries and loads them into the car in the lot. She glances this way and that for any sign of a mattress store up the main street but none seem to be in sight. She'll have to ask Aunt Edie when she gets home. She climbs back into the car, starts it up again, and cruises out of the parking lot.

When she gets back to Ashwood, Beatrice carries the bags of groceries into the kitchen, no sign of Aunt Edie yet. She's probably resting upstairs. Beatrice is a little relieved to know they both had a rough night. Hopefully, tonight is different. She spends the next half hour finding where things go in the fridge and the pantry, doing her best to respect Aunt Edie's organization. When she's finished, she eats a banana and then wanders upstairs, the door to Aunt Edie's bedroom closed.

Beatrice gets her work notebook from her room so she can take notes on the furniture upstairs. The attic doors are in a small alcove on the third floor of the house where Aunt Marley's bedroom is, along with the twins', and Beatrice's mom's. All of the doors up here are shut, and Beatrice suddenly finds herself feeling like she's in one of those dreams where Ashwood is a labyrinth. She would wander through the hallways and rooms but would find herself going in circles, with no way out in sight. The gold doorknobs glisten in the sunlight pouring through the windows behind her. Dust collects in the corners and on the wainscot. She wonders how long it's been since Aunt Edie tended to the upstairs. It looks like it has been touched just as much as her old room was.

The attic doors are wooden and thick, with pink installation foam peeking out from the cracks on the sides. A little gold latch keeps the doors together and with a flick of the finger, they open. Beatrice hunches through the doorway and up the step leading into the drafty old attic where the rafters stretch from the pointed ceiling down to the wooden floor. A triangular window is across the room overlooking the backyard. Beatrice reaches her hand out in front of her to yank the string that activates the single light bulb dangling above her.

The attic has always creeped her out as a child. She remembers playing Hide 'n Seek with the twins one time and she thought it would be a good idea to hide up here among the old decorations and forgotten furniture. She crouched behind an old orange chair that spun around and around, fumbling for a comfortable position in the dark when she heard a noise across the attic. Beatrice perked up at the sound, her head peeking over the back of the chair. An old plastic Santa Claus in mid-wave with a sack of toys at his feet stared at her with beady black eyes. He moved.

Beatrice's eyes widened at the sight and she rapidly blinked to make sure that the darkness of the attic wasn't playing tricks on her. He moved again and a piercing scratching noise began, like long nails scraping against the wooden boards of the floor. Beatrice yelled, throwing herself through the other junk and out the doors.

Now, as an adult, the room isn't any less scary. That same plastic Santa stands with the other Christmas decorations, still waving after all these years. Tubs and boxes stack upon each other, creating a maze of sorts with random junk and furniture on its sides tossed around. Weak cardboard boxes are labeled in handwriting ranging from Aunt Marley to Grammy Astrid to Beatrice's mother and most of them seem as though if they move, they might just split open and tear.

"You're being paranoid, Beatrice," she tells herself, opening her notebook and finding that old orange chair to sit down in. She pulls an old end table with clawed feet closer to her, searching for any signs of nicks or special grooves. Sometimes she can find certain imperfections that are usually made by the Amish on purpose.

She didn't need to go to college to do what she loves. Perhaps her passion for old things comes from living in this very house with a bunch of older people. Beatrice always used to ogle at the furniture, curious about the way things were made and by whom and where they once sat in other people's homes. She loved finding scratch marks and chipped legs, proof that they've been used and worn throughout the years, proof that they have personality and not just something made in a factory. Beatrice used to stand in front of the bookshelf downstairs, staring up at it like it was the biggest thing in the world. And it was, at the time. But now, it's just a dusty old bookshelf that hasn't been moved for decades.

Beatrice puts her notebook in her lap, her other hand holding her phone over the paper to give herself some more light. She turns the end table this way and that, recording the stone surface on the top and the featured drawer on the front. It's a little hard to open but that's not uncommon. With a slight sanding on the bottom, it should work just fine. She gives the table the name Sandy, as she does with all of the furniture she researches. Furniture deserves names, too—

The doors to the attic slam shut, making Beatrice jump so far in the air, her notebook skids across the dirty floor and in between a few boxes. Immediately breathless, Beatrice looks over her shoulder at the doors, wondering if Aunt Edie even knows she's in here.

"Aunt Edie?" Beatrice calls, hurrying over to the doors, the pink installation fur mocking her, laughing because she's stuck inside and knowing that when she touches them, she'll itch immediately.

Beatrice finds two skinny pieces of wood nailed together in the shape of a cross, something they used for the Halloween decorations outside in their makeshift graveyard. She uses it to knock against the doors.

"Aunt Edie?" Beatrice calls out again worriedly, slamming the wood against the doors as hard as possible but with the foam, it muffles the sounds. "I'm in here! I'm in the attic!"

There's no response. She uses the wood to push against the doors instead, hoping the latch isn't secured but they don't budge. Suddenly, Beatrice feels like a little girl again, the way she felt as a child up here in this drafty old attic with Santa staring her down and dust bunnies collecting at every turn. This is the stuff she didn't miss about this house: the fear when you're alone. The worry about being next in the long line of Millstone ancestors who have met untimely ends.

Beatrice stomps her feet loudly on the floor, half hoping that Aunt Edie hears her but also hoping she falls through and gets out of this place. She jumps and stomps as loudly as she can, desperate for Aunt Edie to realize she's up here. A minute later, the doors swing open and Aunt Edie appears, fear splashed over her face.

"Oh, thank God." Beatrice tumbles out of the attic as though she can't breathe. And then she realizes, she couldn't. The air in there is so heavy, so suffocating. If she would have spent another minute in there, she could've become a rotting body by the time Aunt Edie knew she was missing.

"What the hell are you doing locking yourself in the attic, my dear?" Aunt Edie looks at her like she's an alien. She's wearing a baby blue silk dress with white lace tracing the hem. She has a fresh face of makeup on, her eyebrows shaded in with a black pencil.

"What?" Beatrice demands, still breathless. "I didn't. *You're* the one who shut the doors."

Aunt Edie *tsks*. "Now why would I shut the doors? Why would I even be up here?"

"How in the hell would I even be able to lock it from in there?"

Beatrice's eyes flicker from her aunt to the doors of the attic. Aunt Edie's bedroom is on the second floor and this top one *does* look like it doesn't see much life, anymore. It's not like she passed by and shut them, not realizing Beatrice was inside. Beatrice shakes her head, running her hands up the length of her face and then raking her fingers through her hair. The familiar stress and paranoia are falling upon her again like they had done to the adults when she first lived here. The house is drafty. They could have just shut on their own. But what about the latch? How did that lock itself?

"Well, I don't know," Aunt Edie answers helplessly. "I was downstairs."

"You're right." Beatrice decides though she isn't confident about her decision to brush this off like it's nothing. "It was probably just the wind."

"I'm going out into town," Aunt Edie informs without another thought about the situation. It's as though this didn't even happen or isn't that big of a deal. "Did you need anything?"

Beatrice shakes her head, not doing too much thinking of her own. Her eyes flicker back to the attic doors and then to Aunt Edie. Why didn't she just tell Beatrice what she wanted earlier? "No, but thanks."

"Very well then, darling." Aunt Edie glides to the stairs, descending them like she's floating. "Don't go locking yourself in more rooms, either. I don't know how long I'll be out."

Beatrice turns the attic light off without fully stepping inside. She'll handle this another day when she knows Aunt Edie will be home. And with that, she shuts the doors.

Chapter 5

Beatrice is lonely when she finds herself the only one inside Ashwood.

Aunt Edie has been gone for over an hour now and Beatrice has finally shaken off the feeling the attic gave her. She makes herself a Nutella and peanut butter sandwich with some fresh fruit and settles down at the dining table. She takes a massive bite out of her sandwich and scrolls through her contacts to call up Clara. Reception up here in the hills of Silver Creek isn't the best. Since being here, Beatrice has missed three phone calls from Clara and a few text messages that she had responded to earlier, promising to call her when she can.

Clara answers on the second ring. "Oh my God, finally. You had me scared you were face down in a ditch somewhere."

"Sorry, things have been kind of hectic." Thankfully, Beatrice doesn't have to look her in the face when she lies to her about where she is. Clara would flip her shit if she found out that Beatrice was here and not somewhere still in New York. This conversation will be much easier if Clara doesn't have to see her face.

"Are you okay?" Clara orders, concerned, in that motherly way. "Where are you? Did you find a place yet?"

"I'm in Connecticut," she lies, stuffing her mouth with a few blueberries to cover up the falseness leaking through her teeth. "I was having a hard time finding a place *and* a roommate so Declan sent me on this business venture. I'm at an old bed and breakfast doing some research."

"Oh." Clara sighs in relief. "Well, that's comforting to know. How is it?"

Beatrice glances around at the quiet dining room and silent kitchen. "Cozy, I guess."

"Well, are there people there?" Clara wonders, rustling following right after. "This is how girls like you get kidnapped—you think somewhere is safe when in reality, the owner of that cozy little bed and breakfast turns out to be an axed murderer with his mother's corpse in the basement."

"I think you've been watching too many Halloween movies." Beatrice takes another bite of her food.

"I'm just being proactive," Clara claims casually. "Giving you all the inside scoop on what's going to happen if you aren't smart."

"You know I'm smart," Beatrice argues back.

"Sometimes," Clara jokes.

"Sorry, I didn't call you sooner."

"It's fine, I'm just glad you're okay," Clara tells her before something clatters over on her end. "Dammit, Rico! What did I tell you about the swords?"

Beatrice grins, taking another bite of her sandwich. "Is the apocalypse going on over there?"

"I'm taking the kids shopping for Halloween costumes and they clearly don't know how to *not touch anything!*" Clara fires the last part at the kids. "I should go before we're thrown out of the store."

"Okay," Beatrice says. "I'll call when I can. Reception is trash up here."

"Be safe," Clara instructs. "It's a crazy world out there."

It's something she always used to tell Beatrice before leaving the house. She hangs up and sets her phone down next to her plate. When she's done eating, Beatrice washes her plate by hand, dries it, and returns it to the appropriate cupboard. On her way through the front hallway, she gasps, a figure looming outside on the front lawn. She can see him through the frosted windows on both sides of the front door, a shadow staring up at the house.

Beatrice's eyebrows pull together, taking slow steps toward the front door. She's dealt with enough Ashwood creepiness today. She doesn't need any more of it. She opens the front door to get a better look at the guy standing at the edge of the front yard. He's tall and skinny, wearing a multicolored plaid shirt and ripped jeans. He has an eyebrow piercing shining in the sun and his hands are a bit dirty, Beatrice can see from where she stands.

"Can I help you with something?" Beatrice demands a little bitchier than she intended.

The guy perks up, as though Beatrice just invaded *his* privacy rather than vice versa. "Excuse me?"

"No, excuse *me*," Beatrice shoots back. "You're on my lawn."

"Okay, old man."

Beatrice squints. She remembers Aunt Edie mentioning little punks coming up here on Halloween to get a little look at *the* Ashwood house.

How all of them would creep up along the hedges across the street, daring one another to ring the doorbell. But this guy looks too old to be doing that kind of bullshit.

"Wait a minute," he says when Beatrice finds herself too stunned by his words to react. "It *is* you."

Beatrice shifts from foot to foot. "Depends on who you mean when you say *you*."

"Beatrice Millstone." He starts up the yard, gaping at her like she's some kind of newly found fossil or something. He gestures to himself as though she should know him, too. "It's me. Xander."

Beatrice's jaw drops an inch. *This* is Xander? The same kid that would chase her with worms on sticks? The same boy that would challenge her to pizza roll-eating contests? The same one that thought nothing odd of Ashwood, despite the constant happenings here? He's standing in front of her with that same boyish smile he had when they were kids. His black hair sweeps over his forehead, his slightly slanted Philippine eyes a shade of caramel in the light. He has a few dainty tattoos on his hands and he has gone from being some stranger on the edge of the lawn to someone she used to call a friend.

"Holy shit." Beatrice finds herself saying in surprise, her eyes rapidly blinking in his direction. "You still live around here?"

He nods his head and points down the hill where he used to live. "I still live with Nana. She's not doing so good nowadays, so I never moved out."

"Oh, I'm sorry." She always feels so awkward responding to something hard for someone else. Over the years, she has tried mirroring how other people were around her when they were told about *her* family but she was never smooth with her responses.

Beatrice remembers attending calling hours for Clara's mother when she was sixteen. Instead of giving her condolences to Clara's father and Clara's siblings, she simply told them that everything looked good—which was right after viewing the body. Poor choice of words at a poor time but what else could she say?

"Nah, don't be." His shoulders bounce up and down. "She's ancient. We kind of have this bet going on when we think she's going to pass. I've been winning."

Beatrice folds her arms, growing a bit uncomfortable. "Isn't that a bit morbid?"

"I thought so, but Nana's like that."

"Oh."

"I heard that you were back," Xander says in disbelief, looking her up and down like he still can't believe it's her. "I thought it was some story people were telling for Halloween this year. You and the rest of your family have been the main characters in those things for quite some time. Center stage and all that."

Beatrice craves to hear more. She knows the shit people say about her family is nothing but a bunch of bogus shit-talking, but part of it intrigues her to a certain extent. Part of her wants to be a fly on the wall when these stories are shared. She wants to see who is talking about her and what context they put her and her mother in. She wants to create a list of all the true things they're saying and all of the false ones they've only heard from family and friends of theirs. Xander is an outsider who has never left Silver Creek. He probably knows a lot more than Aunt Edie.

"Do you want to come in?" Beatrice offers, her stomach still growling with hunger. That lunch wasn't enough. "I was just about to make some lunch."

Xander nods, not thinking anything of it. Strangers would probably vigorously nod their heads like rabid bunnies, desperate at the chance to hop inside for more information. Beatrice leads the way into the foyer, shutting the door once Xander is inside.

"So, what do you do?" Beatrice starts small, the way adults like them usually do after not seeing each other after all this time. She never wanted herself to be the kind of person to ask another what they *did*, yet here she is. She also never wanted to be this broke, either, and look how that turned out. "Work, wise."

"You really want to know, Beatrice?"

Beatrice nods, glancing at him over her shoulder. He always said her name so much that Beatrice started liking it back then. It made her sound less like an old bag in a rocking chair.

"I went to grad school and got a fat-ass degree in psychology," Xander explains proudly. Even his walk is the same: a foolish wander toward a cliff's edge without a care in the world, blind to how steep the path eventually gets but yet, never caring. "Now, I am certified in counseling drug addicts and troubled marriage couples and kids who have behavioral issues."

Beatrice stares at him in awe when they arrive in the kitchen. That is a much different path than she thought he would take. When they were younger, they would play a game called Careers. They would each pick a career and live their lives. Beatrice always chose to be a vet, lining up her stuffed animals on the front porch. Xander always pretended to be a chef, making pies out of mud and garnishing them with pine needles and berries from the woods. Sometimes they would swap or choose completely different jobs but they were almost always a vet and a chef.

"Wow," Beatrice says, impressed. She roots through the freezer for something quick and easy to throw in the oven. The only thing she's willing to spare is the pizza rolls. "I am impressed."

Xander snorts, settling down at the breakfast bar and rubbing his palms together. "Yeah, that was all sarcasm. Nana says I'm bad with that."

Beatrice holds up the pizza rolls and he nods his head. "So, you didn't go to grad school?"

"I didn't even go to college," he responds. "In all seriousness, I paint houses."

Now *that* is something he would have chosen in Careers.

"Do you make good money doing that?" Beatrice spills the processed food onto a cookie sheet after setting the temperature for the oven.

"Enough." His shoulders bounce up and down again. "What about you? What is it that you do?

"I work at an antique shop," Beatrice answers, leaning against the counter. "I do research for furniture pieces, mostly. We're hoping to expand to online so that we can ship and then I'll be in charge of entering details and all that."

Xander looks genuinely impressed. "That sounds cool."

Beatrice is glad that someone thinks so. Whenever she mentions her job to other people, they treat it like she's a part-time worker, assuming she's currently in college to get a useless degree. It's nice having someone interested, other than Clara.

"It has its moments," Beatrice responds casually.

Silence falls over the kitchen, the only sound being the oven. Beatrice traces a heart in front of her with the tip of her boot, cursing herself for being so poor at small talk.

"So your nana's dying," Beatrice breaks the silence. "That must suck..."

Xander grins but Beatrice isn't sure why. "Uh, yeah. It does. The circle of life, I guess. You're born to die, at the end of the day."

Beatrice has never thought about death that way. Her mom used to tell her that death was sort of the start of another life, of moving forward into a new realm of some sort. Whether that be here in this world or somewhere else entirely. It sparked a curiosity in Beatrice that she still has to this day. In high school, she watched a series of documentaries about spiritual and religious belief systems, touching on what philosophers believe happens after a human leaves this earth. Where does everyone go? Same place? Opposite places? Stuck where they died for all of eternity?

"Well, you seem to be dealing with it rather well," she points out thoughtfully. "That's good, right?"

"I don't think she's ever going to leave," Xander admits. "And I say that in a positive way, of course."

"What do you mean?"

"Well, dying is just a mindset, Beatrice," he replies. "Scientists claim that energy can never be created nor destroyed, which means our vessels or souls or whatever you want to call it remain."

"Remain where?"

"Everywhere."

Xander soon changes the subject back to Trinkets and Treasures and they migrate through the conversation while they wait for the pizza rolls to bake. They chat about the years they haven't seen each other, and how Xander finished public school with barely passing grades. They talk about how Beatrice had a hard time at her own schools, constantly an outcast and forever The Girl from Ashwood. Xander fills her in on more of his nana's heart condition and how he probably has the same one but he's too scared to officially find out because hospitals and doctor's offices make him want to vomit. Beatrice talks about Clara and her two sons and what it was like living in New York, how everything is so pretty and nice and dreams are coming true until you realize how broke you are. Beatrice then concludes with how she wound up back here to do some work for Aunt Edie before the house goes on the market and how she's planning on bringing some of this furniture back to the city.

"So you'll probably be in town for quite some time then, huh?" Xander looks hopeful. He's that same little boy who used to wait on the outskirts of Ashwood, waiting to be spotted by Beatrice to invite him over.

"If all goes well." Beatrice takes the pizza rolls out of the oven, nearly burning her thumb on the cookie sheet. She uses a spatula to scoop them up, tossing almost every single one onto a paper plate until it's a giant heap of steaming pockets of sauce and fake sausage.

"Beatrice, can I admit something?" he asks.

"Yes." She sits down with him, the plate of pizza rolls in between them now.

"I was sad when you left," Xander confesses shyly, his cheeks growing a slight red. "I waited for a week outside of your house for you to come back the night you left."

Beatrice plucks a pizza roll from the top of the pile and stares at him. "You did?"

He nods his head. "Nana told me I was a fool for even trying to wait up for you. She said that you had bigger things on your plate to deal with than some boy down the street."

It's the half-truth. What happened that night *was* seriously big. But, if they're having truth time, then maybe Beatrice should spill something, too.

"I begged Clara to take me back here before we left," she admits after biting the corner of the pizza roll. "I kept saying that if I was going to leave, I wanted to say bye to you, first. I don't think she could understand me through my wails, though."

"Don't sweat it, Beatrice." Xander reaches for a pizza roll and softly blows on it to cool it down. "You know what they say, though. Everything comes full circle. Here we are, sitting in your kitchen eating pizza rolls."

She laughs an honest laugh. "Life is strange like that."

Beatrice wonders how to bring up Ashwood and its legacy in the town. She wants to know more about neighborly gossip and if people sit around campfires talking about the Millstone family curse the way camp counselors talk about Jason Vorhees. She doesn't want anything sugarcoated. She wants the whole truth and nothing but. Aunt Edie might know a lot from the old folk, but what are the younger people saying? Is it even safe for her to go out in town again or will some mob bombard her with orders to go back to where she came from?

"So, if you sat outside the house after I left, what was my aunt doing?" Beatrice asks casually, wondering if Aunt Edie was just as sad at her being gone as Xander was. She kind of doubts it.

"She didn't come outside." Xander's brow furrows and he's looking at her as if she should already know that. "I thought maybe she would open the front door and tell me to get lost but she never did. I started to wonder if she died, too, in here. She was cooped up like a hermit. I can't blame her, though."

Beatrice sinks her teeth into a pizza roll, impatient. The insides burn the roof of her mouth almost raw. She hides behind her hair as she breathes in through her mouth to cool it down, resisting the urge to spit it out. She thinks about Aunt Edie shielding herself in the house, not bothering to take Beatrice back under her wing. She recalls some argument Clara had over the phone with someone outside of the police station. She was pacing back and forth in front of the automatic doors, telling the person on the other end that she would be insane to let Beatrice return to *that* house. Perhaps it was Aunt Edie?

"So," she says after her eyes stop watering. "What can you tell me about this place?"

Xander grins, eating the pizza rolls without being burned at all. "This is your childhood home. Don't you know all the things about it?"

"Not anymore," Beatrice states. "You're around it more than I am. Do people talk about it? Do people come up and tell scary stories in front of it or some shit? That's what I've been hearing."

Xander lets a laugh out his nose. "Kids aren't really doing that stuff nowadays. They're smoking weed and taking naked photos of themselves."

That's reassuring on a level Beatrice didn't even know existed.

"So, no one comes up here at all?"

He shrugs. "I mean, I don't really keep an eye out for it. If your aunt didn't still live here, I bet a kid or two would do that kind of shit. But again, it's not like I keep an eye out for them."

"I see."

"I mean, even after the week I waited for you to come back, I'd come up here and check in," he goes on, curiously studying a pizza roll in his hand. "I don't like to call myself a Peeping Tom but that's what I was. I used to look through the front window to see if you had come back and I didn't know."

Beatrice feels terrible for not trying harder to call him, to force Clara to look his nana up or something, or to call Aunt Edie and give her a message to give to Xander. The thought of him climbing up the hill all by himself just to peer through some glass in hopes she had returned makes her sad.

"Sorry, Beatrice," he mumbles. "Didn't mean to depress you."

"You didn't," she assures. *The house does.* "It's just, being away from something so long makes you think about a lot. About the past and now the present."

"I'm guessing it's not a good feeling."

She shakes her head, peeling apart a pizza roll in her hand, numb to the burns being inflicted on her skin. "No, not the best."

"Well, at least this place wasn't abandoned," he points out, shoving another roll into his mouth. "Your Aunt Edie tried hard to keep this place rented out year-round. There were always flyers for it in town."

Beatrice wipes her fingers on a napkin. "Really? Always?"

"Most of the time," Xander answers. "That's a whole other story itself."

Beatrice scoots to the edge of the stool, wanting more. There's something about this place that teases her mind. She remembers when she would live here and hear those strange noises all over. She and Juniper used to race to find the sources of those noises. The one who found them the fastest would win. Just as Beatrice would round a corner, the source of the sound would disappear. She would open cupboards and doors, convinced she was going to win. But every time, they both lost. Tricked into throwing in the towel.

"What do you mean?" Beatrice asks.

"Well, I mean, that most of the girls who rented this place out are like, missing." He's whispering now, almost like he's afraid he'll get in trouble for mentioning any of this to her. Maybe he'll even get scolded for eating with her.

The word *missing* echoes through Beatrice's mind and she suddenly no longer wants to eat. "I'm not sure what you mean."

"I remember seeing a few of them arrive," he explains. "One of them had these huge gages. You know what gages are, right, Beatrice?"

"Those ugly ear hole things?"

He nods his head. "She had those. And I remember thinking about what odd accessories they were. Then, like, two weeks later, she ends up on a news segment about being missing. Nana was watching the news, Beatrice, not me. So, I looked at the screen and I thought, *Hm, I remember seeing those gauges.* And it turns out it was her."

"Was she ever found?"

He shakes his head. "None of them were. Another girl with this nasty green hair lived here too. She was a complete hippie. Stayed less time than the gages chick. And you know those columns in magazines where they put the missing people?"

Beatrice nods.

"She was in there. They used a mug shot of her, but she had blue hair then," Xander explains intently. "There's been a few guys but not a lot. They're mostly chicks and they don't end up staying. One week they're here, the next, they're not. It gets super weird around this time, too. Nana thinks it has something to do with the Burned Man."

Beatrice's mind buzzes with recognition. She doesn't know where she heard that, but the title of a man with that mysterious name rings a bell with her. "Why does that sound familiar?"

"Because I told you about him before, Beatrice," he informs. "Shortly before you left. You were crying about… the twins."

Beatrice winces, pushing the plate of pizza rolls away from her. She remembers lashing out at Xander, ordering him to never say their names again when he asked if there was any follow-up on Jax and Juniper's whereabouts. She then cried on his shoulder as they sat on the porch steps. He told her that he thought it had something to do with the Burned Man.

"It's an old story," Xander says, now, recapping for her. "But there's this guy who lives in an old shack in the woods behind our houses. He has these terrible burn marks from his real house burning down. The insurance didn't cover anything so he moved out into the woods and only comes out now and then. Apparently, he's listed as a sexual predator online. Did you know you can find that stuff online?"

Beatrice nods and gestures for him to go on with the story, growing a little impatient.

"Well, Nana thinks that he preys on the girls who stay here," Xander proceeds, his eyebrow slightly raised. "Think about it. This house is pretty high up on this hill. No one really comes up here but Aunt Edie. And now that she's the only one that lives here, it makes it so easy for him to snatch one up and do what he does."

"Have the police investigated anyone?" Beatrice croaks, suddenly feeling like she's no longer in her home but in the middle of some serial killer Netflix documentary. "Have they looked into this guy who lives in the woods?"

"They tried but he had no evidence linking him to any of the girls," Xander explains. "They searched his house and everything, but they came up with nothing. Their investigations don't last awhile. They get distracted by something else, something bigger and not as important as missing girls. Beatrice, did you know that most disappearances end up in death during the first 48 hours of them being gone?"

"I didn't know that," Beatrice replies. "But now I do." *And it's unsettling as hell.*

She glances around the kitchen, feeling cold. She wonders if she will become one of those missing girls, just another name on a long list of cold cases that will forever go unsolved. Why didn't Aunt Edie mention any of this to her? Why is she just now learning about all of this information from an old friend when Aunt Edie herself could have given her the rundown on this place? And why hasn't this been brought up on any of the websites dedicated to Ashwood? One would think that hardcore fans would include this in their little articles and forums, gushing about how these mysterious disappearances only happen at Ashwood. But that, of course, would ruin the whole belief that the Millstones have a curse on them. That belief system is a hell of a lot more scandalous.

"I should leave." Xander disrupts her thoughts, scooting his stool out away from the bar. "I've been in your hair for too long already."

"Yeah, Aunt Edie will be home soon, anyway." She gets up from the stool, unsure what to do with the rest of the pizza rolls on the plate but her head is too filled up with other information to care right now.

"It was really nice seeing you again, Beatrice," Xander says on his way to the front door. "It was a good surprise. I'm glad I came up to see if the rumors were true myself."

Beatrice smiles at him, opening the door. "Me too. Come over whenever you'd like. And hey, I might even need you to paint a few walls or something."

Xander salutes. "I'm your guy."

They say goodbye and Beatrice finds herself alone in the house once more. She ties her hair into a ponytail on her way up the steps, wondering when Aunt Edie will be home. She shuts her bedroom door behind her and snatches her laptop from her bag propped up against the bedside table. Beatrice settles down in the window seat, gnawing at her nails as she waits for it to load. The information Xander shared with her is too much to ignore. First, she had to come back and deal with the House Things weighing heavily on her mind. Now, she learns the truth about the tenants that used to live here, most of them missing.

Beatrice pulls up Google and types into the search engine: *Missing Girls, Silver Creek, Massachusetts.* The results load in seconds, spilling out news articles and small advertisements asking if she has seen this person or that person. Beatrice selects the IMAGES tab, photos of all these different girls popping up on the page. She squints at the screen, scrolling down until she finds the one Xander described with the gages or the green hair. Gage Girl appears just a few rows deep, a selfie of her wearing a beanie and her pierced tongue out. She clicks it.

A website dedicated to missing people in the state loads onto the screen in alphabetical order. Beatrice blinks at the number of pages available. 1168 pages of missing people. Beatrice bites the inside of her cheek and clicks the back button. She downloads the picture of Gage Girl and then opens a new tab. Even though she online dates, doesn't mean she's dumb about it. Every picture a guy has sent her, she has downloaded and then reverse image searched it into the internet to make sure she isn't getting catfished. She's only come across one guy who sent her pictures online but that was because he was a model. And guess what his name was.

Beatrice uploads the picture to the site, and a little popup box informs her that the internet is being searched for the image with a loading bar beneath it. Beatrice impatiently drums her fingers against the laptop and perks up when it finishes. Gage Girl's selfie pops up, the same one used on the missing person's site. Beatrice clicks the link and is led to a Facebook account belonging to a girl named Nova Price. Scrolling down it, Beatrice reads the bio located under the cover photo of her skateboarding at a local park. The bio reads: *If you're living without passion, you're already fucking dead.*

The photos on the page depict her with the same group of people, all of them with pierced faces and checkerboard clothing. There's one of Nova and a friend standing together outside of a tattoo and piercing place, nipple rings showing through their shirts. The caption reads, *I'd flash my new tit rings but I'm not trying to get banned LMFAO.*

Beatrice clicks out of the pictures, none of them showing any sign of living at Ashwood. Thankfully, Nova's account is nowhere even close to being private. All of the girls that Beatrice has met like Nova, think social media is the devil and don't post anything on it, keeping all aspects of their life private. But Nova has no shame in sharing her life with the world. Even her posts are public. The last one Nova ever made reads: *Yooooo if I go MIA, send a search team LMFAO.*

The post makes bile rise in Beatrice's throat. It's dated two years back in the month of July. Beatrice moves to the next post, all of them becoming more and more understanding:

For everyone who is concerned: Yes, I've found a place to live.

Can't pay rent. Can't pay utilities. Can't pay for food. I'M LIVING MY FUCKING LIFE, YO. There's a picture of her drinking outside at a bonfire with a few people standing around in the background. She's flipping the camera off, her middle finger erect and a bitchy grimace splashed across her face.

FUUUCCKKK. If anyone knows of any places hiring, lmk

The posts before this one are random shares and tagged photos.

Nothing about Ashwood or the path that would lead to her demise of any kind.

Beatrice goes back to her other tab in search of the girl with green hair. She finds two in the county but one of them is a fourteen-year-old runaway. The other is a twenty-something female with a button nose and plump lips, a mug shot as her missing person's photo—and blue hair in the shot, just like what Xander said. Beatrice runs the same course as she did with Nova. She downloads the picture of Green Girl and plugs it into the image reverse site. She watches the same loading bar inch across the pop-up box until police records are pulled up about the mysterious girl with the mug shot. The link leads her to the county police's site where mug shots are laid out on a screen like a sea of criminal activity. Green Girl's vibrant blue hair color catches Beatrice's attention right away and she clicks.

Her name is Lila Seckondorff and she was arrested for trespassing and then refusing arrest. Beatrice opens yet another tab to type her name into Google. Her Instagram shows up first and Beatrice is led her to the account, which features 567 followers and 69 posts. A string of emojis covers her bio with no words. The grid of photos on her profile features artsy portraits and pictures from protests, marches, and flea markets. In one photo, she poses in an empty room, sunlight lined across her face as she wears a navy blue shirt with *Feminist* printed across it in yellow letters. In another photo, she's lying in the grass, tiny white flowers decorating her newly dyed green hair. Beatrice clicks on the last photo Lila took, the familiarity screaming through the screen.

Lila is sitting on the front steps of Ashwood, her knees pinched together and her elbows resting on her thighs. Her head is tilted to the side and she's casting a peaceful smile at whoever is taking the photo. The caption reads: *Finding my peace.* What is *that* supposed to mean? Since when is there ever peace in this house? Beatrice notices *See More...* under her caption so she clicks on it. A vertical line of bullet points breaks the caption away from the camera emoji at the bottom with a colon and a tagged user on Instagram. Beatrice doesn't spend much time on social media but she gathers that this means the tagged user is the one who took the photo. Beatrice clicks on her handle.

The username is Alice_Down_the_Rabbit_Hole and she could be a model. With a profile dedicated to professional portraits and shoots of her in the iconic *Alice in Wonderland* dress, she poses next to trees and in fields of grass and dark woods, becoming the character with all of these shots. Her bio consists of an email for bookings and Beatrice considers reaching out to her to ask questions about Lila. Just to make sure she hasn't become another missing girl, too, Beatrice clicks on the last photo she uploaded, one of her peering down an actual rabbit hole. October 1. That was just two weeks ago.

Beatrice copies and pastes the girl's email into her own, her thumbs hovering over the keys. She sinks her teeth into her bottom lip, debating on what she should say and how she should say it and if she's going to come across as some amateur detective researching all the missing girls here. She takes a breath and starts typing, her fingers flying over the keys as fast as her brain is spewing her a brilliant excuse.

Hey, Alice! I hope that's your real name. But I recently moved to Silver Creek and I stumbled upon your friend Lila's IG page. I was led to yours from her posts and I would just LOVE to do a piece on you for my writing class. I know this sounds insanely weird, but we have to interview with local people and your IG is too interesting not to follow. Big Alice in Wonderland *fan here so it would be an honor. If not, that's cool too. I've attached my number at the bottom of this page if you're interested. Or you can email me back. Thanks in advance!*

—Beatrice Montgomery

Ashwood. Before.

Nine-year-old Beatrice left her bedroom with a high ponytail one November morning. She tightened it as she walked across the creaky floorboards beneath her, proud of herself for not needing her mother's help. The house was still mourning, it seemed, now that Grammy was dead. Suicide. She was going a little insane in the years leading up to her death but no one thought anything of it. They figured it was because of Grandpa Hugh's death. Aunt Marley claimed that it was quite possible to lose your mind when a loved one died. Beatrice hoped and prayed that night that she would never lose hers.

Mourn is such a weird word, Beatrice thought to herself on occasion now. It's a word that should only be used as an antonym for *night*.

Beatrice noticed Aunt Edie standing at the other end of the corridor with her back turned toward her, gently swaying from side to side like a woman with no balance. Beatrice stopped in her tracks, her head tilting to the side. Aunt Edie was talking but there was nobody there so she must have been talking to herself. Talking, talking, talking. That was all that she was doing. Beatrice wondered if it had something to do with Uncle Eli talking to the house outside like he did, as though it was a real person.

Beatrice stayed toward the walls as she crept closer to her aunt because the sides of the hall were always far less creaky than the middle. As she got closer, she could hear Aunt Edie's voice, that dark and seductive tone she once tried teaching Beatrice but her mother put a stop to it. Aunt Edie had been extra vain lately, according to Aunt Marley and Ma. She was dying her hair with boxed colors more than usual and she spent her days lathering her skin with lotions and creams to stop herself from getting wrinkles that were already there. She'd place warm tea bags on her eyes to prevent bags from forming, and she would even dip her head into pots of hot milk to strengthen her hair growth. Nothing worked. In fact, Beatrice was pretty sure that everything Aunt Edie did to stop herself from looking any older than she was, was making her look far worse. Kind of like an old witch from a fairytale.

"I don't want to sleep anymore," Aunt Edie was saying to the invisible space in front of her. She was wearing one of her usual long silk dresses that looked like a nightgown until Beatrice stepped closer and realized that it actually *was* a nightgown. Baby blue, stopping at her ankles. She was shaking her head at no one, as though they were responding. "I just want to wake up."

Beatrice swallowed, afraid to approach her. Living in a house with several old people got scary sometimes, especially when Aunt Edie would have one of her sleep episodes; which would consist of her wandering the house in the middle of the night. She had even wandered outside before and woke up in the woods.

"Let me wake up," Aunt Edie begged, her voice wobbly with tears.

"Aunt Edie?" Beatrice asked quietly, reaching out and touching her back with the tips of her fingers.

Aunt Edie whipped around, her poorly dyed brown hair pinned away from her face, hanging in stringy strands down her shoulders. Her eyes were glossed over like she was wearing grey contacts or like she was suddenly blind. She stared right at Beatrice, frightening her enough to send her a few stumbling steps backward.

"Darling Bea." Aunt Edie held her hand in front of her as she took a few shaky steps forward, as though she was a deer learning to walk for the first time. A pleading expression flooded her face and instead of gaining sympathy from Beatrice, she terrified her. "Please, help me wake up."

Beatrice's eyes grew wide as she slowly started taking steps backward, her heart thundering within her chest. She felt like she was in one of those old Japanese horror movies Xander brought over one time on VHS. Beatrice would shield her eyes the whole time and Xander would watch with so much interest Beatrice often wondered what else he watched without his nana's supervision.

"But you're already awake," Beatrice squeaked.

"Aunt Edie is sleepwalking, dear," she told her, looming over her great niece like a terrible child abductor looking for innocent prey. The lines in her face seemed deeper and her eyes were bugging out of her head, growing so wide Beatrice thought they might just pop out. "Help me wake up. *Now*, sweetie."

Beatrice's tiny chest heaved in and out as the hallway began growing shorter and shorter behind her, the wall being way closer than she expected. Her back reached the end, the wainscot digging into her spine. As her aunt got closer, Beatrice built up enough strength in her throat to scream as loudly as she could, mouth open and throat swelling up as she shoved enough out of her as possible.

Aunt Edie came to a stop in front of her, rapidly blinking the gray from her eyes as she stared down at her wrinkly hands like she'd never seen them before. Her nails were painted blood red and they were trembling, like how Beatrice did when she would wake from her own nightmares. Aunt Edie exhaled and grabbed her stomach like she was about to be sick. Beatrice watched her quietly, not saying anything.

"Bea, what are you doing?" She looked at her in confusion, breathing heavily and gasping for breath. "Are you all right?"

Beatrice blinked, mirroring her puzzled expression. "You were sleepwalking, Aunt Edie. You wanted me to wake you up."

Aunt Edie thought to herself as though she just remembered. She looked more awake now and she ran a slender hand over her hair. "Oh, right. Sometimes my dreams grow a life of their own. Like *Jack and the Beanstalk*." She got to her knees to be at eye-level with her. "What do you say we make some peanut butter brownies? I think I know where Grammy Astrid keeps the recipe."

Chapter 6

Beatrice wakes up to the sound of pattering rain hitting the bedroom windows. It takes her a few seconds to blink herself out of the disorientation, sitting up in the daybed, yesterday coming back to her like the sun emerging from behind the clouds. She did hours of research on the missing girls who once stayed here in Ashwood, making a long list of them in one of the notebooks she picked up on her second day here. She filled the lines with their first and last names and included their ages—which ranged from early twenties to thirties. She couldn't track down each one of them online, but she did find that some were students at the community college, and others were not.

Beatrice thought that she would find some sort of pattern between them all, something familiar about each of them that would make them the same kind of target. She knows that a lot of serial killers and kidnappers would have some sort of type about their victims. Whether they be people who don't have many family members so nobody would miss them when they're gone, or they all have blond hair, or they all jog the same trails at state parks. But even through all her digging, Beatrice couldn't find one thing that would make them all fall under the same umbrella.

Except for them all once living here.

Her laptop is open next to her against the wall, the screen black. Beatrice catches a glimpse of herself in the reflection. Her hair is wilder than usual, knotted and twisted together on one side. One of the itchy yarn blankets from the hall closet is pulled up to her waist and she feels like her head has been hit with a bag of bricks. She shuts her laptop and fumbles for the charger plugged in next to the bedside table. She jabs it into the side of her computer and then stretches her arms over her head. She doesn't remember hearing Aunt Edie get home. She was too sucked into the deep vortex of stalking these girls that she wasn't even paying attention. She laid down just for a few minutes and hibernated enough into a dream world.

Beatrice rises from the bed and opens her bedroom door, the cold draft wrapping itself around her bare ankles. She peers out the tall window at the end of the hallway. Aunt Edie's car sits in the driveway, buried in the early morning October fog. Beatrice jumps at the touch of a hand on her shoulder. She whips around to find Aunt Edie herself standing in front of her, calmly blinking in confusion.

"What are you doing up so early, child?" Aunt Edie asks her.

"I uh, fell asleep early last night," Beatrice says honestly, listening to her heart thump between her ears. She doesn't know why, but she suddenly feels cornered. "What time did you get home? I didn't even hear you."

Aunt Edie shrugs her bony shoulder. "I don't know."

Beatrice blinks when she doesn't say anything else. Maybe it's an old lady thing—forgetting the important things and letting time slip away through her wrinkly old fingers. Or, maybe Aunt Edie doesn't want her to know where she's been. Beatrice wouldn't doubt it.

"Well, okay," Beatrice says finally. "I guess I'll get dressed, then."

"Bea, darling, were you in the attic again today?" Aunt Edie asks when Beatrice moves around her to get back into her room.

Beatrice looks at her over her shoulder. "In the attic? No. I just got up."

"Then were you yesterday?"

"No. Why?"

"The doors were open," she answers. "I try to keep them shut. The draft that comes from it is just awful."

"I will keep note of that."

Beatrice hides away in her room, putting on a flannel shirt and army-green jeans. She's almost too afraid to come out and have breakfast with Aunt Edie downstairs. She would rather stay cooped up in here, doing more research on those missing girls and where they are, and why they all stayed here and then suddenly vanished from thin air. *Poof.*

But, if Beatrice spends another night on this shitty mattress, she's going to be losing a lot more sleep. She slips her wallet into her purse and starts for the day. She decides to skip breakfast and go straight to brushing her teeth, rinsing her mouth out with Listerine. Aunt Edie is in the kitchen making tea by the time Beatrice comes downstairs.

"I'm going out to buy a new mattress," Beatrice says to her. "I shouldn't be very long."

"Are you sure you want to do that today?" Aunt Edie holds her large black mug in her hand, dipping her teabag inside of it like a yo-yo. Up and down, up and down, up and down…

"Yes?" Beatrice basically guesses.

"You've barely made any progress on the house." Aunt Edie waltzes toward her to the doorway of the mud room where Beatrice stands. "And by barely, I mean none at all."

"I know, I'll get to it," she promises. She's only been here for like, five minutes. "You don't need everything done by a certain time, do you?"

"No, of course not, but I just want to make sure you're getting your use out of the house," Aunt Edie explains. She's different today. Not as flighty or carefree as she usually is. She seems on edge, almost bitter about something Beatrice can't put her finger on. "You are getting good use out of it, aren't you? What with your work and all?"

"Oh, yes, of course," Beatrice blubbers, nodding her head a little too fast. "I've even sent pictures of the stuff in the attic to my boss and he is going to love everything even more in person."

She smiles now, looking relieved. "Well, that's good to hear."

"Yeah." Beatrice awkwardly fiddles with the strap of her satchel bag, feeling like a little girl again caught doing something she isn't supposed to be doing. "If that's all, then?"

Aunt Edie nods, a tight smile playing across her lips. "Be safe."

Aunt Edie's car hums loudly as Beatrice steers it down the hill, wet yellow leaves sticking to the windshield as she cruises through the heavy fog rolled out in front of her. She passes Xander's house at the bottom of the hill and then cruises into town. Silver Creek is still sleepy by the time Beatrice finds a Mattress Queen store on the corner of Arlington and Chenoweth. There are a few dog walkers out and an old couple power walking down the sidewalk but other than that, nobody. Good.

"Hi there!" an enthusiastic college-aged guy welcomes Beatrice into the store. The white button-down shirt he's wearing seems a little too big for him but he seems too excited to be alive today to even care. "Welcome to Mattress Queen! What can I do for you today?"

"I need a mattress for a daybed," she answers. "You do have those, right?"

"Over here." He leads the way down the long aisle of model mattresses with spongy tops and memory foam surfaces and signs about fall sales until they reach the corner of the store where the mattresses with daybed dimensions are displayed. "What kind were you hoping for? Memory foam? Something a little less stiff? You can test out any of these."

"I just need the second to last cheapest," she informs impatiently.

He looks at her quizzically. "Second to last cheapest?"

She nods her head. "Not the cheapest, but the one just above it."

"What an odd request."

"It's not something I'm going to be sleeping on for years to come but I need it to have enough back support." Beatrice sighs, unreasonably annoyed.

Realization blankets his face as he points a finger at her. It's almost as though the freckles dancing across his pale white skin perk up, too. "Hey, I know you!"

Beatrice studies him. From his ginger red hair and lanky body, he doesn't ring any bells. "The feeling isn't mutual."

"You're that girl who grew up in Ashwood," he gushes.

It has finally happened. Someone who isn't friends with Aunt Edie knows of her and probably thinks he's very well educated on the happenings at Ashwood, convinced he knows the ins and outs of what took place there. Beatrice could refuse and claim that she's someone else, a divorcee from Rhode Island. A real estate agent just outside of town. A schoolteacher with a husband and a child. Or, she could shrug it off and nod. Alive and in the flesh.

"Am I?" Beatrice plays dumb, turning her attention onto the mattress he pointed to seconds ago. "Guess I didn't notice."

"What are you *doing* here?" the guy gushes. He folds his skinny arms over his narrow chest, leaning in a little, ready to bite into whatever gossip Beatrice is willing to spill. "You haven't been here in *ages.*"

Beatrice isn't sure if she's more annoyed at his emphasis on random words or that he's talking to her as though she's some glamorous celebrity. She glances over her shoulder at the front door of the store to make sure no one else is coming in. She considers lying and making up some excuse on why she could be back in Silver Creek but that seems a lot more difficult rather than just explaining her work. It's not like she has to go into specifics of how she's broke and now relying on a family member that she hasn't seen in years to pay her to do some housework. That would just sound pathetic.

"I'm in town for some work," she answers honestly.

"*Work?*" the guy goes on, adjusting his folded arms and wrinkling his shirt in the process. "What is your work? Oh my God, I thought you lived in New York."

"I still do," Beatrice snaps at him impatiently. "And no offense, dude, but I came here to buy a mattress. If I would have known I was going to be interrogated like this, I would've gone somewhere else.

Mattress *King* or something."

"That doesn't exist." A flashy smile spreads across his chapped red lips.

She's trying her best to not sound too bitchy but it's hard when strangers know what city she lives in and ask personal questions about why she's back in her hometown. Sure, people come back to the places they grew up all the time but she doubts that they're bombarded with questions as annoying and intrusive as these. She can't say that she's too surprised. Judging by the obsessive bloggers online, it was only a matter of time until she bumped into one in real life.

"I've been meaning to come into your store," he goes on, clearly not finished with his questions. "It would be a long drive for me but I love vintage."

She observes him. "You know where I work?"

"I'm sure I could find it." He shrugs. "There's a page I follow about you, I hope that doesn't sound weird. But your family is like, my religion. Everyone here still talks about you guys."

Beatrice winces, plopping down on a mattress to give it a try, hoping this will steer him away from asking anything else. She's never understood why people are so fond of other people who are in the public eye. They're humans, too. They walk the same earth, breathe the same air. Why is it that these people are so easily pined over just for being talked about?

"I don't like memory foam," Beatrice tells him.

"Is it true that the twins are still missing?"

The question makes the walls of the mattress store start closing in around her. She suddenly feels squished between two giant ones, suffocating her while her screams and cries for help are muffled by the padding. She tries not to think about her cousins. Jax and Juniper made a few headlines after their disappearances, their freckled faces splashed over the news. Aunt Marley lost her mind after they were taken. Beatrice thinks they *all* kind of lost their minds when that fateful day happened. She tries not thinking about it because that day was a blur and made little sense to her at all. She thought her dreams were trying to tell her what happened to Juniper and Jax but her mother insisted that she was simply imagining.

"I want this one," Beatrice tells him. "And I expect a discount or else I call your boss and let them know you harassed me about my home life the entire time I was here."

He's no longer smiling with glee and it brings Beatrice a twisted joy.

The mattress fits awkwardly in the back of the car, half of it hanging out the back and strapped in with bungee cords. Beatrice shoved it in her entire self, telling the guy she didn't need his help. After spending a few minutes pushing and shoving and grunting, it settled inside once she inched the front seat up almost directly to the steering wheel to the point where she should have just smashed her face against the windshield. The drive back to Ashwood is haunting. Not because of the skeletons hanging in storefront windows or ghosts dangling from tree branches, but because the memory of Juniper and Jax sifts through her mind. Their laughs echo off the walls inside of her head, the sounds of their pattering feet against the driveway ringing out from endless summer afternoons. They would now be twenty-two if nothing happened to them. Alive, spending their birthdays together. Finding love. Going to college or not going to college. Paying their phone bills and posing for pictures on social media. They would be safe.

But that's the thing about Ashwood: it's not safe, no matter how much love is spread through those rooms. It stands proud on its hill, strong against the winds. A house made up of so much structure and stability that everything inside must be weak and flimsy just to balance it all out. Including those who walk among it.

Beatrice's brow furrows when she pulls into the driveway to find two other vintage cars parked alongside each other, orange and red leaves spilled over the tops as though they've been sitting here for a while. Beatrice leaves the mattress in the car as she makes her way inside, wondering if Xander or his nana is visiting. She can only hope.

A laugh echoes through the sitting room when Beatrice slips into the foyer.

"Exactly," a woman's voice is saying. "I just don't see the point in any of it. It's not like they're being used at all. Am I wrong, Marilyn?"

"No, Ruth, you're absolutely right." Beatrice recognizes her voice to be the woman from the store the other day, claiming that she used to come over when Beatrice was younger and play poker with Aunt Edie. Guess her story about knowing Aunt Edie checks out. "But stealing things from other people's yards can still land you in some hot water. Even if they're just flowers."

"I suppose I'd have to ask my lawyer about that one." A long slurp follows and the gentle *clink* of a teacup lands on a plate.

Beatrice peeks around the corner into the sitting room, where she feels like she's just stepped into an expensive coffee table book about styling mansions and how to host successful dinner parties. Aunt Edie sits on the sofa with a teacup in hand, steam floating out the top in long white ribbons. Marilyn is seated on the stiff chair to the left, her long legs folded out in front of her, while a dark-skinned lady is on the other chair, her fingers threaded together in her lap.

"Beatrice darling, you're home." Aunt Edie perks up, smiling at her. Seems like her attitude from earlier has left. "Please, come join us for tea. We were just having one of our garden club meetings."

Beatrice takes a safe step into the sitting room, glancing around for proof of other people. "Your garden club consists of just the three of you?"

"We're the presidents," the lady Beatrice doesn't know speaks up proudly. She's wearing a pink blazer and matching tweed skirt, a white gaucho hat covering her head. "Well, Edie is the president. Marilyn and I are vice."

"Beatrice, it's so nice to see you again." Marilyn smiles at her, showing off her straight, peril-white teeth.

"I don't believe you've met Ruth yet, Bea." Aunt Edie gestures to the lady in pink before taking a sip of her tea. "Ruth and I go way back."

Ruth smirks, sending a glance Aunt Edie's way. "We sure do."

If Beatrice didn't know how horny Aunt Edie was back then for guys, she would believe that Ruth was her lover.

"Beatrice works with antiques," Aunt Edie says proudly as if she's a mother with the duty to show off her child to other moms at a PTA meeting. She sets her cup down on the floral-printed saucer plate on the coffee table. "She's in town to pick up a few things from the attic. Lord knows how desperate it is to be emptied."

"I have a few pieces that you could take with you," Marilyn offers. "When Pete died, I didn't know what to do with any of the damned things. He was a collector."

Beatrice perks up, leaning her shoulder against the threshold. "What kind of antiques did he collect?"

"Those god-awful western plates." Marilyn rolls her eyes so hard that they nearly get stuck in her pretty little head. "You know, the ceramic ones that are only designed to be hung up on the wall? They have cows all over them and pigs and men wearing cowboy hats. They were the most hideous thing I ever allowed in my house."

"I doubt they're as hideous as Madeline's art," Ruth growls next, rolling her eyes just as hard. "I keep telling her to create something bright and full of life. All she wants to do is make sexual organs the size of bookshelves. I just don't get it. Maybe I will never understand the artistic world nowadays but if it's anything like that, I don't think I want to."

"Ruth's daughter is an artist," Aunt Edie informs Beatrice. "Where does she live again, Ruth?"

"As of right now, Prague," she answers stubbornly, pursing her blood-red lips. "She thinks that her traveling the world is going to help her creativity."

"That could be true," Marilyn comments thoughtfully.

"Yes, but if it's true, and she's making these sculptures that look like gentiles, then what is she doing to open her creative windows?" Ruth rants, shaking her head in disgust as she reaches for her tea again. "I'm sorry, but I don't want my daughter running around the world opening her legs just for the sake of art."

Beatrice laughs because Ruth is genuinely funny. Other people open their legs for a lot of other things but Ruth isn't ready to hear *that*. It's odd seeing other people inside Ashwood. It was even weird seeing Xander here but that was only because it pushed her back in time so hard she nearly got whiplash. But these two other women, clearly not caring about any of the rumors they heard about this house, sitting here enjoying their time with Aunt Edie. Do all the members of this garden club know about Aunt Edie being a Millstone? Do any of them know the truth? Has Aunt Edie confided in these two other women about the things she witnessed here? The thought of someone else knowing the truth, someone outside of the family, almost frightens Beatrice but she doesn't know why.

"Well, I will let you guys get to your planning," Beatrice announces louder than she intends. "I'm going to haul my mattress upstairs."

"Okay, darling." Aunt Edie smiles again. "Let us know if you need any sort of assistance. Ruth and Marilyn would be happy to help."

The women cackle together as Beatrice makes her way outside. She opens her car door, trying not to call herself pathetic again for intending to sleep on a mattress of this size. It's not forever, though. She hauls it out of the car—a battle in itself—and glances up at the house, where movement catches her eye in the upstairs hall window. Beatrice feels her ears go hot for a second as she stares up at the glass, the thin curtains softly moving as though whoever was up there ducked behind it.

Her eyes then flicker to the windows of the sitting room, where Ruth is nodding along with something Marilyn is saying, Aunt Edie, sipping her tea again. Beatrice's stomach tightens into a tangled mess of knots. What the hell did she just see upstairs?

A crow swoops down, disrupting her thoughts but making her even more shaken up than she already is. She quickly starts for the front path leading inside, not entirely careful with the mattress in the process. When she pulls it up to the second floor, nothing is up here. The curtains remain untouched and the three women are still in the front room chatting about gardening tips they hope to go over in the next meeting.

Breathless, Beatrice makes her bed, coming up with all sorts of reasons why the curtain could have moved. It's an old house. Drafts come through here as often as dust collects in the corners. It's not unusual. But, Beatrice's childhood flashes before her eyes. Growing up with the unknown House Things as though they were pets. Weird gurgles from the basement or footsteps in the attic became normal, something to not be afraid of. But Beatrice has been out in the world. She has learned from more than enough resources that those things are in fact, not normal. It is not normal for Great Granny Ophelia to suddenly drop dead at the dinner table or for her husband to fall asleep in the bathtub and accidentally drown. Or for Grandpa Hugh to die in his sleep with a snapped neck. Or for Uncle Eli to fall through the basement stairs, his shoes completely off when he was found. Or for Aunt Marley to scream until she died in the kitchen. None of that is normal. Yet, it was her reality and the longer she spends time within these walls, it still is.

Chapter 7

Beatrice skipped dinner that evening and settled for pretzels and Nutella, promising herself she wasn't going to fall back into her unhealthy diet of skipping full meals, but she can't bring herself to sit across from Aunt Edie at a table and pretend like she hasn't been snooping into the recent past of Ashwood, as though countless girls haven't stayed in this house and suddenly vanished from thin air, just like Juniper and Jax.

So, she made some excuse about having to do some work on her laptop and that she was already behind on a deadline that doesn't exist. She felt a little bad making Aunt Edie eat by herself downstairs but she's probably used to it by now. Technically, Beatrice didn't lie. She *did* have work to do on her laptop, just nothing to do with the antique store. She spent hours of her evening trying to hunt down more girls who lived in Ashwood. The first night she dug into all of this, it was a little more complicated than she thought it would be. She researched every single missing girl in the county in hopes not all of them stayed here at the house. But over a fifteen-year course of Aunt Edie being by herself and renting out a room, it was bound to draw in a few innocent victims. That's what Ashwood does and did for roughly fourteen young people. Fourteen people that the police have no leads on whatsoever and who lack any sort of solid connections from the world. People who have been swept under the rug for being lone wolves or abandoned.

This morning, Beatrice changes into a black and white striped sweater and jeans with holes in them that aren't supposed to be there. She pulls her hair into a ponytail, gathering the locks through her fingers when she hears a *ding* come from her laptop open on her bed. She glances at it over her shoulder, seeing the little mail icon pop up in the bottom corner of her screen. She dashes over to it, pulling up Gmail and hoping that it's Alice, Lila's friend who took that photo of Lila for Instagram.

Sure enough, a new email waits to be opened at the top of the screen from Alice's booking email. Beatrice opens it.

Hi, Beatrice. Yes, my real name is Alice. And I'd be happy to do an interview with you! First one, OMG. But I hope this gets to you in time. I'm gonna be leaving town for a little bit tomorrow so today is really the only day we can meet until I'm able to return. Hope to hear back from you soon. Xx, Alice.

Beatrice slowly breathes through her mouth, nervously drumming her fingers against her laptop once again. She feels like she does before she goes on one of her little Tinder dates. She quickly types back an email with a place and time, hoping it gets to her straight away. Beatrice ventures out of her room, shutting the door behind her and heading downstairs to catch breakfast before she has to meet Alice. She turns her phone's notifications on full sound. When she reaches the bottom of the stairs, Aunt Edie stands in the doorway of the house, her eyes glued to the front lawn. She's slightly swaying from side to side, the way she used to do when…

"Aunt Edie?" Beatrice asks softly, afraid to approach her. She finds herself in her young girl self again, wondering why old people had to be so weird and why Aunt Edie slept-walk so much.

Aunt Edie doesn't answer. She's continuing to train her eyes on nothing outside but yet on everything at once. And then, she speaks. "They're in the house."

The words send a rush of worry through Beatrice's veins. She doesn't dare say another word, hoping to get a few crumbs of information on whatever the hell it is she's talking about. *Who* is in the house?

"All over," Aunt Edie continues, shaking her head. "They're all over the *fucking* house."

Beatrice listens to her tone getting more and more angry. Should she wake her? Or should she just let her do her thing and keep listening? Is she talking about the girls that were here before her? Or is she talking nonsense, as her sleepwalking episodes usually go?

Suddenly, Aunt Edie snaps her head around to stare at her great-niece. Beatrice's eyes widen, her lips parting. She looks exactly how she used to look back then with her grey, glazed-over eyes. Her jaw is clenched, lips turned down into a frown. She reaches her arm out in front of her, exposing the wrinkles crawling up her skin like vines. Her fingers are wide apart, as though there should be webs in between.

"Bea," Aunt Edie whispers.

"You're sleepwalking, Aunt Edie," Beatrice tells her gently, grabbing hold of the banister to the stairs. The little girl inside of her wants to sprint back up to the safety of her room and not come out until she knows Aunt Edie is awake again. But the adult side of her wants to stay put and make sure she doesn't do anything reckless or dangerous.

"Wake me up, my dear," Aunt Edie croaks, stepping toward her. "Wake me up, goddammit!" She's screaming now, the veins in her neck threatening to burst open. "Wake me up, wake me up, wake me *up!*"

Beatrice lets out a pitiful yelp, stumbling backward on the steps when Aunt Edie lunges for her. The edge of one of the stairs digs into her back and she cries out again, crawling up onto the landing. She clears her throat and the scream that follows is ear-piercing enough to crack the ancient window that is plastered next to her. She remembers the feeling of screaming this loudly, pushing all of it from the bottom of her stomach and out her throat.

In seconds, Aunt Edie is blinking herself into the real world, swallowing a ball in her throat as she reaches the sphere-shaped wood at the bottom of the railing to gain balance. She breathes for a few seconds and Beatrice doesn't say a word. Even though she wants to demand to know if her sleepwalking ever stopped and what is it that she's always dreaming about? What is she so afraid of that when she's sleepwalking, it puts her into this trance she'll die from if she never wakes up?

"Was I sleepwalking?" Aunt Edie wonders aloud breathlessly.

Beatrice nods. *Isn't it obvious?*

"Oh." She purses her lips, twisting her hands together as her eyes flicker back and forth in front of her. She reminds Beatrice of the sidewalk crackheads back in New York. "Sorry you had to witness that, sweetie. Getting old is not as it's all cracked up to be. Would you like some breakfast?"

Beatrice eats with her because she's too scared to say no. The last thing she needs is Aunt Edie dreaming of her rejection and coming into her room at night for some sick revenge. The entire meal, they chat about what else Aunt Edie needs done with the house and how she has a garden club meeting this afternoon. While she spoke, she was back to being carefree, sarcastic Aunt Edie. It's as though she didn't sleepwalk at all. But Beatrice saw the whole thing, just like how it used to be when she was a kid.

She wants to ask her all sorts of questions, especially about the contents of her words. What is in the house? Is she talking about the House Things? Is she talking about the girls? Beatrice can't hold her tongue anymore.

"What about the girls that stayed here before?" Beatrice asks bluntly, shoving a French toast stick into her mouth, syrup sticking to her chin.

Aunt Edie looks caught off guard, delicately splitting open one of her sticks with a butter knife. She glances at her like she cares about what she's asking but her eyes are also demanding for her to not ask such a nosy question. "Pardon?"

"You mentioned that you rented out one of the rooms here to college students and people who were looking for places to stay," Beatrice reminds her, attempting her best to sound as casual as possible but she doesn't think it's working out as well as she would like. "What room did they stay in?"

Aunt Edie flicks a strand of wavy white hair away from her face and looks unsettled by the question. She stabs at her French toast stick with her fork, politely shoving it into her mouth, probably to give her enough time to think of an answer. It feels like it takes her a lifetime to swallow and make eye contact with Beatrice again before finally speaking. "Your mother's old room."

The answer isn't what she expects and Beatrice finds herself gripping the edge of the table with all her might. She blinks a few times, wondering if she heard her correctly. Through all the years that members of this family have died, their rooms have always remained untouched. Even the twins' room. Even though they were never pronounced dead, their rooms were still made up, waiting for their return, sealed shut in the meantime.

"What?" Beatrice asks quietly.

Aunt Edie sighs, pushing her plate away from her. "I knew you were going to be upset about this. That's why I never told you about it."

Beatrice can't entirely be upset. She really can't. What did she expect Aunt Edie to do? Keep her room when her mother didn't live here anymore? No one had any say over what Aunt Edie did with this house when everyone was gone because they were all either dead or missing. Beatrice hates herself for thinking it but why wasn't Aunt Marley's room ever touched? Both of her kids are missing and it's false hope thinking Jax and Juniper will one day make a triumphant return. Beatrice is still here, though. Why would Aunt Edie get rid of her mother's room out of all the rooms in this house?

"I'm not upset."

"I helped raise you," Aunt Edie says. "I know when you're lying."

"Where is all her stuff?"

"It's packed up in the basement," she answers, sounding annoyed. It's as though Beatrice doesn't have the right to ask about her mother's belongings. Like the question itself should be stashed on some high shelf and forgotten about. "And to be frank, darling, you don't have anything to be angry about. If you wanted any of your mother's belongings, you could have made a visit or two. You could have called. But you didn't. What was I supposed to do with all of it?"

"Leave it where it was and put your tenants in Aunt Marley's room?" Beatrice snaps at her.

"Aunt Marley's room is too close to the attic."

"So?"

"*So*, it gets drafty." Aunt Edie grits her teeth. "As I've said."

Beatrice holds back her thoughts. It's a dumb excuse and Aunt Edie knows it. *It gets drafty my ass*, she thinks to herself, no longer hungry. She wants to sit here and fight, but the rest of the breakfast is filled with an awkward silence, the only sound being the scraping of Aunt Edie's fork against her plate. Whatever. Beatrice won't stay mad for long. All her mother's old things are in the basement. She'll just bring them with her when she leaves.

Once she brushes her teeth, Beatrice sets out to meet Alice at the Coffee Bean. She's too stubborn to break the thick silence between her and her aunt so she doesn't ask to use the car. She will walk, it'll be good for her. She hikes her bag further up her shoulder on her way out of the driveway, trying to tell herself that it's unrealistic of her to be upset with Aunt Edie for giving up her mother's room instead of Aunt Marley's. Sure, it's a little sour of her to want Aunt Marley's stuff cooped up in the basement but anything is better than her mom's being wiped clean.

She isn't sure if they're going to have to talk about all this by the time she gets home. Usually when a conflict of sorts arises inside of their family, they never really say what they're thinking. They just kind of step over the situation like it's poison ivy. Her mother used to tell her that she gets her stubbornness from Aunt Edie herself so who knows how long this might last.

Beatrice wanders down past Xander's house, where a few fake tombstones are planted in the front yard for the season, dramatic *RIP*'s across them in red. She considers stopping by and saying hello but that might be weird. She ventures on into town, making a mental note that she should go walking more often because this is a hell of a workout and she's ready to find a damn bench. The Coffee Bean is a little café sandwiched between a tiny gym and a vegan restaurant that wasn't here when Beatrice was growing up. She spots Alice right away, perched in the front window, her silky blond hair spilling over her shoulder. She's wearing white and blue striped fingerless gloves, her hands around a steaming mug of hot apple cider. As Beatrice walks through the door, she studies her a little more, taking in her piercing blue eyes and petite nose, her lips two thick lines of pink. She really *could* be Alice from Wonderland.

"Alice?" Beatrice asks, though she already knows who she is, and kind of feeling underdressed compared to this real-life cartoon character.

"Yes." Alice looks up at her and then snaps into realization as though she forgot why she was here in the first place. "Beatrice Montgomery?"

Beatrice winces at her lie-of-a-name but she nods, smiling, and takes a seat across from her. She tells the barista that she'll take a green tea and then focuses back on the girl across from her. "I'm so sorry this was such short notice. I didn't find you until the last minute."

"Oh. No biggie." She doesn't look bothered. "My life is a never-ending rabbit hole of spontaneity. I'm just honored that you felt like I would be a good subject for your interview. Do you go to school around here?"

"Uh, yeah," Beatrice lies, promising herself she will make it up to the universe later. But, it *is* a plus that this girl doesn't seem to recognize her as a Millstone. She can be anyone she wants to be right now with no past behind her and no future in front of her. "I'm getting my degree in journalism."

"Oh, nice," Alice says, nodding. "My brother tried that and then dropped the major when he realized how much writing he had to do."

Beatrice thanks the barista when her tea arrives and she roots through her bag for one of her many notebooks, dropping it onto the table and clicking her pen alive to look more like the part. She can play a character, too. "So, what made you run with this whole Alice vibe?"

"I was named Alice," she explains goofily. "So I've always been fascinated with the world of Wonderland. I thought it would be cool to kind of live like Alice if that makes sense. This world that we live in now is too serious. Too real. Wonderland, though, is here, but you just need to know where to look."

Beatrice scribbles some of this down just for show. "And is this your full-time career? Modeling?"

"Eh, we'll see." She shrugs her tiny shoulders before taking a drink of her cider. "I'm not really one to plan the future. I just go with the flow."

"I see." Beatrice writes this down in a script so messy she can't even read her own writing because she really couldn't care less about this girl's modeling career.

"Can I ask you something?"

Beatrice takes a sip of her tea. "Shoot."

"Why were you creeping on Lila Seckondorff's Instagram?"

The question makes the tea sloshing down Beatrice's throat nearly stop. She loudly swallows the rest of it, politely coughing into her elbow. It's a reasonable question. If Beatrice was in Alice's position, she might just ask the same thing. She dabs at her mouth with a tiny square-shaped napkin, suddenly feeling like Aunt Edie and her garden club.

"I wouldn't call it *creeping*," Beatrice stalls.

Alice's thin eyebrows slide up her forehead. "I would. I can't even tell you how many messages I get on social media about her. All of them are creepers, all of them are snooping."

Beatrice flicks a strand of hair away from her eyes. "Is that not something you want? People looking into her disappearance?"

Alice squints, suddenly looking guarded. She's not the same vulnerable girl she was a few seconds ago. She's a tougher Alice, the one after she leaves Wonderland, not the one she is before following that damn white rabbit. "Is this actually an interview about me or is it one about her?"

Well, that didn't last long.

"Okay, fine." Beatrice drops her notebook on top of her bag and leans over the table. "Your friend Lila isn't the only girl to go missing from Ashwood."

"How the hell do you know she lived in the Ashwood house?" Alice spats, her guard only going up higher.

"Because..." Beatrice tries thinking of some excuse to give her. The last thing she wants is for people to think that just because she has family ties to that house, she's suddenly a walking bad luck charm. Just being in her presence might rub off on someone. She might as well be added to the list of superstitions with walking under ladders or opening umbrellas indoors. "Because I'm staying there, now, too."

Alice's eyes widen but quickly return to normal size as though reminding herself to not show too much emotion. "What does this have to do with me?"

"I wanted to figure out what you knew," Beatrice admits, proving to the universe she kept her promise. "If Lila wasn't the only girl to go missing from there, then how much is being kept in the dark and why?”

“That old hag had something to do with it,” Alice mumbles into her mug before taking another drink, her eyes shifting from side to side.

“Edie?” Beatrice asks. “Edie Millstone?”

Alice sighs, running her thumbs up and down the side of the cup. “Don’t take what I say too seriously. That bitch did not like me.”

“Why?”

“She had some rule about bringing people to the house,” she informs her. “She told Lila that since it was such a tourist attraction, bringing people inside might be a little dangerous to her and everything in it.”

Beatrice could easily see Aunt Edie saying something like that, but that doesn’t mean she was honest. Take Ruth and Marilyn for example. She lets them inside without another thought on whether their intentions are good or not.

“I guess it was understandable,” Alice continues. “I wouldn’t want people coming to my house, either, if it was some legend.”

“So, you’ve never been inside of it?” Beatrice questions.

Alice shakes her head, thoughtfully staring up at the ceiling, remembering. “No, not really. I like to think of myself as a very intuitive person and that house had a bunch of weird shit about it. Old lady living by herself away from town, lures young girls inside, and then… *poof!*” She bellows loudly, making Beatrice jump. “They’re suddenly nowhere to be seen. Sounds like some *Hansel and Gretel* type shit, does it not?”

“I guess it does,” Beatrice agrees, not realizing how odd it sounds coming from someone else. “Did Lila have any bad feelings about moving there? Didn’t she know what happened in the past in that place? What was the process of her finding it, anyway?”

“She saw an ad in town,” Alice tells her, leaning back in her chair, the wood creaking against her weight. She glances over at three teenage girls making their way into the café. “She was desperate to find a place. She was crashing on my couch at the time and couldn’t afford anything. So, she agreed to move into Ashwood to help that lady clean and run errands for her and whatnot. Kind of like an assistant.” She pokes her head out in front of her. “But just between you and I, what kind of old bag needs an assistant? The lady isn’t even crippled. And from the looks of it, she could get around just fine.”

“Why didn’t Lila just keep staying with you?” Beatrice tries not to sound judgmental, as she's quickly realizing that she and Lila have some things in common. Beatrice could've easily stayed in the city and crashed with Clara until she got through this rough patch but she opted to return to Silver Creek instead.

"I couldn't quite afford to have her live with me, either." An embarrassed blush appears on both of Alice's cheeks. "And to work for that Edie lady, you have to live in the house or else you don't get the job."

"Didn't she hear the stories about Ashwood?" Beatrice snaps, wishing she could go back in time and wave her arms over her head to stop Lila from doing something that could become the downfall of her entire life. She wishes she could stand guard in front of the house itself, stopping all those girls from wandering inside to their demise. "Hasn't she heard the stories?"

"It's not something she believed in," Alice tells her, her tone of voice mirroring the snippiness in Beatrice's. "It's not like anyone from that house has come out and said any of the stories that get spilled around is true. I mean, all that stuff is fun to talk about but a lot of people around here don't really care if it's true or not." Her face falls as she stares at Beatrice for a beat longer. "Please don't tell me you're one of those people who believe the hocus pocus that happened there."

Beatrice straightens up. She bites her tongue, wanting to tell her that she, in fact, was actually *there* to witness the *hocus pocus* inside of those walls. That she listened to her aunt scream her head off in horror until she finally died. How she had gone to one too many funerals in her childhood and how she had to watch Jax and Juniper get swooped up out of the yard.

She decides against it, not wanting to rattle any type of base that she's already created with Alice and getting more information from her.

"I dunno," Beatrice plays along, pretending to be an outsider. "Who are we to judge if we weren't there to see anything on the inside?"

Alice snorts. "I'm sorry, but I'm not about to believe that some family in *this* town of all places have some weird curse on them that forces them all to die in totally weird ways. That shit doesn't happen in real life."

"You said yourself that Wonderland is here, you just need to know where to look," Beatrice challenges, running her thumb up and down the length of her cup.

"Why are you defending that place?"

Beatrice crosses her ankles under the table. "I'm not. But I think you'd be surprised if you knew what was real and what was fake. Just because we can't see something, doesn't mean it's not there."

Alice studies her for a few beats. It makes Beatrice uncomfortable enough for her to hide her face by taking a long drink of her tea.

"Have you seen something there?" Alice finally questions.

"What do you mean?"

"You seem to be knowledgeable about all that weird shit going on inside." Alice rests her elbows on the table. "Have you seen anything firsthand?"

"Did Lila?"

"Like I said, she didn't believe in that sort of thing," Alice says again. "And if she did, she never told me any of it."

"How many times did you go there?" Beatrice bites the inside of her cheek, hoping she isn't pushing too hard too fast. If this girl is leaving tomorrow, though, Beatrice doesn't have enough time for small talk.

"I told you that I never went inside."

"I know, but how many times were you *there*? On the grounds."

Alice shrugs her shoulder again. "I don't know. Two, maybe? I didn't stay long. That day I took the picture of Lila on the porch steps is the day I brought the stuff she left at my place. That was when the old hag told Lila she wasn't allowed to have guests inside."

"And the police have no leads on where Lila is?" Beatrice inquires. "Or any of the other guys and girls, for that matter?"

Alice looks helpless. "I guess not." She pauses. "I have a friend whose husband works on the police force. She told me that a lot of them don't believe in that haunted stuff, anyway. It's not like they all fall into the conspiracy theory of thinking that just because someone moves into that house, they're going to vanish."

"Was Edie questioned by the police?" Beatrice finds herself asking next, her mind buzzing with doubt and regret. She tried scouring the internet for anything to tell her that Aunt Edie was brought in for questioning but obviously, she found nothing.

Maybe this wasn't the best idea coming back here. Maybe she should've taken Clara's offer to crash on her couch until she could save up enough to find a place on her own with another stranger as a roommate. Perhaps the biggest mistake she has made this far in her life was calling up Aunt Edie and asking to come back home for a little bit. It seemed shaky at the start, but that was simply because she would be returning to the House Things and the memories she buried there a long time after leaving. But now, discovering this new truth, this new horror, taking place on the grounds of her childhood home is all too much. She should run back to Ashwood right this minute, collect her things, and get the hell out.

"What do you mean?" Alice asks, bringing her back into reality.

"Was she asked about Lila or any of the other girls when they disappeared?"

"I don't know." Alice is now starting to sound annoyed. She's taking more drinks of her cider, probably running her plan through her head to get the hell away from Beatrice. "I would think so since she's the one who reported Lila missing in the first place."

The information makes Beatrice's blood run cold and for a split second, she finds herself feeling somewhat… *hopeful.* If Aunt Edie was guilty of anything, she wouldn't go running to the police to encourage the start of an investigation, right? Or is that just a brilliant way of covering up whatever she's done?

Alice breaks Beatrice out of her thoughts when she speaks again. "You should probably get out of there while you can."

"What makes you say that? I thought you said you didn't believe in any of that hocus pocus people talk about."

"I don't, but that doesn't mean I trust the house owner." Alice takes a long drink of her cider, finishing it off. "Look, I don't think I have the answers to any of the questions you're looking for. I don't know what happened to Lila or any of the other people who stayed there. And now that I realize you only asked me here to interrogate me over my missing friend, that's my cue to leave."

"Do you blame me?" Beatrice says pleadingly. "Don't you want to know where Lila is?"

Alice is already standing up from her chair. She studies Beatrice for what feels like an eternity. "Look, sometimes being blind to the truth isn't such a bad thing."

And then, she's out the door, the bell to the café jingling behind her.

"**B**eatrice," a voice whispered in the night.

Beatrice's eyes slowly flickered open, adjusting to the darkness of her room surrounding her. Juniper's tiny face loomed over her, her red curls framing her chubby appearance and her plump lips slightly parted. Beatrice sat up a little on her elbow, glancing at the alarm clock on the bedside table. 3:42 am.

"Juniper?" Nine-year-old Beatrice croaked tiredly, scratching her head. "What are you doing up?"

"I keep hearing things," Juniper told her, obviously wide awake. It seemed like she had already been up for at least an hour. She glanced toward the door and then back at Beatrice. "The House Things."

"So just go back to sleep," Beatrice instructed groggily, reaching for an extra pillow to cover her face with. She grabbed hold of her nameless plush elephant by the ear and tucked it under her chin.

"I can't." Juniper tossed the pillow away from her.

"You can, but you didn't even try." Beatrice sighed, tossing her blanket off her to go put Juniper back to bed.

"You don't know that I didn't try," Juniper whined, staying put on Beatrice's bed. "It's scary out there, Bea."

She was just three years younger than Beatrice but she was already so complex. A little girl, fearful of whatever is living inside of this house with them. But she was also a little girl who claimed she wasn't afraid of anything—but only when the sun was up.

"They aren't going to hurt you," Beatrice recited exactly what Grammy Astrid told her when she was scared of the same things Juniper was talking about then. "Think of them as pets."

Juniper's upper lip rose and she shook her head. "Pets don't thump the ceilings."

As if on cue, Beatrice listened to the footsteps on the ceiling. She listened as they pattered across the hall like they were racing something else to an unknown finish line. Beatrice perked up, her brows pulling together. She'd heard the thumping before, but never this loud, this... *urgent.*

Slowly, Beatrice made her way to the door of her room, only

opening a crack big enough for Juniper to have squeezed through. Juniper follows her, their footsteps weighing heavily on the old wooden floorboards. Beatrice opened the door fully, peeking her head out as the footsteps slowed down. She craned her neck to stare at the ceiling, but nothing seemed amiss.

"Don't you hear it?" Juniper whispered loudly.

"It stopped," Beatrice whispered back.

Then suddenly, the footsteps came charging toward them on the ceiling. It sounded so hard and so fast that for a second, Beatrice thought whatever it was could put a hole through the ceiling itself. She gasped and for some reason, ducked her head, as she pulled Juniper back into her bedroom, slamming the door shut behind them.

"I want Mommy." Juniper sounded like she was about to cry.

The footsteps stopped just outside the door, above the doorframe as though waiting to be invited inside.

"It's okay," Beatrice told Juniper, swallowing the ball in her own throat. She quietly turned the notch on her doorknob to lock them inside, backing away from the door.

The girls squealed when three heavy knocks on the door came after. It sounded like they were using all of their energy to lift their arm, pound it against the door, and then let it drag down the wood. The cycle repeated. Beatrice's heart hammered within her chest, so loud that she was sure Juniper could hear it, too, only to echo the action. She put a protective arm in front of her cousin as they found themselves completely on the other side of the room by the window.

"He isn't very nice," Juniper whispered.

Beatrice snapped her head to the side, staring down at her as the moonlight from outside shone through the glass window. "What?"

"The man on the ceiling," she hissed, pointing a stubby finger at the door. "He's mean."

"How do you know?" Beatrice asked, wondering if this wasn't the first time Juniper had been in contact with one of the House Things. How does she know it's a him?

"Because he talked to me before," Juniper replied in a quiet voice, the pounding on the door sounding again. She jumped, her eyes glued to the door, and then finally looked back up at Beatrice. "He's Uncle Eli."

Chapter 8

After she met with Alice, Beatrice returned home and microwaved what was left of the pizza rolls from Xander's visit. She made her way back up to the attic—propping it open with an old box of board games—and settled inside.

The attic is threatening to cool down her food but Beatrice doesn't entirely care at this point. The faster she gets her work done, the quicker she can get out of here. On the other hand, the slower she gets her work done, the longer she has a place to stay. She shoves a pizza roll into her mouth, scanning the junk in the attic, some of it covered with stained white sheets while other pieces of antique furniture carelessly collect dust.

Beatrice looks around the floor for any sign of her work notebook, but she hasn't seen it since the last time she was in here when she got locked in. She stuffs her face with the remainder of the rolls and sets the plate on a three-tiered shelf before starting to move a few dirty boxes around covered in cobwebs. She finds one filled with ancient sports equipment, another cluttered with linen that smells like mothballs. She notices her book lying face down against the wooden floorboards, going to grab it when she jumps at the sound of her ringing phone.

Beatrice yelps, reaching into her back pocket for her phone. Clara is calling. Her stomach ties itself into a knot and she can't resist the urge to decline it. She doesn't want to keep talking to Clara on the phone, not if it's going to make her feel extremely guilty for lying to her. Clara would march down here herself and not only yell at Beatrice for twisting the truth, but she would go in on Aunt Edie as well with bottled up resentment.

"Hey," Beatrice answers, putting the phone to her ear.

"There you are," Clara says, exhaling on the other end so hard that the speaker rustles with air. "You do realize that I still get concerned for you when you don't check in, right?"

"I know," Beatrice replies.

"Then why don't you?"

"Because I have a lot going on," Beatrice says honestly. At least she can tell her a *little* bit of the truth… right? "I have tons of work that I've been doing."

"Oh, that's great!" Clara exclaims happily, as though she had nothing to worry about in the first place. "How *is* the bed and breakfast, anyway? Are they feeding you good enough there?"

Beatrice nearly forgot she told her she was in a B&B in Connecticut. "They make really good pizza rolls."

Clara sighs heavily. "Please tell me your meals have not consisted of garbage food heated by a microwave."

"I put them in the oven… the first time." Beatrice grins, sitting down in the plush orange chair that for some reason smells like cat piss.

"You need something more substantial."

"I eat just fine," Beatrice claims, crossing her legs in front of her. "I'm sorry I haven't been checking in as much. This place is kind of weird."

She's been itching to talk about her recent findings to someone that isn't her stuffed elephant. She hasn't seen Xander since that day he stopped by to find out if the rumors of her being back in Silver Creek were true. And who else is she going to talk to about girls that vanish out of thin air after staying in Ashwood? Aunt Edie?

"What do you mean?" Clara wonders aloud and then pauses. "It's not haunted or anything, right?"

"No, nothing like that." Beatrice glances around the attic. "Lots of disappearances in town, apparently, over the years. It's odd."

"Well, maybe you can include that in one of the bios for the furniture," Clara jokes, banging a few pots and pans. "There are some real freaks out there who would buy a piece or two with the sole knowledge of it being from someone who has mysteriously disappeared."

Beatrice snorts. "Doubt it."

"I'm serious," she goes on. "Do you realize how many twisted people out there would sell their souls for Jeffrey Dahmer's glasses?"

"Good point."

"Well, be careful out there," Clara warns. "I don't want to have to come to rescue you from some psychopath."

Beatrice grins but it slowly fades as she thinks about the guy with the burns Xander told her about. Could that guy be somehow responsible for the disappearances?

Before Beatrice responds, she hears a voice from downstairs.

"Beatrice?" Xander calls out to her, his deep voice ricocheting off the walls of Ashwood like a bouncy ball until it reaches her ears.

"Hey, I'm going to have to call you back," Beatrice tells Clara, rising from the chair. "Someone just got here."

She hangs up and makes her way out of the attic, trotting down the stairs to find Xander standing inside the opened front door, a blood-red leaf sticking to his shoulder. Beatrice tilts her head when she finds him standing by himself, the driveway still scarce of Aunt Edie's car.

"The front door was open," Xander tells her, his hands in the pocket of his black denim vest, a checkered shirt underneath. "I'm not trying to break in, I swear."

"It's an old house." Beatrice approaches him, doing her best to hide the fact she's creeped out by the open door. She gestures for him to come inside and so he does. "Doors open and close by themselves all the time. I got locked in the attic the other day."

"I guess that's something to get used to."

"I guess," she agrees, shutting the door. "What brings you by?"

"It's going to sound extremely desperate and maybe a little weird but the last time we talked, you mentioned that you might have a few jobs for me around the house," Xander explains, glancing at the faded wallpaper and the splintered trim. "I was going to have a look around, see what needed to be tended to." He pauses, looking at her. "That is, if the offer still stands, Beatrice."

"Of course it does," she says, relieved to know she'll be getting *some* help around here. Aunt Edie has made it clear that she won't lift a finger to do anything when it comes to the housework and even though Beatrice is the one that is in charge of this, she can't do it alone. Plus, having Xander here might not make her as paranoid. She will just have to split the cost of what Aunt Edie is paying her. "I was thinking about the wallpaper. I don't know much about interior design, but I think it's pretty outdated."

Xander leans in close to inspect the wallpaper. "You can say that again."

Beatrice decides not to lamely repeat herself. Scaring off her only friend with her dumb sense of humor won't benefit her.

"They look like they're…" Xander trails off, studying all the faces that stare back.

"Screaming?" Beatrice finishes for him, folding her arms over her chest. When she was a girl, she would spend a lot of time staring at the wallpaper, all of the ghosts staring back at her with their little mouths open in the shapes of ovals. She wasn't fearful back then, but if she stared at them long enough, she could hear a million distant rings, as though every one of the faces was beginning to scream.

"Yes, screaming, Beatrice," Xander agrees and then straightens himself back up. "What else?"

They wander through the house together, Xander testing the strength of the railing to the stairs and studying the hinges and knobs on the doors. They talk about paint colors for the hallway and pass some ideas back and forth on a matching trim color. Xander ends up rambling about the different strengths of brick used for the fireplace and how a professional would have to come in and tear it up before he could touch anything around it.

"What about the bedrooms?" Xander asks when they reach the third-floor hallway, glancing around at all the shut rooms around them.

Beatrice shrugs. "What about them?"

"Shouldn't I take a look at them, too?" He tilts his head to the side, the same way he would when they were kids. "Or does Edie want them untouched?"

"Apparently not all rooms," Beatrice mumbles under her breath, still a little bitter about her mother's things being put in the basement. "But I'll have to ask her about it. As far as I know, they still look exactly like they have since…"

Xander looks weary. "You mean, you haven't looked in one?"

Is that so crazy? Beatrice grew up in this house. With all the death that followed, the doors to the deceased's bedrooms were sealed and locked, stuck in place and time for eternity. Almost like gravestones. They remained full of stuff and a life that was left behind but never visited. Beatrice knows that other families visit cemeteries when a loved one dies. They walk to their graves with flowers or keepsakes. But the Millstone family has their own plot near the woods in the backyard, as though keeping their rooms the way they were wasn't enough of a reminder of who they lost.

"We usually never went in them," Beatrice admits. As a kid, she was comfortable telling him all about the weird quirks and things about her family and her house because when you're a kid, you don't worry about your best friend judging you. But standing here as adults, she feels a little ridiculous and she can't put a finger on why.

"Why not?"

"I guess it was easier to pretend," Beatrice nearly guesses, stuffing her hands into the back pockets of her jeans. "I know, it's weird, but it was normal for us."

"Well, maybe just a peek won't hurt," Xander challenges, wrapping his fingers around the old knob to the twins' room. Beatrice doesn't have to try and protest. The door doesn't even budge when Xander tries opening it. "Is it locked from the inside?"

Beatrice gets a heat flash—which is only supposed to happen to old ladies, right? She stares at the door she hasn't looked at since being here, faced with it after all these years. She remembers trying to pick it days after Jax and Juniper never came home. Beatrice tried her very best to worm her way inside to find any clues that could lead to their disappearance, but Aunt Edie told her it was too late. The room was already locked. After that, Beatrice never tried, naïve to believe that just because they no longer lived here, meant that there was no way of getting into their room.

"Yes," Beatrice answers, pointing to the keyhole on the golden knob. "There's a key that goes to it."

"Do you know where it is?"

Beatrice studies him. She's seen a lot of movies where a guy this good-looking and nice turns out to be some serial killer stalker or something. By the end of the movie, he'll have her tied up in the basement and she will have to outsmart him to survive.

"You seem awfully determined to see what's inside," Beatrice challenges flatly and then she thinks of him wandering through the front door. What if he came in himself and the door downstairs wasn't even opened, to begin with? "Why so interested?"

"It's kind of my job?" he nearly guesses. "Business has been slow as of late. Nana's medical bills are stacking up. And I want to show you and your aunt that I am professional, Beatrice. But, if you'd rather do the bedrooms yourself, that's completely okay with me."

Beatrice bites the inside of her cheek, studying the door. She has run from the memory of Juniper and Jax for long enough. Even though she isn't open to recalling that day she last saw them, perhaps finally opening the door to their room might be a start.

"Come on, I know where the keys are kept."

Beatrice leads the way to the grandfather clock on the second floor, a clock that has never stopped ticking for as long as Beatrice has known it. She stands in front of it, her reflection staring back at her as Xander stares, too, confused.

"I don't get it," Xander says honestly, rubbing the back of his neck. "We wait for the top of the hour to get them or something?"

"No." Beatrice gets to her knees, where the little cabinet beneath the shelves of the clock sits, unopened, with a large lock covering the thin crack between both doors.

It's made up of a chained magnet to be slid through a maze taking place on both sides of the door, unlocking whatever it is attached to on the inside of the cupboard. Beatrice used to ask her mom why they had a lock like this one and she told her that it was to keep the children out—almost like she only meant Jax and Juniper and that somehow Beatrice didn't count. Beatrice remembers asking why they couldn't just use locks like normal people. Her mom looked up at her with such confusion that Beatrice second-guessed her question.

"Oh, Bea," she had said. "Because we aren't normal people."

"Wait, are you serious?" Xander asks her now, disrupting her thoughts. "You have to play some maze to unlock the doors?"

"It was Grandpa Hugh's idea, apparently," Beatrice answers, using the pad of her finger to move the magnetized ball through the maze, the metal scraping together against the edges and corners. "He didn't want any of us kids getting our hands on these."

"What was the worst thing he thought was going to happen?"

Beatrice shrugs. "Wish I knew."

She fiddles with the magnet, the edges of the maze no longer smooth with youth. It's old and a little bit of rust flakes off the metal as Beatrice moves the ball through the tiny corridors. It takes her several minutes until the ball finally clicks into place at the finish line and the lock undoes itself with a single *click*.

"Whoa." Xander sounds lamely impressed. "Good thing you did it. It takes me way longer to do those mazes on the backs of cereal boxes."

Beatrice grins and reaches inside, where a sea of skinny black keys are waiting to be used. Seeing even just one sends Beatrice back to her childhood, recalling watching the grownups use them as though their bedrooms were their little apartments, keys that Beatrice had never once used. She hungrily licks her lips, showing Xander the chunky keys now in her hands. "Take your pick."

It takes them four tries to find the appropriate key to Jax and Juniper's room. Every key in that cabinet doesn't belong to a bedroom, they could go to the chests inside of the locked bedrooms or the China cabinet in the kitchen, or the drawers in the study. All the keys look the same but with different grooves and edges made specifically for their assigned lock.

The door to the bedroom creaks open and Beatrice finds herself standing in the doorway, an assembly of sparkling dust sailing in front of her. Twin sleigh beds made of oak are against the wall to the left, the plaid comforters tucked in neatly and the pillows unfluffed. A bay window is on the other side, a long narrow chest locked beneath it. The wallpaper is patterned with sailboats, meeting a thick rug stretching from the door to the other side of the room. A bulky dresser sits across from the beds, a series of drawers supplying their clothes. Before they disappeared, Aunt Marley was looking into getting a wardrobe for them.

"Talk about deja-vu," Beatrice says, looking around in disbelief. "It looks exactly the same."

She remembers running through here with Juniper, giggling together as they hid from Jax. She remembers bringing board games up here at nighttime, the three of them fighting in whispers about who cheated when they should have been in bed. She remembers dropping toys into that chest under the window when it was time to clean up. So many memories float around Beatrice, just like this dust, shining brightly in the sunlight, but not even the slightest bit of a twinkle in the dark.

"Did you expect it to look any differently, Beatrice?" Xander stands next to her, almost like he's afraid to move any further inside. Beatrice can't blame him.

"I guess not," she admits, taking another tentative step into the room. And like all the other rooms in Ashwood, this one creaks just as much. "It's just weird. Uncomfortably weird."

"Understandable." Xander stays put still, looking around at the trinkets on the dresser and an antique doll perched on a shelf toward the ceiling, the glossy eyes staring down at them as though she's waiting to be taken off and changed into a nicer dress.

Beatrice runs her hand over the end of Jax's bed, tracing her fingertips through the grooves in the woodwork. If she focuses hard enough, she can see him in the bed right now, tucked away under the thick blankets, whining about having to sleep. But he would be safe. He would be warm in the walls of Ashwood. He would be protected from any outside source coming to do him harm. Sure, he might face the darkness that lies inside Ashwood itself, but at least he would have time to change his fate.

Beatrice's eyes slide over to where Juniper's bed is. She, too, would be propped up on all those pillows, opposite of her brother by looking forward to sleep. She would wear that big, toothless smile with her curly orange hair a mess and all over the place in a wild tangle. She would squirm under her blankets, say goodnight, and quickly start to doze. If she would have never grabbed that hand…

Beatrice loudly clears her throat to stop herself from thinking. She looks over her shoulder at Xander, who is still cautiously remaining at the door. "So? Do you think anything needs to be done in here?"

"For starters, that vent could use some work." He points to the old metal vent at the bottom of the wall clear on the other side of the room, collections of dust stuck in the grate. "But yes, we could paint in here, too. The floor might need something done. Seems like it's sloped."

Beatrice puts her hand back on Jax's bed, thinking. "Maybe I could take the beds back to New York. They're old enough to be in the store. Declan would love them."

Beatrice holds her breath as she glances around the room again, gnawing at the inside of her cheek. Her memories of the twins are assaulting her mind like muggers, angry and filled with rage. She has blocked out her cousins for this long. Stepping back into their sacred space like this after all these years is something she isn't sure she was prepared for. She almost feels like she's disrespecting them by being in here when it's all her fault they're not here in the first place.

"I'm sorry," Xander apologizes quietly, still lingering close to the door. "I shouldn't have pushed you into coming in here."

"No, you didn't," Beatrice responds, flicking a strand of hair away from her face. "I would be dumb if I thought that I was going to come back here and not face any of my inner demons."

"You've got a lot of them." Xander flashes his boyish smile and Beatrice sends one back in return, equally boyish. "Plus, some therapists might even say that this kind of thing is therapeutic."

She arcs a brow, slipping her hands into the back pockets of her jeans. "So now you're saying that I need therapy?"

"I think there would be something wrong if I thought you *didn't* need therapy," Xander replies coyly.

After locking the room up, Beatrice walks Xander to the front door, the two of them chatting about picking a day to get started on everything. The conversation crashes Beatrice's mood more than it already was in the first place. She's got her work cut out for her to make this place look a *little* nice for it to be bought. But she's glad she isn't alone. Having Xander here to help makes this whole burden a little less unbearable. At least she can have other social interaction that isn't just Aunt Edie.

She shuts the front door behind him and heads back up to the attic to get all that furniture up there logged into her notebook and take more pictures for Declan. The room is just how she left it and she considers hauling all of it out into the hallway to study it instead of this dusty old attic where the "draft" can pull the doors shut at any minute.

"Get over yourself, Beatrice," she whispers to herself, the floorboards creaking as she peeks around the box to reach for her notebook which has now started collecting dirt. She picks it up and plops back down on the orange chair, finding a leather rocking chair stool next to it.

Beatrice leans over to flip the stool, in search of any tags or proof from some manufacturer. She opens her notebook when she doesn't find anything on the stool but her blood runs cold when she stares down at the open page on her lap. Blinking down at the page, her left hand starts to tremble and she suddenly feels like she's in one of those terrible nightmares where everything starts to happen in slow motion. No matter what move she makes, it will never be fast enough to complete the task at hand. Her eyes move over the words in her notebook, the letters big and shaky in a script that isn't her own, used with a crayon that she's probably never seen. The two words make Beatrice want to scream, mostly because she knows she didn't write them at all.

Welcome Home.

"They're so tiny," four-year-old Beatrice claimed as she stood on the kitchen chair, staring down at the twins in Aunt Marley's arms.

Jax and Juniper were only one, but their red hair had come in like wildfire. While Jax's hair was in wispy thin strands, Juniper's ringlets looked like curly fries. Aunt Marley had one of them on each hip, smiling for miles in a way Beatrice has never seen her wear before. Her mother used to tell her all the time how much she loved Beatrice and how she was her entire world. That feeling must be the same way Aunt Marley felt about the new babies.

"They are, aren't they?" Aunt Marley agreed happily. "Their daddy would have been happy."

Beatrice tilted her head. She often wondered where Aunt Marley's ex-husband went. She never remembered hearing a thing about him after he passed away at the end of the driveway. Beatrice didn't know the details.

"Would you like to hold one?" Aunt Marley asked her, as though the babies were large pieces of fruit and not tiny little humans with frail bones and squeaky noises.

"Yes!" Beatrice exclaimed and listened to what Aunt Marley told her.

She settled in the chair she was standing on, dusting the invisible dust off her thighs as her aunt gently handed her Jax. She took him carefully, listening as Aunt Marley instructed her to support his head and to make sure that his legs didn't slip off her lap. Beatrice stared at the baby smiling up at her, faint freckles sprinkled across his nose and cheeks. He was far heavier than any of her baby dolls and his face was so much more realistic, too. Beatrice found herself wondering where they ever got the idea to make baby dolls, as they're a lot harder than actual babies. Why wouldn't they just sell real babies like this at the store? That way every little kid in the world could *really* know what holding one felt like. Jax also had lime green eyes, whereas all of the baby dolls Beatrice had played with, were black and hard and nowhere near as squishy.

There was a slow stomping upstairs, making Beatrice and Aunt

Marley both look up at the ceiling. They sounded like footsteps, slow and steady, dragging across the hallway floor.

"What is that noise?" Beatrice asked Aunt Marley, still thoughtfully staring above.

"I'm not sure," she replied. "The only ones here are us and Uncle Eli."

Beatrice curiously stared at the ceiling again, listening to the footsteps make their way across the hallway and down the staircase. She craned her neck for a better view around the wall, wondering why on earth Uncle Eli would be walking like one of those zombies she saw on television. Aunt Marley, too, adjusted herself to get a better look.

"Uncle Eli?" Aunt Marley called out.

He didn't respond. His eyes were glued to the ceiling as he slowly made his way across the foyer and down the hallway, framed by the bookshelves on either side of him. His forehead was sweaty and Beatrice watched as his knees trembled with every step he took toward the mudroom. His bottom lip was quivering, and Beatrice watched him closely, realizing that it started to look like he was following something. Kind of how her mother looked when she was following a fly in the kitchen, her hands cupped in front of her, ready to squash it between her palms. Uncle Eli looked more sad, though. Sort of like he was going to cry.

"Uncle Eli," Aunt Marley said again, her thin eyebrows pulling together in worry. She adjusted Juniper in her arms. "Are you okay?"

"H-help me," he croaked, wrapping his fingers around the doorknob to the basement.

Aunt Marley rose from the kitchen chair and tucked Juniper back into the highchair. But it was too late. Uncle Eli had already embarked down the basement stairs and a horrible splintering sound followed right after with a cry from Uncle Eli himself. Beatrice jumped out of fear and Jax tumbled out of her arms and onto the floor.

"Jax!" Marley cried, scrambling to pick him up.

"I'm sorry, I'm sorry, I'm sorry, I'm sorry," Beatrice quickly told her, Jax's wails lighting up the room with a feeling of unease. Juniper started mirroring her twin.

"Honey, go check to see if Uncle Eli needs help." Aunt Marley was vigorously rubbing her son's head, tears streaming down Jax's ruby-red cheeks, his eyes nothing but slits now. "It's okay, honey, you're okay…"

Beatrice got up, guilt hanging over her like a storm cloud as she hurried to the basement. But what she and Aunt Marley heard wasn't some accident that Uncle Eli had. What she saw was something else entirely. For a split second, she could have sworn she had seen Uncle Eli on the ceiling, bleeding out of his stomach. But he wasn't up there at all. No, he was *in* the stairs—which was awfully odd, because people aren't supposed to be *in* stairs. They're supposed to be *on* them. Uncle Eli's entire bottom half sank through the wooden steps, his upper half slumped in front of him. The stairs were stained with blood, a color that would take a lot of scrubbing to get out.

"Uncle Eli?" Beatrice croaked over the sound of Jax's—and now Juniper's—cries from the kitchen.

But Uncle Eli did not answer. Uncle Eli was dead.

Chapter 9

Beatrice stands in the steam-filled bathroom after her shower that evening. The house smells like stuffed peppers and Aunt Edie is humming to herself in the kitchen downstairs. She must have gotten home during Beatrice's hour-long shower, where she scrubbed and scrubbed at her skin, attempting to clean herself after what she read in her notebook up in the attic.

If she were a little girl again, this wouldn't come as too big of a surprise. She would think Jax or Juniper wrote it with one of the many crayons they would carry in their pockets, writing and drawing on any surface they could find. But Beatrice is not a little girl anymore, and the twins do not live here. So who the fuck wrote that in her notebook? One of the House Things? Beatrice shakes the thought from her mind, telling herself that it's not something she should leave Ashwood over. But every red flag that is popping up in her mind is telling her to get the hell out. She's taking mental note of them all but it's too early to leave now.

She lets her hair air dry as she slips into a pair of sweats and a striped cardigan. She tosses her dirty clothes into the hamper in her room, trying to mentally coach herself to go back downstairs to join Aunt Edie for dinner. Maybe she should talk to her about this. Maybe she might know a thing or two. Perhaps more stuff similar to this happened in all the years Beatrice no longer lived here. Maybe, just *maybe*, Aunt Edie will be relieved that she can talk about this kind of stuff to someone else, someone who will understand what she has been living with all her life. She makes her way down the steps and into the kitchen, where Aunt Edie is waltzing across the room with plates and silverware, setting the table.

"Oh good, you're out of the shower." Aunt Edie smiles brightly at her, as though their little tiff this morning at breakfast never even happened. The pink fur on her mesh robe sways in the air like they're all waving at Beatrice and just as chipper as Aunt Edie seems to be. "Here, sit down. Let me make you a plate."

Beatrice swallows and finds her spot at the table. "Are we expecting company?"

"Not that I know of." Aunt Edie glances at her over her shoulder, dishing out a stuffed green pepper onto the China. "Why do you ask?"

"We only ever had stuffed peppers when we were celebrating something," Beatrice responds, pulling her sleeves over her hands. "And I figured we would do something short and sweet tonight given our little argument this morning."

"You're not still thinking about that, are you?" Aunt Edie sets her plate down in front of her before reaching for her own. "Sweetie, family members fight. They argue. It's completely natural. No need to get your panties in a twist."

Beatrice reaches for her fork, too shaken up to eat.

"And anyway, stuffed peppers are too good to only make for special occasions," Aunt Edie goes on, her red pepper nearly splitting open from the stuffing. "Wouldn't you agree?"

"I guess," Beatrice mumbles as her aunt sits across from her with a satisfied smile. Beatrice clears her throat, using the edge of her fork to cut through the pepper. "So, I was thinking about earlier a lot today. And no, I'm not going to argue about it all again, but I wanted to let you know that when I leave here, I'll probably take my mom's stuff with me."

"I would sure hope so," Aunt Edie says, scooping up the meat onto her fork. "When I go, I'm hoping a lot of this stuff does, too."

"What are your plans?" Beatrice asks, finding herself more and more desperate for a casual conversation so she won't have to bring up what happened in the attic. She managed to stay up there earlier to jot down everything she could about the furniture, busying her mind with work and keeping her hands busy. "For after you sell the house, I mean."

"I am going to travel," she answers proudly with her chin jutted into the air. "Marilyn and Ruth are coming with me, of course. The three of us realized that life is way too short to spend every day looking at things you've already seen a million times." She looks around the kitchen and points to the ugly pig statue in the corner that Beatrice's mother loved, but everyone else hated. "See, that pig, for example. I have spent every day for over eighty years seeing that damn thing. And I don't gain one benefit from it. But traveling the world and seeing things I've only ever looked at in pictures is an experience I want."

"That sounds great."

"It is, isn't it?" Aunt Edie agrees, her teeth scraping against her fork. "And, I'm not even too worried about how fast the house sells. I've got a fair amount of money tucked away that can be used up."

Beatrice stuffs her mouth with food so she doesn't have to answer. It must be nice being her age sitting on a shitload of money without a care in the world. She's ancient. Her days are probably numbered. Beatrice has her entire life ahead of her and she only has a few cents to her name. Her envy starts radiating out of her skin but she bites her tongue.

"Unless, of course, you would want to keep the house," Aunt Edie offers after taking a generous sip of wine. She's staring at her, completely serious. Her eyelashes are curled upward, and the corner of her mouth is tugged up her pasty white cheek.

Beatrice blinks twice. "Are you seriously asking me that?"

"Yes, Beatrice, I'm seriously asking you that." Aunt Edie laughs, reaching for her wine again, her fingers slipping through the stem so elegantly that she almost looks like a ghost passing through the glass. "It's a nice house when you think about it. There's plenty of room, a big yard, secluded. And above all, you grew up here."

"That's exactly why I wouldn't want it."

"*I* grew up here," she reminds her, her lipstick smearing across the glass when she takes another drink.

Beatrice's head tilts to the side. She faintly remembers hearing about Aunt Edie growing up in this very house, only to get older and not leave it, convincing her older brother, Lachlan, her younger brother, Hugh, and his wife, Astrid, to stay here with her when all the other Millstone family members died. Beatrice has always known that more branches of their family tree had taken up this house back in the day. It's been passed down from generation to generation like sentimental jewelry or clothes. The walls of Ashwood are lined with memories and portraits of those who once walked here and have since been buried six feet under in the plot out back.

"And you see how well I'm doing, don't you?" she finishes.

"Yeah, but this isn't exactly the kind of house I would want." Beatrice treads carefully. She knows how dramatic Aunt Edie can get about a lot of things. The last thing she would want is to start the second fight of the day over another meal. "Plus, it'll be fun to make it a little more modern."

Aunt Edie's brow furrows as though the thought of modernizing the house for it to be bought had never occurred to her. Perhaps she thought a fresh paint job and securing a few shelves might do the trick but no one is going to want to buy this place if it looks like something out of the early 1900s.

"Well don't change too many things, now," Aunt Edie warns. "The house still needs its charm."

"Aunt Edie, can I ask you something?" Beatrice blurts after swallowing a mouthful of stuffing. She dots her mouth with her napkin, looking up to find Aunt Edie nodding her head.

"You can always ask me anything you want, dear," Aunt Edie has always told her this, even when Beatrice was a little girl. She used to cup Beatrice's tiny hands into hers and look her right in the eye.

"If there is anything in this world that you are curious about, you can ask me," Aunt Edie would tell her. "Or if there are any questions you have and you're too afraid to ask your mom. I can answer anything you want to know."

It felt so reassuring at that time. It felt like Beatrice wasn't a child, fearful of asking the wrong questions to the wrong adults. She could go to Aunt Edie about anything that bothered her. Though she rarely did, Beatrice is now seeing this as the perfect opportunity to take her up on that offer.

"Do things still happen here?"

The question rings through the kitchen like an alarm but Aunt Edie seems to be unbothered. She takes another bite of her food, staring down at her plate as she thoughtfully chews. Beatrice watches, waiting. After a loud swallow, a fake smile plasters across Aunt Edie's lips.

"I don't have the slightest clue of what you're talking about," she tells her.

Beatrice glares a little. "You know exactly what I'm talking about. The weird stuff that has always gone on here. The unexplained things, the noises, the feelings. The House Things."

Aunt Edie wipes her mouth with her napkin, staining it with her lipstick. "Every house has its thing."

"That's always what people told me when I was younger," Beatrice says. "But when I left here, I realized that wasn't the truth. I was the only freak who had stuff like this happen."

"You're not a freak."

"You didn't answer the question."

"I'm not quite sure what you're asking."

"Bullshit."

"Language, Bea."

"Something was in the attic," Beatrice deadpans, her voice bouncing off the pretty China laid out between them. Aunt Edie is nervously looking everywhere around the dining room, anything she can look at that isn't Beatrice. The plants in the corner. The thick red drapes framing the windows. The painting on the wall depicting a man and a woman riding in a carriage. "Something *wrote* in my book."

She looks at her quizzically. "What was written?"

"*Welcome home*," Beatrice answers. "And you say that this house is drafty but I'm starting to wonder if it's something else entirely."

"Like what?"

Beatrice stares at her. She's never admitted it out loud, even when she was a kid, the rest of her family would shrug these things off like it was nothing. And then they would all get confused about why this Millstone family curse would strike and one of them would turn up dead in a strange and unusual way that didn't make sense. They would walk around like each of them were slowly losing their minds until they couldn't take any more and they would turn up dead. How could Aunt Edie ignore all this? How could she still live in this house so peacefully after all this time? Were they losing their minds? Were they seeing things that weren't there, to begin with? Or were there really things there, lurking in the shadows and doing things they knew they could get away with?

"Like ghosts?" Aunt Edie guesses when Beatrice doesn't say anything. She laughs before Beatrice has a chance to answer. "You honestly think there are ghosts in this house?"

"I don't know what to think," she snaps at her. "Have you been sleepwalking all these years?"

Aunt Edie's smile fades. "Pardon?"

"I've found you sleepwalking," Beatrice explains, resting her elbows on top of the table and pushing her plate away from her. "You seem to be very delirious when it comes to your sleep habits, no offense. So, I'm wondering if you have been like this for the last fifteen years, and if so, who's been waking you up if it wasn't me?"

"You're being dramatic," Aunt Edie claims, squinting her eyes. "My sleep habits are just fine."

"Really?" she challenges. "Because I remember being a kid and you begging me to wake you up sometimes because your dreams were too much for you to take. And it seems like very little has changed."

"It's the opposite, actually," she says. "Things change a lot more as you get older. You'll realize that one day, I hope. We think that we are safe when we sleep. We think that the minute we're tucked away in a dream, we have the deepest level of security." She's gently shaking her head so soft it's almost not even happening. She's no longer staring at

Beatrice but at a faraway view somewhere over Beatrice's shoulder. "But it's the most vulnerable state a human can be in, you see. We open ourselves up to a world beyond our control, to places that don't want us to leave. Lonely places in the deepest corners of our minds, desperate and alone."

Beatrice stares at her, suddenly feeling an overwhelming sense of discomfort, a feeling that's nearly been constant since being back.

"So, we do things out of character to try and get out of those dreams," Aunt Edie proceeds. "We try clawing our way out but sometimes it's not enough. Sometimes you need to invite someone else in to rescue you from those places. Because if you don't get out fast enough…"

When she trails off, Beatrice isn't quite sure she wants her to continue. She clears her throat, tucking a lock of wet hair behind her ear. "I see."

"You don't," Aunt Edie says, still politely smiling at her. "But maybe you will. One day. When you're older."

After dinner, Beatrice cleans up while Aunt Edie runs herself a bath upstairs. She washes the dishes, dries them, and puts them away. She wipes down the counters, too, and even sweeps the floor, just to keep herself from spending too much time with her thoughts while she's alone. The conversation about dreams with Aunt Edie is still trying to replay itself through Beatrice's mind and she would like nothing other than to stop it from happening.

Perhaps the only reason Beatrice finds herself in such an uncomfortable mindset is that she's had her own fair share of nightmares within this house. She has even woken up outside a time or two from sleepwalking. She remembers going to Aunt Edie about it, asking if there was something wrong with her.

"There is nothing wrong with you, darling," Aunt Edie told her, propping her up on her bony knee. "I sleepwalk, too, you know."

"You do?" Beatrice asked as though she didn't know at the time that Aunt Edie would roam Ashwood in the dead of night, her silk nightgown spilling behind her as she glided down the halls.

Aunt Edie nodded her head. "It's quite normal, actually."

"But my dreams aren't nice ones," Beatrice said. "They're scary."

"Dreams aren't real, though," Aunt Edie argued with her gently. "They put us in different places in our minds, but they can't touch us. What we see or what we feel inside them might feel very real at that time but when we wake up, it's nothing to be afraid of."

"So, it's not bad if I go outside?" Beatrice wondered aloud, thinking of all the possibilities that could happen if she ventured out the front door and into the night.

"No, it's not," Aunt Edie promised.

"But what if I get lost?"

"Ashwood is your home, Bea," Aunt Edie said, stroking her cheek with her bony knuckles. "You're always going to find your way back here. Here is a place where you're forever safe."

Beatrice shuts the kitchen light off and climbs the stairs up to her bedroom. *Forever safe.* Yeah, right.

Beatrice wakes with a jolt from a blood-curdling scream coming from downstairs. Her mouth is cotton dry and she blinks in the dark surroundings of her childhood room. For a second, she almost forgot that she was at Ashwood and not stuck in a dream instead. She listens to the scream from the kitchen, hearing it bounce off the walls with no place to go. She isn't positive that it's taking place in the kitchen, but something inside of her is saying it is. This scream sounds all too similar to how Aunt Marley sounded the last night Beatrice was here.

Beatrice throws her legs over the edge of the bed and scurries out of her room. The hallway is silent and black, a soft sliver of moonlight cutting across the floor from the window near the stairs.

"Aunt Edie?" Beatrice calls out worriedly, nearly falling down the entire flight of stairs to the landing. She grips the railing to catch herself, the yelling only getting louder, like someone has been lit on fire. She's never heard something more terrifying in her whole life.

Beatrice reaches the bottom and races toward the kitchen—which is empty. Beatrice stops in her tracks, breathless and confused. There's a ringing in her ear but not from the volume of the loud screaming she just heard seconds ago, but from a deadly silence that has popped in out of nowhere. She looks around but every seat in the kitchen remains empty. Even the dining room to the left is scarce from any sort of activity.

"What are you doing down here, child?" Aunt Edie's footsteps peel off from the stairs as she descends, tying a mint green robe around her toothpick figure.

"I heard a scream," Beatrice answers honestly, finding herself looking around for any sign of Aunt Marley. But the only faces that stare back are those in portraits on the walls and Aunt Edie. "I thought someone was down here."

"A scream?" Aunt Edie echoes. "The only sound I heard was you calling for me and then your elephant stampede down the steps." She growls to herself. "Someone might need to make a trip or two to the gym."

"That doesn't make any sense." Beatrice hears the desperation in her voice and she knows she looks and sounds both equally pathetic. But she heard what she heard. "I heard a scream, just like…"

Aunt Marley. But she can't bring herself to say the name. Not only will she continue to come off like a paranoid little girl, but she will also look like she's losing her fucking mind. She runs her hands up and down the length of her face. Perhaps that dream talk with Aunt Edie at dinner did a number on her.

"Go back to bed, dear," Aunt Edie instructs. "You need more sleep."

The entire rest of the night, Beatrice found herself tossing and turning and then more tossing and turning. She gave up around 4 something and pulled out her laptop to check her email. She sent Declan the photos of the furniture yesterday but he has yet to respond. She sifts through her bookmarked sites, mostly consisting of information about the girls who stayed here before she did. She considers clicking on one of them to do more research but she decides against it. She's already lost her mind once this morning, she doesn't need to do it for a second time.

Beatrice changes into a black crewneck and jeans, running a comb through her curly hair and then sitting in her window seat, bringing her knees to her chest. She watches the early morning fog roll through Silver Creek, up the hills, and through the trees stretched out behind the grounds of Ashwood. The family plot sits in front of it, the graves crooked like teeth, jutting out of the earth. Beatrice locks eyes with the stones, curiosity nagging at her like a fly that won't leave her alone.

She stuffs her feet into her combat boots and starts out of her room. She gently shuts the door behind her, the stairs creaking on her way down. She makes her way to the mud room, glancing at the kitchen, where she stood hours before, determined to find the cause of that horrible screaming that she never ended up finding. Beatrice slips out the door and into the yard.

The grass is wet with dew, tiny droplets scooped together onto the blades of grass like clear peas. The fog thins out as Beatrice approaches it, embraced by the mist, the graves ahead of her waiting to be tended to. She stops in front of them all, frowning. She looks at the names etched into the stone, each of them consisting of *Millstone*—even the females that kept the family name or never married. This is Beatrice's first time staring at her mother's grave. Aunt Marley's is next to it, their names engraved with their birthdates underneath. Beatrice imagines Aunt Edie doing all the manual labor to make sure they were buried side by side after that fateful night. Beatrice didn't even go to her own mother's funeral. Doing so would have meant her returning here just days after Halloween.

The other graves among the plot stare back at her, their names catching Beatrice's attention. Beatrice has never even heard of some of these family members, death snatching them up long before she was even born.

Up ahead, Beatrice notices the path she and the twins used to take whenever they would venture into the Jungle—that's what they called the woods. It seemed so much bigger at that time when Beatrice was just as childish and carefree. All three of them had their entire lives laid out in front of them—just like that path into the Jungle. Beatrice finds herself stepping onto it, lost in the trance of the fog pouring through the trunks and branches.

The floor of the forest is covered in colorful leaves, all of them different shades of reds and oranges and yellows and golds. Juniper would have loved seeing how vibrant these woods have gotten over the years. Beatrice continues through, twigs and sticks snapping beneath her feet. Two birds fly overhead, their wings spread out as they soar against the wind, turning this way and that with nowhere to go and forever to get there.

Beatrice continues forward, realizing that the path that she and the twins would return to whenever they drifted too far off, has now since overgrown. She can't imagine Aunt Edie coming out here for any reason—least of all to take care of the woods. It was Beatrice's job to make sure that their paths were clean and easy to find. She and Xander would whack away shrubs and weeds with sticks, pretending they were fighting creatures from some magical land.

She isn't sure how long she's been walking until Beatrice finds herself so far away from the entrance that she can't see it anymore. But, there is something up ahead, something that was never there before. Or maybe, it was there all this time and she's never come out this far. Her mother would always tell her to stay close to the entrance in case she needed her. And so, she obeyed. But now, being out here, she realizes just how big the Jungle is. It's filled with heavy trees and thick roots crawling out of the dirt. It has bird nests high up in the branches, and deer tracks through the mud.

But none of these things is what catches Beatrice's attention. There's a small shack up ahead, off the path and carpeted in thick green moss. It has a worn-down wooden door, and a rusty lock keeping it shut. It seems like it's only one story high and lacks any sign of windows. Beatrice feels like she's in some sort of children's story, where she wanders into the woods, only to be lured inside a house by an evil witch who wants to eat her for dinner. She thinks of Alice bringing up *Hansel and Gretel* during their coffee date.

Beatrice's conversation with Xander flashes through her mind the day he came and welcomed her back to town. He told her that his nana thinks the missing girls from Ashwood have something to do with the Burned Man—the old guy that lives in the shack here in these very woods. There is something oddly familiar about the house, though Beatrice can't put her finger on it. She hears a twig snap loudly behind her, making her whirl around but the woods are scarce of any life but her own.

Beatrice starts back the way she came, her urgency a lot stronger than it was when she came out. She hops over a fallen tree, the sense of no longer being alone nagging at her from behind. She pumps her arms at her sides until she runs and runs and runs all the way back to the yard of Ashwood. She pants breathlessly, tumbling out of the Jungle. Beatrice glances over her shoulder and she finds herself yelling, unable to catch her footing. A flash of a person's body has emerged from behind a thick tree with flaky bark, the figure slowly disappearing back behind the trunk. Beatrice guns it back for the house, slamming the door to the mud room shut behind her and flipping the lock so violently she's surprised it doesn't break.

Breathing hard, Beatrice presses her palms against the door, squeezing her eyes shut. Who the *fuck* was that? And why were they in the woods? She's seen a lot of things in this house that weren't there. Whether they were always figments of her imagination or they were something a lot more dangerous, she grew privy to it. But after all these years, being back here is making her realize that she is home. And it's a nightmare.

Beatrice attended Uncle Eli's funeral wearing a plain black dress with sleeves that stretched to her wrists. Two strands of hair were pulled away from her face and pinned in the back with a green butterfly clip, and the black tights her mother picked up for her that day were itchy and uncomfortable.

Beatrice and the rest of the Millstone family stood in the backyard of Ashwood, where the family plot sat, dedicated graves to family members that had passed before. Uncle Eli's body was hauled off just a couple of days ago when he fell through the basement stairs. Aunt Marley couldn't stop screaming, louder than the cries of the twins. Beatrice couldn't move away from the basement door. She couldn't take her eyes off Uncle Eli slumped over the wooden steps the way he was, so unnatural for a human to be in such an uncomfortable position. Aunt Marley had to physically drag her away, shielding her eyes with a sweaty palm.

A tall man dressed in black with a little white strip in his collar stood in front of the family, reading out of a strange black book that Grandpa Hugh always said religious people lived by. Beatrice wasn't sure what that meant but it was much too large of a book for her to pick up. She looked around at all the other adults, listening intently as Uncle Eli's body sat in front of them next to the hole that was the same size as his height. He was wrapped in environmentally friendly sheets—something Beatrice's mother insisted on because it was a family tradition.

Aunt Marley sadly stared down at the sheet, Jax and Juniper both sleeping in their double stroller in front of their mother. Grammy Astrid and Grandpa Hugh stood together near the grave, both of them frowning, yet their expressions unreadable. Aunt Edie mourned the death of her husband by sobbing into her fur coat, tears springing out of her eyes as she clenched a tissue so hard in her hand that her knuckles were a beaming white color. Beatrice's mother stood next to Beatrice, holding her hand and softly stroking it with the pad of her thumb.

She had sat down with Beatrice and explained how Uncle Eli will never come back from where he now was. Beatrice was confused at first, wondering what she meant. She explained the cycle of life, how humans are born as babies—like the twins—and then they grow up and when they get really, really old, they die. They go off to some other land where everything is pretty and made of candy. Well, she didn't say that everything was made of candy, but Beatrice had been watching *Willy Wonka and the Chocolate Factory* on VHS and if there was one place that would be happy and pretty, it was a factory that only had candy in it.

Once the man in black stopped speaking, Beatrice watched Aunt Edie crouch down next to her dead husband. With the help of Beatrice's mom, they both gently pushed Uncle Eli into the hole. Beatrice was confused, as she noticed Grandpa Hugh grabbing a shovel, Aunt Marley joining him.

"What are you doing?" Beatrice asked them when she realized they were now shoveling dirt on top of his body, like they were going to trap him in there, stuck underground forever.

"We're burying him, kiddo," Grandpa Hugh answered, as though he had done this many times before today. And he had. The tombs of Millstone family members behind him proved it.

"But…" Beatrice stared down at the weird shape that Uncle Eli now was and forever will be. "He won't be able to breathe with all that dirt on him."

"He's dead, baby," her mother whispered to her gently, stroking her cheek with her knuckle. "His soul is gone, that's what happens when we die. When we are born, our souls are kept in our bodies. But when we die, they go to that happy place we talked about."

Beatrice suddenly felt an overwhelming sense of sadness. She watched as her family started to bury her uncle, dirt being tossed on top of him. The sound of the sharp edge of the shovels digging through the dirt pile rang out through the empty yard. Beatrice began shaking her head.

"But he'll get cold down there." Why couldn't any of them see this? Why couldn't any of them realize that sleeping in the ground is no happy place? "There are worms and bugs and if there is a lot of dirt on top of him, he won't be able to get out."

"Honey, his soul is not inside of him," her mother tried explaining again. "It's just a body. Think of it as a costume. A costume we wear our entire lives." Her eyes sparkled in the early summer morning sun, making her skin look smooth and shiny. "Costumes don't last forever. So, when we die, we have to wear a new one in the happy place."

"But, still," Beatrice said, her eyes flickering down to the heap of dirt now covering the sheet Uncle Eli was wrapped in. "He's going to get cold."

"He's fucking dead!" Aunt Edie snapped angrily, making the strange man in black jump a little. He cleared his throat and adjusted the book in his hands. Aunt Edie was glaring at Beatrice. "He can't feel *anything*!"

Beatrice clamped her mouth shut as she watched her aunt sob hysterically over the grave that her husband was now in. She thought about apologizing but Aunt Edie herself had once told her that she should never apologize for anything unless she knows what she's apologizing *for*.

"It's okay, Bea," Aunt Marley encouraged her with an equally sad smile the rest of them were wearing. "Aunt Edie is just a little fragile today."

"With good reason," Aunt Edie spat. "My husband is dead and we are burying his body in our backyard."

"It's nothing we haven't done before," Grammy Astrid mumbled to herself, her husband nodding in agreement.

Aunt Edie swallowed the ball in her throat, gathering the collar of her fur coat in her bony hands and tugging it together. She looked at Beatrice on the other side of the grave. "I'm sorry, Bea. Aunt Marley is right. I'm a little fragile today."

Beatrice nodded but didn't say anything. All of this seemed way too grown-up for her to chime in with anything. She looked over at Juniper and Jax waving their chubby hands in the air and having no clue that they were attending the burial of an uncle they won't ever remember except in photos. Without saying anything, Beatrice's mom handed Beatrice a smaller shovel than the rest of them had, catching her off guard.

"The dirt will keep him warm," she had promised.

And so, Beatrice started burying him—which she would later find out was a family tradition. Millstones didn't let other people bury them. Millstones buried each other.

Chapter 10

When the sun comes up over Silver Creek, Beatrice blinks through it peering in through the window, finding herself on the stiff couch in the sitting room. A throw pillow is stuffed under her neck, causing a knot to swell between her shoulders. She must have dozed off after coming in here to unwind after her run through the Jungle.

Beatrice shakes the thought that anyone else could have been in those woods except for her. It would be naïve to think that those woods are empty *all* the time, but was someone actually following her? If not, then why would they hide behind a tree? What if it wasn't some*one* at all? Perhaps it was some*thing*.

She stands up, her shirt now wrinkled but she's too groggy to care. A pulsing headache moves through her head on her way out of the sitting room, that is now alive with sunlight. She rubs the back of her neck on her way into the kitchen, where Aunt Edie stands at the sink with a potted plant placed under the running water. She glances at her over her shoulder.

"Are you feeling all right, darling?" Aunt Edie asks her, flipping off the faucet with a flick of her wrist. "Came downstairs this morning and found you passed out on the sofa. You looked like me throughout my early twenties."

"Yeah, I just had a rough time sleeping last night," Beatrice admits tiredly, padding over to the coffee machine, where a mug waits for her. "Thanks for the coffee."

"I figured you'd need it," Aunt Edie says, returning the plant to the windowsill. She dusts her hands off as though the act was a handful. "I know that when I sleepwalk, I always wake the next morning needing a little extra caffeine."

Beatrice snaps her head to the side to look at her. "I didn't sleepwalk."

Aunt Edie's brow furrows. "You didn't?"

Beatrice shakes her head. When she was younger, she would find herself in these weird spells of walking during the night but she was able to distinguish what had happened the next morning. She doesn't remember sleepwalking. She heard the screaming, she couldn't sleep, she took a walk, and then passed out in the den.

"Why, did you hear something?"

"I'm always hearing things," Aunt Edie tells her with a tight smile. "Any-who, I'm going to meet Ruth and Marilyn in town. Would you like to join?"

Beatrice shakes her head once more as she gulps down the coffee. She wipes her mouth with her sleeve. "No thanks. I should probably pick up some paint today. Xander offered to help with some of the renovations."

"Xander?" Aunt Edie looks confused.

Beatrice thumbs over her shoulder toward the direction of Xander's house. "The guy from down the street? He used to come over when he was little?"

"Oh. Him." Aunt Edie slowly slips her arm into one of her obnoxious fur coats and then reaches for her hat on the island. "You haven't mentioned that you've been seeing him."

Beatrice studies her, wondering if there is some sort of bad blood between the two of them. Xander was left all by his lonesome when she escaped Ashwood that fateful Halloween. Perhaps Aunt Edie ordered him to stop coming around when he would wait for Beatrice to return. Maybe he left that part out when he was telling her about the years she missed away from this place.

"Is that not okay?" Beatrice asks after a beat of insanely awkward silence.

"Of course, yes," Aunt Edie says. "Tell him hello for me."

She's out the door in seconds, bustling to her car in the driveway. Beatrice watches her leave from the front window and then takes a breath. She stands in the foyer, waiting to hear or see something that will remind her of her childhood. But the only sound is the ticking grandfather clock upstairs where the keys were held. Beatrice perks up at the thought of all those keys now in the jewelry box in her room. She didn't bother putting them back the other day with Xander, just in case she needed more of them for the other rooms in the house.

Beatrice goes up to her room, quickly opening the lid to her jewelry box—the twinkly music immediately starts to play. She slams it shut when she gathers the keys in her hand, marching up the stairs to the third floor. The attic waits at the end of the hall, but a few doors before that is her mother's old bedroom—now the guest bedroom for the tenants Aunt Edie recruits.

The missing girls are still weighing heavily on Beatrice's mind. She considers interrogating some of the town's residents, demanding to know what they know and to gather information on what people believe happened. Do they, too, believe that the Burned Man in the Jungle had something to do with their disappearances? Do they think Aunt Edie is involved? Has Aunt Edie ever been questioned by the police for this? Why isn't more being done?

As all of these questions swim laps through Beatrice's head, she tries key after key until the appropriate one meets the lock and it clicks open. The hinges squeal as Beatrice pushes it free with her boot. The room is dead silent and reminds Beatrice of an old motel. The bed is a full-sized one, with two bedside tables on either side. There's a blood-colored rug running from the door clear to the window on the other side that overlooks the family cemetery and the hill that leads to Xander's house. There's a bulky wardrobe against the wall and a small dresser with a lamp sits next to it. A closed door that leads to the Jack and Jill bathroom—which Beatrice's mom would share with Aunt Marley—is to Beatrice's right.

There is nothing left of her mom in this room. Actually, there is nothing left of anyone that stayed in this room after her. It lacks any sort of personal touch or creativity. It was simply just a room for people to stay in. Just like a hotel.

Beatrice isn't sure what to do next so she opens the doors to the wardrobe, expecting to find something that will give her a slice of information. It remains empty, except for the wire hangers slung over the bar at the top. She blows air out of her mouth and curiously opens the two drawers on the bottom half of the wardrobe, telling herself that she's looking for the sole reason for those missing girls but a small part of her is almost anxious to find something that once belonged to her mom. The contents of the left drawer, though, take Beatrice by surprise.

A single Polaroid picture is left abandoned in the drawer, familiar green hair catching Beatrice's eye. Lila Seckondorff, Ashwood's last resident before Beatrice, is in the photo, her arm outstretched in front of her holding the camera. Terror bathes her face in a look so familiar, Beatrice can feel it, too. She reaches inside to pick it up by the corner, afraid to leave any sort of evidence on it that would link it back to herself. Just over Lila's shoulder is a figure in the darkness, silhouetted by the moonlight peering in through the window of this very bedroom. The figure's body belongs to a man and Beatrice's heart sinks to her knees when she notices the snapped neck and broad shoulders.

A ball forms in Beatrice's throat as she slowly sinks to the floor, her breathing growing heavier and more staggered. Grandpa Hugh never woke up on Christmas morning when Beatrice was seven. Instead, Grammy Astrid found him with a snapped neck next to her, his lips parted and his eyes glossed over like the dead. Now, he's in that photo, haunting from the shadows of Ashwood. Beatrice is too terrified to look at the photo again, but when she turns it over, black letters dance in front of her vision: *Man with the cracked neck. Only appears in pics.*

Beatrice considers this, biting down so hard on the inside of her cheek that she tastes blood. This sounds like a note or a reminder. Beatrice has researched and made notes about a million and one different pieces of furniture, she knows how clipped they can sound in the head. Reading these words on the back of the Polaroid makes her think of herself, her own little reminders she would scribble down in her notebooks. If that's the case, then there's a chance that there could be more. More Polaroid pictures that were taken by Lila, maybe even all of them including some sort of note or reminder on the back.

Beatrice stuffs the photo in the back pocket of her jeans before darting back into the hallway, locking the room up. She needs to go into town to get that paint and maybe ask Xander if he's available today to get started on painting the guest bedroom. She throws on her denim jacket and impatiently waits for her phone to connect to service in order to call a cab. She waits outside because being inside is now giving her horror movie vibes. Seeing Grandpa Hugh in that photo floods back all kinds of memories Beatrice has forgotten since being so far away from this house. She remembers seeing that same exact figure—a shadow—in pictures years before she left here. She remembers him standing with them all in Christmas portraits, looming in the background of the pictures from her ninth birthday, framed in a window during snapshots from a family barbecue. He was always in the background, the whole time. And no one said a damn thing about it when he would appear in the pictures, like everything was so normal. Like that's how he always was: a black blob floating in the background. How could this have been overlooked and so *normal* for all of them?

The cab arrives and the smell of cigarette assaults Beatrice's nostrils when she climbs into the backseat. She tells the woman driver to head to Home Depot and the car lurches out of the driveway, the tires squealing in the process.

"Ashwood, huh?" The driver glances at Beatrice through the

rearview mirror. She looks like she's somewhere in her forties with aging lines decorating her face and smoky gray eye shadow smeared across her eyelids.

"Yep." That's all she's going to say.

"That's gotta be an adventure." The woman sniffles, wiping her nose with her wrist. "Heard a lot of horror stories about that place. And when I say *horror*, I mean straight up *horror*. Like demon movie type shit."

Beatrice resists the urge to roll her eyes. She and her entire family might have avoided the talk about Ashwood being haunted by ghosts her entire life, but there is no way there are any signs of demons in those walls… even if that's what the mood is becoming inside. If that were the case, Aunt Edie wouldn't have stayed there her entire life and Beatrice wouldn't have come back. But, she needs this lady on her good side if she wants to ask a couple questions about Lila and the other missing girls from there.

"Didn't a few girls go missing from there?" Beatrice asks casually, adjusting her bag in her lap.

The lady coughs a smoker's cough without covering her mouth. "That's what the papers say."

Beatrice arcs a brow. "But you don't believe them?"

"I believe they're missing, all right, but that doesn't mean they went missing *inside* of the house," the driver explains, cruising to a stop sign and braking. "Just because they lived in that house during the time they went all MIA, doesn't mean their place of residence was the cause."

"Then what else could it be?"

She glances at her again before she starts through the intersection. For a second, Beatrice thinks she's going to accuse her of being snoopy but if she's Ashwood's newest innocent resident, she should know a thing or two.

"I hear a lot of those girls were troubled," she explains. "Their parents didn't do none of those press conferences like you're used to seeing when an everyday girl vanishes out of thin air. Not a lot of people were lookin' for them other than their friends—and even they gave up, I hear."

"What do you mean they were troubled?"

"I mean that they were either broker than broke or they ran away from their lives in other places," she responds with a heavy sigh. "Apparently some of them even ran away from their homes before." She clears her throat, draping her chubby wrist over the steering wheel.

"I read all about those girls when they would pop up in the papers. My boss says as a cab driver, it could help some people out if I actually pay attention to who gets into my car."

She pronounces car *cur.*

"Which, sorry to say it if I'm wrong, but I don't believe every single person who has stayed in that house has gone missing," the driver continues. "Like I said, some of them were troubled. They would go from place to place without a plan. When a new opportunity came up, they would flee. Did you know a couple of 'em had warrants out for their arrests?"

It was something Beatrice did come across in her research. Most of the crimes weren't severe. Petty theft, trespassing, one of them got in trouble for indecent exposure.

"And you think that's what some of them did? Just fled?" Beatrice wonders if that could be true. If she was ever labeled as a missing person, though, the first thing she would do is let people know that she's perfectly okay. Unless some of these girls were so troubled they were mixed up with the wrong sort of people and never looked back.

"There's a chance," she confirms, orange leaves whirling down from the trees lining the street ahead. "But what do I know? I'm just a cab driver."

Home Depot's Halloween section is noisy with decorations that make all sorts of spooky sounds and battery-operated movement. Beatrice walks right past it and scans the wall of paint sample colors. She decides to do a mustard yellow, even though she thinks it's ugly. She's not the one who will be sleeping in it. As she waits for the employee to get back to her with a bucket, Beatrice sends Clara a text asking how she's doing. She leans against the paint counter, gnawing on her bottom lip as she considers the new information and opinions the cab driver gave her. What if she's right? What if every past resident at Ashwood didn't suddenly vanish from there, but a handful of them ran away? What if a few of them were mixed up with some bad people and they had to change their appearance and names like on TV? Or what if they realized the kind of stuff that was taking place inside of Ashwood itself and fled the first chance they got? Perhaps it might be time to ask Aunt Edie a thing or two about everything.

When Beatrice climbs back out of the cab after returning to Ashwood, she finds Xander standing on the porch, cupping his hands against the glass to peek inside. He jumps when he hears the car door being shut and he spins around.

"Hey," Xander says. "There you are, Beatrice."

"Here I am," she replies. "It's funny to find you here. I was even going to swing by your place and ask if you were available to help paint."

A small part of her is a little iffy on letting Xander help redo a few of the things needed done in the house—a small greedy part of her. She would rather take all the money herself, she needs every cent, but there's no way she's going to know the ins and outs of things that need done.

"Well good minds think alike, I suppose." He goofily grins, taking the paint bucket from Beatrice so she can open the front door.

"I also wanted to talk to you about a thing or two," she admits, not really sure why she feels so nervous to let him in on everything she knows so far. It's almost like she's sharing a whole big secret that she shouldn't be spilling.

"That sounds intriguing." Xander follows her inside, using his free hand to scoop his black locks away from his eyes.

"I found this today in the guest bedroom." Beatrice shows him the Polaroid of Lila.

Xander's eyes widen when he notices Grandpa Hugh standing in the background. "Holy shit."

"I thought the same thing," Beatrice agrees and then flips the photo over for him. "Correct me if I'm wrong, but it almost sounds like there were more. Like she was making a note on this one, just like she did on a few others. Unless I'm over thinking and going crazy."

"What, like an entire collection of Ashwood ghosts?" Xander asks jokingly but Beatrice is nodding her head, seriously. "Oh. Really?"

"I mean, it might be farfetched but it kind of sounds like it could be true, doesn't it?" Beatrice asks hopefully, wondering if she's just doing a lot of wishful thinking on things that might not even turn out in her hand.

Desperation is bubbling inside of Beatrice at this point. Her subconscious encouraged her to come back here after all this time and maybe face the haunts of her past, to truly decide if her family has some curse on them or not. Now that she's here, she is reaching for any sort of string that will prove to herself that her family was never crazy or cursed. Maybe it's just the house.

"I suppose it could be," he concurs, rubbing his chin with an index finger and almost looking like Shaggy from *Scooby-Doo*. "But you didn't find any other pictures?"

Beatrice shakes her head. "No. And Lila was the last girl to stay here before I came and that was a year ago. Her stuff could be long gone by now."

"So, let me get this straight…" Xander puts down the bucket of paint on the staircase landing. "You actually think there are ghosts in this house?"

"I don't know what they are," Beatrice admits. "But just because a house is haunted, doesn't mean it's being haunted by *ghosts*."

"Then what do you think is in here?"

It's a question that has swam through Beatrice's thoughts for the last twenty-five years. A question that keeps her up at night, a question so heavy that it has been living inside of her head ever since she was a little girl. So, she can only think of two words for whatever is stuck inside this house. The same two words that were given to her as a kid. A phrase given because a truer one lacks.

"House things."

Beatrice ran across the creaky floors of Ashwood, her feet padding against the floorboards. Xander raced behind, his footsteps louder and echoing off the surrounding walls and making the framed photos twitch.

"No running in the house!" Grandpa Hugh roared from behind them at the end of the hallway.

Beatrice and Xander burst into giggles on their way down the steps, Beatrice reaching the front door first.

"I win!" she proclaimed proudly, her chin in the air.

"I couldn't keep up," Xander said breathlessly. "You know this house way better than I do. I'm at a disadvantage, Beatrice."

"But you're here just as much as I am," she challenged, folding her arms over her chest.

"We wanna play!" Jax exclaimed, stumbling out of the sitting room. Juniper was behind him, wearing a mint green sun dress and sandals, her usual curls in ringlets framing her chubby face.

"You guys are too little to run through the house as fast as we do," Xander told them and Beatrice suddenly felt way older than she actually was.

Jax ignored Xander and looked at Beatrice with pleading eyes. "*Pleeaaasseee?*"

"How about we go on an adventure?" Beatrice suggested. The last thing she would want is Juniper crying when Grandpa Hugh yells at them again for running in the house.

To the four of them, going on an adventure meant wandering into places they weren't supposed to be or spying on the adults. Their first adventure was bringing the twins into the Jungle—only to have Aunt Marley barely scold them for running off with no adult supervision. But they've been back in there a few times after that, and Aunt Marley didn't seem to mind. They've also filed into the attic and looked through dusty old board games with missing parts and faded lettering. They found really old Halloween masks and even put them on, scaring each other in the dimness of the room.

"What kind?" Juniper asked, mirroring Beatrice by folding her arms out in front of her.

"We can look in the basement," Beatrice suggested, her eyes flickering down the hall to the mud room, where the door to the basement was.

Xander perked up. "I've never been in your basement, Beatrice."

"There's a first time for everything, right?" Beatrice smirked and then led the way down the hall, the three others trailing behind her like a train.

They were always told not to play in the basement, whether it be by Grandpa and Grammy or Beatrice's own mother. It had been three years since Uncle Eli fell through, and the adults of Ashwood had been more adamant than ever in making sure the kids didn't come down here. But technically, they weren't going down to play. They were going to snoop through things and maybe find new games they hadn't grown bored of yet.

"Are you sure we're allowed down there?" Xander whispered loudly, even though the only adult inside was Grandpa Hugh. Everyone else was outside enjoying the summer sun.

"We're not allowed anywhere in this house," Beatrice mumbled and opened the door.

"Maybe we'll find dragons down there!" Jax exclaimed excitedly as they all began to file down the flimsy wooden steps.

Jax had been on a fantasy kick, lately, ever since Aunt Marley brought home a large collection of fantasy books. She'd been reading them to him and Juniper every night and then the next day, Jax would come up with a game about the book that was read to him the night before. He would talk about dragons and castles and creatures with horse butts and human faces.

"Or wendigos!" Juniper added, just as excited.

"Wendigos aren't real," Xander claimed when they reached the bottom.

The basement was dingy, made up of four gray brick walls that stretched out to make the room in the shape of a rectangle. The washer and dryer sat under the basement window—masked in thick cobwebs and dirt. A bunch of storage things cluttered the back corner, with a small step ladder leading into the crawl space.

"I'm scared," Juniper whimpered, looking around and clearly no longer excited. She rubbed her hands up and down her arms. "And cold."

"It's not that bad," Beatrice assured, looking around some more.

"And I'm sure there are some really cool toys down here if we look in the right place."

The twins held hands as they ventured further into the dark basement, their heads snapping from side to side as though something was going to jump out and grab them. Xander seemed fearless, though, casually strolling next to Beatrice further into the shadows. Beatrice, on the other hand, had a strange sense that something was off. Like the four of them weren't the only ones down here.

Thump, thump, thump.

"Did you hear that?" Beatrice whirled around to peer at the ceiling, which consisted of wooden boards to stabilize the floor above, spider webs draped from board to board.

"Hear what?" Xander asked.

"No," the twins answered at the same time.

"It sounded like footsteps," Beatrice replied.

"It was probably Grandpa Hugh," Jax assured. "Or did you forget that he's inside?"

Beatrice wanted to explain that it didn't sound like the thumping noise was upstairs, it sounded almost like it was on this very ceiling.

"Hey, check it out!" Jax picked up a heavy sword out of a box marked *Grandpa Hugh's. DON'T TOUCH.* "It's a real sword!"

"Whoa, careful with that," Xander warned.

"Beatrice, he's gonna hurt himself," Juniper whined stubbornly— probably upset there wasn't a matching sword to fight her brother with.

"Oh calm down, Juniper," Jax spat. "I'm only just looking at it." He brought the hilt closer to his face, his face growing red as he covered his mouth with his free hand, giggling into it.

"What's so funny?" Beatrice asked curiously.

"There's a naked lady on this," he replied.

Beatrice, Xander, and Juniper all craned their necks when Jax held it out to show them. Sure enough, a lady resembling a mermaid was engraved on the metal hilt, her long hair not even bothering to cover up her exposed breasts. Beatrice looked away, suddenly feeling a little dirty. But before she had time to think about it, nails dragging against wood peeled off through the room.

Juniper's eyes grew as big as her fists and she looked around at the others, blinking a few times. "What was that?"

"I heard it that time, too." Xander looked over his shoulder.

Over the boxes and the plastic tubs was the crawl space, its wooden doors protectively shut with a rusty lock latched over both. Beatrice and the others all stood in silence, staring at the doors and waiting to hear another sound. Her eyes had adjusted to the dark by then, making the doors easy to lock her gaze with. Slowly but surely, the noise came back: a scratching sound starting from the top of the other side of the cubby's doors, slowly raking down them.

Chills shot up Beatrice's spine as though she could feel the wood curling up beneath her own fingernails. Then, the basement went silent. The scratching noise stopped and whatever was walking around upstairs had gone quiet, too. Beatrice opened her mouth to suggest that maybe it was an animal that needed help. Raccoons could sometimes get stuck under the foundation of the front porch so maybe it had wiggled its way inside somehow. But before she could speak, she was stopped.

Suddenly, a horrifying bellow came from behind the crawl space doors in a croaky, hoarse voice that Beatrice could only describe as *decaying*.

"Run!" Beatrice ordered, grabbing Jax by the arm to drag him away while Juniper and Xander were already sprinting for the stairs.

The four of them scrambled up the same staircase Uncle Eli died on, thrashing against the walls and each other, desperate to crawl out of the stairwell and into safety. Beatrice felt herself break the fall of Jax as they all clambered out of the mudroom and onto the floor.

"I want mommy!" Juniper cried, tears flooding her big green eyes. Her plump lips were aimed downward, quivering like she was on the verge of tears.

"What was that?" Xander hissed at Beatrice like this was all her fault. Like she *knew* what was going to happen when they went down there. She was just as terrified as the rest of them.

"There you all are," Grandpa Hugh stood in the doorway of the mudroom, the kitchen behind him. He was holding a sweaty glass of lemonade in his hand, his eyes flickering from the four of them to the opened basement door. His eyebrows made one large line over his eyes, just under the wrinkles in his forehead. The short hairs stood off his ears and the dimple in his chin looked like an eye staring at them. "What in the hell are you doing on the floor?"

"We heard something in the basement." Beatrice quickly stood up when everyone else stayed silent. She dusted off her thighs, swallowing the huge ball in her throat.

"It was scary," Jax chimed in, shoving his ring finger into his mouth to gnaw on—a bad habit of his that Aunt Marley had been trying to get him to stop.

"What does that have to do with you being on the floor?" Grandpa Hugh didn't even seem bothered that they were all scared out of their minds. Shouldn't he have been more concerned about his grandkids? Shouldn't he have already been racing down those steps to figure out what they were talking about? He just stayed put, looking at them like they were crazy to lay on the floor but not crazy to think that there was something lurking downstairs.

"Did you not just hear me?" Beatrice heard herself snap at him. She never talked back to adults. For one, she never needed to. And for two, the grownups here were always a lot tougher than they let off—for obvious reasons. "There was something in the basement. Behind those weird doors on the wall."

A look of realization flickered over Grandpa Hugh's face. The lines in his forehead wiggled a little and he adjusted the glass in his hand. He wiped his brow with the back of his wrist. "Are you talking about the crawl space?"

Beatrice nodded her head, the others following suit.

"It was loud," Xander finally spoke up when a ringing silence filled the room, the only sound being the chirping birds through the summer breeze outside.

"And like Jax said, it was scary," Beatrice added.

Grandpa Hugh stared at the basement door for a long time before taking a cautious drink of his lemonade. He wiped his upper lip with his thumb after swallowing. "Why don't you guys stay out of the basement for the time being? You shouldn't be wandering down there anyway. It's not a playroom."

"What's down there?" Juniper asked him before Beatrice could nudge her to keep quiet. Beatrice knew the adults don't like too many questions asked about the house.

"What do you mean by that, kiddo?" Grandpa Hugh chuckled, as though the question was ridiculous. And perhaps it was. "It's just a basement. A bunch of junk is down there."

"But what about the noise we heard?" Beatrice heard herself ask. Again, before she could stop herself. "It sounded like an animal or something."

Grandpa Hugh didn't look worried in the slightest, which honestly scared Beatrice a little more than whatever happened downstairs. He put his free hand on her shoulder. "It's just the house. That's all."

Chapter 11

Beatrice and Xander quietly painted the walls of the guest bedroom after they sorted through every other drawer and hiding place inside to make sure they weren't missing something else important. As Beatrice runs the paint roller up and down the walls, she can't stop thinking about the Polaroid that now sits in her jewelry box, safe from anyone trying to find it.

She could be over thinking the whole thing but that's what Ashwood does to a person: your mind goes stale with paranoia, making you second guess the world in ways you didn't know existed. It's an odd talent that a house can have, but one that has spread through these walls like wildfire. If Beatrice is right, and there are more photos that Lila took, recording every occurrence and happening inside of Ashwood, then Beatrice just needs to know where to look.

"You okay over there?" Xander asks from the other side of the room. "I can pretty much hear your brain gears turning."

Beatrice glances over her shoulder and forces a tight smile. If she thinks any more about this, she really *is* going to lose her mind and Xander will see her just as crazy as the other members of her family. That's the last thing she needs. "I'm fine. Just have a lot on my mind."

"You can ramble about anything," he offers, carefully using his brush against the brown trim near the floor. "I like to think of myself as a good listener, Beatrice. That's pretty much the only thing Nana and I agree on, actually."

"How is she doing?"

He shrugs a shoulder and hesitates to respond. "I mean, she could be better, but I suppose at least she's not six feet under—if that makes sense."

More than you know.

"It makes perfect sense." Beatrice plunges the roller into the paint tray, the ugly mustard yellow splattering a bit onto the hardwood. "It's hard when you know a loved one is going downhill."

"Very long hills, at that," Xander adds, wiping his face with his wrist and smearing paint across his cheek.

"Do you have any other family?" Beatrice asks curiously.

When they were younger, Xander knew everything about Beatrice's house: the people inside, the weird things that would happen at random times, the deaths. He would come over after the family funerals and offer his shoulder for Beatrice to cry on—in which she never used. But he very rarely ever spoke about his own family. He would bring up his Nana every now and again but it was never a long conversation. Now, Beatrice wonders if poor little Xander had an annoying childhood of Beatrice giving him details about another one of her family members dying or going missing when she never bothered to ask him about his own.

"Pardon?" He glances at her like he's caught off guard by the question. Beatrice almost snorts at his politeness.

"It's weird." Beatrice realizes. "We grew up together, in a way, but now that I think about it, I know very little about your family. And you know everything about mine."

"Yeah, well, they're not as exciting as yours," he jokes. "But like I said before, it's just me and Nana. My aunt and uncle have been hiking through Iceland for I don't even know how long."

Beatrice arcs a brow. "What's in Iceland?"

"Does anyone really know the answer to that question?"

She grins, going back to painting. "Good point."

"But I do think they own two donkeys out there or something," Xander goes on, sounding a little embarrassed. "They sent a postcard to us a couple years back of the donkeys getting married."

Beatrice laughs, imagining how ridiculous those photos must have looked and sort of wanting a framed copy for the store. "You're kidding."

"I honestly wish I was, Beatrice." He chuckles, shaking his head and dipping his brush back into the paint bucket. "But, no. In a year or two, I'm betting we'll receive another postcard announcing the birth of their first baby."

"You lie when you say your family isn't as interesting."

"Nah, I still stand by that."

Beatrice doesn't want her family to be interesting. Growing up as a Millstone, she thought all of this unusual stuff was normal. It wasn't until she moved in with Clara that she started to feel a little like the rest of society, what normal looks like for *them*. Comparing it to her childhood here in Ashwood is like comparing blue to brown. The contrast is too much. It makes Beatrice crave a regular childhood like regular kids. A childhood where funerals weren't held in the backyard and when uncles weren't walking ceilings and the House Thing in the crawl space wouldn't yell for help in the middle of the night.

The thought makes Beatrice consider what Aunt Edie told her about what she did with her mother's belongings. All of it is in boxes in the basement. If Lila went missing during her stay at Ashwood, and she didn't have much family, is it possible that Aunt Edie kept some of her stuff?

"I can hear your brain gears again," Xander tells her, sticking his tongue out a little as he carefully drags the paintbrush down the length of the wall. "You're making me start to worry about not hearing my own."

"Aunt Edie told me that she put all of my mom's things in the basement when she made this room the guest room," Beatrice explains, setting her roller down in the paint, ignoring it when the handle slips inside.

"So?"

"So, what if she packed all of Lila's things up after she never came back and put them down there, too?"

"I suppose that's a thought," Xander agrees, a glob of paint dripping off the bristles of his brush. "But I haven't been down there since…"

The Scratch in the Crawl Space. That's what they called that thing the day the two of them were down in the basement with the twins. Beatrice can't even remember why they were down there in the first place. But she recalls the four of them, standing in that dingy basement Uncle Eli died in, and listening to the ear-piercing sound of nails digging into the crawl space's doors, starting from the top and making their way all the way to the bottom. That was the last time she went to the basement. Even when she told her mother about what the four of them heard, her mom sat her down and explained that they had to bury Grandpa Hugh's brother when Beatrice was just a baby, as his skeleton was found inside.

Beatrice still doesn't know how it happened, but the brother, Lachlan, somehow locked himself in the crawl space that was never used back in the day. No one could hear him screaming or clawing at the doors to get out. Everyone above assumed he had just went missing or that he ran away like he kept promising to do. He spent his whole life down there in that basement, never coming up into the real world, afraid of everything that went on up there. Probably afraid of the sun, too. And according to family stories, one day he claimed that he was going to leave Ashwood. Silver Creek, too, for that matter. He would flee and start a new life somewhere else, where he would wake in the sunlight every day versus cooping himself up in the lonely basement of Ashwood.

Years later, his bones were found by Aunt Edie in the middle of the night and he was put to rest in the family plot.

"Yeah, me either, actually." Beatrice notices, rubbing the back of her neck. "But it wouldn't hurt to look around, right?"

For a flash of a second, Xander looks afraid. But then he shakes it off and nods his head. "Yeah. Might as well. Lead the way."

Beatrice does as she's told, leading the two of them to the first-floor mudroom, where the basement door stares back at them, looking like it hasn't been used in ages. Beatrice runs her tongue over her teeth, debating on whether she should try talking herself out of it now or not. She should. Uncle Eli dying on the steps was one thing but hearing something in that crawl space is another. Returning to the forbidden room in the house makes her stomach churn.

"We don't have to look, if you don't want to," Xander suggests from next to her, his hands in the pockets of his jeans. "I don't blame you. The last time we were down there, it was freaking weird."

"We're just looking around for a quick second or two," Beatrice assures herself more than she does him. "We'll look for any boxes marked with Lila's name and bring up a few. We won't be down there long."

Xander nods but doesn't say anything. Beatrice finds herself feeling like a little girl again, standing next to her best friend as they explore the mysteries of Ashwood, scared out of their minds, but determined to look fear in the face. She flicks a strand of wavy hair away from her eye and quickly opens the door to the basement. She stays to the side of the steps, not wanting a repeat of what happened to Uncle Eli taking place. Xander follows suit, hanging onto the rail for balance. They reach the bottom and very little has changed.

More cobwebs are strung up in the corners and create a film against the cylinder brick walls. The washer and dryer look rusted at the bottom with no signs of use. Beatrice remembers Aunt Edie telling her about laundry the first day, and how she usually just does everything by hand nowadays. She promised that Beatrice was more than welcome to use the washer and dryer whenever she would like if she wasn't interested in doing her laundry by hand. But after seeing the way they look, Beatrice is going to have to pass.

Boxes and tubs and old decorations that never got used clutter the back corner of the basement, stacked in front of those sinister crawl space doors. Beatrice doesn't stare at it for too long. Instead, she roots through her pocket for her phone as a source of light.

"Wow," Xander speaks first. "This place hasn't changed a bit, has it?"

"Not by much, that's for sure." She takes a few steps toward the soggy cardboard boxes in front of her, all of them stacked and unstable with the corners splitting and edges poking through. "So, I guess just look for anything that might belong to Lila."

"Don't you think that's a little difficult when neither of us knew the girl personally?" Xander wonders aloud but begins shifting boxes around anyway, a Virgin Mary statue with a missing nose poking up out of one of the boxes. He winces at it and pushes the box to the side before pulling another one closer.

"Yeah, but like I said, Aunt Edie could've labeled a box of her stuff when Lila went missing," Beatrice says back, setting a light box onto the floor before rooting through the one beneath it. It's a shoe box consisting of tangled gold jewelry that probably isn't even real. Beatrice tosses it to the side. "You probably think I'm crazy. And paranoid. Among a bunch of other things."

Xander tilts his head, glancing over his shoulder as he squats down to rummage through a box he can't lift without it falling apart. "Why would you think that, Beatrice?"

"Because I probably sound just as delusional as every other person who has lived in this house." She's saying her thoughts aloud, because she's realizing that it's true.

What if there's really nothing for her to figure out? What if the girls who stayed here that eventually went missing aren't some part of a mysterious conspiracy theory surrounding the happenings here at Ashwood? What if the gossip is true, and some of those girls fled Silver Creek because they were on the run from whatever bad chapters they found themselves caught up in? Is Beatrice paranoid enough to believe that the House Things had something to do with all this? That they're the cause of these disappearances? Or that the house itself swallowed them whole and Aunt Edie somehow had something to do with it? After all, she and Beatrice are the only two the house hasn't touched and Aunt Edie is the only one that has stayed here.

"I think it's brave," Xander says flatly, picking up a dusty framed photo from the box in front of him. "I guess that's one trait this place has taught you, right?"

She frowns. She's never thought about Ashwood teaching her anything positive. Beatrice looks over as Xander uses his sleeved elbow to rub off the dust on the Victorian-styled portrait, grey eyes staring back at him.

"Who's this chum?" Xander asks.

"Hmm," Beatrice grunts, stepping over to loom behind his shoulder. The man is tall and lanky with shoulder-length hair in thick waves. His smile is faded and his eyes are filled with sadness, staring back at the two of them like he's begging to be saved from the barrier of the frame. "That's Lachlan. Grandpa Hugh's brother. He's the one that was locked in the crawl space and died."

Xander's eyes flicker through the darkness to the crawl space doors and then up to Beatrice. "You couldn't have made up a lie about who he is? At least while we're in the basement?"

Beatrice opens her mouth to answer, but she's disrupted by a sound so familiar, her body goes numb. Sharp nails dig into the wood on the other side of the crawl space doors, sinking into them like a knife easing into a tub of butter. The tips of Beatrice's fingers buzz at the thought of nails being raked down wood the way she's hearing it. Xander doesn't move. He stays squatting, his eyes glued to the doors. Beatrice can't find herself to do anything. The sound is piercing the air like a spear soaring through an open field. Beatrice has forgotten to breathe, she realizes, just as the familiar scream rings out from behind the doors.

Just like when they were kids, Beatrice and Xander scramble to the stairs, taking two at a time to return to the ground floor. Beatrice slams the basement door behind her and quickly switches the lock, breathing heavily as she pins her back against it, her heart thundering inside of her chest.

"What the hell was that?" Xander demands breathlessly. His eyes are huge, his forehead lined with worry wrinkles, and his lips chapped and parted. If Beatrice stares at him long enough, she might just remember that they're no longer children. But seeing that old familiar expression of his sends her back into a time warp, like most things in this house continue to do for her.

Beatrice shakes her head, unsure what to say. On one hand, she can't answer him honestly because she doesn't entirely know the whole truth herself. Then again, if she tries telling him that it could be Lachlan, then she would for sure confirm to him that she's insane.

"It's just... Great Uncle Lachlan," she tells him, confirming that her words sound just as bizarre out loud as they did in her head.

"Okay, look," Xander begins, still panting for breath. "I've seen a lot of weird stuff go on in this house, Beatrice. And I've heard all sorts of horror stories that people share about this place. And you might have grown up believing that there were things called *House Things* but I'm starting to believe that's just a different way of saying *ghost*."

"They're not ghosts."

"Then what are they?" Xander sounds like he's growing more and more impatient. Beatrice has never seen this side of him before. Not when they were kids, arguing about who got to play what role in the games they made up. Not when they'd fake fight with swords and weapons but accidentally hit each other with the sharp edges. "Because if you're saying that your grandpa's brother accidentally locked himself in there all those years ago, and no one has ever opened it up, wouldn't you think that his ghost is stuck inside?"

Beatrice puts her hands on her hips. "So, what are you saying? That you want us to go down there and open the doors? To let out whatever kind of *spirit* is stuck on the other side?"

Xander only considers it for half a second, letting his shoulders lift and then drop. "It doesn't seem like such a bad idea."

"Fine." Beatrice opens the basement door back up, gesturing for him to return back down those steps and into the pit of darkness waiting at the bottom. "Knock yourself out."

Xander stares at her, clearly debating on what he should do. They lock eyes and Beatrice can tell he's actually considering it. There is no way in hell Beatrice would ever do something like that. She remembers seeing Grammy Astrid after her death just a few times before finally leaving Ashwood. She would tell her mother about the sightings and her mom would always inform her not to bother the House Things, that this is their house just as much as it is for people who haven't yet died. So that's what Beatrice did: she ignored the flickers at the end of the halls or the walking on the ceiling from Uncle Eli. She would pretend she didn't hear Lachlan during the night or that an old lady filled her bedroom frame every time she woke from a dream. The House Things were to never be disturbed.

"I should go," Xander says finally, rubbing the back of his neck with a hand. "Nana is probably waiting on me to prep dinner."

"Okay."

Xander awkwardly crosses through the mudroom and starts for the front door. Beatrice follows him, cursing under her breath at adult situations. When they were kids, nothing like this would have made them uncomfortable with each other. But as people get older, they get guarded and sensitive and things get made into a whole big spectacle that isn't even worth it at the end of the day.

"Thanks for your help today," Beatrice says when Xander opens the front door. "With the paint and all."

"No problem," he responds. "I'll be back tomorrow to help some more."

He's gone in the blink of an eye and Beatrice shuts the door, Ashwood's silence making her ears ring. She shuffles back down the hall to the mudroom, glaring at the basement doorway as it mocks her entire existence. Half of her wants to go back down there with every flashlight and candle she can find in the house to search for Lila's things. She'll get what she needs and come back up here without anything to worry about. But Lachlan in that crawl space still sends chills up her spine. So, closing the door again, she decides it will have to wait.

Beatrice's eyes flashed open, gasping for breath. The smell of dirt assaulted her nostrils and the big round moon in the sky loomed over her like it was mocking her existence.

She grabbed a handful of the dirt at her side to make sure that she was awake and no longer dreaming. Letting her eyes adjust to the night, Beatrice slowly brought herself up in order to discover that she was in the garden. Aunt Marley's and her mother's newly planted flowers were crushed beneath Beatrice's weight, petals plucked off their stems and littered around her like broken glass. She began to breathe heavily, scared out of her mind.

"You were just sleepwalking, Beatrice," she told herself over and over again to reassure her that she wasn't in fact losing her mind, she just got carried away with sleep. This wasn't the first time and it probably wouldn't be the last. Aunt Edie did this sort of thing all the time. It was nothing to be fearful of.

She got to her feet and dusted the dirt off her sweatpants that were way too small for her now. Beatrice froze when she noticed a figure her size wandering near the Jungle. From the looks of it, he was definitely a boy, but too tall to be Jax and too short to be Xander. Beatrice stood, watching, not sure what to do. Maybe she should run inside as fast as she can and wake up every adult in the house. Maybe she should duck behind a shrub and not head inside until he went away. The most ridiculous thing she could do was to demand to know what on earth he was doing in her yard.

"Hey!" Beatrice called out, unafraid. He was a little boy. It wasn't like he could hurt her or anything.

He looked over his shoulder but his face was masked in the shadows of the trees and the structure of Ashwood. He stared at her for just a few seconds before taking off toward the other side of the house. Beatrice leaped over the newly planted azaleas and raced through the backyard, the noises of a summer night ringing through her ears.

"Hey!" Beatrice yelled again when the boy was running so far ahead of her, he somehow reminded Beatrice of the Gingerbread Man, dashing through town and determined to not get caught. "Stop!"

The boy didn't stop. He kept running until he reached the front lawn, letting out a small chuckle before turning for the driveway. Beatrice pumped her arms at her side, flinging her legs out in front of her as fast as they could carry her. She slipped on the wet grass rounding the corner into the front yard, but the boy was gone. The only thing that caught Beatrice's eye was the wide- open front door. She swallowed, her eyebrows pulling together as she tried regaining her breath. Glancing over her shoulder at the empty street and then back at the house, Beatrice was suddenly scared to go inside. Was he in there?

"Bea?" Aunt Edie appeared in the doorway of the house, a bumblebee yellow nightgown stopping at her ankles, a white robe draped over her shoulders with a furry collar. She took a tentative step out onto the porch, looking around for some sort of clue to tell her what Beatrice was doing outside in the middle of the night. "Are you all right, sweetie?"

"I saw someone," Beatrice said, pointing to nowhere in particular. The boy vanished from thin air. "There was a little boy out here."

"Are you talking about Xander?" Aunt Edie asked after a pregnant pause.

Beatrice shook her head. "No, I know what Xander looks like."

"Well, what did this boy look like?"

Beatrice opened her mouth three times before answering, cursing at herself for not being faster to get to the mysterious boy quick enough. "I don't know, it was dark."

"So, then, it could have been Xander," Aunt Edie told her slowly, holding her hand out to beckon Beatrice back inside. "Come on, let's make some hot chocolate."

"Don't you think it's a little too warm for hot chocolate?" Beatrice followed her into the foyer, giving one last look over her shoulder for any sign of the boy that somehow got away.

"Hot chocolate always tastes better in the summer," Aunt Edie replied, locking the front door behind them before they started for the kitchen. "Just like how ice cream always tastes better in the winter."

"I think I slept walk," Beatrice admitted when she found herself sitting at the dining room table with her aunt, a big mug of hot chocolate in front of her. Tiny marshmallows swam through the hot milk, growing soggy.

Aunt Edie nodded her head without looking too surprised. "I figured as much. The Millstone clan comes from a long line of sleepwalkers. There's nothing you should be concerned about."

Beatrice's brow furrowed. "But I woke up in the garden."

"Trust me, darling, I've woken up in stranger places." Aunt Edie grinned, wringing her hands together. "Sleep can be a greedy thing, Bea. When we are unconscious, sleep has a way of demanding to be entertained."

"Like a person?"

She nodded again, this time softer. "Yes, like a person. Walking while we sleep isn't the worst thing that could happen. We're just adventurous, that's all. We can sleep peacefully when we're dead, that's what I always say."

Beatrice never heard her say that. She takes a sip from her hot chocolate, giving herself a liquid mustache. "There was a boy outside. I think he was around my age. But it was too dark to see his face."

Aunt Edie looked concerned now and then painted a forced smile across her lips. "Honey, I know Xander comes around a lot of the time—"

"It wasn't Xander," Beatrice cut her off, beginning to feel unsafe. She didn't want strangers in her yard during the middle of the night. What would she do if one of them climbed up to her window and peeked inside? What would any of them do if something terrible happened to Juniper or Jax?

"Then do you have another friend that would be wandering the grounds this late at night?"

Beatrice shook her head. "No."

Aunt Edie reached across the table and wiped away the chocolate from Beatrice's upper lip. "I'm sure it was just a dream."

Chapter 12

Beatrice wakes that night with a violent jerk, her body tingling from the unexpected sudden movement. She's sweaty under her bed blanket and her mouth is sour with sleep. Her crocheted elephant stares at her with its button eyes from the window seat across the room. Her eyes adjust to the darkness of her room and as she blinks, she notices her bedroom door opened to her right. Beatrice turns her head to the side, where the dim glow of the hall light illuminates a silhouette standing in her doorway.

Grandpa Hugh stands there with his neck craned in a way that makes his head hang to the side. A bone bulges out, cutting through the air like a broken tree branch. Beatrice tries to let out a scream but she can't find the strength to push one out of her. Her hands begin to tremble, as they would when she was a little girl, tucked away in her bed and witnessing such a disturbing image. Sometimes, she would pinch herself to be sure that she wasn't having some horrific dream or imagining things that were never really there. But it's a strange thing, seeing something so terrifying that it paralyzes you. Beatrice can't bring herself to pinch her wrist or her palm or even her thigh. Instead, Grandpa Hugh watches her with his snapped neck, in no rush to move or say anything at all. He just watches her with dead eyes.

Time goes on for an eternity, it feels. Surely, it could've just been a few minutes, but Beatrice is almost sure that if she were to reach up and feel her hair, strands would come out in brittle gray ribbons. Then, something weird happens, something that usually never happens when Grandpa Hugh joins her at night. Two small figures appear on either side of him, both of their red curls reflecting the light behind them. Beatrice recognizes their clothes right away: Jax's corduroy overalls and Juniper's velvet blue dress. It's Juniper who waves her over, motioning for her to get up.

That's when Beatrice knows this is a dream. It isn't real life. Ever since the twins went missing, Beatrice never saw them again. It wasn't like her other family members, where after they died, she still got to see glimpses of them every now and again. The twins were different. So, Beatrice finally gets her limbs to cooperate and she kicks off her covers, fumbling out of her bed and sliding on the heap of clothes on the floor in the process. The twins and Grandpa Hugh are already making their way down the hall by the time Beatrice leaves her room, the lights on the wall lit up ever so softly.

She can't even hear the creaking of the floors under her feet as she makes her way down the narrow hall. Jax and Juniper hold their grandpa's hands as they start up the flight of stairs leading to the third floor. Beatrice's brow wiggles, wondering where they're going and why. She follows them, anyway, reaching the top and finding the three of them staring at the door to the guest room. Beatrice's mother's old bedroom.

The smell of drying paint wafts out into the hall and for some odd reason, Beatrice immediately feels lightheaded. Jax, Juniper, and Grandpa Hugh are all staring at something inside of the room, blankly, like there is nothing in front of them but a black hole designed to suck anything that comes in its way.

"Hello?" Beatrice speaks like they're strangers. The words roll out of her mouth like they're made of syrup: thick and slow. She takes a wary step closer to them. "What are you guys doing?"

None of them say a word. They stare ahead into the room for several more beats before Juniper turns her head to stare Beatrice in the face.

"You're next."

Beatrice wakes, gasping. Sunlight pours in through the windows and before she can sink further into her mattress to process the nightmare, she realizes she isn't on a mattress of any sort. Instead, she's lying on plastic covering, surrounded by paintbrushes and freshly dyed walls. The guest room lingers around her, still and oblivious as to why she's waking up in here. Beatrice's bones ache as she sits up, her neck throbbing with a knot in the back and her collarbone out of place. She rubs her head with a hand and rotates her shoulder, telling herself not to freak out, that this is nothing she needs to worry about… yet.

She's slept walk before. Ashwood has that power over the people inside. Aunt Edie knows all about that. In fact, she still does it. But what about that dream? What about Grandpa Hugh and seeing the twins for the first time in years? Isn't that something? Sure, she's dreamed of the day she last saw Jax and Juniper, but they never looked so much more alive than they did in that slumber. Her heart hammers loudly in her chest at the thought of them being House Things along with everyone else on the family tree. But she shakes the thought. She doesn't want their fate being as miserable as everybody else's. She refuses to put them under that same twisted category as all the Millstones before them.

"Beatrice, darling." Aunt Edie is in the doorway with a wrinkled hand over her equally wrinkled chest. She's staring at her with wide eyes, her hair freshly curled and the sunshine yellow dress she has on nearly blinds Beatrice from the floor. "What on earth are you doing in here?"

"Sorry," Beatrice mumbles, standing herself up and ignoring the throbbing pain shooting through her head. "I must've slept walk. I had the strangest dream."

"It looks like it."

Beatrice looks at her to wonder if she is trying to rag on her appearance, but then she notices Aunt Edie's gaze trained on the wall on the other side of the room. Beatrice looks over her shoulder and the sight makes her thundering heart drop to her knees. The newly painted yellow wall is now covered in red handprints, all over. One pair after the other after the other after the other...

Then, in the middle, where an expensive piece of art should be hanging, are huge red letters in the same paint: *YOU'RE NEXT.*

Beatrice covers her mouth with a hand that is not covered in any sort of red paint. She looks around for any sign of the color red but there is none to be found. Only yellow and a bit of primer. Beatrice takes a step away from the wall, her mind buzzing with thoughts and activity too fast to even attempt for it all to slow down. She didn't write that. And she definitely didn't dip her hands in paint to do some preschool project inside of the guest room. She thinks about the twins and how they used to dip their hands in things all the time, leaving trails through the house like tiny monsters. *You're Next.* She can practically hear Juniper's voice echoing through the room.

"What on earth did you do?" Aunt Edie finally demands, sounding more annoyed than confused. She looks both disappointed and horrified, her eyes flickering back and forth to the message on the wall and then at Beatrice. "What would make you write such a thing?"

"I didn't do that," Beatrice blurts before she can form a more believable sentence. "The twins did."

Aunt Edie looks stunned. Her lips part and she stares at Beatrice for an ear-piercingly silent pause, rapidly blinking and unsure how to respond. "What did you just say?"

Beatrice opens her mouth to tell her that it was Juniper and Jax but there is no way she's going to take that seriously. Beatrice can't blame her, either. She would be looking at her the same way Aunt Edie is right now if the roles were reversed. Part of her thinks that Aunt Edie might give her a shot, since they're both sleepwalkers, disappearing into the night like bored owls. But this is different. Neither of them had ever done something like this in their sleep before. Sure, they might have wandered up and down the stairs for hours on end or ventured out into the yard. But they never redecorated a room.

"Like I said, it was a dream," Beatrice tells her, suddenly feeling desperate to be believed. "I'll clean it up."

"I would hope so." Aunt Edie pads out of the room, glancing over her shoulder before disappearing down the hall.

Beatrice runs her hands up and down her face, her stress levels inching higher and higher. She needs a shower. It might help wash this delusion that has been absorbed into her skin, sinking beneath the surface like a cancer.

She grabs a fresh change of clothes from her room and roots through the hall closet for a large towel. Beatrice strips off her clothes when she shuts the bathroom door behind her and stares at herself in the boxy mirror above the sink. Her hair is matted down on top of her head, just as desperate to be clean as the rest of her body. She blinks, a flash of Grammy Astrid appearing over her shoulder.

Beatrice lets out a scream, cowering to the side of the room and for some reason focused on covering her bare chest. The room remains empty, though, as it has every other time Astrid has appeared in the mirrors of Ashwood, forever watching from the other side of the glass.

Even the scalding hot water in the shower isn't hot enough for Beatrice. She stands under the showerhead, the water running through her hair and down her skin in tiny waterfalls, tracing her body like paths on a map. Her eyes remain shut for the entirety of the shower, blocking out anything she might see if she opens them. One might think that the horrors of your childhood home would remain with you forever and ever. That you would never forget the feeling of essentially being haunted.

But Beatrice has forgotten that indescribable feeling. Sure, she remembers most things about living here when she was a kid. She remembers her family members and the House Things and seeing flashes of them throughout the days. She recalls the noises they would make in the night and how the other living adults would shrug it off. And yes, she knew that it was a very abnormal upbringing. But if there is one thing that she has truly forgotten, it's what it feels like to constantly be watched; to always feel like you're never alone. As a kid, she never cared. But as an adult, it's freaking her out. And it shouldn't. Adults shouldn't be scared of things like this. Children should be the ones living in fear of seeing dead relatives. Their minds are supposed to be innocent, tainted when they see the things Beatrice has seen and experienced. But it seems to have done quite the opposite.

Beatrice wanders downstairs after her shower, the soft patter of rain hitting the exterior of Ashwood like tiny bullets. Aunt Edie is at the dining table, bills and envelopes and paperwork laid out in front of her.

"Have you eaten breakfast?" Beatrice asks, making her way to the coffee machine at the counter.

"I met up with Marilyn and Ruth earlier this morning," Aunt Edie answers, shuffling some of the papers around. "And the rest of my day is now dedicated to figuring out what to do with this damn place."

"Selling, wise?" Beatrice pours her coffee in a mug patterned with pastel flowers.

Aunt Edie nods with a heavy sigh. "No one is going to want to buy this house. Not after all the town gossip and rumors."

"People enjoy buying houses they think are haunted." Beatrice leans against the counter, her fingers wrapped around the mug. She is going to talk and talk and talk for as long as her aunt will let her. Anything that might keep her from going upstairs to paint over that message in the guest room. "Even those bad ghost hunting shows no one watches."

"But this place isn't haunted in the way they think," Aunt Edie corrects quietly.

Beatrice runs her tongue over her teeth and she takes a few steps through the kitchen and to the dining area in the turret. She plants herself down in the chair across from Aunt Edie, the heavy question that's been weighing on her mind since she got here pushing its way to the tip of her tongue.

"Aunt Edie, I have to ask you something," she begins, catching her aunt's attention. "What happened to the girls that rented out the upstairs?"

Aunt Edie blinks at her, fear flashing over her face for just a split second before returning to normal. "What is it that you're asking, dear?"

"Well, it's come to my attention that they've all kind of... vanished," Beatrice explains. "I heard through the grapevine that a lot of the girls that used to live here were very much alive and present... until they weren't."

"That goes for all humans, though, right?" Aunt Edie faintly smiles. "We're all very much alive and present until we aren't."

"But these were younger girls," Beatrice pushes. "And they're all still missing."

"There's a difference between someone missing and someone that is simply MIA," Aunt Edie explains to her, threading her slender fingers together on top of the table. She stares at her for a solid minute until speaking again. "During the past fifteen years, I have had a total of twelve girls who stayed here in that guest room. Girls like them, girls young and pretty and with their whole lives ahead of them, go missing all the time. Some of them, yes, got themselves into tough situations that they were running from so they didn't stay long."

"So they just packed up and left?"

"More or less," she answers. "I believe I've only had four flee off into the night."

"But what about the other ones?" Beatrice orders impatiently. "What about the ones that didn't just run off?"

Aunt Edie shrugs her bony shoulders helplessly. "Your guess is as good as mine, darling. They were here one day, and then gone the next. There has been a lot of speculation about this, too, so don't think you're the first one."

"I'm not thinking that."

"I figured you of all people would understand, though," she proceeds, her head gently tilted to the side. "You know what it's like growing up in this house. The things that happen, the unexplained. It would scare anyone off, I reckon."

"But what if it could be explained?" Beatrice suggests. She knows that her aunt is going to call her crazy for volunteering an idea like this but screw it. "What if the things that go on here can be explained?"

Aunt Edie stares at her in bewilderment. "I'm not sure what you mean."

"We can have someone come take a look," Beatrice offers. "A specialist to see if it's haunted and stuff."

Aunt Edie throws her head back in laughter, her white teeth brightened like little lights inside of her mouth. "Oh, sweetie. That's a cute thought."

"Cute?" Beatrice echoes in annoyance. "There have been things in this house ever since I can remember. And it could've driven everyone you rented out that room to out of here because it's not normal. The way I grew up was not normal. The fact you still live here is not normal. Doesn't any of this freak you the fuck out?"

Aunt Edie is looking at her in shock, her hand to her chest and her teeth no longer lit up like Christmas. "You might be an adult now, Beatrice, but that does not give you the right to speak to your great aunt like that. I refuse to have that language be used in this house against me."

"Well maybe I refuse to walk around here like everything is normal," Beatrice argues back. "I made it out of here. I've seen other things. You grew up here and never left. This is all you know. And I'm here to tell you,

Aunt Edie, that everything you know is not okay. I shouldn't see my dead grandmother in a bathroom mirror. I shouldn't be dreaming of Grandpa Hugh and his neck or seeing Uncle Eli on the ceiling—"

"Stop it!" Aunt Edie roars, standing up and slamming her palms against the table. A blue vein in her neck bulges, threatening to burst and cover the entire room with a dark shade of red. "Stop it right this instant, young lady, or so help me I will throw you out of this house, do you hear me?"

Beatrice stares down at her mug of coffee, too scared to look her aunt in the face. She doesn't think that she's ever been screamed at by her before. Aunt Edie used to tell her all the time when she was a girl that she was her favorite. Beatrice would say the same back to her. But now, the thought of bringing up the fact that Ashwood is not a normal house and that these family occurrences are beyond regular, speaks volumes. Aunt Edie is nowhere close to accepting the fact that she is living in a space that might as well be black mold. But then why is she ready to put it on the market?

After having coffee for breakfast, Beatrice stands in the guest room, staring at the dried red paint splattered across the walls in handprints that are too small to be hers. She thinks about going to Xander's to tell him about what happened but she'd rather not go back downstairs and encounter Aunt Edie again. Plus, when he left yesterday, it was a little awkward after she told him to go downstairs to open the doors to the crawl space.

Beatrice presses her hand up against one of the many red handprints, confirming that they're way too small to be her own. Which means she didn't do this. Then who did? As she begins to paint over the mess with yellow, her mind wanders back to the twins. She could easily see them wandering through here with messy hands, smacking them against the wall to create a mural of what looks like straight out of a Charles Manson crime scene. But even after Jax and Juniper disappeared, Beatrice never saw them again, not like how she did with the adults.

Beatrice keeps her mind busy, quickly rolling enough paint on the wall to get it to dry as fast as possible. She works at a fast pace, wiping her brow from sweat every so often but managing to get the job done as fast as possible. The rain continues to hit against the window on the far side of the room, dribbling down the glass and blurring the yard. Beatrice dusts her hands off when she sets the roller down, satisfied with her work. She takes a breath, turning to look at the wall with the oak wardrobe against it. That one is next. Maybe Xander will even stop by later to help and their tiff from yesterday will be nonexistent.

Beatrice grabs hold of the side of the wardrobe, grunting as she tries scooting it away from the wall. The clawed feet drag against the wooden floor, digging into it enough to scratch.

"Shit," she mumbles under her breath. She wouldn't really care if the house wasn't being put on the market to be bought. But Ashwood needs to be sold as soon as possible.

Beatrice crouches next to the wardrobe, her hands running along the deep groove that's now in the floor. Her brow furrows when she follows the groove further across the hardwood, a trail that was made previously—which means it's been moved before. The scratches stop just a foot or two away from where the wardrobe is now, prompting Beatrice to get back up and move it some more.

She does it slowly, careful not to make too much noise. The last thing she needs is Aunt Edie marching up here to rip her a new one again. The heavy wardrobe groans against its own weight and Beatrice's face pinches with strength as she moves it as far as she can to where the prior tracks in the floor stop. The large vent toward the bottom of the floor is the only thing that catches Beatrice's eye. She crouches to the floor again, squeezing the upper half of her body between the back of the wardrobe and the wall, her fingers sliding through the grate of the vent and lifting the door off.

Beatrice stupidly gasps at the sight. There isn't a lot inside, but a small purple box made of velvet is covered in dust. It seems to be the only thing in there. It's the size of Beatrice's jewelry box and the purple is so deep that it almost blends into the darkness of the vent. She snatches it up and maneuvers herself out of the tight space. Dust floats off it with a gentle blow. There's a glimmering gold clasp in the front, with a single keyhole staring up at her. Beatrice tries opening it, knowing it won't work. Screw patience.

Beatrice bashes the box against the corner of the wardrobe and the flimsy lock undoes itself, bending and now, forever useless. Eagerly, Beatrice opens the box, a small stack of Polaroid photos inside, along with a few trinkets and stained newspaper. The first thing that catches Beatrice's eye is the clump of newspapers stuck together by a baby blue paperclip. She carefully spreads them out on the floor in front of her, bold headlines in capital letters screaming at her:

ASHWOOD DEATH SPARKS CONTROVERSY.

MILLSTONE FAMILY CURSE STRIKES AGAIN.

IS ASHWOOD HAUNTED? THE TRUE STORY BEHIND THE HORROR.

All of the articles are things that Beatrice has already read, for the most part. She remembers even finding Samara Hamilton's Facebook page a few nights ago during her research. She of course never saw the articles about Aunt Edie but it's good to know the cops in this town aren't completely stupid. But how was she proved innocent? It's not like Beatrice *wants* Edie to be guilty, but the fact Ashwood is a constant in a long line of disappearances raises reasonable suspicion.

The next thing in the box is a necklace that looks all too familiar to Beatrice. It's fake gold and very long. So long that it used to hang all the way down to Beatrice's mother's bellybutton. The locket is in the shape of a squid and when it used to open, a picture of the two of them would be inside. Beatrice holds the necklace between her fingers for a long time, staring at the worn clasp and green chain. She wrestles with the locket for a few seconds before it pops open. Sure enough, the same photo that was inside all those years ago stares up at her, the two of them with their faces smashed together when Beatrice was just a baby.

She slips it around her neck and hides it under her shirt, wondering where it was found and why it was put in here. The Polaroid photos are next. Beatrice doesn't want to get her hopes up in thinking that they're the rest of whatever collection Lila could have had before she disappeared, but it wouldn't make sense if they weren't. She reaches for the tiny stack, squinting at the blurry picture on the top. The white curls, the saggy cheeks, the purple eye shadow painted over wrinkly eyelids. The photo depicts Grandma Astrid standing in the bathroom mirror, framed in the darkness. Beatrice flips the photo over to read Lila's writing: *The lady in the mirror.*

The next photo shows Lila's thumb covering half of it. The other half is blurry and dark and there doesn't seem to be anything unusual. In fact, it looks like something that was taken on accident, printed against its will. Beatrice turns it over: *The man on the ceiling.* She goes back to the front side, holding the picture closer to her face. It takes her a minute, but sure enough, there's the figure of Uncle Eli, racing across the ceiling upside down.

The third Polaroid is of a blond woman running from the camera in a lace dress. She's glancing over her shoulder and looks to be in about her twenties. Her arms are stretched on either side of her, clambering out the mudroom door and into the night, running for the yard. It looks like Bobby Jo, judging from the dress. Beatrice isn't quite sure where she falls on the long line of Millstones but she remembers Aunt Edie showing her Bobby Jo's photos in an album in the study.

"She was so beautiful," Aunt Edie told her, holding out a photo of Bobby Jo on her wedding day. "Everyone thought so."

"Where is she now?" Beatrice asked, perched on the arm of the leather sofa.

Aunt Edie sighs, tucking the photo back into the plastic holder of the album. She turns the page. "She was trampled by a horse."

Bobby Jo died on her wedding day. The man she was marrying apparently died of a broken heart days after. Beatrice recalls hearing Aunt Marley once say she thought that her fiancé killed himself because he couldn't handle the loss of his almost-wife. She also had a twin sister, Barbara Jean, who died from hypothermia the year before after accidentally being locked outside during the coldest night of the winter. Beatrice flips the Polaroid over to find this one titled: *Runaway bride?*.

Beatrice's heart hammers in her chest as she moves on to the next picture. Aunt Marley stands in the kitchen and the sight is horrifying enough that Beatrice almost lets the Polaroid slip from her fingers. Aunt Marley's mouth is stretched open so much that the back of her throat is visible. Black lines trace her entire face and her jaw hangs all the way down to the base of her neck. It looks like she's screaming. The title on the back reads: *The screaming woman.*

The next one is really blurry and Beatrice finds herself staring at it for what feels like an eternity. She can make out the blades of grass in the backyard, dead flowers sprouting out from the dirt in a square shaped section of the lawn. Beatrice brings the photo closer to her face for any more clues but she finds nothing. She flips the photo over instead and again, in Lila's handwriting: *The thing in the garden.*

Beatrice has no idea what that means. What thing in the garden? The photo under that one confuses her, as well. It was taken on a sunny afternoon day and it depicts the green shed in the back of the yard. There's a dark shadow toward the right hand side of the shed. The caption on the back reads: *The noise behind the barn.*

The final picture is of Beatrice's mom. Even though Beatrice can't see her face, she sees her back facing the camera as she descends down the stairs. Her dark hair spills over her shoulders and she's still wearing that plain white t-shirt she had on the night they tried to leave. Beatrice's eyes flood with unnecessary tears so she flips it over, wondering what the hell kind of nickname she was given. *The quiet one.*

"Beatrice?" Aunt Edie calls from downstairs, disrupting Beatrice's thoughts.

She quickly wipes a tear away and stuffs everything back into the box, shoving it under the wardrobe. She wipes her face again with the inner part of her elbow before marching out of the room and down the steps to the foyer, where Aunt Edie is waiting with her champagne-colored purse slung onto her shoulder.

"I'm going to meet Ruth and Marilyn again. Would you like to join?" she asks stubbornly, as though she's a child being forced to ask Beatrice out after their fight.

Beatrice considers it. It would be nice to get out of here for a bit—even if it's with Aunt Edie. But then again, she has so much work to do around the house before they can even entertain the thought of officially listing it.

"I have a lot to do around here," Beatrice reminds her. "I should finish painting the guest room and there are a few doors that need adjusted and—"

"That can wait." Aunt Edie flaps her hand in Beatrice's direction. "Come on. We're going apple picking."

"Found you!" Beatrice tagged Juniper on the arm when she found her cousin crouched under the desk in the upstairs study.

"Not fair!" Juniper whined, crawling out from under the heavy oak piece of furniture. "You're older. You find places faster than me."

"Not true!" Beatrice argued back even though she knew that Juniper was right.

Hide and seek was a game that never got old in Ashwood. Beatrice and the twins could race through the house time and time again and find new places to hide from each other without worrying that their secret locations would lose their touch. Plus, even though Beatrice was nine, it was a simple enough game for Jax and Juniper to catch onto, as they were only six.

"Um, yes true." Juniper popped out her hip and blew an orange ringlet out of her face. "You always are smarter because you're older."

"I wanna play with you guys." Jax wandered into the study, pulling up his baggy pants that fail to stay on his little waist. He refused to wear a belt because he would tell his mother that it made him feel like he was being pinned down.

"I guess we can play one more round," Beatrice agreed.

"Fine." Juniper started for the door. "But I'm counting because hiding is too hard!"

Beatrice and Jax returned to the foyer with Juniper—who shoved her face into the corner by the front door to start counting, her voice muffled by the walls. Beatrice spun around to creep back up the stairs while Jax wandered up behind her.

"Where are you hiding?" Jax asked her loudly when they reached the second-floor hallway.

Beatrice deadpanned, shooting him a look. "I'm not going to tell you. The last time I did, you told her where I was hiding after you were found."

"I did not!"

"Did to."

"Okay, well why don't you tell me where you hide so that I don't hide with you?" Jax smiled brightly, his toothless grin facing up at her.

"Why don't you hide in Grammy's and Grandpa's bathroom?" Beatrice suggested. "You know how much the carpet makes Juniper not wanna go in there."

"Good idea!"

And with that, Jax scrambled off to find Grammy Astrid's very pink bathroom while Beatrice took the steps to the third floor two at a time, the attic at the end of the hallway waiting for her arrival. She tiptoed across the floor, listening to Juniper's counting go from twenty-something all the way to fifty, somehow. She sped up with her words and Beatrice quietly opened the doors to the attic before slipping inside, the fluffy insulation on the inside brushing against her arms.

The attic was cold, as they were now moving into the winter in just a couple months. The raindrops outside pattered against the roof of the house, sounding like a million tiny footsteps racing over the shingles. Beatrice squinted through the darkness, the only source of light being the window straight ahead. Dust floated in front of her vision and Beatrice found herself crawling through the labyrinth of boxes and forgotten furniture. She found a comfy enough spot next to a large plastic pumpkin they had brought back inside once Halloween was over. She pulled her knees to her chest and pressed her back up against a tub labeled *Lena— School Stuff*.

Even though it was hard to hear noise all the way up in the attic, Beatrice could faintly make out her cousin's footsteps dashing through the rooms downstairs to find Jax and Beatrice. Beatrice patiently waited, staring at the attic doors and wondering if Juniper was smart enough to see that they were opened a crack. As she waited, a shadow passed by over a stack of boxes holding Aunt Edie's summer wardrobe. Beatrice snapped her head to the side, blinking and expecting to see a rat or something or maybe a bird or Jax himself. But a whole other figure caught her eye near the window.

A woman with a low black bun at the nape of her neck faced the glass, her hands folded together in front of her. Her back faced the rest of the attic and she was wearing an eggshell white dress that stopped at her shins, a red apron tied around her waist. Beatrice's eyes grew to be the size of golf balls and she slapped a hand over her mouth. The woman was humming quietly to herself, almost swaying back and forth—like the gentlest breeze could have blown her over.

Beatrice scooted away, crouching as small as she could behind the Victorian sofa in front of her. She bit down on her bottom lip, wondering if this was what heart attacks felt like. The organ in her heart literally felt like it was going to explode and in a matter of seconds, she would cover the entire attic with blood sputtering out of her mouth and ears. She perked up when she heard the attic doors open but the person inside certainly was not Juniper.

A boy with a friendly smile emerged into the attic and he pulled the doors shut behind him. He was wearing a blue sweater vest and corduroy shorts, socks pulled up to his knees, clogs covering his feet. Beatrice somehow recognized his body shape as that boy in the yard a few months back, the one who she chased, and he somehow disappeared inside. He was one of the House Things and the woman must have been, as well.

The boy watched the woman but didn't say anything. Beatrice could only see a sliver of his face from where she was now, desperately trying to crawl her way to the doors of the attic. She stayed put, afraid to swallow because swallowing too loudly would give away her presence and she wasn't ready to face either one of them. Beatrice slowly slid herself against the wooden floor of the attic, holding her breath in the process to make sure she was as quiet as she possibly could be. The sofa in front of her moved not even a centimeter and Beatrice froze.

The woman and the boy were now both staring at her in silence, their eyes circles of black holes, like someone had gauged them out with a very sharp spoon. The scream that escaped Beatrice's throat was so loud her ears began to ring. She scrambled across the attic, knocking a box over to have a bunch of old porcelain dolls fall out in front of her. She stomps on their parts on her way to the attic doors but they were securely shut.

"Help!" Beatrice yelled at the top of her lungs, throwing her arms against the pink foam mocking her. She could almost hear it laughing at the fact that it was thick enough to block out her noises. She rammed her shoulder against the doors but they only budged a little, the gold latch on the other side strong enough to keep them shut.

Glancing over her shoulder, Beatrice screamed again. The woman and the boy were standing side by side just two feet away. The woman's hands were clasped together at her waist and her head hung to the side. The boy's mouth was in the shape of a tiny smile.

"Bea?" Grammy Astrid called from the other side.

"Grammy, the doors are shut!" Beatrice stated the obvious, feeling like she was about to burst into tears.

The doors flung open and Grammy Astrid was in the hallway, her eyes big and her eyebrows sloped up toward one another in concern. She reminded Beatrice of the time Grandpa Hugh found her stuck up here. It was really the only time she had ever seen her grandfather show real concern over her, scooping her out at a rapid pace.

"What's wrong?" Grammy Astrid asked. Her patience had been wearing thin with everyone lately, it seemed. "Who shut the doors on you? And what were you doing in there?"

"We were playing hide and seek," Beatrice answered, hearing her voice tremble with fear. She looked over her shoulder but the boy and the woman were gone. She could feel her whole body shaking as more footsteps sounded at the end of the hallway.

"Beatrice?" Her mother came racing toward her, Juniper trailing behind, pointing a chubby finger at her.

"Found you!" Juniper bellowed. "You lose!"

"The game is over, Juniper," Beatrice spat, letting her mom engulf her into a hug. "Someone shut the attic doors. I was scared."

"Who in the hell would shut the doors?" Grammy Astrid asked in annoyance before her eyes slid down to Juniper, who was staring up at everyone with her big, moon-shaped eyes. "Juniper, did you shut the doors?"

"No," Juniper answered. "I was downstairs."

"Juniper, if you did this—"

"It wasn't her," Beatrice's mom cut Grammy off. "I could hear her downstairs. Unless it was Jax."

"He's hiding," Juniper told her flatly and then reached out to grab onto Beatrice's arm. "Maybe it was the House Things."

She said it in a whisper, which sent chills down Beatrice's back. She thought about telling them all about the other two people that she saw in the attic but Juniper was right, they're House Things. Beatrice clung to her mother's shirt, feeling too old to be so shaken up but every time she blinked, she could see those two pairs of missing eyes staring down at her like something straight out of a nightmare.

Chapter 13

One of Silver Creek's most visited places is the pumpkin patch and apple orchard located on the far outskirts of town where cornfields and patches of woods bleed into the next town over. The ride there is awkward and quiet, Beatrice slumped in the passenger seat of Aunt Edie's car, while Aunt Edie herself steers it through the back roads of town, humming quietly to nothing since the car radio is a void of fuzzy static.

"You're quiet today." Aunt Edie breaks the silence between them, glancing over at her. "If you're still thinking about that little argument we had this morning, that's childish, darling, it really is. We're grown adults, you know. There is no need to continue this petty drama." She rolls down her window a little, letting in crisp fall air. "You should know that I am not one for the theatrics."

Beatrice looks at her, debating on continuing the fight but there's nowhere for her to go when it gets too ugly. Besides, Aunt Edie has every right to believe what she wants to believe. Beatrice isn't going to sit here and try to convince her that Ashwood is a place where bad things happen for some unknown reason. She might not have seen it as a child growing up there, but her eyes are open now and she's realizing more and more that the things that take place within those walls are anything but normal. They're terrifying.

"You're right," Beatrice agrees. "It was stupid."

Aunt Edie smiles satisfyingly to herself. "That's what I like to hear."

Beatrice sits up a little more in the seat, watching other old Victorian houses blur by, their age and history on full display. "So, is this a tradition of yours? Apple picking with your friends?"

She feels childish asking a lady of Aunt Edie's age such a question, but then again, Aunt Edie has never acted older than thirty.

Aunt Edie laughs as though the question was actually funny. "I suppose a little bit. Marilyn brings her grandchildren. There are three of them. Triplets. Could you imagine shoving three entire babies out your hoo-ha?" She clucks her tongue, taking a turn at a stop sign. "Anyway, she invites Ruth and I along and then we usually make homemade applesauce with the apples we pick on Halloween."

"Do you get trick-or-treaters?" Beatrice wonders.

"We do," she confirms. "You'd be surprised how far children are willing to walk just for some candy."

There are other reasons they're walking that far, Beatrice wants to say but she bites her tongue like the good niece that she is.

"And then of course, the grandchildren like to visit the pumpkin patch, too," Aunt Edie proceeds, glancing at her rearview mirror to check the lipstick painted across her lips. "It'll be a glorious time."

Beatrice climbs out of the car when Aunt Edie pulls into a muddy parking lot with cars lined up in rows. The rain has stopped, but the brisk cold nips at Beatrice's nose as she shuts the car door. She slips on her knitted gloves that have pretty much fallen apart by now but she wears them anyway with however much dignity she has left at this point.

"There you two are," Ruth greets them when Aunt Edie and Beatrice walk through the lot to find Ruth, Marilyn, and three blond girls waiting near the gazebo where admission is held. Ruth's dark skin is glowing, despite the gloominess lingering above them in the sky. She's wearing a sunshine yellow raincoat and a red skirt, making Beatrice immediately think of mustard and ketchup. "We were starting to think you weren't going to show."

"I had to drag Beatrice out of the house kicking and screaming," Aunt Edie lies and greets her friends French-style with a kiss on both of their cheeks.

"Who are you?" One of the triplets ask, pointing a finger up at Beatrice. They have to be somewhere around nine or ten years old.

"I'm Beatrice," Beatrice answers in a chipper voice. Her adult life consists of avoiding children at all costs. They're weird and messy and most of them are kind of bitches. But she would never say anything like that out loud. The last time she did was to a mom at Clara's son's school play and it did not end well. "What are your names?"

"Go on, introduce yourselves," Marilyn tells her grandchildren, rolling her bluish gray eyes. "Sorry, they're not the best at communicating unless it's with each other."

"I'm Ella," the middle girl says with her arms folded over her chest. She's wearing a baby blue headband in her hair, her face pinched in an annoyed expression. "This is Aurora and that's Wendy."

"It's nice to meet all three of you." Beatrice paints a fake smile on her face. She is going to suck up to them like her life depends on it. She isn't really in the mood to walk with Aunt Edie and her two friends the whole time like an awkward fourth wheel. "You guys ready to pick out some apples today?"

"No," Aurora answers next, her own pink headband slicking back her locks of gold. She has faint freckles sprinkled across her nose and it reminds Beatrice of the same freckles the twins used to have.

"Okay…" Beatrice glances up at Marilyn and her aunt, unsure how to respond. "That's great."

Marilyn pays for everyone's admission, all of them fastening their bright orange bracelets to their wrists before heading off with burlap sacks toward the open field of apple trees, where they're planted in long rows creating canopies of shadow over the grass. Beatrice fiddles with one of the loose buttons on her flannel jacket, watching the three girls prance ahead into the field like Disney princesses.

"Don't sweat their attitude," Ruth whispers from next to her, taking the rear of their line with Beatrice. "They're such pretty girls but my God, they can be such little twits."

Beatrice snorts at how unexpected Ruth's choice of words are. "I would've tried saying something a little nicer but you kind of nailed it."

"Marilyn's son doesn't know the first thing about discipline, I can tell you that much." Ruth adjusts her hefty purse on her shoulder and then gazes around at the trees that have worked all season to produce the fruit. "So, how is it being back in Silver Creek? I'm sure you're experiencing a lot of different waves of nostalgia, yes?"

Beatrice nods, crouching down to the ground to pick up a ruby red apple wet from the rain. "Yeah, it's definitely a weird trip to be back. But I'm not hating it."

"Silver Creek is a lot of things but hateful is certainly not one of them." Ruth ducks under a low hanging branch, reaching out for a dangling apple.

"How long have you lived here?"

"Since I was a little girl," Ruth answers, reaching for another apple barely hanging onto a low-hanging branch. "When I said that your aunt and I go way back, I wasn't kidding."

The mention of someone else knowing Aunt Edie years ago when she was just a little girl makes Beatrice perk up like a dog. She's only ever seen ancient pictures of Aunt Edie back when she herself was growing up in Ashwood. None of her family members did a whole lot of discussing what the house was like back then. But, Aunt Edie did used to spend a lot of time talking about herself and her adventures here in town. But it was all from her own perspective.

"What was she like?" Beatrice wonders aloud, glancing over her shoulder to make sure Aunt Edie is still busying herself with Marilyn in deep conversation several trees down. The triplets are prancing over fallen limbs and sticks, apples crunching beneath their feet. "Aunt Edie, I mean, back then."

"She was pretty much the same as she is now," Ruth tells her casually, slipping her arm through the loops of the burlap sack. "Extravagant, dramatic. Mysterious. She was a force to be reckoned with, that one. And I'm not just saying that because she grew up in Ashwood."

It's odd, hearing someone laugh about Ashwood. It seems like the blogs and articles and conversations Beatrice has researched on her childhood home, people believe laughing about a house so cursed could come back and bite them in the ass. But maybe since Ruth has known Aunt Edie for so long, the thought of Ashwood being some home to the devil or some similar bizarre theory, is just that: bizarre.

"Edie had a hard time making friends," Ruth explains a little more quietly now. She purses her lips, her eyes flickering to Aunt Edie in the distance. "So did I, being one of the only black girls at our school. We were an unlikely friendship but one that I am so thankful for. I'm sure she feels the same."

"Was Ashwood talked about a lot?" Beatrice blurts, her questions getting the best of her. "Did a lot of people talk about it the way they do now?"

Ruth shakes her head. "No, not at all. It was a pretty normal house. People didn't start paying attention to any of the deaths happening inside of it until way later when ancient residents like myself realized how much the Millstone family had been through. But, when you think about it, your family was fairly large back then. Death was going to take its toll in one way or another."

"What do you think about Ashwood?" Beatrice knows that it's a loaded question, one Ruth has probably spent a lifetime avoiding, being friends with Aunt Edie and all. But Beatrice is genuinely curious to know the answer from an outsider looking in. Xander thinks it's haunted, he just doesn't know by what. But Ruth has a different viewpoint from where she stands.

Ruth still has a pinched smile on her face, and she tilts her head gently to the side. "I'm not sure I understand the question."

"Well, you must think something is weird about it, right?" Beatrice urges, shifting her weight to one foot. "You can't honestly tell me that you don't think anything is weird about Ashwood or any of the stuff that happened inside."

"I don't know that house like you do," Ruth responds. "Or like anyone who has lived there. Do I think it's completely coincidental that members of your family have disappeared and died in mysterious ways? Of course I do. But the world is a huge pool of coincidences."

Beatrice squints. She's never believed in coincidences. It was a word that was never used in her house growing up, even after she left Ashwood and moved in with Clara. Coincidences don't happen. Everything in the world is planned out so intricately that whenever something is meant to happen, it is going to happen, no questions asked. Timing is everything in a universe like this one: where people love and people die and roads close and storms tear through cities like wildfire. Everything happens the way it is supposed to.

Despite growing up in Ashwood, where death and disappearances happened all too regularly, Beatrice is a little shocked that she and her family didn't look at them like coincidences. They simply claimed they were all *accidents*, happening never on purpose but far too often.

"Something tells me that you don't believe in coincidences," Ruth says, studying her face.

Beatrice shakes her head a little. "No, I don't."

"To each their own."

The apple picking continues and Beatrice keeps to herself for a little longer, letting her conversation with Ruth seep into the cracks of her brain. Ruth carries on, clearly not thinking as hard as Beatrice is about anything. She's laughing with the triplets, chasing them around a few trees and scooping up more apples in the process. Beatrice follows them all toward the corn maze when Aurora won't shut up about doing it.

"Are you sure you want to do this, Rory?" Marilyn asks her once again as they approach the entrance, a college couple coming out of the exit several yards away. "This is the adult maze, not the children one."

"Well, that's good because I'm not a child." Aurora folds her arms over her chest and pops out her hip. She looks ten years older than her actual age and this is one of the reasons Beatrice can't stand children. "I want to do it and I want to do it *now*."

Brat.

"We'll wait out here," Aunt Edie announces, gesturing to her and Ruth. "We'll put the apples in the car then meet you guys at the hayride."

"Okay," Marilyn agrees and then smiles at Beatrice. "I'm going to need someone young with me to handle these three."

Beatrice fakes a smile and tries shooting her aunt a look for her to stay but she's already making her way to the lot with Ruth by her side. Beatrice takes a breath and starts for the entrance. These things scare the hell out of her. She only ever did it once, and that was enough. Her mom brought her to this exact maze when she was a little girl the same week Uncle Eli died. It was her poor attempt at making Beatrice feel like life was happy and carefree again. That even though people die, doesn't mean the living should, too.

Beatrice had gotten all lost in the maze without her mom when a big crowd of laughing high school kids came roaring through. She was shoved into the mud and before she knew it, her mother was gone. She panicked, calling out for her mom over and over again, running in circles through the maze and fearing she would never get out. She ran in circles and faced dead ends, turning around and desperately looking everywhere for any sign of her mother. It wasn't until she wound up back to where she started that she found her mother standing in her white and green flannel coat and jeans, looking lost herself.

"Mommy!" Beatrice raced to her, throwing her arms around her waist and pressing the side of her face against her mom's belly. "Where were you? I couldn't find you anywhere!"

"I was right here, Bea." She put a hand on her daughter's head, smoothing back her hair. "Those kids came in and we separated for a few minutes."

It felt like hours. No, it felt like *days*. No, it felt like years. Beatrice looked up at her, the fall sun trying to peek out from behind the gloomy clouds above.

"I was scared," Beatrice confessed.

Her mother looked worried and she got down to her knees. "It's so nice to be out of the house, isn't it?"

Beatrice shrugged, nodding her head.

That night when Beatrice's mother was tucking her into bed, she showed her the squid locket around her neck and the photo of them inside. She told her that whenever she was wearing it, they won't be driven insane and apart from each other. That they would always find their way back, no matter what.

"You okay, sweetie?" Marilyn breaks Beatrice from her thoughts, looking at her curiously. "Seems like something is on your mind."

"Oh, I was just thinking about the last time I was here." Beatrice clears her throat, not wanting to get into specifics. "By the way, I haven't done one of these in forever so if we get lost, then I will take full responsibility, but I still can't be blamed for it."

Marilyn smiles, glancing up ahead at the girls arguing over which path they should take next. "No worries. Corn mazes have never been my thing, either, so we can both take responsibility."

"Deal."

They walk in silence for a few paces, Ella leading the way, determined and looking a little pissed off. The other two follow in her footsteps, their little fingertips grazing the cornstalks on either side of them.

"They're quite adventurous," Beatrice says, reaching for a conversation topic to have with Marilyn.

"Oh, extremely," Marilyn agrees, almost rolling her eyes. "I often tell Edie that they remind me of you and your cousins."

Beatrice winces. She needs some sort of warning before people bring up the twins. She needs a huge sign with blinking lights alerting her whenever Jax and Juniper are going to be brought up in conversation. It's a topic she needs to prepare for before speaking on it.

"They're always running around getting their hands dirty, staying out until sunset," Marilyn goes on, slipping her hands into her crisp white coat. "They're nothing like these kids today, I can tell you that much. They're all cooped up inside with a screen shoved in their faces. It's insulting to the hard work parents back then worked with."

"I hear you."

"So how are the renovations coming?" Marilyn asks next. "Edie tells me that you agreed to do some work for her around the house so she can sell it?"

Beatrice nods, stepping over an abandoned piece of corn in the middle of the path. "It's coming a little slowly. The neighbor down the street agreed to help with a few things I have no experience in."

"The neighbor?"

Beatrice nods again, stiffening against the cold breeze zipping through the cornstalks and making them rustle. "Xander."

"Oh," Marilyn squeaks, staring at Beatrice in awe, as though she is some long-lost friend she's running into at the airport or something. "Right. I forgot about him. Wow, he's still around after all these years?"

"His nana has some health issues, so yes," Beatrice responds, glancing up ahead at the girls but she sees only two blond heads.

Aurora and Ella are skipping together, chanting, *"Devils and ghosts, they'll give you a fright! Black cats and witches, on Halloween night! Lure one with candy, chocolate, precisely. When the kids are in costumes, they will do nicely!"*

"Where's Wendy?" Beatrice asks Marilyn, glancing over her shoulder to make sure she wasn't left behind anywhere.

Marilyn slows down in her tracks, following Beatrice's gaze. "You're right. Where did she go?" She looks up at the other two again. "Ella, Aurora, where is your sister?"

The girls turn around, menacing smiles pasted over their mouths. They look like some alternate version of the twins from *The Shining.* Beatrice is waiting for them to demand for her to come play with them and she balls up a fist in case they do.

"We don't know," they say in unison.

"What do you mean you don't know?" Marilyn demands impatiently, her cheeks growing pink. "She was just here a second ago. And now what? She's just gone?"

"Wendy?" Beatrice starts back in the direction they came, peering through the cornstalks for any sign of Wendy's blond curls or pale face. "Wendy, where are you?"

"I'm serious, I don't know!" Ella claims back with Marilyn when Beatrice hears her scolding them further.

Beatrice picks up her pace, feeling like the path is closing in on her. As if she wasn't feeling enough like a child since being back in Ashwood, here she is racing through a corn maze trying to find someone else. She hurries around the corner, nearly colliding with two guys holding hands. She whips her head around this way and that, a ball of panic swelling in her throat.

"You okay?" One of the guys asks.

"Have you seen a little girl?" Beatrice orders. "She's blond and her name is Wendy and she has a white headband on."

The second guy with facial hair shakes his head. "We haven't seen anyone in here but you so far."

Beatrice darts back to where the others should be waiting but they're gone, too. "Marilyn?" Beatrice calls out, swatting a leaning cornstalk out of her way. Her feet sink into the mud beneath her and she is now jogging through the empty corridors of the maze, no one in sight. "Aurora? Ella?" She calls out louder this time, pumping her arms at her sides. "Wendy?"

"Yes?" Wendy appears on the path ahead, just up a small hill. She's looking as innocent as ever, the gray clouds behind her matching the dress she has on under her coat.

"There you are." Beatrice exhales, taking long strides toward her. "Where were you? Why did you run off?"

"Because Ella and Aurora were being mean," Wendy claims, looking down at her rain boots. "They're always being mean. And they wouldn't believe me that the path I chose was the way out."

"That doesn't mean you can just run away without telling an adult," Beatrice tells her, her beating heart slightly slowing down.

"Well it's not my fault they *like* getting lost," Wendy whines. "I thought that if I could find my way out before them, I could prove them wrong."

"Well don't do that again," Beatrice snaps at her. She doesn't know how to talk to kids at her age and quite frankly, she doesn't want to start learning now. "Your grandma and I were worried about you."

"Sorry."

"You found her," Marilyn calls out from behind Beatrice, the other two at her side. "Wendy, what on the earth were you thinking?"

"Told you she ran off just for attention," Aurora tells her grandmother. "She's always doing this."

"Am not!" Wendy shoots back.

"Are too!" Ella chimes in with Aurora.

"We aren't going to fight here, you can wait until we get home." Marilyn grabs hold of Ella's and Aurora's hands, starting up ahead.

The sight of Marilyn's white hair blowing in the breeze, walking into nature with the kids at her side sends chills down Beatrice's back. She watches her disappear around the corner, just like how she had watched the lady in white disappear into the woods all those years ago with the twins. But she was having a dream. Her head was all fuzzy from a fever and her mother told her she was just dreaming. But now, the vision of this long white hair blowing in the breeze on a cloudy day has awoken something in Beatrice, something telling her that she was not dreaming. The realization sends her stumbling back a couple steps. She reaches out to the side to grab on to a cornstalk but she drags it out of the muddy earth instead.

It was Marilyn. She was the last to see the twins alive.

"I'm not feeling well," nine-year-old Beatrice told her mom when she found her in the study, rooting through large stacks of books in front of her. Beatrice's brow furrowed. "What're you doing?"

Her mom jumped at the sound of her daughter's voice, putting a hand to her chest. "Bea, you scared me. You can't sneak up on people like that."

"But I said I didn't feel well." Beatrice put her own hand to her stomach, feeling like all of her insides have been turning around and around, trying to get her to throw up this morning's crepes and bacon.

Beatrice's mother looked more worried now and she tossed the book on her lap to the side to get up. She marched over to her daughter and cupped her face in her hands as though she could tell if something was actually wrong just by looking at her. "Is it your stomach?"

Beatrice nodded just as the door to the study opened again and the twins emerged in the doorway.

"Beatrice, come play with us!" Jax exclaimed, trotting across the floor to grab his cousin's hand.

"Yeah, we're playing the royal game in the Jungle!" Juniper said after, twirling around in a dress patterned with green apples. "And I'm going to be the princess."

"That means you get to be the prince or the guard because I call being the dragon!" Jax rolled his head back as he attempted to roar loud enough like a dragon would.

"Kids, I think Beatrice is going to have to sit out for this one," her mom told them. "She isn't feeling well. It might be a cold and I don't want her playing outside."

"But why?" Juniper frowned. "My mom says that colds aren't anything to be worried about. You just gotta suck it up and deal with it until it goes bye-bye."

"Well she will deal with it with a lot of bed rest." Beatrice's mom held her close as she ushered everyone out of the study. "If she's feeling better tomorrow, then you guys can go out and play in the woods.”

“Ugh, fine.” Jax sighed dramatically and looked at his sister, a smirk sneaking across his mouth. “I’ll race you to the trees!”

They went stampeding down the steps while Beatrice followed her mom into her room, and onto her bed. One of the things that the Millstone family was proud of was their good immune systems. They didn’t ever worry about catching the flu or some other illness from someone else. Sure, they were always raised to wash their hands and cough into their elbows, but they never truly got ill from anything.

“Feels like you might have a fever.” Lena put the back of her hand against Beatrice’s forehead. “Tell you what. I am going to go downstairs and make you a huge bowl of Grammy Astrid’s secret chicken soup. You will nap and when you wake up, you’ll feel all better.”

Beatrice smiled groggily at the thought of no longer feeling like a slug. She watched her mother pad out of her room, and she stayed lounged on her bed for a few minutes, shutting her eyes. Her head throbbed with pain, sweat dotted across her hairline. Her eyes flickered open to the sound of Juniper’s laugh from outside, floating all the way up to her window.

Beatrice swung her legs off the bed and ventured over to her turret window, where she settled on the cushioned bench. She watched as Jax and Juniper play-fought with long sticks, racing each other toward the Jungle. She smiled sadly, wishing she could just go out and join them and let her body beat this little flu sometime later. But something white and bright caught her eye from the edge of the woods. Beatrice’s smile faded as she noticed an older lady standing among the trees, her face shielded by branches and fall leaves. She must have said something because both Jax and Juniper looked over at her, too.

Beatrice watched as the lady in white beckoned them closer to the woods like they were tiny cats, being lured to a bowl of fresh milk. Her lips parted and her eyebrows bunched together in confusion as she watched both Juniper and Jax drop their sticks and start wandering over to the lady waiting for them feet away from the family plot. Beatrice wanted to scream, she really did. She wanted to throw her hand through the glass and call out to them. She wanted to remind them of all the stranger danger lessons Aunt Marley had given them, warning them about strange men in white vans claiming they had candy to give.

But no matter how hard Beatrice tried to shout out a warning or call for her mother, she couldn't speak. She stayed put in the window, her hand pressed against the glass. She watched the lady take both of their hands, the three of them venturing into the Jungle like a trio out of a fairy tale. It wasn't until her mother returned to her bedroom with a tray of soup that Beatrice groggily woke up from what she thought was a nightmare.

Chapter 14

Beatrice quickly climbs out of the car when Aunt Edie pulls into the driveway. It's been too long of a day and she doesn't want to spend another moment with anyone but herself.

"Bea?" Aunt Edie calls after her as she gets out of the car at a much slower pace. "Are you all right, darling? You've barely breathed the whole way home."

"Fine, I just have to use the bathroom," Beatrice lies, rushing inside and not bothering to shut the front door behind her.

As she climbs the stairs to her room, her mind buzzes with Marilyn's face and that haunting image of her luring the twins into the woods behind Ashwood, just like how she walked with Aurora and Ella today in the maze. She couldn't bring herself to say anything to the lady during the entire rest of the maze. She kept Wendy close, only making small talk with her to pass the time until the girls were able to find the exit. She didn't even say goodbye to Marilyn, only Ruth and the triplets—who only gave her a wave farewell.

Witnessing the twins' disappearance has been something that Beatrice thought was a dream. Was it? That day was a blur and Beatrice's head was as fuzzy as TV static. One minute, she was watching the twins from her window, the next, she was watching a woman in white whisk them out of the yard, and then she was waking up. It had to have been a dream. She didn't say anything more to her mom when she was told that her imagination got the best of her.

Aunt Marley spent the whole night roaming the woods once the twins didn't return. That was when Beatrice told her mom about her dream, that the twins were taken.

"It's just a dream, Bea," was all her mother said as she tirelessly peered out into the backyard from the dining room window.

The family made call after call to the police station and neighboring businesses, telling everyone to keep a lookout for Juniper and Jax. Everyone agreed that they would keep their eyes open but nothing ever came of it. The Millstones planned their own search party, hunting through the woods for any sign of them but it was too late. Whatever had happened to them was already done and they were gone.

Beatrice drew herself a bath that evening and she slipped into the scalding hot water with a lack of suds. She doesn't care about that part, though. She's more focused on burning her skin until maybe it boils off and she grows a whole new suit of armor. One that isn't covered with guilt over the disappearance of her own cousins. That wasn't a dream. Beatrice didn't know better back then, especially with her sleepwalking spells. But seeing Marilyn today rang so many alarms for her. She doesn't remember her being around back then so it's not like she dreamed of a total stranger. It really did happen.

She gnaws at her bottom lip, wondering what the hell Marilyn could have been doing with the two of them. She must have known Aunt Edie at the time, due to their conversation at the store when Marilyn told her that she remembers her when she was just a girl. And she remembers Xander. So why would she lure them out of the yard and what was she planning to do with them? Does this mean she might have something to do with the eight girls who have gone missing here? Has she played some part in their disappearances, too? Does Aunt Edie know anything about this or is she oblivious?

Beatrice shuts her eyes, her heart thundering loudly in her chest with these new revelations. She shouldn't have come back here. She should've just stayed as far away as possible. Her life was good. It wasn't the best, but there wasn't much to complain about. There wasn't much she sat around stressing over or scared of. But the thing about Ashwood is that it doesn't care how many years someone might spend time away from it. It's a memory that will stay in the back of your head forever, patiently waiting for your return. And when you do, it'll be like you never even left at all.

After her two-hour long bath, Beatrice climbs out of the tub, her entire body red from the water's temperature. She reaches for the towel waiting for her on the counter, drying herself off in aggressive movements. By the time she leaves the bathroom, the sun outside has officially sank behind the trees of Silver Creek, surrendering to the night. Beatrice marches downstairs, to where Aunt Edie is lounged in the sitting room, the stem of a wine glass slipped through her long skinny fingers. She once again looks like something out of a renaissance painting: taking up the entire sofa without a care in the world and surrounded by things she deems luxurious: figurines if naked men, gold candlesticks with ancient white candles, glass flower vases, and dusty books with ribbons for page markers.

"There you are," Aunt Edie greets her when Beatrice steps foot over the threshold. "I was beginning to think you drowned in that tub."

"Aunt Edie, we have to talk." Beatrice isn't going to be able to sleep tonight until she gets this off her chest. She needs to talk to her about what she knows about Marilyn and how the image of her taking the twins from the yard won't stop playing on a loop inside of her mind. It's going to drive her insane far before Ashwood does.

Aunt Edie sighs, swinging her legs over the edge of the couch and getting up to make her way to the bar cart squished between two bookshelves. She picks up her bottle of wine, her movements jerky and unbalanced. How long has she been drinking?

"What now, Beatrice?" Aunt Edie asks, the red wine sloshing into her glass. "If you're looking to pick another fight about this house, it's going to have to wait until the morning when I can gather my thoughts."

"I'm not looking to fight about that."

"Oh. Wonderful." She spins back around and takes a heavy drink, loudly swallowing. "Then what is it? You're not pregnant by Xander, are you?"

Beatrice finds herself taken aback and she quickly shakes her head. "What? No. Of course not."

"Right. Of course not," she echoes her before collapsing on the sofa again. "Then please. Enlighten me."

"Marilyn was the one who took Jax and Juniper from the yard the day they went missing," Beatrice sputters before she can think twice about it and stop herself. Aunt Edie is tipsy and on the verge of being fully drunk. Maybe this *could* have waited until the morning. "I know that sounds crazy but I only just remembered today. I remember seeing her take them."

Aunt Edie stares at her for a solid beat before tossing her head back in laughter, nearly spilling her wine onto her lap. "Oh, Bea. What a confused little girl you are."

"I'm not confused," Beatrice snaps. "I blocked that entire memory out for years, thinking it was a dream. And seeing her today sparked it back up and I remember. I'm not confused anymore. It was her. She was standing in the woods and the twins were playing outside and she said something to them and they went over to her and she took them into the Jungle."

Aunt Edie is no longer laughing. She's squinting at Beatrice like she can't see her that well from where she sits. "You were nine years old when that happened."

"So?"

"So, you were just a girl," Aunt Edie clarifies. "You didn't know what was happening."

"Maybe I didn't then, but I do now," Beatrice points out, desperation bleeding into her tone of voice. Why isn't she believing her? Because her loyalty lies with Marilyn? Because she's never seen Beatrice grow into the adult she is? Because she will forever see her as her little great niece and nothing else?

Aunt Edie takes another drink but doesn't say anything, fingering the rim of her glass with her nail.

Beatrice sits down next to her on the couch. "Why don't you believe me?"

"Because it's hard to take someone's word for this type of stuff in a house such as this one," Aunt Edie responds, her voice raspy—something that's always happened when she drank too much. It's like her throat rejects the booze so much it goes hoarse. "May I remind you that I grew up in this very house? I've seen a lot of things that I thought were there but really weren't."

Beatrice stiffens, a super-cut of every horrible thing she has seen in this house flashing before her eyes. "What do you mean?"

"I mean that houses like this, old and historic, find ways to complicate things." Aunt Edie looks around them at the walls, the dim lamp lit up next to the sofa casting only half of her face in the light. Her fingers touch the couch cushion beneath them. "They make us think certain things or see things that aren't even there at all. It makes things difficult to differentiate illusion and reality."

"So now you're going to try telling me that everything we've seen growing up has never really been there?" she challenges, obviously not convinced.

"No, I'm not saying that," she protests in an aggressive tone. "It's just... I know how things might look on the surface. But there is always something more to it than what meets the eye. That is something you need to learn."

"So you knew Marilyn was going to take them?" Beatrice's heart picks up speed inside of her chest. This can't be happening. If Aunt Edie admits to this, admits to knowing what happened to the twins after all this time, she's packing her things tonight and getting the hell out of here.

Aunt Edie sighs, shutting her eyes for a few seconds. "I didn't. I knew she was going to stop by that day. She told me afterward that she had taken the twins into the woods to play with them."

Beatrice's brows pull together. "That makes no sense. Why would a friend of yours come all this way just to play with some kids?"

"She saw them out by themselves, I don't know." Aunt Edie is now slurring her words but that doesn't stop her from taking another drink, resting the glass on her knee as she thoughtfully stares ahead, the memories of years prior coming back to her. "I asked her what they did when they went into the woods and she said that they had run off after a little bit of playing their fantasy game. She couldn't find them anywhere."

"So, she left?"

"She was scared."

"You're defending her?" Beatrice stands up from the couch. "Why didn't you say something?"

"What was I supposed to say, Beatrice?" Aunt Edie threw her skinny arm in the air. "Marilyn was my best friend and what she did was harmless. It wasn't her fault that they ran off and disappeared."

"Yes, it is," Beatrice shoots back. "If what she told you was true, she had one job and that was to keep an eye on them. How do both of them suddenly disappear without a trace?"

"I don't know."

"How could you not have said anything?" Beatrice roars, her face morphing into anger and resentment, the two of them going hand in hand with one another. "You could have told Aunt Marley. You could have gone to the police—"

"So could you," Aunt Edie fights back, glaring her ocean gray eyes at Beatrice. "Before you go pointing your finger at someone else, you might want to check your tone."

It's taking everything inside of Beatrice not to snatch her glass from her aunt's hands and throw it against the wall. But if she does that, then she'd have to be the one to clean up the mess and that defeats the whole purpose. This whole time, Aunt Edie knew more about what happened to Juniper and Jax, yet did nothing about it. She told no one. Marilyn got to walk around Silver Creek playing dumb while the twins were out there somewhere, lost or dying. Beatrice was a little girl who thought she was dreaming. When she told her mom about it, she wasn't taken seriously, so why in the hell would she think what she saw was real life?

But where does this woman's loyalty lie? With some friend over her entire family? Is there more to it all that she isn't telling Beatrice?

Maybe Beatrice should've waited to get angry until she could hear full details. It would have been impossible, though. She has spent the last sixteen years feeling guilty for not saying anything about the lady she saw luring the twins into the Jungle. She spent sixteen years avoiding the thought of her cousins, fearing that guilt might take over and literally kill her. But now, Aunt Edie has held this piece of the puzzle so close to her chest it had to take a few glasses of wine for her to speak up.

"I will never forgive you for this." Beatrice storms out of the room and she hears Aunt Edie say something from behind her but she doesn't stop walking until she reaches her room.

Beatrice wakes to the sound of an owl.

It's large, with golden yellow eyes and black and brown peppered feathers. It lands on the tree branch above her, staring down at her as though she's its new prey. Beatrice takes a breath in through her nose, caught off guard by the creature looming over, its head twitching every few seconds to look at her from different angles. She wants to scream, but her lips feel like they've been sewed together with needle and thread.

Beatrice's eyes widen at the Jungle spilling out around her. A small piece of her mind suggests that she could be in any patch of woods in any place in America. But she recognizes the twisted trunks of the trees, the familiar bed of leaves coating the forest floor, the ivy snaking up around thick, fallen branches. She quickly sits up and realizes she's in a dream when she feels no pain from the ground in her back at all. She looks around again and then back up at the owl, the moonlight casting its light through the branches above.

She scrambles to her feet, screaming at the sight of Jax and Juniper standing up ahead. Beatrice feels bad for being scared of them, but she can't help it. They're both wearing similar versions of the white dress Marilyn wore the day she took them from the yard. And, like usual, they're standing alike, too. They have their little fingers thread together in front of them, interlocked.

"What are you guys doing?" Beatrice asks breathlessly, the owl's head flickering back and forth between her and the twins, as though it understands English. "You shouldn't be out here."

"Neither should you," the twins say in unison.

Jax perks up, his silky orange hair glowing. "Beatrice, come play with us!"

"Yeah, we're playing the royal game in the Jungle!" Juniper says happily, the dimples in her cheeks deepening the broader she smiles. She twirls around in her dress, the same way she did that day they invited Beatrice outside to play with them. How different would it have been if she had gone? If she never had that cold? "And I'm going to be—"

"The princess," Beatrice finishes for her in a faint whisper.

"That means you get to be the prince or the guard because I call being the dragon!" Jax leaps into the air—way too high for a person his height or age. His feet plant themselves back onto the ground and he pretends to breathe fire out of his mouth. "Come on!"

The twins race off through the trees and Beatrice shakes her head in disapproval. Part of her has the urge to tell them that she doesn't feel good and that her mother is going to make Grammy Astrid's chicken noodle soup recipe. But the other part of her is screaming at her to follow them, to play.

Jax races forward, continuing his fire breathing sounds while Juniper climbs onto a fallen tree, resting the back of her hand over her forehead, bathing in the blue tinted moonlight above.

"I am the greatest princess!" she proclaims loudly, her tiny voice bouncing off the surrounding trees. "And this is my tower!"

"I'm here to rescue you," Beatrice says desperately, looking from Juniper to Jax. "I'm here to rescue both of you."

Jax snickers. "Beatrice! Dragons can't be rescued."

"Yes, they can." She hurries over to him until she's on her knees so that they're eye level. "Everything in this mess of a world can be rescued, you just have to know its weakness. And I know yours." She looks over at Juniper. "I know both of yours."

"Dragons don't have weaknesses," he asserts proudly, but a small whimper seeping through his voice proves otherwise. "We are fearless."

"But it's okay to not be," Beatrice tells him softly. "Not every dragon has to breathe fire. You don't have to do things just because you don't want to seem afraid. The world is a scary place. It's harmful and bad things happen. You have a right to be scared."

Beatrice realizes that her voice is no longer her own, it's someone else's, saying things she would never say to them back then. But perhaps that is the point. Perhaps the whole point of being stuck inside of this dream is her mind's way of coping with the truth behind their disappearance. Maybe this is her way of saying all the things she could have told them back then that might have stopped Marilyn from scooping them up and them getting lost in this huge patch of woods.

"Why are you saying this?" Juniper asks, perched on the fallen tree from behind them. "We're trying to play a game, Beatrice."

"Because this isn't a game anymore," Beatrice tells her, getting back to her feet to look at Juniper. A wet mist hangs in the air, dotting the colorful fall leaves in tiny droplets. "Something terrible happened to both of you and I want to save you from that. I *need* to save you from that."

"Well, you know how you said that not every dragon needs to be fearless?" Juniper challenges.

Beatrice nods, frowning.

"Not every princess needs saving."

Suddenly, Beatrice hears a twig snap from behind and she whips around to find Jax gone from his spot. She whirls around again, Juniper missing now, too.

"Guys?" Beatrice hollers loudly, spinning around in circles, waiting to see a glimpse of their white dresses or orange hair from behind one of the trees but she doesn't see them anywhere. "Jax?" she calls out, taking long strides through the trees. Her lips feel numb, now, like they've just been injected with something. "Juniper?" Beatrice looks behind a tree stump but there's no sign of either of the twins.

With every call of their names, Beatrice can feel her mouth getting harder and harder to work. Her lips tickle, and she's starting to sweat, dashing through the Jungle at a frantic run. She brings her fingers to her lips when her breathing goes heavy because she's now no longer breathing through her mouth. Thick vines are sewn across her lips when Beatrice touches them, and she tries to scream but she is silenced. Beatrice tries tearing at the plant keeping her from speaking, but they don't budge.

The more she claws at her skin, the more blood gets caked under her fingernails. She spins around, suddenly forgetting how to leave the Jungle. But how can she without the twins? Beatrice looks this way and that, catching glimpses of some shack in the distance, appearing through the trees like an eye blinking in front of a keyhole.

"**I**'m losing my mind," Aunt Marley said from behind the closed door.

It was the summer after the twins had gone missing, which means they had officially been away for a year. Grandma Astrid died last November and Ashwood felt emptier than ever now. Beatrice found herself at a loss for words. Xander still came over and spent some time with her, doing his best to not bring up her mess of a family life right now but every now and again, he would slip up and Beatrice would find her mood crashing like a car into a tree.

The day was hot and sticky, unusually muggy for the end of August in Silver Creek. Beatrice spent most of the day outside, playing in the hose under the supervision of Aunt Edie—who was mixing alcohol into her lemonade and asking a lot of questions about Xander. Beatrice wondered if Aunt Edie had the impression that Beatrice had a crush— which she didn't.

"I can't do this anymore," Aunt Marley said next from inside of the bathroom, her voice muffled into either a towel or Beatrice's mother's shoulder. "It's impossible."

"It's not impossible," Beatrice's mom said back encouragingly. "We're going to find them, Marley. I promise."

Beatrice stood outside of the bathroom, her ear to the door. Everything was so weird around Ashwood, lately. Yes, the twins were gone and Grammy Astrid was laid to rest in the plot out back, but her mom and Aunt Marley were doing a lot of whispering and sneaking off together without telling people where they were going or why. Aunt Edie, obviously, paid no attention. She was either drinking herself into an abyss or pretending like everything was daisies and rainbows. She claimed that her alcoholic beverages helped her sleep at night and she hadn't been doing any sleepwalking lately. She then offered a drink to Beatrice and that set her mom *off*.

"Do not promise me something so stupid, Lena," Aunt Marley snapped at her sister. "We both know what happened."

"Not for sure, yet."

"We know enough," Aunt Marley said, her voice thick with tears.

"We need to figure out what the fuck is going on or I am going to go crazy, do you hear me?"

Beatrice leaned closer to the door to pick up on anything else but their voices dropped too low under the sound of the humming air conditioner for her to gather their words. It must be a pretty serious conversation if Aunt Marley is using foul language.

Before she can move away from the door in time, it flung open and Beatrice's mom and her aunt emerged in the doorway. They both stared down at her in awe and for a second, Beatrice wondered if they forgot that another child was alive in this house, still. She stared up at them, her mind scrambling to come up with some excuse but she couldn't seem to find one quickly enough.

"H-hello," Beatrice stammered.

"Bea, what are you doing out here?" her mom asked, looking worried. She glanced up and down the hallway, expecting to find maybe Aunt Edie out here, too.

"I was just going to use the bathroom," Beatrice lied. "I didn't know anyone was in there. Sorry."

"Did you hear what we were talking about?" Aunt Marley asked her. Her stringy brown hair had thinned out ever since the twins went missing. It hung in a braid down her back every day and she didn't bother with makeup anymore or dressing in something other than a hoodie and sweats.

Beatrice quickly shook her head. "Not a word. I just got up here."

"Good." Aunt Marley marched down the hallway, her braid swinging from side to side behind her.

Beatrice's mom watched her sister until she was out of sight. She then looked down at her daughter and got to her knees. "What did you hear?"

"I just said I didn't hear a word."

"I know when you're lying." Beatrice's mom didn't give it another thought. "So tell me what you heard."

Beatrice sighed. She could never really lie to her mother. She tried many times but she always knew her too well to know when the truth was being bent. Beatrice lifted her shoulders and let them fall. "Just that Aunt Marley thinks she's going crazy if she doesn't find Jax and Juniper."

"Oh."

Beatrice studied her mom's expression, unable to read it. "Why does she think she would lose her mind?"

"It's just a figure of speech, sweetie." She kissed Beatrice's head and padded off down the hall.

Even though Beatrice could never really tell when her mother was lying to *her*, she could always put her finger on when she wasn't being the most honest person in the world. Saying *It's just a figure of speech* might as well translated to *Aunt Marley doesn't have a screw loose about her and she is perfectly fine.* When in fact, she most certainly was not.

Chapter 15

Beatrice spends Tuesday finishing painting the guest room. She dusts and sweeps it as much as she can to try and stage the look for when the house is ready to be listed. She then spends the rest of her afternoon on the phone with Declan, discussing the pieces of furniture in the attic that can be shipped to the store at the end of the week to be there by Monday. Beatrice also stayed cooped up in her room, updating Clara on her stay at the bed and breakfast place she lied to her about when she got here. She managed to not stay on the phone for too long, knowing that her guilt about lying to her would eat away at her in no time so she kept the conversation short and sweet.

The weather outside is stupidly happy for such a glum day. Despite keeping busy with stuff, Beatrice's mind keeps wandering back to Jax and Juniper and how they were lured into the Jungle by Aunt Edie's friend—which she knew about this entire time but said nothing, fearing it would make the situation scarier than it already was. In truth, Beatrice isn't even positive about why she didn't share that information. She was nine at the time. Why do nine-year-olds do anything? Beatrice told Aunt Edie the truth last night when she said she would never forgive her for this. Wherever the twins are, their life was cut short because both Marilyn and Beatrice didn't mention anything the day they vanished. But Marilyn is far more to blame. She was the adult. *She* was the one that took them to play in the Jungle. Not Beatrice.

Is what Aunt Edie said true? That Marilyn brought the twins into the Jungle to play for a bit and then they suddenly vanished? One minute they were there and the next they were gone? Just like that? Or is there something lurking under the surface?

She listens to the front door close downstairs and Beatrice finds herself alone in Ashwood once again. She picks up the box she found in the vent of the guest room, laying out the Polaroid photos Lila took in front of her on the window seat. Beatrice has seen these images enough times in real life to know exactly what Lila was feeling when she took these. Beatrice never wondered why none of her family members tried catching the House Things on camera because they never thought anything of it. This was their house just as much as it belonged to the House Things.

As Beatrice holds the photo of Aunt Marley between her fingers, she thinks about her dream from last night. She thinks about how the twins looked so comfortable in those woods and it makes Beatrice feel sad for them. They loved the Jungle so much. To go missing or to have something terrible happen to them there hurts Beatrice to her core. Her eyes flicker up to the backyard, where the woods sprawl out at the back of the property. Beatrice gnaws on the inside of her cheek, flashes of that shack swimming through her thoughts. She remembers Xander telling her about that legend of the man that supposedly lives there, all burned and charred.

Deciding to grow some balls, Beatrice stuffs her feet into her duck boots and throws on her flannel jacket, shutting her bedroom door behind her and locking it with the key she still has from the grandfather clock. As she heads down the stairs, the doorbell rings, making her jump. Beatrice glances out the window, even though she already knows the one person it could be.

"Xander." She opens the front door, where Xander stands on the porch wearing a denim jacket over a plain white t-shirt. "Hey."

"Hey, Beatrice," he echoes. "I come bringing trim."

Beatrice's brow wriggles in bewilderment. "Trim?"

"For the upstairs hallway," he elaborates. "I figured that since you wanted to paint that, too, we could rip the old trim off, paint, and then take care of that."

The renovations. Right.

"Oh, yeah." Beatrice runs her fingers through her hair, her mind jumbled with preoccupied thoughts. "That's great. Thanks."

He observes her, squinting a little. "Did I catch you at a bad time or something? I can come back tomorrow—"

"I was just about to take a walk," Beatrice interrupts him, now thankful for his presence. She was going to walk alone through the Jungle, determined to find that shack that was in her dream. But maybe that's the one mistake the girls that lived here before her did: they went wandering out alone into those woods, never to return. "In the woods."

Xander raises his eyebrows, caught off guard. "Are you serious?"

"Should I not be?"

"I didn't know you were still going to… snoop," Xander tells her, searching for the appropriate word. "I figured the other day in the basement freaked you out enough."

"Trust me, I've experienced worse," she promises under her breath and sneaks a look at him. "I don't want to drag you into anything, but would you wanna join?"

The corners of Xander's mouth pull up into a smile. "I thought you'd never ask."

They embark out of Ashwood and across the backyard, Beatrice stuffing her hands deep into her pockets. The only way she is going to get answers is to figure things out for herself. Clearly, Aunt Edie doesn't know how to speak the truth and she isn't going to find much of anything if she's cooped up inside. Sure, finding Lila's Polaroid collection is a step in the right direction but it doesn't give her answers as to why everyone here before her is no longer around or if Marilyn played a part in them going missing, too.

"I found the pictures Lila took," Beatrice says as they enter the woods, a place she used to find so wholesome and freeing. It was her own hideout, a getaway when Ashwood got to be a little too much. But now, those memories of playing in here with Juniper and Jax are forever tainted by the last playground the twins ever played on.

Xander looks impressed, his eyebrows springing up again. "Wait, really? Where? And how?"

"They were in a secret box in the vent behind the wardrobe," Beatrice explains, reaching up to touch the squid necklace tucked inside of her shirt. "Lila also found my mom's necklace that was in there, too."

"What were the other pictures of?" Xander ponders.

"Family members," she answers sadly. "Not only ones I knew, but ones that died ages before I was even born."

"How was that?" Xander glances at her.

"I don't know," she says. "I mean, these disappearances of the tenants Aunt Edie moved in makes me wonder if she had anything to do with it but if that's the case, then did she have anything to do with anything that happened to my family?"

"No." Xander doesn't sound convinced. "You don't honestly think your aunt is grim enough to do anything to harm the rest of your family, do you?"

"I never considered it," Beatrice steps over a thick branch with ivy wrapped around it. "I always thought she was lucky enough to be the last one standing. Maybe that the house even needed her to stay…"

Alive. It's the only word Beatrice can think of but she doesn't say it because she knows how odd it would sound. Ashwood isn't a living thing, she knows that. But that hasn't stopped her or any other Millstone from treating it as such.

A canopy of leaves shielding them away from the bright blue sky looms above, all of the orange and red leaves tickling each other in the wind. As Beatrice finds them walking and walking, she considers telling him about what she remembered at the corn maze yesterday about Marilyn. She should tell him. They're kind of in all this together now and it would feel really good to get some things off her chest without worrying if it will spark a tiff, like with Aunt Edie.

"I remembered something I sort of blocked out the other day." Beatrice clears her throat, trying her best to sound casual.

"What's that?" Xander almost trips over a root stretching out of the earth. He stuffs his hands into the pockets of his jacket out of embarrassment.

"My aunt had this friend who apparently would visit the house sometimes," she begins. "Aunt Edie and I met up with her yesterday and I had this sudden vision of her from the day Jax and Juniper went missing, of her walking into these woods with them. Hand in hand. I thought it was a dream back then but now I'm for sure convinced that it wasn't."

Xander's eyebrows pull together. "I'm not following, Beatrice."

"This whole time, I didn't know that what I saw was true," Beatrice goes on. "I told my mom and she said it was only a dream so I believed her. I didn't remember falling asleep, I only remembered seeing the twins play and then I was waking up. And now, if I would've tried harder to tell everyone what I saw…"

Silence falls between them and Beatrice suddenly wonders if she has said too much. She did. She scared him off. He's going to tell her that she's the one at fault for what happened to the two of them and no one else's.

"It's okay," he finally says.

"Is it?" Beatrice yanks out a thin strand of hair. "The twins could still be here if I would've told another person about the dream. Maybe someone would've taken it more seriously."

"Our brains are weird… slimy balls of nerves and signals and thoughts," he says. "You were a kid, living in a strange place, and saw something strange. It might not have even looked that weird at the time but honestly, I don't blame you. I would've thought it was just a

House Thing if I saw that."

Beatrice shoots a look of appreciation at him, fully regretting not staying in touch with him after all this time.

"Wait, do you think this is a good idea?" Xander slows down in his steps when they notice the shack up ahead, lingering behind the trees like a black shadow.

"We walked all this way." Beatrice glances over her shoulder, the army of trees behind her blocking her view of the path they've embarked on. "We can't walk back now with no answers."

"But my nana told me that this guy is listed as a sexual predator online," Xander reminds her, his eyes flickering over to the house looming ahead of them. "Shouldn't we take that into consideration?"

"There's two of us and one of him." Beatrice rolls her shoulders back in an attempt to seem tougher than she actually is. She'd be lying if she said she wasn't freaking out a little bit but one of them has to hold it together and it sure as hell doesn't look like that's going to be Xander. "I think we got it handled."

Xander sighs and reaches for a thick branch on the ground with a sharp end to it, reminding Beatrice of a wooden stake. "Okay. But if I end up getting slaughtered first, tell Nana I love her."

Beatrice takes a breath as they continue forward through the trees, slowing down in their steps when they finally reach the shack: a shitty old house with the siding falling apart and the roof nearly caving in. There's a chimney, smoke pouring out the top and floating off into the sky, mingling with the tree branches looming over the roof. There's a wooden old door nearly blocked by shrubs and a broken chair that looks like it's been chewed through by an animal.

"Yeah, I think it's time we turn back," Xander whispers to her. "This looks like something out of a serial killer documentary and I don't know about you, Beatrice, but I don't really want any screen time in a movie like that."

"It's fine," Beatrice claims, trying to convince herself of the words just as much as she's trying to convince him. "It's just a house. The poor guy had his first one burn down. We can't blame him for being stuck with something like this."

"Are you forgetting the part where I said he's listed as a sexual predator?" Xander hisses at her louder this time, growing more and more impatient. "Let's just go back. We can try and do some research on this guy before he—"

"Who's there?" A very tall man with a slim frame comes barreling out the front door, making Beatrice squeak as she stumbles backward over a branch and falls to the forest floor.

Beatrice's breathing grows rapid and heavy as she stares the man up and down. He's wearing chunky brown combat boots and ripped cargo pants. His shirt is tattered all around the hem and his skin is cratered with burn marks and scars. His face is something like Beatrice has never seen before, his eyes two black holes and he has no nose. Beatrice hates herself for it but he immediately reminds her of something crawling out the depths of Hell—where she will be for just thinking that way.

"Who the hell are you?" The man is holding a hunting rifle, aiming it directly at Beatrice. Xander has disappeared behind one of the thick trees, scared out of his mind and pulling the collar of his jacket over his mouth.

Beatrice clears her throat, staying on the ground as she raises her hands in the air. "P-please don't shoot. My name is Beatrice Millstone. I live on the other side of the woods."

The man blinks, lowering his rifle just a few inches but not low enough for Beatrice to feel anywhere close to safe. "Millstone. You live in Ashwood."

His voice is raspy, giving Beatrice the hint that he smokes at least two packs of cigarettes a day *or* the fire that burned down his house tainted his lungs forever. Does that happen to people?

"Yes," Beatrice sputters, really wishing Xander would have stuck around with that stake. Bastard. "I uh, just moved back for a little. And I read about the missing girls."

He lowers his gun completely now and Beatrice tries her best to read the expression on his face but all she can see is annoyance and scars. "I didn't have nothin' to do with that shit."

"I didn't say you did."

"But that's where you're getting, right?" He glares. "You think that the man who lives in a shack in the woods had something to do with those pretty little girls goin' missin'."

"I actually was hoping you could tell me a little bit more about the woods itself." Beatrice slowly starts to stand, still holding her hands in the air even though he's completely turned down his gun. "If you saw anything, any of the girls."

He clucks his tongue, studying her. His head is bald, reflecting the sun from above. "Are you with the police or somethin'?"

"No, just doing personal research," Beatrice quickly answers, not daring to drop her hands. "It's clear that the cops in this town don't really have an agenda to find out what happened. And it seems like the long list of girls that have gone missing stayed in my house, so…"

"You can come inside if you want," he finally growls after a beat.

Beatrice swallows. Her gut is telling her that the man is harmless, but her mind is screaming at her to run the hell away. Xander told her that this guy is listed as a sexual predator. How dumb would she be to agree to go into this man's home?

"I have some tea," he adds when Beatrice doesn't say anything. "Or if you wanna talk out here, we can do that. I know what the rumors are about me so I ain't gonna blame you."

"Tea sounds nice." Beatrice takes a few steps toward him and she looks around for any sign of Xander. "Xander?"

He peeks out from behind a bush, wide eyed, his gaze going from Beatrice to the man like he's watching a ping-pong match.

"Wait out here," she instructs as the man starts leading the way into his house, leaves crunching under his big boots. "I'll only be a minute."

"Don't go in there!" Xander hisses at her desperately, shaking his head so vigorously it might just roll off his neck. "You're going to wind up in the guy's basement!"

"Just be on the lookout," Beatrice orders and then follows the Burned Man inside of his shack.

The walls are plain wooden boards nailed together like a makeshift home. It's freezing inside, probably because of lack of insulation. There's a crackling fireplace in the only room in the house, just across from a small kitchen area where the man is already pouring Beatrice a mug of tea. She looks around for any sign of life but there is nothing. There are no pictures of family members hung up on the walls, no signs of pets, no TV in sight. Just a bed, a kitchen, and a fireplace.

"The name's Fred, by the way," he introduces himself before coughing into his elbow, passing her the mug and plopping down at the tiny round table across from the fridge. Beatrice follows suit but doesn't have any plan on drinking this tea. "Yeah, a burned man with the name of Fred. Trust me, I've heard all the jokes already."

"I wasn't going to make one," she replies politely, wrapping her fingers around the mug. It's hot enough to do damage if she were to throw it on him in self-defense. There's also a knife block next to the sink. A ceramic bowl sits on the round table. A log poker is propped up against the brick fireplace.

"So, you got a friend out there?" He jerks his head to the front door.

The burns covering his face make Beatrice feel sick to her stomach—but hopefully not in an offensive way. She's never seen someone with so many scars before.

"He's my neighbor," Beatrice answers, thumbing over her shoulder. "I told him this wouldn't take very long, so…"

"Why do you want to know about those missin' girls?"

"Why wouldn't I?" Beatrice counters, feeling uncomfortable the longer he stares at her. She grips the mug tighter with both hands and averts her gaze away from him. "It seems like a lot of people in this town completely ignore the fact that they're still missing. It's not right."

"What's it got to do with you?" he interrogates. "It ain't like you live here."

"No, but if I were to go missing, I would want someone looking for me," Beatrice says honestly and awkwardly. She flicks a strand of hair away from her eyes. "Besides, they all lived in Ashwood leading up to their disappearances. Every last one of them. There are a lot of theories on what happened but I think the only person that would hold a vital clue would be you."

"And why's that?"

"You're not too far from Ashwood," she explains. "And a lot of bad things can go on in woods like these so I was just guessing that you might have seen a thing or two in your years of living here." She pauses, realizing Xander never told her how long he lived here. "In fact, when did you move in here?"

"Goin' to be about seventeen years now, I think," he answers, his elbow resting on the back of his chair, his entire body slumped. He stares at Beatrice for a long pregnant pause, maybe waiting for her to drink but Beatrice isn't taking the bait. "I didn't choose to live here, ya know."

"I heard about your first house burning down, yeah," Beatrice says sympathetically. "I'm sorry."

"You say *first house* like this piece of shit counts as one." He sighs heavily, glancing around his surroundings in disgust. "I was forced out here by the good ole residents of Silver Creek, you know that?"

Beatrice shakes her head. "N-no, I didn't."

"They was accusin' me of sleeping with the girl down the street," he explains to her, a bird flying past the window outside. "I didn't touch her. But when you're accused of something so goddamned mental, it goes on file. Never went to jail for nothin' because they couldn't prove it. I dunno who, not sure I even want to know, burned down my house."

Beatrice stares at him sadly. She isn't going to take everything he says to heart, but if any of this is true, she feels sorry for him. There are so many people in the world that can get away with this type of stuff and live their lives in freedom. But false accusations can literally ruin lives. But again, Beatrice isn't believing every word he says.

"Insurance wouldn't cover it," Fred goes on. "So, I found this piece of trash out here and settled my shit inside. Not that I had much of it, but…"

"I'm sorry to hear that," Beatrice says honestly—but not too honest because who knows if he's telling the truth or not? "Life can be cruel, I guess."

"Life is more than cruel, little girl," he warns her with a pointing finger. He lets his hand drop back down onto the top of the table, creating a loud *thud* and making Beatrice jump. He smiles at her fear, his teeth crooked and yellow like little spikes. "It's a monster, thirsting after misery."

Beatrice winces, ducking her head. It makes her think of Ashwood.

"I don't get much company," Fred tells her as if that's something that isn't obvious. "I appreciate visitors."

Beatrice clears her throat and takes a fake sip of the tea. "So in these seventeen years that you lived here, you must have seen something, right? Something unusual? Maybe one of the girls?"

"Why should I keep answering your little questions?" he wonders aloud. "Whatchu got for me?"

"What do you want?" Beatrice worries he's going to say either money or sex. It's the national anthem and she has zero to offer with both of those things.

"To keep this off the record."

Beatrice blinks. "That's it?"

"Whatchu mean?"

"That's all you want?" she asks, taken aback. "For me to not tell anyone about this?"

"Like I said, I don't get much visitors." Fred takes a loud drink of tea, putting the mug back onto the table and fingering the broken handle. "What I say stays between us."

The way he's looking at her makes her uneasy. She's almost afraid of what will happen to her here more than what she fears will happen to her in Ashwood.

"Yes, I won't say a word."

"Not even to your boyfriend outside."

Beatrice ignores the comment, leaning forward a little. "So I'm guessing this means that you saw them? One or two of the girls, then?"

"I'd seen a few of them, yeah." Fred shifts in his seat, setting his jaw back but he doesn't say much else about it.

Beatrice blinks. "Do you mind if I ask what you saw?"

"What do you think I saw?"

Beatrice second guesses why she's here at all. Maybe this was a mistake. Maybe Fred is just some miserable old man living in the middle of nowhere and desperate for company. Maybe him luring her in here is part of some plan that would make headlines years in the future when her body finally gets found. Does he want money or something? Some sort of trade for information? Because if so, Beatrice can't give him much. Like, nothing at all.

"I don't know, that's why I'm here," she responds a little impatiently.

"I remember seein' a girl or two over the years but there was only one I saw running through the trees screamin' her little head off," Fred recalls, blinking at something over Beatrice's shoulder, his recollection staring back at him. "I remember it was night and she was wearing this bright red dress—which is what caught my eye in the first place. She was runnin' and runnin' like a chicken with its goddamned head cut off, I'll tell ya."

"What did you do?" Beatrice leans forward a little. "Did you help her? What was she running from?"

"I couldn't see," he admits. "The screaming stopped soon enough, though. And she didn't run this way. She circled back around to the house. I thought it was some drunk party girl so I didn't think nothin' of it."

"Did you go to the police when you realized she went missing?"

He shakes his head, a smirk covering his face. "If I went to the police, you really think they would take an accused pedophile who lives in the woods seriously? And if they did, they would find a way to pin it all on me."

"That's the only weird thing you saw?" Beatrice feels her shoulders slouch. Yes, the girl in red running through the woods is definitely a start, but it's not going to get her anywhere near a lead for more information.

He shakes his head again, leaning forward. "There was somethin' else I saw about a year after I moved in here."

Beatrice slides her mug of coffee away, resting her arms on top of the table. "I'm listening."

"I will never forget it."

Beatrice blinks, her heart picking up the pace again—not that it ever slowed down but she can feel it threatening to break through her ribs. Sixteen years ago is when the twins and Marilyn wandered into the Jungle together.

"I saw this lady in white." Fred's words fill the room like an elephant taking over, breaking through the walls and ramming the entire shack to the ground, the sentence carries so much weight.

The lady in white is no doubt Marilyn. She's been in the back of her head after all these years, holding evidence to the day the twins disappeared. And now, there is a man sitting in front of her who saw the same woman she did. This confirms everything. She wasn't some confused little girl who was caught up in a dream. It was real.

"She had two kids with her," he goes on and Beatrice flinches. "I dunno, they must've been around five or six. Maybe I'm wrong, I ain't ever had kids. But they were small."

"What happened?" Beatrice demands, feeling like she's literally going to go insane if she doesn't get this answer. She thought she was the last to see them alive before they vanished under Marilyn's watch. But Fred seems to have taken that role for now.

"They were running, all of them holding hands," he explains. "I was out skinnin' a squirrel for lunch and I remember lookin' up to see the three of them runnin'. The lady was older and looked like she was in a hurry. For a minute, I wondered if they was running from an animal. A bear, maybe. But they wasn't. Nothin' was behind them."

"And then what?"

"The kids started to slow down." Fred glances at his scarred hands in front of him on the table. "They were lookin' tired at first, but then I realized how green they was lookin'."

Beatrice finds herself confused. "Green? Like they were feeling sick?"

He nods his head. "They couldn't run anymore and the lady was trying to pull them further but they couldn't push themselves to follow her no more."

"So, what happened?"

"They fell," he answers. "It's that simple. And not in some tiresome way out of running for too long. They looked sick. The lady wept over them, her tears dripping all over their bodies like magic, I'll tell ya. She covered their bodies with leaves, scattering all kinds of different leaves over their faces and arms and legs until they were just as blended in with the rest of the woods. I couldn't believe my eyes when I saw what she was doin'. I wanted to say something but I ain't ever been frozen with fear like I was in that moment."

Beatrice's eyes flood with stinging tears. She's had enough common sense to know that Jax and Juniper didn't live long—or at all—the day they went into those woods. She kind of always knew that something terrible had happened to them. But being told that she was right, that something did happen to them just minutes after leaving the backyard and they didn't live long enough to make it out of the woods breaks Beatrice's heart into a million and one pieces. Hearing the way it happened makes Beatrice want to puke. Picturing them falling over together and Marilyn covering them up with leaves like they weren't even people. Fury rages through Beatrice's veins.

Beatrice blinks through her tears, realizing Fred's own eyes are filled with them, too. Her lips part to ask him why he's crying but he speaks up before she can.

"So I did what I thought was right," Fred whimpers, glancing at her and then back down at the table. "I was made to be this monster to this entire goddamned town. I was looked at as a pedophile. A predator. Someone who could never do good around kids."

Beatrice wipes away one of her tears, listening closely.

"So I did what that lady in white couldn't." His voice cracks and he swallows the ball bulging out of his throat.

"What did you do?" Beatrice nearly whispers.

"I felt for a pulse," he explains, finally making eye contact with her again. Tears cascade down both of his cheeks, splattering against his forearm. "I checked on both of them and they ain't had one. So I got my shovel out the house..."

Beatrice feels like her lungs have collapsed. She grips the edge of the table, her mind buzzing with disbelief and revelations. The legs of her chair screech against the floor as she pushes herself back a few inches. "Wait... you...?"

"I buried them." He's crying harder now, his eyebrows sloped up toward one another. "I was so determined to show the world that I wasn't a monster. That I could be trusted. That I have a heart and that they were all wrong to do what they did to me. They burned me at the stake for touching a child I never touched in the first place, you see. I thought I was doing right, giving them kids proper burials."

Beatrice puts a hand to her stomach, feeling the urge to puke.

"And then the family came," Fred says after a beat of silence.

Beatrice snaps her head up to look at him. "What family?"

"Yours. The Millstones," he answers, rubbing his hands together, the sound making Beatrice want to peal her ears off her head. "I saw them all that night. They came through them woods like the police themselves. They were calling out the names of them kids. And I remember them all runnin' so fast to find them. They would run over their graves, circle around them over and over again. And I couldn't say nothin' to them. Because if I did, they would've thought I was responsible, when I wasn't. It was that lady or whatever they was runnin' from. But ain't no one would've believed me."

He wipes his nose with his wrist, a glob of snot sticking to his skin.

"But they were right there the whole time," he adds sadly. "I couldn't bury proper graves but they weren't that far down. And I remember pleading that the family would dig a little. That they would find them—"

"You could've said something," Beatrice growls, shaking her head. "You knew this whole time and you let me and the rest of my family wonder for years what happened and where they were."

"I'm sorry." Fred's voice cracks again. More tears drip off his face and onto his knees. He quickly wipes them away with his shirt. "I thought I did the right thing. For me. To prove to myself that I wasn't this monster these people painted me to be. That I could be a good person, do good deed."

"What good is that deed if you leave the family in limbo like that?" Beatrice is breathless and is two seconds away from shattering this mug over Fred's head. She's trembling with anger.

"I don't know," he answers, looking up at her. His face is no longer scaring her, just angering her. "I didn't want to involve myself in any other legal shit. I thought stayin' outta all that crap was good for me. Ain't nobody was gonna believe me if I told them what I saw. Them cops aren't very friendly—"

"You ruined my family's life." The words are nasty and Beatrice doesn't mean them. But she feels just as guilty as he does. She could have said something more, too, even years after what she saw that day. But she didn't. Beatrice, Marilyn, and now Fred all get to play as puzzle pieces in what happened to the twins. All three of them had some sort of insight to that day, yet all of them were quiet. Jax and Juniper deserved better than that. Way better.

Beatrice leaves the shack, flinging herself out the front door and gasping for the fresh air of fall waiting for her outside. Xander is throwing questions at her but she isn't in the mind space to answer. She's stumbling towards the path they took to get here, Xander hurrying after her but Fred does not attempt to join them outside.

"Beatrice, what's going on?" Xander asks.

Beatrice throws up when she's a good several yards away from the shack, chunks sticking to the pretty sea of leaves in front of her.

"Holy shit," Xander mumbles, putting a tentative hand on her back. "Okay, you don't have to say anything—"

"He buried them!" she cries, sinking to her knees and feeling her mascara clinging to her cheeks like glue. She looks up at Xander, feeling herself be so very vulnerable with him, something she doesn't usually do with people at all. But here she is, crying like the pathetic grown woman she is about her two dead cousins that went missing over fifteen years ago. "They… died, somehow, and Marilyn tried covering it up but Fred buried them thinking he was helping."

Fuck the residents of Silver Creek for painting Fred in such a horrible light. Fuck Fred for doing what he did or for bending the truth or for whatever really happened to the twins. Fuck Marilyn for not speaking up and for… what? What did she even do? What part did she play in their demise? Did she give them something before Fred could see them through the trees? Did she poison them? Fred made it sound like she was just as surprised at their fall as he was watching it. Was Marilyn surprised by this or was something not supposed to kick in until they were out of the woods?

Lastly, fuck Beatrice herself for never saying a damn word to anyone else all those years ago. Screw any part of her that convinced herself she was dreaming, that immediately listened to her mom when she told her it was just a dream. If Beatrice told one more person, the likelihood of the twins being rescued or found was so much greater.

"Come on, let's get you home." Xander wraps an arm around Beatrice's torso and they start through the woods again, any sense of Beatrice's sanity being left behind.

Fall came to Silver Creek and it was Beatrice's favorite time of year. She looked forward to the leaves changing and decorating for Halloween and trick-or-treating with Juniper and Jax. But it had been over a year since they vanished and the magic that usually came with the autumn leaves was nowhere to be found.

In fact, Beatrice was pretty sure that the new season brought the opposite. Aunt Marley was nowhere near sane and she would make visit after visit to the police station, asking them if they had found any leads as to what happened to Juniper and Jax. Beatrice's mom was keeping to herself more, drowning herself in the books in the study after hours and wouldn't come out until well into the next morning. Aunt Edie was normal, pasting on a smile and dripping in her jewels like nothing was amiss. Beatrice found herself clinging to Aunt Edie more, as she was the only one that made her feel comfortable enough to smile.

Beatrice was splayed out on her bedroom floor, sheets of white paper laid out before her, colored pencils spilled out around her. She couldn't stop drawing the House Things lately. She drew the chattering teeth she heard outside the windows during the wintertime. She drew a huge black scribble with noise-making squiggly lines around it to represent the screaming in the crawl space. She was now working on the little boy she had seen in the attic with the woman at the window. She had seen another little girl with large red hives on her skin a few weeks back for a split second at the end of the hallway, too. Beatrice would have to draw her next.

"You're a real good drawer, Beatrice," Xander said from across from her, his own artwork in front of him on different sheets of paper. His illustrations consisted of faces all morphing together at different scales and sizes. He kept mentioning his inspiration being someone named Pablo but Beatrice had never met him before.

"You think so?" Beatrice scrunched her face up as she looked at her drawings. "I don't think they're that good."

"Well of course you don't," Xander said. "My nana told me that no artist thinks they're going to be the next Vincent van Gogh."

"Who's that?"

Xander raised his eyebrows so high that they nearly stretched to the back of his head. "You've never heard of good old Vincent, Beatrice?"

She shook her head, shading in the navy blue on the little boy's shirt. "Nope."

"Well maybe you should start educating yourself on well-known artists," he suggested thoughtfully, shaking his thick black hair out of his eyes. "One's favorite artist can give very good details about a person."

"Let's do something else." Beatrice set down her pencils and sat up. "This is making me tired."

"Okay." He tossed his own pencils into the pile of wooden colors. "What now?"

"Let's ask mom if we can use the camera," she suggested, excitedly getting to her feet. "We can film a stop animation movie of the pumpkins outside!"

"I'm game!"

The two of them wandered out of her bedroom, the door creaking shut behind them. As they start for the stairs, Beatrice perked up at the sound of talking from the other side of the bathroom door near the stairs. She put her hand out to stop Xander from walking, both of them leaning closer toward the door.

"What is that?" Xander whispered to her.

Beatrice shrugged, stepping closer to the door and wondering if it's another one of her mother's and Aunt Marley's secret conversations they'd been having a lot lately. Xander joins her in pressing his own ear to the door, Grammy Astrid's voice ringing out on the other side.

"I don't know what you want me to do," Grandma Astrid was saying. A beat. "I just want to stop seeing you."

"Who is she talking to?" Xander asked quietly.

Beatrice helplessly shrugged her shoulders and continued to listen.

"But you're everywhere I look and it's scaring me." Grammy Astrid did indeed sound terrified. There was a *clink* and she went on. "I can't even look at myself anymore without seeing you. And I'm bringing this up now because you seem to find it funny but I am done."

"You're never done," someone responded back but the voice belonged to someone Beatrice had never heard before.

Boldly, Beatrice reached out and wrapped her fingers around the shiny gold doorknob, gently pressing her shoulder against the door and easing it open. There Grammy Astrid stood at the sink, another face staring back at her. Two faces, actually. One was very much her own, bathed in fear and worry. The other was of a lady Beatrice somehow recognized, though she didn't know from where.

Resisting the urge to scream, Beatrice staggered away from the bathroom when she realized that the lady in the mirror was just that: inside of the mirror. She wasn't a person standing next to or behind Grammy Astrid. It was like the mirror was a window, but it wasn't.

"Beatrice!" Xander called out, following her down the stairs. "What are you doing? Are you all right? Did you see something?"

"I saw something, yeah," Beatrice said back breathlessly, glancing up the stairs to make sure Grammy Astrid wasn't following.

"Well, aren't you going to tell me what it was?"

Beatrice considers it but Xander is her only friend. Sure, he knew about all the weird stuff that went on in her house but she felt like her friendship with him was on thin ice because of it all. One more weird thing taking place when he was present was for sure going to drive him away sooner or later. She didn't want that happening. She didn't want to scare him off.

"It was nothing," Beatrice lied. "Just Grammy without any makeup."

Chapter 16

"**T**hey're dead," Beatrice reiterates when she and Xander find themselves back at Ashwood, seated in front of the fireplace in the parlor. Aunt Edie is still out doing who knows what and even though the sun is still beating down on Silver Creek, Beatrice can't stop shivering.

"Is there anything I can do?" Xander asks cautiously from the armchair next to her. He's been nervously biting his lip ever since they got back, clearly unsure what to do with Beatrice when she's in this sort of state. He's never seen her like this before and Beatrice hates herself for allowing him to.

She shrugs—which she has found herself doing a lot lately. She thinks about the twins, unable to get that horrifying image of her and the rest of her family members walking over their graves, oblivious to the fresh dirt under the leaves, unknowing that Jax and Juniper were right under their noses the whole time. They just didn't know where to look. She thinks about Fred and how terrible of a person he turned out to be. Not saying anything, not giving Beatrice's family the closure they needed was just as bad as the secret Marilyn is holding close to her chest, too.

Marilyn. Beatrice has yet to decide what to do with this newly found information. She could go to the police, turn that bitch in for her part in this mess and for keeping her mouth shut about it. But Beatrice would want to confront Marilyn on her own before she misses the opportunity. Or she could spill the news to Aunt Edie and show her that this friend she thought she's had for this long is no friend. Friends do not watch their friends' great niece and nephew die and not say anything to anyone at all about it. On the other hand, perhaps Aunt Edie already knows.

It's quite clear that ever since Beatrice has returned to Ashwood, Aunt Edie hasn't exactly been the most forthcoming with information regarding the things that go on in this house. She refuses to acknowledge the House Things and plays dumb whenever Beatrice brings up the missing girls. She can't be trusted. Telling her this piece of news might make her the next big target on whatever sinister list

185

seems to be created under this roof.

"Maybe we should talk to your aunt when she gets home," Xander suggests as though he read her thoughts. His voice is weak, wary. "If Marilyn is her friend—"

"Then she might already know," Beatrice finishes for him, pulling the itchy throw blanket tighter around her back. "Either Aunt Edie knows nothing about what happened to Jax and Juniper, or she and Marilyn are close enough that she already knows all of the gory details."

"But if that's true, then why wouldn't she say anything?" Xander ponders. "Why wouldn't she try and do something about it?"

"Because she's the type of person to only give a shit about herself." Beatrice shoots him a look, feeling her hair turning gray one strand at a time. "Sorry to drag you into all this. You don't have to stay."

Xander reaches over to put his hand on her knee for a few short seconds. "I don't mind, Beatrice. Actually, being with you in this house is doing a lot of good for me. I tend to do better with nostalgia."

Beatrice forces a grin. "You say *nostalgia* like it's a good thing."

"It can be, sometimes."

"Not in Ashwood."

"You might have a point." He pushes out a laugh and then leans back in the armchair. He looks around at the high shelves crammed with books and figurines and small trinkets collected over the years. "I give you a lot of credit for staying here, though. I wouldn't be able to last a day."

"You don't give yourself enough credit." Beatrice pulls her legs beneath herself.

Xander stares at the crackling fire in front of them, the sky outside suddenly blanketing over with stringy clouds. "You'd be surprised how scared I am of most things, Beatrice."

She arcs a brow. "I'm listening."

Xander sighs and waits a few seconds before continuing. "Well, terrified of sloths."

Beatrice finds herself laughing, something she hasn't done in much too long of a time. Part of her tries to be sad about the realization but she pushes it down. "Sloths? You're actually serious about this?"

"Okay, have you ever seen those things move?" he asks her. "They look like things from a whole other planet!"

"Some people find them cute."

"And those *some people* are delusional." Xander tilts his head back thoughtfully, squinting his slanted eyes as he considers what is next on the list. "Snakes never really scared me until Nana made me watch this movie about them being on a plane. I hate the thought of driving my car into a body of water and drowning."

"I can agree with you on that one," Beatrice affirms quietly.

She's always had this weird dream growing up of her in the bathroom on the second floor of Ashwood. She would be lying in the tub and suddenly, someone or something would push her head underwater. She would flail her arms and legs this way and that but the pressure of two hands on top of her head wouldn't let up. She would scream and scream under water, her vision blurred by bubbles scattered around her face. Beatrice would never finish the dream. She would wake up gasping for air and pretty sure that she could feel water filling up her lungs.

"Small spaces, too," Xander goes on, his eyes trained on the flames in the fireplace, no longer wearing a small grin, but a frown. "I developed that fear here, actually."

"Wait, here?" Beatrice echoes. "Like, in this house?"

Xander nods his head.

"How?"

"It was when you and I were playing hide and seek with the twins one time," Xander recaps, tucking a leg underneath his other. "I thought it would be a good idea to tuck myself away into your aunt's wardrobe. Aunt Edie, that is." He pauses, his frown deepening and Beatrice finds herself almost feeling guilty for his adult fear of small spaces but perhaps her guilt over Juniper and Jax is seeping into every other aspect of her existence. "And then, the weirdest thing happened."

Beatrice blinks, waiting for him to continue and wondering on a scale of one to ten, how strange it's going to compare to everything else that's happened here.

"Someone locked it," he tells her, confused, like it's happening all over again. "I could hear it, someone turning that little clasp on the outside that keeps the doors shut. And I remember saying that I was in there. I was screaming quite loudly, calling out to whoever was on the other side but no one was there. And if they were, they didn't help." Xander doesn't look too bothered by it now but the tone in his voice makes Beatrice remember the child version of himself. "I started kicking the doors, throwing my fists into them like some sort of mad man. It felt like the entire wardrobe was getting smaller, yet I was somehow getting larger. You know, kind of like that movie about the girl falling down the rabbit hole."

"*Alice in Wonderland*," she says.

"Yes, that." Xander thinks before going on. "I tried looking out the crack between the doors and I could see someone's shadow on the floor but they weren't doing anything to help me. At first I thought it was you playing some kind of prank but the shadow was way too big to be yours, Beatrice. So I kept screaming and screaming but no one could hear me. I was stuck in a way I'd never been stuck before in my whole life. I felt like I had truly gone mad."

"I don't remember any of this," Beatrice says honestly. She tries thinking about a time when she saw Xander's knuckles bleeding or him telling her about this during their game but no memory comes to mind. It saddens her for him even more, now. Picturing him stuck in that wardrobe with no way out is a feeling Beatrice has had so many times herself before. She might not have been physically stuck in Aunt Edie's wardrobe, but she had been stuck in so many other positions before because of locked doors.

"I never told you," he croaks.

"Why?"

"I wanted you to think I wasn't scared of anything." He wears a side smile on his face, making Beatrice see him as the little boy she grew up with even more now. The one she would make mud pies with, the one she would race through the Jungle with twigs in their hair and dirt on their knees. The Xander that would comfort her when another one of her family members died in some big mysterious way.

"But I've shown you when I'm scared," Beatrice states. "I wouldn't mind comforting you every now and again, you know."

"Yeah, but back then it was different." Xander looks back at the fire again. "We were kids."

"Exactly," she murmurs under her breath. "We needed a whole lot of comforting."

"You don't think you got that?"

Beatrice stares at the blazing fire, thinking hard about his question. She recalls her childhood being this weird experience no one on this earth will relate to. The twins could have, but they aren't here. She is the only living child to have grown up during that time. She saw strange and unusual things but was raised to believe that was normal.

"I think I got told a lot of the time to not be afraid of the dark," she confesses, tugging at a loose thread in the blanket covering her. "I was told to not be afraid of the things that I saw."

Beatrice remembers staring at Grandpa Hugh's shadows in the back of glossy images from holidays and backyard cookouts.

"I was told that the things in this house aren't anything to be afraid of," Beatrice goes on, recalling that woman in the mirror, talking to Grammy Astrid, a sinister smile covering her lips. "That I should look the other way if I saw something scary." A pause, the sound of the fire the only thing filling the room for a long beat until she goes on. "And I did. I looked away every single time. And I don't know why I did, because I heard all about how even the adults would pretend to not see what was there. They would look the other way just as much as me. And then they would end up… dead. And I remember wondering if that was because they pretended to not see the impossible. If they turned a cheek without knowing what would happen to them."

"I don't think that's the reason they wound up where they are now," Xander tells her gently.

"Maybe not," Beatrice agrees with a slight shrug once again. "But whatever the reason, it was no coincidence."

Beatrice's eyes flutter open and she feels a knot in her neck almost immediately. She winces at the pain, finding herself still curled up in a ball in the parlor's armchair. She looks over at where Xander was seated but he is gone and the fire has died down, the room now dark with night. Burning embers flicker from in front of her. She rubs the knot forming in her neck, slowly stretching her legs out in front of her. The wind is strong outside, whistling through a cracked window somewhere on the ground floor. Thin tree branches rake their ends against the turret's windows, prompting Beatrice to awaken.

What time is it? And when did Xander leave? She recalls the two of them making pointless conversation about work and Xander's life at public school but she doesn't remember falling asleep. He must have left after she had already dozed off. Beatrice rubs her eyes with her palms and stands from the armchair, stretching her limbs over her head and she pops her neck in several different spots, feeling a lot looser. She goes to start for the stairs, wondering if Aunt Edie had gotten home yet but the figure looming in the threshold stops her cold.

Her mother's thick brown hair spills down her shoulders and she's wearing the plain white t-shirt she had the last night they spent here at Ashwood. Her jeans are pulled up high on her waist and she's staring at her daughter with the tiniest hint of a smile over her lips. The sight nearly sends Beatrice into a trance, the entire room threatening to turn itself upside down. She reaches over to put her hand on the back of the armchair to keep her balance.

"Mom?" she asks breathlessly, not bothering to pinch herself to see if this is another one of her weird dreams or not. She doesn't want to know.

"Sweetheart," her mother says, the corners of her mouth pulling up into a sad, grateful smile. She takes a tentative step closer to her but doesn't reach out to touch her like Beatrice was anticipating. "I don't have much time."

"Before what?" Beatrice asks impatiently, wondering if Aunt Edie is going to appear next and scare her mom off. "Are you alive?"

The expression that her mother makes is the same one she wore the day she told Beatrice that they aren't like any ordinary family. She shakes her head a little, her eyes growing sadder and sadder the longer Beatrice finds herself staring at them. "Oh, no, sweetie. I'm not alive. But you won't be either if you stay in this house."

"Why would you say that?"

"Because it's not safe for you here," she says quickly. "You need to get out. Now."

Beatrice shakes her head at her. There is no way in hell that she's leaving. She's spent over a decade knowing nothing about what happened to her mother. Now that she has the chance with her standing directly in front of her, the last thing she wants to do is leave. She can't.

"I'm not leaving," Beatrice argues. "I don't care if something bad happens, I want to be with you—"

"You're going to get hurt," her mother warns in a heated whisper. Her hand hovers in front of Beatrice's cheek, like she's too scared to make skin-to-skin contact. "And I wouldn't be able to forgive myself if I didn't try getting you out of here before that happens."

"I don't know what you're talking about," Beatrice rambles, desperate for any other piece of information that can tell her what the hell is going on.

"It's not safe," she whispers, her voice so close that Beatrice can feel it deep in her ear like a bug. Goosebumps explode up and down her body and in the blink of an eye, her mother is gone.

She looks around the dark parlor, a sliver of moonlight filtering in through the window and across the sofa. Nothing seems amiss and her mother is nowhere to be seen.

"Mom?" she whispers in the dark but she gets no response, only the crickets outside seem to chirp and the whistling of the wind grows stronger. "Mom, where are you?"

Beatrice checks behind the couch and the other side of the curtains for any sign of her mother, like they're playing one of the many rounds of hide and seek that took place within these walls. She remains in the middle of the room for five minutes, waiting for her mom to come back, to feed her more information on why she needs to leave now and what kind of danger she'll be in if she chooses to stay. When she doesn't return, Beatrice sighs out of her nose and bites the inside of her cheek, wiping more sleep from her eyes as she walks through the foyer and up the creaky stairs to her room.

She expects to see her mother in here when she opens the door but she doesn't get her hopes too high. One of the many things she has learned about Ashwood is that the House Things often choose when they want to be seen. She can't just snap her fingers and make her mother appear. It doesn't work like that. But if it did, she would be absorbing as much answers as her mother is willing to give her.

She may have played a little dumb when her mom told her she was in danger, but she wanted that conversation to last as long as it possibly could, even if it meant Beatrice getting hurt in the end—maybe she deserves it at this point. She doesn't care what it would have taken to just speak with her mom for more than a minute. As Beatrice slips under the covers of her old bed, she remembers the dream she had of the twins and Grandpa Hugh leading her into the guest room and telling her that she's next. She thinks of the paint on the walls, warning her again. And now, her mother's visit demanding her to leave.

Is Beatrice on the verge of becoming one of these House Things? Is something going to happen to her the same way things happened to her family and all those missing girls? She considers what she would be called in Lila's collection of Millstone family members. *The oblivious one. The confused. The lost one.* Or something a little more blunt: *The stupid girl walking straight to her death.*

Beatrice tied her bright red converse to her feet and pulled her hair into a messy ponytail. She gave herself a nod of approval in the mirror above her dresser and then skipped out into the hallway. Even though it was cold outside for November, Beatrice was still going to meet up with Xander to rake some leaves together and build a nest. She knew the twins would have loved it and even though thinking about them made her awfully sad, she was trying her best nowadays to not think about that kind of stuff. It only brought her down and she knew that all of the remaining adults in Ashwood were already so low. She would hate to see them go lower.

"It's about time," Xander called out to her when Beatrice slipped out the side door of the mud room. "I've only been waiting for seven and a half years, Beatrice."

Beatrice grinned at him. "What an odd number to come up with, Xander."

He shrugs, dirt already smeared across his cheeks as though he had already been playing outside for hours. But with who? Xander didn't have any other friends that Beatrice knew of. She heard Aunt Edie talking a lot about jealousy but Beatrice never really knew what it meant. Perhaps it's the feeling that she is feeling now, kind of upset that Xander would be playing with other kids instead of her.

"You sure it's a good idea to build this thing?" Xander asked as he followed Beatrice to the back of the yard where the shed stood, bracing itself against the autumn wind. "Nana told me that it's supposed to snow tomorrow."

"So?"

"So, wouldn't it be a waste to build a nest if it's just going to get snowed over?" Xander wondered, his studded bracelet sliding up and down his arm. He was going through a punk phase and even tried coloring his hair with red sharpie. It didn't show up in his black hair.

"Who cares?" Beatrice said when she approached the shed doors, pulling them open. "What else are we going to do today?"

"We could do something inside," Xander suggested and then thought again about his words. "Actually, yeah, let's stay out."

Beatrice looked at him over her shoulder, her brow furrowing. She turned around to face him, her hip popped out to the side. "Wait, are you afraid of my house?"

"Why would you think that?"

"Because you suggested to play inside and then you thought about it and said no," she stated, her arms folding in front of her. A weird sense came over her, almost like she was feeling defensive over Ashwood—which is an odd thought because Beatrice started to discover that the longer she lived here, the bad memories began to overtake the good ones. She shouldn't be sticking up for a *house* in general. Least of all, Ashwood.

"I just thought that if this was going to be the last good day of fall, we should enjoy it," Xander chirped, glancing up at some of the falling leaves blowing out of the woods. "We get so few of them, don't we, Beatrice?"

She studied him and then reached for two of the rakes inside of the shed. "You sure do say my name a lot, you know."

Xander looked at her worriedly. "Is that a bad thing?"

She shook her head as they started to rake up some of the brown crunchy leaves that blanketed the yard. Xander followed suit. "No, not a bad thing. Just interesting."

"Well I like being interesting," Xander responded, using his rake to start gathering up a small pile of leaves. "It's far better than being boring or normal or simple or any of those other dreary words people like to use."

Beatrice glanced over at the entrance to the Jungle, where she noticed Aunt Marley coming through the trees. As usual, the corners of her mouth were aimed down, her head hanging low. She never looked as sad as she would when she'd come out of the woods without any sign of her kids. That familiar gut-wrenching feeling that had been eating away at Beatrice came back in the pit of her stomach.

"What are you doing with the rakes?" Aunt Marley asked tiredly, purple bags under her eyes and her hair a greasy mess on top of her head.

"Building a nest made out of leaves," Beatrice told her happily, hoping that some of her lighthearted energy might rub off on her. "We're gonna pretend we're in *Where the Wild Things Are!*"

"Jax loved that story," Aunt Marley said, her eyes glossy as she stared down at the start of their leaf pile.

Beatrice ached for her. She could only imagine how difficult it was going through the woods over and over again with no idea where to start and where to end. Who was to say that the twins were still even in there?

They could have been escorted out from one of the many other sides.

Xander cleared his throat, his gaze filtering back and forth from Beatrice to Aunt Marley. "Do you wanna join? There's another rake in the shed. We are going to need all the help we can get if we want it to be as big as we're hoping for it—"

"I'm going to lie down," Aunt Marley cut him off, not making eye contact with either one of them as she started back toward the house, her shoulders slumped so much she looked like she had a hunchback.

"I feel bad for her," Xander said to Beatrice when Aunt Marley was out of earshot. "She must be going through such a hard time."

"She is," Beatrice confirmed, going back to raking. "We kinda all still are."

"She's hanging in there, though," Xander pointed out optimistically, as he usually did about this kind of stuff. It was why Beatrice had appreciated him so much. "I hear that a lot of parents who lose their children, kill themselves."

As if on cue, Beatrice heard an ear-piercing shatter come from behind. She whirled around, expecting to see Aunt Marley breaking china or something on the lawn. What she saw instead would forever haunt her after today. Grandma Astrid's body was in midair, falling out the tall, rectangular bathroom window. It was like watching a fork drop from a table. The two ends would become unbalanced until her body would hit the ground with a horrifying *crack* that would make Beatrice scream.

"What in the world?" Xander dropped his rake.

Beatrice covered her mouth with both of her hands, her feet glued to where she stood in the yard. Her screaming was muffled by her palms and she watched as her mom came racing around the side of the house with Aunt Edie close behind her. Aunt Marley was screaming from the bathroom, appearing in the window's frame and calling down to the others.

And then, everything went black.

Chapter 17

Beatrice can't stop thinking about seeing her mother last night. Maybe she should hunt down some sorcerer that is able to rewind time so she can go back and relive those few seconds over and over again until the world ends. She thinks about what her mom might be thinking of her, now. She wonders if she's worried or is watching her at this very moment. Perhaps she's silently urging her to get the hell out of here, like how she told her to last night.

Beatrice should listen. She should pack up her things right this instant and leave. But there is something inside of her that is pulling at her to stay, a magnet yanking her into these walls and bidding her not to leave. She has to find out what happened to these girls. If she doesn't, who else will? Are they all a part of the same conspiracy as Beatrice's dead family members or are they separated? Also, staying could mean seeing her mom again and there isn't a single thing in the world that would make Beatrice pass that opportunity.

"I don't know what to do," Beatrice tells her plush elephant, holding him in her hands. "Why can't you speak and tell me all the answers?"

Beatrice jumps at the sound of her ringing phone. She reaches over, fumbling for it sitting on her nightstand. Early morning sun filters through the windows on the other side of the room, slowly easing Beatrice into more of a consciousness. She blinks at the screen to find Clara's name staring back at her. She clears her voice from sleep and puts the phone to her ear.

"Hey, Clara," she answers casually, trying her best to sound like the girl staying at a bed and breakfast rather than a black hole in the shape of a gothic house.

"Hey," she says back, rustling going on behind her somewhere. "Just thought I would check in with you again. Our last conversation yesterday was cut short."

Clara's kids are more needy than babies—something Beatrice would never tell Clara, of course, but it's a very well observation that anyone would be able to make from meeting them. Yet, people still wonder why Beatrice is very firm on never having children. Ever.

"That's okay," Beatrice tells her. "I have a lot going on over here, too."

"So work is going well?" Clara sounds more attentive today and Beatrice can hear her sit down. "You're getting it all worked out?"

"Yes," Beatrice says honestly—because she is. The movers for the antique furniture from the attic are supposed to be coming this weekend to deliver it to Trinkets and Treasures back in New York. The only other work she's been slacking off on is the house renovations but Clara doesn't even know about that part. "I'm shipping it all out this weekend and Declan is covering the cost so luckily, you won't have to worry about me paying out the ass for that."

"Beatrice, I told you I would be more than happy to give you some money." Clara's voice grows serious. "Your mom would have my head on a stick if she found out that you were struggling the way you are and I wasn't doing anything to help."

"You have helped me. A lot," Beatrice says truthfully. She can feel her teeth starting to ache with the next lie rolling off her tongue. She keeps mentally reminding herself that she doesn't have much other options but she knows that's not the entire truth, either. "I don't need help. I'm completely fine."

"That's a lie and you know it."

Beatrice needs to change the subject. Clara has done what she could for her since Beatrice left this house all those years ago. She would feel terrible taking money out of her sons' mouths just because she made the bad decision to room with someone who left her with the very expensive rent in a New York City apartment.

"I saw Mom last night." The words escape Beatrice's mouth before she can even attempt to stop them. But, maybe it's a good thing she couldn't. Maybe talking about it will make it more real than the few seconds she had with her mother. It's not like she can talk about any of this with Aunt Edie. "Not in person, obviously. I think I dreamed it."

"What would make you dream that?" Clara asks. "I thought you stopped having dreams of that night."

"It wasn't of that night, though," Beatrice responds, Halloween night flickering through her mind once again like a candle in a jack-o-lantern. "She talked to me for a little bit and then I woke up."

"How did that make you feel?" Clara sounds like a therapist now, something she often sounded like without even trying. She has always been genuinely concerned for Beatrice's wellbeing… which makes lying to her that much more difficult.

"Good," Beatrice says honestly. "I think I needed it."

"Well, that's good," Clara agrees. "It beats you waking up in the middle of the night screaming."

"I think anything would beat that," Beatrice mumbles, her mind wandering off to the weird dreams she's had here lately about the twins and Grandpa Hugh and her sleepwalking habits coming back to her like a toxic ex-boyfriend. "Anyways, how are you doing? How are the boys?"

"They're boys," Clara grumbles. "Sometimes I think about getting pregnant again just so I can have another girl around here."

"Are you forgetting about your wife?" Beatrice snorts.

"She doesn't count," Clara jokes. "She acts more like them than she does a grown woman."

"I miss you," Beatrice tells her after a beat of silence. She thinks that it might make up for her sneaking behind Clara's back by being here but it actually makes her heart ache even more. She has a lot of kissing up to do once she leaves here.

"I miss you, too," Clara chirps. "But after this weekend, you'll be back and we'll figure out where you go from there."

The door to Beatrice's room gently eases open and Aunt Edie sticks her head inside. Beatrice stiffens, clearing her throat.

"Listen, I'm going to have to call you back," Beatrice says into the phone, trying to make her voice quiet enough for Aunt Edie not to hear but it doesn't look like she's planning on giving her proper privacy.

"Okay, no problem," Clara responds unknowingly. "I love you, be safe. It's a crazy world out there."

"I love you too." Beatrice hangs up the phone and sits up more in her bed, surprised that Aunt Edie isn't sticking to her stubborn ways and waiting for Beatrice to make the first move. Silence has been bubbling between them since their fight about Marilyn and the twins the other day. It's been awkward around the house. Beatrice has been doing a lot of walking on eggshells and Aunt Edie has pretty much been MIA.

"Good. You're up." Aunt Edie makes her way into the bedroom without an invitation. She's wearing an emerald green cape thing with a black jumpsuit, chunky gold jewelry to accent it all. "We need to discuss something."

Beatrice tosses her phone to the foot of her bed and swings her legs over the side. "If we are going to do more fighting, can I at least have coffee first?"

"Oh, darling, I didn't come up here to argue with you," Aunt Edie assures, sounding somehow sympathetic. "I've realized that there really is no point in arguing with someone that won't see outside of their own narrow mind."

Beatrice glares at her. "I don't have a narrow mind. I have every right to be mad. Marilyn took Juniper and Jax into the woods that day and who knows what happened? You might."

"You honestly believe that I wouldn't do anything if I knew what happened to those children?"

Beatrice studies the look on her aunt's face. She can't fully say that Aunt Edie is cold hearted enough to let something bad happen to Juniper and Jax. She can't one hundred percent guarantee that Marilyn hurt them and that Aunt Edie knew about it. But the fact that she knew Marilyn was in the Jungle with them the last day they were alive speaks volumes.

"I don't know what anyone is capable of anymore." Beatrice walks over to her dresser to run a brush through her hair. "If you didn't come up here to fight, then what do you want?"

"There's been a suicide."

The words catch Beatrice off-guard and she snaps her head around to look at her aunt. She isn't sure why, but she quickly runs through the broken family tree, trying to discover which one of her family members have died next. But then she remembers that she and Aunt Edie are the last two apples.

"That man that lived in that house in the woods," Aunt Edie goes on, rubbing her hands together, her rocky rings clunking against each other. "Apparently he shot himself late yesterday evening."

Beatrice slowly sets her brush back down on her dresser, letting her mind race with thoughts buzzing so hard that her head might just explode. She could cover her entire childhood room with brain chunks and blood. Talk about a renovation.

Yesterday's conversation with Fred gave Beatrice a huge chunk of information about something that she has wondered about for years and years. She might not know the full details about what happened to Jax and Juniper the day they died, but she knows Marilyn was with them when they did. She fled the scene in a panic and Fred buried them for a proper burial. He kept his mouth shut when Silver Creek was rocked by their disappearances *and* when Beatrice and the rest of her family came flooding the woods to find them. Leaving his house with Xander yesterday, part of Beatrice did wonder whether what Fred told her was honest. There was a chance that he was bullshitting her the entire time. But if he killed himself over the guilt of what he knew, it would all make sense for it to be true.

It was no secret how startled Beatrice was at that newest revelation. It was no secret that Beatrice felt hatred toward that man for never giving any of them a piece of mind for this many years. Guilt is an odd thing for a human to carry. It has such sharp teeth, little daggers that will eat at you until you break. It chews through your skin and then your flesh until it is able to gnaw at your bones. And then, there's nothing left anymore after that. Guilt wins most of the time and in Fred's case, it was victorious.

"Why aren't you saying anything?" Aunt Edie demands when Beatrice doesn't speak.

Beatrice looks at her. "What do you want me to say? I didn't know him."

"I suppose I'm waiting for you to accuse me of murdering him cold," Aunt Edie says dramatically. "That is what I'm capable of, right? You think I'm some cold-hearted murderer who didn't care about Jax and Juniper and let them die?"

"I never said they were dead."

"They're dead."

Beatrice swallows, remaining emotionless. She knows Aunt Edie can feed off people's emotions, able to manipulate them when she senses weakness. "Sure, that's a thought we've both had for years but their bodies were never found."

"I'm aware," Aunt Edie snaps at her. "Anyway, darling, I have a garden club meeting today so if you're going to be here, please keep the noise down."

She glides out of the room and Beatrice shuts the door loudly behind her and rolls her eyes. She plants herself back down on her bed, holding her face in her hands. How can she attend a garden meeting with all this? Fred killed himself because of what he told Beatrice yesterday. She needs to talk herself out of feeling bad for him but she is already failing miserably. Sure, Fred was already carrying such grief with him during all these years but if it wasn't for her showing up at his house and pulling his past out of him, it wouldn't feel fresh. He wouldn't have felt the need to introduce the tip of his gun to the roof of his mouth. Beatrice would be ignorant to believe that she didn't somehow play a hand in this man's demise. The thought alone sends a mess of knots through her stomach, tightening together like thick ropes and pulling at her heartstrings.

After changing into a stained Nirvana shirt and ripped black jeans, the piece of paper tucked under the jewelry box on the dresser catches Beatrice's eye. She stares at it for a long time, considering opening it up after fifteen years. It was given to her by some lady at the front door before the Halloween Beatrice left. The lady showed up with a blond bob and a pencil skirt, handing Beatrice a piece of paper with information on grief counseling offered here in town. Beatrice asked her mother about what that was and her mom explained it was for people to seek help when a loved one dies. She was so mad that some lady was trying to advise a nine-year-old to seek therapy but now that Beatrice thinks about it, she should have went. It could have stopped a long chain of PTSD Beatrice now lives with. She snatches it off the dresser and stuffs it into the back pocket of her jeans.

Beatrice makes her way down to the kitchen for a huge mug of coffee. She listens to Aunt Edie greeting Marilyn and Ruth at the front door, inviting them inside. Beatrice peeks over her shoulder at Marilyn, setting her jaw back. Her wispy white hair framing her face makes Beatrice want to tug at it until it falls out, leaving her bald. Her navy-blue pantsuit looks ridiculous to wear for a freaking *garden club* meeting. And those white kitten heels might even be sharp enough for Beatrice to drive it through her temple.

Stop it, Beatrice, she wills herself to stop thinking such vile thoughts about another human. She is unable to stop herself, though. She has so much anger pent up after this long, that she feels like she needs to rid herself of it somehow. If thinking terrible things about the lady who played a major part for what happened to the twins helps her just a little bit, then so be it. Marilyn is just as guilty as Fred is for what happened to Jax and Juniper, yet here she is walking around town like she doesn't have a care in the world. What does she do before going to sleep at night? Does she think about what happened? Does she even care about the terrible thing she played a part in? Or does she sleep soundlessly with a fluffy pillow and a heavy blanket?

"Beatrice, hi," Marilyn greets her as she comes waltzing into the kitchen, wearing that plastered smile Beatrice wants to swat off her face. "It's a pleasure to see you again."

Beatrice manages a tight smile because she doesn't trust herself to speak yet.

"Are you going to be joining us for garden club today?" Marilyn roots through the cupboard for her own mug, making her way to the coffee machine on the counter. She acts as though she's some news anchor in the break room, chatting it up to a colleague. "Your aunt, Ruth, and I are always taking in new members."

"Gardening isn't really my thing," Beatrice answers. "The whole digging things up and then burying them isn't my style."

"Well, I suppose it's not for everybody," Marilyn replies over the sound of the coffee sloshing into the mug.

"But it's your thing, isn't it?" she says as equally dry as she is blunt.

Marilyn eyes her but doesn't let her fake smile fade. "Pardon?"

"The whole burying things, thing," Beatrice says. "You're good at that stuff? I guess you'd have to be if you're a co-president of a garden club, huh?"

Marilyn seems to relax a little, laughing. "Of course, yes. I'm nowhere near as talented as Edie, though. That woman has a gift, I'll tell you."

"You know, that garden out there wasn't always tended by Aunt Edie." Beatrice manages to talk low enough for Aunt Edie and Ruth to not hear from the parlor as they start moving furniture around for the other members that will be here soon. "My mom and my Aunt Marley used to take care of it when I was growing up here. Aunt Marley is the one that had the twins."

"The twins?" She shows no sign of recognition. She has a poker face that Beatrice wants to punch.

"Juniper and Jax," she clarifies, knowing damn well Marilyn is aware of who she's talking about. She had already mentioned them in conversation before but now she wants to play stupid?

"Ah. Yes, I do believe your aunt mentioned something about that," Marilyn speaks, remaining casual. She glances at the coffee machine, drumming her manicured nails against the countertop, impatient. "They took lovely care of it. I'm impressed."

"Looks like people are arriving," Ruth says excitedly from the foyer, peering through the front windows out into the driveway.

"It's just such a shame what happened to them, don't you think?" Beatrice pushes, feeling like she's stepping on Marilyn's throat with no intention of letting up. "I mean, they were only six. They didn't even get to reach double digits."

"Tragedy truly is something no one can explain," Marilyn agrees, fixing her eyes on Beatrice. "I guess that's what happens when you open Pandora's box."

Beatrice squints. "Pandora's box?"

"You know, the box that was opened that released every cruel curse?"

"I know what it is but I don't think that's to blame for… well, *anything*," Beatrice says. "That's why they call it a myth."

"I better go." Marilyn strides through the kitchen when her coffee is finished. "It was nice chatting with you." She heads into the foyer, greeting the other ladies spilling into Ashwood with cheek kisses and smiles.

Beatrice doesn't even realize that Aunt Edie is marching her way until she's right in front of her, scowling.

"What do you think you're doing?" Aunt Edie hisses at her, clenching her jaw so tight that it looks locked.

"What do you mean?"

"Don't play me like a fool, young lady." She points a finger in her face. "You are to not question my guests when they are in this house. You do not live here anymore. This is not your home. You are a guest here, too, so I will not put up with your antics."

"I don't know what antics you think I'm trying to pull." Beatrice plays innocent, simply because she knows it will piss Aunt Edie off enough. Maybe then her true colors will start to show regularly and everyone a part of this stupid garden club meeting will see her for who she really is. Maybe Beatrice will, too. "I was just making small talk with one of your friends. I didn't realize that was a crime."

"You used to be a lot better at lying." Aunt Edie marches back into the parlor, putting on a pretend smile for her guests and ushering them into the room, everyone starting to find their seats.

Beatrice rolls her eyes. Whatever. She has more important things to be taking care of, anyway. Leaning against the counter, Beatrice pulls the ancient advertisement for the grief group out of her pocket. The style is very 90's but it includes a location and time slots. The green digital numbers on the microwave inform Beatrice she has forty minutes until the next meeting—if this thing is even up to date. It's not like she *needs* some group of strangers sharing their thoughts and feelings about their dead loved ones but what could it hurt? Her entire family is dead and she is left with an aunt who is starting to hate her more and more by the day. And now, she seems to be the cause of a suicide to a man she doesn't even know. Sitting in a church basement with other people who might relate doesn't seem like the worst decision she's ever made.

After downing the rest of her coffee and checking online for details about the modern-day times for this group, Beatrice calls up the taxi service to come pick her up. She doesn't want to intrude on her aunt's little garden club meeting to bother her for her car. Plus, she needs to stop relying on Aunt Edie as much as she can. She rinses her mouth out with Listerine and by the time she's done, the dirty yellow cab is pulling up the round driveway.

Even after fifteen years, the grief group is still running in the church basement on Whipple Boulevard, as her online search confirmed. The same flyer that's been sitting in Beatrice's room after all this time is the same one hanging on a bulletin board inside the front doors. Beatrice steps out of the way of a middle-aged man brushing by her to get to the basement stairs. She rubs the back of her neck, debating on whether she should leave. This is stupid, isn't it? What good is this going to do for her—
"Are you here for the grief group?" a voice interrupts her negative decision making and Beatrice jumps. It's the same lady that showed up at her doorstep all those years ago. It's as though time in Silver Creek simply doesn't exist. She still has a blond bob but today, she's wearing black slacks and an ugly brown blazer. She has almond shaped eyes and two lines on either side of her lips because it seems like she never stops softly smiling. Some people might find that warm and inviting but Beatrice finds it weird and strange. "Sorry, didn't mean to scare you."
"No, you're fine," Beatrice assures. "I'm just naturally jumpy."
"So?" the woman asks after a few seconds. She steps out of the way of a few more people filing in through the church's double doors, not one of them walking through to the main room, but heading for the basement. "Grief group?"
Beatrice glances at the double doors. She should just leave here and not look back. She can search for more clues on the missing girls and how Fred's suicide case seems to be going. But instead, she finds herself nodding and following a heavyset old lady down the steps.
The church basement has a pretty low ceiling. A ping-pong table is shoved to the side, along with a few round tables. Plastic chairs are placed in a circle in the middle of the room near a small table for coffee and doughnuts. Beatrice feels like she just walked into the wrong room. She thought this was a group for grief, not an AA meeting.
"Okay, everyone, if you could find a seat," the blond lady announces to the members and everyone begins doing as they're told. "As most of you already know, my name is Mandy. And it seems like we have a few

new people to welcome today."

Beatrice ducks her head and plants herself down in a chair between an old man with nose hair peeking out of his nostrils and a young girl that looks around her age, her fingers flying over the keyboard of her iPhone. Beatrice feels a little relaxed seeing another person her age here. It makes her feel far less special for experiencing such trauma this early in life.

"Okay, who wants to start us off?" Mandy looks around the group, crossing her long legs in front of her. No one says anything. "Again, this is a safe place. Everyone here knows what you are going through. You don't even have to talk for a long time. Anything you want to say, you can say."

"Okay, I'll start." The girl next to Beatrice tucks her phone into the pocket of her sweatshirt. She runs a hand through her choppy black hair and slouches in her seat. "But I think what I say here might offend, you know, the big guy upstairs."

"In what way?" Mandy looks genuinely curious, leaning over her twiggy thighs.

"Well, ever since my mom died, I hear her," the girl explains, only talking to Mandy as though the rest of the group doesn't exist. "Sometimes it's the middle of the night. I can hear her humming and rustling around in the kitchen. It's as clear as day. And I don't know any of your guys' religious beliefs, but I think it's her ghost."

Beatrice shifts in the chair, ducking her head again to create a curtain of hair on either side of her face. She eyes the doors on the other side of the dingy church basement room. Is it too late to leave?

"A ghost?" The man that walked by Beatrice earlier speaks up on the other side of the circle, next to Mandy.

The girl nods her head. "Yes sir."

He turns to the leader, shoving his glasses further up his nose. "Mandy, I come to this group because I like to relate to other people who have lost family members or people that are close to them. Not to gather around and tell ghost stories."

"Yes, but you can relate to her," Mandy points out. "Usually, when someone we love unexpectedly passes, we find ourselves searching for answers in a number of ways. Last week, you told us that you went rooting through your wife's belongings for any sign of why she might have been where she was when she died." She gestures to the young lady next to Beatrice. "This female is searching for answers, too."

"But I'm not making this up," the girl remarks. "I've heard her."

"Are you sure you aren't dreaming it?" A nice-looking lady asks, yarn gathered in her lap, her meaty fingers holding a crochet hook. "After my brother died, I woke up all the time in the middle of the night thinking I heard him yelling for me in the yard. It went on for three months. I'd be sound asleep, and then I would hear him. So, I would get up night after night and go to the front door. But he was never there. I spent so much time believing that he was, believing that he needed me. But he was already gone. And that was something I had to come to terms with or else I'd never sleep again."

"I could smell my uncle after he died," a man says on the other side of the girl seated next to Beatrice. He looks like he's in his mid-forties, his fingers threaded together in his lap. "Months after he passed, I just kept getting these random whiffs of his cologne. It didn't go away for weeks."

"It's her ghost," the girl says firmly. "I'm not sleeping before it happens so I'm not dreaming." She sits up straighter and Beatrice can feel her growing more and more defensive. "But I get up and by the time I get to the kitchen, everything stops. But I can *smell* her." She glances at the man next to her. "Just like you did. She had this cheap perfume she always wore. And I can smell it so clearly."

"As I often say to everyone here, we do not degrade anyone's religious beliefs," Mandy warns. "Most of you know, I have a wide variety of beliefs when it comes to the afterlife. And often times, I hear stories from people who communicate with the dead and it happens in all sorts of forms."

"In what ways?" Beatrice asks. She realizes it's her voice when she receives a few glances from the other members. She sinks in the chair, waiting for Mandy's answer.

"Well, a lot of the time older people will admit to seeing their dead loved ones shortly before they die themselves," she explains, looking happy Beatrice was bold enough to ask a question. Does she even recognize her? Does anyone here know who Beatrice really is? None of them seem like they do. Or maybe they don't care. "Usually, ghosts or spirits or whatever you want to call them don't speak to us until it's our time to join them."

The statement makes Beatrice grow faint. She thinks about her dead mother and the conversation they had last night about how Beatrice needs to leave Ashwood as soon as possible. That doesn't have anything to do with what Mandy is saying, though, right? Her mother is not a ghost, so it technically doesn't count. Just because they spoke to each other, doesn't mean Beatrice is going to go home to her death.

"Does this resonate with you?" Mandy asks her when Beatrice doesn't respond.

"How do you differentiate a ghost and… something else?" Beatrice feels ridiculous for even asking the question but that's why they're all here. Mandy said it herself: they're searching for something following the death of a loved one.

"Like a demon?" the girl next to her asks flatly. "I hear those can be real bitches."

"Demons aren't real," the first guy speaks up again. "None of what you guys are talking about is real."

"Sir, if you degrade someone else's beliefs again, I'm going to have to ask you to leave." Mandy still wears the tiny smile across her lips and she pats the man's knee before returning her gaze to Beatrice. "It seems to me that you have experienced something of the paranormal realm, yes?"

"I don't know," she replies, shaking her hair out of her face. "Maybe. But I was raised to believe that these things in my house aren't ghosts. They're different."

"In what way?"

"That's what I'm trying to figure out," Beatrice snaps, growing impatient with the lack of information she's failing to receive. "They seem like ghosts. They make noises in the night, and they appear and disappear but they're… they're not always nice. But that's so different from how I knew them when they were alive. They've become these… *things*. House Things, if you will. And they stick to certain corners and places of the house and they act in ways I don't remember them acting when they were living. They do things that I don't think normal ghosts would. And then there are some that I know nothing about and don't even see them all that much anymore." She folds her arms over her chest, hearing herself ramble. "And my cousins are dead, and they've been haunting my dreams but I only see them there and not in real life. And I played a part in what happened to them and the guilt is literally eating me away to the point where I don't think I can take much of it anymore. That, along with the guilt of being the cause of someone killing themselves all because of what he did to those same two cousins of mine."

She looks around at the strangers, who are all staring at her with wide eyes and O-shaped mouths. None of them have been dealing with anything as bizarre as what Beatrice is going through. Perhaps it was a mistake coming here. Maybe this was a bad idea. She thought sitting in a circle with strangers might do her some good but it's turning out to confirm that she's losing her marbles.

"That does sound intriguing," the leader says with a hand to her chin. "I don't really think the term *House Things* is accurate for whatever you're experiencing but are you sure they're not ghosts?"

Beatrice feels herself deflate, her hope that someone in this group could help her out depleting. She stares into her lap. "I was told that they're not ghosts."

"Whoever told you that is lying," the girl with the short black hair whispers loudly to her.

"It's okay to be scared," the crocheting lady speaks up again, her eyes on her work. "The houses in this town have been around for a long, long time. In structures as old as the ones we have here in Silver Creek, we're all bound to bump into a ghost or two."

"Why are they here?" Beatrice leans forward a little.

She's not quite sure what to make of this. Did her family tell her that the things in their house were just *House Things* so she wouldn't get scared? Have they simply been dead people this whole time, wandering the grounds as ghost versions of themselves? Beatrice has spent her entire life thinking of them as other forms of paranormal entities. And what about Lila's Polaroid photos? She named one of them *The thing in the garden* and another *The noise behind the barn.* And what about Uncle Eli walking the ceilings? Those all seem too strange to simply be ghosts.

"There's plenty of reasons why a spirit might not move on," Mandy answers smoothly. Her voice is like honey. "Most people believe they have unfinished business they need tending to before they cross over. But a lot of the time, spirits either don't know they're dead or they're stuck on a loop of playing the day they died over and over again."

"Why?" A middle-aged man wearing a baseball cap asks in a gruff voice. "The whole loop, thing. Why?"

"Think of it as a glitch," Mandy replies after giving it a thought. "The death system is like any other system and there is always bound to be some sort of glitch."

"How does a glitch get fixed?" Beatrice demands impatiently.

Mandy shrugs helplessly. "That is something I cannot answer. I don't think anyone really can."

"Wait, aren't you that girl who's living in Ashwood now?" Someone asks but Beatrice doesn't know which one of them it is.

"Excuse me, I have to go." Beatrice gets up from the chair so abruptly, she sends it a few feet back toward the white brick wall. She marches out of the main church basement room   and up the steps, pushing herself out the double doors ahead.

"Why did you even come?" Beatrice mumbles, tearing up the flyer from her pocket and letting the pieces float into a nearby trashcan. She runs her hands up and down the length of her face, a newspaper-stand several feet away catching her eye. An old picture of Fred covers the front of the magazine, the headline reading: *Suicide in Silver Creek.* She takes out her phone to once again call a cab.

$$\cdot \!=\!\!\!\Rightarrow\!\!\otimes\!\!\Leftarrow\!\!=\!\cdot$$

Chapter 18

Once Beatrice returns to Ashwood, she climbs out of the cab and hands the driver a few limp bills—despite still not having the luxury to be spending all this money on getting rides. At this point, she doesn't really have the mind capacity to think about money. Her thoughts have been taken over by Ashwood's status.

"Xander," Beatrice greets her friend when she finds him climbing the porch steps.

"Beatrice." He whips around, clearly caught off guard. He puts a hand on his chest. "You scared the shit out of me. Where were you?"

"I was in town." She's going to not tell him about her little failure at a group therapy meeting. If she went and everything went smoothly and she left there feeling like a star, that's one thing. But she hurried out of there like the church was burning down, eager to get away from those people and conversation. She'd rather not go around telling others about it. "What are you doing here?"

"We never got to do the trim yesterday for the hallway," he reminds her. "I wasn't sure if you were interested in getting that done today or not since your aunt has people over. If the answer is no, don't worry about it."

"No," she answers, starting toward the side yard. "Not that I'm busy for the entire day but I have other matters I want to check in with before then."

"Like what?" They start across the yard, Xander wandering with her blindly and struggling to keep up with her stride.

"Fred killed himself last night," Beatrice tells him quietly, as though sharing the news of his death is going to rock Silver Creek in ways it hasn't been rocked before. Perhaps she feels odd speaking about a death that doesn't have to do with one of her family members. It almost seems foreign.

Xander's eyes widen. "Wait, are you serious?"

"I wouldn't joke about something like this."

"How do you know?"

"Aunt Edie told me this morning and it's all in the papers," Beatrice answers, shoving her fists into the pockets of her jacket. "And that was before we almost got into another fight about everything she knows about the twins going missing."

It feels funny to claim them as missing, when Beatrice now knows for a fact that they're dead—not even buried six feet under. She mentally curses at herself for not getting the proper location of the bodies from Fred before he offed himself. Sure, it wouldn't have changed his fate, but Beatrice could finally put Juniper and Jax to rest the way they deserve after everything.

"Holy shit," he mumbles in disbelief. He watches his feet as they walk, now maneuvering through the trees of the Jungle. "Maybe we should've stayed with him."

"No." Beatrice turns that idea down and then thinks about it. Maybe he has a point. If they had stayed, maybe he would still be alive. Maybe they would have left things on better terms. But then again, she can't entirely blame him for what he did. "He did nothing about the twins. He never gave their own mother the closure she needed. She died without that knowledge and that is something I would never forgive anyone for. Not even myself."

"I understand."

They keep walking through the woods, not saying much. The late October day is cold and there seems to be a lot more naked trees around than there was yesterday. The forest floor has become a sea of autumn leaves. Beatrice keeps glancing up ahead, waiting to see police standing around yellow caution tape with the sound of crackling walkie-talkies floating through the air but the distance remains only of nature.

"So, you know about my aunt's garden club?" Beatrice decides to break the non-awkward silence because she has found it can never be awkward with Xander around.

He nods his head, glancing at her. "She's been doing it for years."

"How come your nana isn't a proud member?" Beatrice asks sarcastically. Anyone in their right mind would stay as far away from Ashwood as they possibly could. Living down the street is close enough. "Sitting around with other old ladies talking about trees and flowers isn't her style?"

Xander laughs. "Not entirely. Plus, she's never really gotten along with Edie, it seems."

Beatrice never knew this. "What do you mean?"

"I don't know any details but it's always seemed like the two of them never truly got along," Xander explains to her. "I don't think they have some infamous feud with each other, but they've kept their distance for years."

"Hmm." Beatrice tries to stop her paranoid mind from venturing off into the mountains of questions she has piling in her head, but she can't help it.

It seems like every piece of information she's learning lately has something to do with things she knows nothing about. It's also no surprise that Aunt Edie keeps coming up as vital parts of all of these things, a key member to everything that happens around here. Beatrice hates herself for it, but she finds herself wondering why Aunt Edie never died all those years ago along with the rest of the adults. She would have, though, if she was in Ashwood the night Beatrice's mom and Aunt Marley were eventually killed. Right?

Beatrice frowns, the image of her mother from last night appearing in her mind again. That faint smile, the smell of her familiar perfume that would now be considered outdated. She can't complain too much about coming back to Ashwood and being hit with all these questions, because she *has* gotten a few answers since returning. She knows now what happened to Juniper and Jax—even though the truth is brutal and gut-wrenching, she has answers.

"There's something I forgot to tell you, Beatrice," Xander says, bringing Beatrice back into reality. "About that game of hide and seek we were talking about yesterday."

"What is it?"

"When I was hiding in your aunt's wardrobe, there was this weird stuff on the inside of the door," Xander explains, glancing at her from the side. He's walking with his head hanging low, his shoulders high, like he's paranoid of being heard by someone who shouldn't hear this. Like he's being stalked by something in the trees, a creature lurking in the shadows.

"Weird stuff?" Beatrice echoes in confusion. "That could be a number of things."

"Yeah, but they were carved on the inside," Xander explains. "The inside of the doors. I could feel them when I was trying to get out, when I was looking for where one door ended and the other one began."

"What were they?"

"I don't know," Xander admits. "It was so long ago, but I don't think they were words. And if they were, they weren't etched in English."

Suddenly, Beatrice is hit with a memory that has been long since forgotten, stashed away in the back of her mind like a shoe lost in a closet. She remembers when she was six and it was Christmas Eve. Uncle Eli died two years ago and in a year, Grandpa Hugh would be next. Beatrice sat in the window of Aunt Edie's bedroom, once the holiday festivities ended downstairs. She was supposed to be getting ready for bed, tucked under the blankets in hopes Santa brought her something pleasant the following morning. But, Aunt Edie told her to meet her up here once they were done downstairs.

"There you are, my darling," Aunt Edie said as she crept into her bedroom, gently shutting the door behind her. She wore a white and red velvet robe, looking like a skinnier version of Mrs. Claus. "We don't have long. Your mother is going to be looking for you."

"What did you want me for, Aunt Edie?" Beatrice asked, taking her eyes off the falling snow outside. The thick snowflakes were blanketing the entire yard and all of Ashwood, sticking to everything and promising a white Christmas for tomorrow.

"I wanted to give you an early Christmas gift," Aunt Edie said, the Christmas music on the record player still playing downstairs. "And I knew your mother would throw a cow if she saw me give you this."

Beatrice perked up, stepping away from the icy window and eagerly rubbing her hands together. Her mother had always tried to teach her not to be greedy but Beatrice couldn't help it. She was a six-year-old, it was in her blood. She patiently waited as Aunt Edie opened the double doors to her bulky wooden wardrobe pressed up against the floral-patterned wallpaper. Aunt Edie's furry robes and boas hung in a line across the bar in all their glory.

"Now remember, you have to keep this just between us," Aunt Edie warned, reaching inside of the wardrobe for the wolf-fur coat dangling off one of the hangers. "I got this for you."

Beatrice's jaw dropped as she reached out to run her fingers through the fur. "Aunt Edie, I can't believe this!"

"I figured you might want your own," Aunt Edie explained, taking it off the hanger to wrap around Beatrice's tiny frame. "You're always coming in here to wear some of my fur coats. It only seemed fitting for you to have your own."

"I love it!" Beatrice slipped her arms through the sleeves and twirled around in it, the coat hanging all the way to her feet. "How do I look?"

"Marvelous, darling, simply marvelous," Aunt Edie encouraged, clapping her hands together as a one-woman audience. She gestured to the body mirror next to the wardrobe. "See for yourself."

Beatrice did as she was told and hugged the coat tighter around herself. Her eyes slid up and down her body in approval. Now she can walk around the house just like Aunt Edie, wearing fur, something her mother hated and claims is *cruel*—whatever that is supposed to mean. Beatrice's eyes flickered to the wide-open wardrobe doors, jagged marks etched into the inside of the wood. Beatrice didn't think twice about it. She gazed back at her reflection in all her luxury, Aunt Edie smiling proudly from behind her.

"Earth to Beatrice?" Xander is now waving his palm in front of Beatrice's face. "You all right? Seems like you just visited the twilight zone or something, Beatrice."

"You're right, there was something on the inside of the wardrobe," Beatrice agrees, trying to force her mind into remembering what was written but it fails. What was it? Was it anything of importance or was it Uncle Eli's doing, completely off the wall and losing his mind? "I remember seeing something, too, I just don't know what."

"Oh, shit." Xander gapes forward at the shack that has now popped up in front of them. They've been walking for this long already?

Beatrice follows his gaze. It all does look like a crime scene of some sort, straight out of the movies. Tape blocks off any chance of entrance and there are a few police officers chatting outside of it, women wearing clear plastic over their bodies coming in and out with items in baggies. There's a photographer on the site too, snapping photo after photo with a reporter standing next to her, chattering into her phone.

"Should we say something?" Xander asks Beatrice in a hushed voice.

"Like what?"

"I dunno," Xander admits. "But you were the last one to see him alive before he…"

Beatrice snaps her head to look at him. "Yeah, so wouldn't that make me look like it's all my fault? With my luck, they'd end up retracting their statement on it being a suicide and turn it into a murder investigation or something."

"But you could tell them what he told you," Xander urges, making eye contact with her. "I know you think of him as a monster for letting what happened, happen, but these cops are going to paint their own theory of him."

Beatrice thinks about what he's saying. He might have a point. Silver Creek created a version of Fred that wasn't ever proven to be true. He was sued for false allegations against him and when no evidence was found, the residents of the town took it upon themselves to take matters into their own hands. They burned his house down with him inside of it. Fred moved out here to get away from everyone and everything, witnessing something so terrifying as two dead children in the woods, that he tried showing the world he wasn't the monster everyone was making him out to be. He buried Jax and Juniper in hopes that he wouldn't think of himself the way other people thought of him.

Now that he's dead, it is only a matter of time until the newspapers start saying that he must have killed himself because of what he did to his neighbor. That he couldn't live with the guilt of touching a girl that young, being listed as a sex offender.

"I'll say something," Beatrice decides. "Stay here."

She makes her way around the last chunk of trees until she reaches the two cops chatting to each other outside of the shack. She clears her throat to make herself known, giving a tiny wave to the female cop as if to say *We're on the same team.*

"Hi," Beatrice speaks when neither of them greet her first. "My name is Beatrice Millstone. I live on the other side of the woods."

"This is a crime scene, ma'am," the heavyset balding cop with pasty white skin says to her. Beatrice hates to admit it but he looks like every stereotypical cop in every cartoon show she's ever watched. The only thing missing is a donut and coffee in each of his hands. "You're not allowed back here."

"I saw Fred yesterday," Beatrice admits before they try hauling her off. "I don't know if that is relevant or not, but I was here."

The female cop has dark skin and wavy brown hair pulled into a bun at the nape of her neck. She reaches into the back pocket for her notepad. "You said your name was Beatrice Millstone?"

"Your family is a part of that Ashwood curse, right?" The cop points a chubby finger at her, his lips parting and making him kind of look like the Pillsbury dough boy.

Beatrice winces at the question but she manages to nod her head. "Yeah, I guess. But I just thought I'd let you guys know that I was here if you have any questions about what happened."

"We're ruling this a suicide," the female cop informs her, her gold nameplate reading *Gomez.* "There was a note found with the deceased."

"Gomez," the first cop snaps at her, his name being *Hudson.* "We can't just go giving this kind of information to random people."

"Who cares?" Gomez rolls her hazel eyes. "It's going in the paper today anyway. Everyone already knows about it."

Hudson sighs and looks back at Beatrice, adjusting his belt as his large belly hangs over the front of it. "Thanks for the information, but it's not needed."

"He was carrying a secret," Beatrice sputters.

The cops exchange a glance with each other before looking at Beatrice, waiting for her to continue.

"I came here yesterday to ask him about my cousins." It might be straying away from the whole truth but it's not like she's taking the stand. A little white lie to the police hardly counts as obstruction of justice. "They disappeared years ago in these woods. Being back in my childhood home made me want to find out what happened to them."

"Are you talking about the Millstone twins?" Gomez asks her, shooting another glance at her partner. "That case was never shut?"

Beatrice blinks. The woman looks more around her age than she does around her colleague's, meaning she could have been just a few years older than Beatrice when the twins were taken by Marilyn. "It shouldn't have been. No one ever found out what happened."

"Hmm." Gomez tucks her notepad back into her pocket. "Because when I first started, I took up some cold case files that were at the station. I remember hearing about the Millstone twins when I was a kid. But that wasn't in the system as unsolved—"

"Are you going somewhere with this?" Hudson snaps at Beatrice, completely shutting Gomez down. "This secret that Fred seemed to be carrying?"

Beatrice licks her lips, the truth on the tip of her tongue. Gomez stares at the ground, looking confused and scolded. Beatrice could tell them what happened, about how Fred was the one who watched the twins die in front of Marilyn and how he took it upon himself to bury them. Their case would be solved. But it now seems like their case as a whole was never a priority. If it was, wouldn't it still be among all the other cold cases in the system?

"He told me he never hurt that girl," Beatrice says honestly. "And he remembers seeing another girl running through here from Ashwood at some point and I think it was one of the many missing women that have not yet been found."

Hudson now looks bored. His face falls, like a child getting an apple for trick-or-treat instead of candy. "That's it?"

Beatrice nods her head. "It's interesting. I've noticed way too many posters around town for missing women. But every time I do research, there doesn't seem to be a lead of any kind. Don't you think that's a little odd?"

"What are you saying?" Hudson folds his arms over his belly, hanging his head to the side. "You saying that the police department here in Silver Creek don't know how to do their jobs? That some little girl like you can do it better?"

"No, it's just disappointing for the families of those women," Beatrice fires back with a shrug. "I know that if it were my sister or daughter or friend, I would be doing everything I could to find out what happened."

"That's the thing, little lady," Hudson says. "Those girls didn't have anyone looking for them. Not a lot of people, anyway. It's kind of hard to build a case around girls that would have much rather been invisible than to be seen by the public."

With that, the cop ducks under the yellow tape to head inside, where the evidence specialists are finishing up. Gomez waits until he's out of ear reach before snatching her notepad out of her pocket.

"Sorry about my partner," she apologizes. "He's not the most professional person to work under, for obvious reasons." She begins scribbling across the paper. "But if you have any information on Fred or your cousins, please call me. I would love to hear it and hopefully put those kids to rest peacefully."

Beatrice takes the folded paper from her and holds it between her fingers. "What makes you think I know something about Juniper and Jax?"

"Because I doubt the last thing Fred told you was that he didn't touch Madeline Winthrop."

The name rings a bell for a few short seconds before Beatrice is able to put her finger on why. Madeline Winthrop. Ruth's daughter.

"What the hell do you mean *did someone push her?*" Lena demanded from the front porch of Ashwood, her arms folded over her chest and her eyebrows in the perfect shape to form a V, wrinkles slit across her forehead. "I know this might look insane to you, but no one in this house is capable of pushing my mother out a window."

Beatrice sat in the grass just below the porch, Xander by her side. They both exchanged a worried look, watching as Grammy Astrid's body was wheeled away on a gurney, tucked inside of a noisy black bag that was far too big for trash. Beatrice plucked at the blades of grass beneath her, listening to the cop speak to her mother in a low voice she couldn't pick up on.

"Wow," Xander broke the weird silence between them. He offered to go back home multiple times but Beatrice assured him that she was fine and she wouldn't mind if he stuck around a bit longer until the police left. "I hope your family does okay after this."

"Trust me, they've had a lot of practice," she mumbled.

"It's a good thing your family isn't religious," he said next, gently bumping her shoulder with his.

Beatrice looked at him. "Why?"

"Nana said that people who kill themselves don't always go to Heaven," Xander explained. "Not that she even believes in God or any kind of afterlife, really, but she heard it somewhere, Beatrice. Apparently killing yourself is a big no-no to religious folk."

Beatrice couldn't even remember the last time God or Jesus was mentioned in her house. No member of her family had ever admitted to believing in such a man. She only ever saw bibles at funerals and Xander once told her all about this stuff last year when someone visited his Nana. He informed her of the bible being a huge book filled with stories that probably never even happened, written by a bunch of old guys way back in the day that has been rewritten a million times since. So yes, apparently it was a good thing that none of them were religious, just in case. But even if they were, it wasn't like Grammy Astrid was leaving them anytime soon. Not really.

"Sorry," Xander whispered. "Am I talking too much?"

"No, I'm just thinking," she admitted, craning her neck to look at her mom and the cop over her shoulder.

"Fine," her mom was saying, shrugging, defeated. She signed some form of paper and when the cop bid her a farewell and climbed down the porch steps, Lena remained where she was, running her hands up and down her face. She scanned the front lawn and then the side. "Bea? Are you still out here?"

"I should go," Xander said, getting ready to race back down the hill and to his house. "You probably have some family stuff you need to get ready for."

"Come by tomorrow?" Beatrice asked as they both rose to their feet.

"Sure." He nodded his head and before Beatrice knew it, he was wandering back home.

Beatrice rounded the bushes surrounding the porch and gave a slight wave to her mom waiting for her outside the front door. She was almost afraid to go inside, wondering what kind of horror would be waiting for her when she crossed the threshold. She couldn't get Aunt Marley's screams out of her head when she appeared at the window after Grandma Astrid's fall. Beatrice winced at the thought, Xander no longer there to act as an anchor to ground her.

"How are you, sweetie?" her mom asked when Beatrice made her way up the porch steps. "Do you have any questions for me?"

Beatrice stared up at her in confusion. "Like what?"

"Like what you saw happen," she answered, pulling Beatrice over to the wooden bench Uncle Eli made near the turret.

Beatrice thought about watching her grandmother fall, the way everyone came rushing outside and the feeling of her heart nearly leaping out her throat. She could still hear her muffled screams behind her hands, and she shook the thought away, managing to look at her mom again. "I don't know. Why would she do that?"

Her mother leaned against the bench, the back groaning under her weight. "I don't know, honey. Some people just... handle things differently, I guess."

"Like what?" Beatrice wondered, raking her nails up and down her thigh.

"I'm guessing Grandma was going through a lot," her mother offered, her gaze drifting out into the front yard as she started to think. Her eyes were wet with tears and her cheeks were rosy. "I think Grandpa dying was a lot for her to handle. Perhaps more than we thought."

"But that was two years ago."

"And people grieve differently." She tapped her daughter's nose with the pad of her finger. "Sometimes people never fully get over it when someone dies."

Beatrice stared down at her sneakers, thinking about the instances in which she saw Grammy Astrid in leading up to today, how she caught her talking to some woman in the mirror and how she would refuse to look at her own reflection. She was so skittish and constantly losing things or scurrying around in the middle of the night or covering up the mirrors in her bathroom. It was a lot. Is that what happens to everyone when their spouse dies? Does everyone patter around their houses, their mind slowly seeping into a puddle of oblivion?

"She was crazy." Beatrice heard herself say before she could stop herself. She quickly covered her mouth with her palm and looked at her mom again. "I didn't mean to say that."

She grinned, unbothered by it. "It's okay, honey. You're not wrong. Sometimes things can drive you to go mad." She reaches up to pull out the squid necklace from out of her shirt, looped around her neck. "That is why I carry this on me at all times."

Beatrice laughed, scooting closer to her on the bench. "Why? It makes you not go crazy?"

Her mother smiled sadly and wrapped an arm around her. "I'm going to share a secret with you, Bea."

Beatrice tucked the few strands of hair that had fallen out of her ponytail behind her ears. She liked secrets just as much as she liked gifts. "Okay."

"Sometimes houses can drive you a little insane," she explained, looking down at her seriously.

Beatrice tilted her head to the side as she studied her, her eyebrows bunching together. "They can?"

Her mom nodded her head, her nostrils flaring a little, like they always did before she cried about something. She swallowed, continuing. "They're more than just structures. Your Aunt Edie will tell you all about that. But, when you're in one for far too long, you go a little stir crazy."

Beatrice thought about Uncle Eli roaming Ashwood, his eyes glued to the ceiling, passing doorways and walking in and out of rooms… until he ventured to the basement and fell through the stairs.

"When you're cooped up inside for long periods of time, your mind fails to be simulated the way it needs to be," her mother went on. "You fail to get contact with the outside world. You don't speak to anyone else but the people you live with."

Beatrice's mind drifted over to Grandpa Hugh, waking in the night and pacing back and forth in his room. She thought about him screaming from night terrors and some of the mornings she found him already up in the morning, not having slept a wink.

"But there is something special about this house," Beatrice's mom said to her, her eyes flickering behind them at the house's pale yellow siding, as though it was listening. "This house in particular can make even the sanest people go mad."

"Why?" Beatrice asked, confused. "What about our house makes it crazier than other houses?"

"I'm trying to figure that out." She gently stroked her daughter's cheek with her thumb and then reached to touch the locket again. "But, that's why I wear this. It keeps me protected from all that bad stuff in there that might make me want to go a little stir crazy."

"It does?" Beatrice perked up, finding herself feeling special to be the cause of her mother feeling safe. She did so much to make Beatrice feel the same, so it was different to have the roles reversed.

Beatrice's mom nodded once more. "Yes."

"Well don't I need one?" Beatrice asked. "A locket with a picture of us inside?"

"Your mind is pure," she responded, looking like she was going to cry again but Beatrice guessed that it had to do with Grammy's death. "You'll be safe for now."

Chapter 19

"I'm confused," Xander says to Beatrice, shaking his head as he is seated on a fallen tree in the Jungle. "The girl that accused Fred of… touching her, was Ruth's daughter?"

Beatrice nods her head. Her thoughts are running at a hundred miles a minute and no matter what she does, she can't seem to get them to shut the hell up. Not only is Aunt Edie shady for living in Ashwood after all these years, the last home to all these missing girls, but now her two friends are also guilty of past sins. Marilyn was there with the twins when they died, and now come to find out, Ruth played a part in what happened to Fred, the cause of why he moved into these woods in the first place.

"This is all too much to be coincidental," Beatrice says to Xander, shaking her head in disbelief. "But I still have no freaking clue what's going on."

"Why don't you just ask your aunt about it?" Xander suggests, placing his palms next to him against the bark. "Doesn't that beat remaining in the dark about all this?"

Beatrice deadpans. "I've tried talking to her several times about stuff and she doesn't budge on anything and it's getting really annoying."

"Then what do you think we should do?" Xander wonders. "You can't exactly tell Marilyn and Ruth that you know about what they did."

"Why not?" Beatrice challenges, glancing up ahead to where Ashwood sits, the women of the garden club spilling out the front door to tend to the garden in the side yard.

"Because that's insane," Xander declares. "And you're only going to piss your aunt off even more. Do you really want to see her wrath?"

"I couldn't give a shit less about that." Beatrice starts toward the house, a new wave of determination coursing through her.

She has wasted so much time slipping into the shadows and uncovering secrets about things and people when they shouldn't have ever been hidden at all. She's had enough. Aunt Edie's friends playing parts in crimes committed around Silver Creek is the cherry on top of the cake and frankly, she doesn't think she can continue living in Ashwood if she's silent. She isn't ready to leave quite yet, though, so she has to play this carefully. She still wants to see her mom—in whatever form she can get her in, but she doesn't want to ignore her request to leave, either.

"Beatrice, where are you going?" Xander follows her, kicking up leaves in the process. "You're being irrational."

"Irrational would be biting my tongue," Beatrice says. "Besides, it's not like I'm going over there and exposing them or anything. I just want to talk."

"Well, I'll wish you luck on that." Xander casually heads for the direction of his house.

"You're not coming with me?"

"For one, garden club really isn't my thing," Xander says over his shoulder. "And for two, I'm too scared of your aunt to stick around for that."

Beatrice sighs. Fine. She can do this by herself. If it's only her, it won't look too much like an interrogation. It's just friendly chatter over some flower talk. That's completely normal in a place like this. She flicks her hair away from her face and marches across the yard, to where the group of ladies are all hovering over the bare garden, potted flowers next to them and ready to be planted, despite being the end of October.

Beatrice blinks at the polka-dotted patterned gloves and how all of the women are wearing matching sunhats, laughing together while their fresh lemonade is on a patio table next to them, their glasses sparkling in the fall sun coming and going from behind the clouds.

Aunt Edie's smile fades when she sees Beatrice approaching but she quickly pulls another forced one across her lips. "Beatrice, darling. Have you gotten your act together or are you going to bombard my guests with more *small talk*, as you liked to call it?"

Beatrice smiles back at her sarcastically. "You're right, Aunt Edie. A walk did me some good. I was hoping to join you ladies."

"We would love that," an Asian woman with shiny black hair claims from the ground. She kind of looks tipsy. What is in that lemonade?

"Yes, Beatrice." Ruth smiles encouragingly, approaching the ladies with two potted flowers in her hands. "We'd love to get to know you a little more."

Beatrice glances at Marilyn, who looks a little unsettled at the idea of her joining them but when she notices she's being stared at, she quickly nods in agreement. A sheep following the herd.

"Okay." Beatrice chirps, finding a space between the tipsy lady and a toothpick-thin one that is popping a pill under her tongue. She puts her hands on her knees, feeling like a schoolgirl again sitting with the sporty chicks at the lunch table: a place she didn't belong at in the first place.

"So, ladies, remember to leave a little space between the petals and the ground," Aunt Edie coaches as though she's been doing this for years and years. Beatrice doesn't remember her ever showing appreciation for gardening or any sort of nature, for that matter. "We're going to be adding some mulch and I want a lot. And make sure your plants are aimed toward the street, we want them getting as much light as possible."

"Shouldn't we be doing this in the summer or the spring?" Beatrice asks the tipsy woman next to her in a quiet voice. "Fall isn't the most suitable weather for gardening, right?"

"These are all flowers meant to bloom in the colder months," the lady informs, adjusting the hat on top of her head. "My name is Shelly. Shelly Chang."

Beatrice shakes her hand and then glances at the other side of the garden, where the other women have dived into private conversations, not rushing the planting of their flowers just yet. She reaches for the potted flower next to her, the yellow petals vibrant and probably able to be seen at night.

"So, how long have you been in garden club?" Beatrice asks Shelly and then remembers she has to dig a hole first. She reaches for one of the unused hoes.

"About four years now, I think?" she guesses, glancing up at the sky. "Honestly, I needed to do *something* after my son was born. Having four kids all a year apart from each other is chaos. Being a part of something with other women is keeping me sane."

Even in Ashwood? Beatrice wants to ask but she manages to hold back.

"Do you have any kids?" Shelly asks in a chipper tone, as though if Beatrice says no, she will offer her deepest condolences. She kind of seems like the type of woman to believe that the only form of success is a husband, a couple kids, and maybe a golden retriever. Oh, and the infamous white picket fence.

"God no," Beatrice blurts before stopping herself. She digs the hoe deeper into the earth, scooping out dirt and making a little mountain next to the hole. "Not that I hate kids or anything, but I'm definitely not at that point in my life yet."

It's a kind-of lie. Beatrice never dreamed of having kids. Perhaps it stems from growing up in a household where everyone died and it left this weird void in her heart that terrified her of having children or even considering the thought of having them. She once dated one of the many Kevins of the world and he analyzed her on their very first date and fed her all this information when she said that she didn't want babies. He was the type to believe a woman's purpose is reproduction.

"Trust me, you're making a smart decision," Shelly stage whispers, grinning. "If I could have waited a little bit longer to have them, I would have. But my husband, on the other hand, he has sperm made of gold."

"Oh, wow…" What the hell is she supposed to say back to that?

"Sorry if that's a little TMI, but it's the truth," Shelly goes on, shrugging one of her shoulders. "What can I say? I'm lucky."

Beatrice scans the other women again to make sure she's in the clear to ask a question that she hopes won't come off as too nosy or gain the attention of others. She softly clears her throat. "So, I heard about that man who died. Fred."

Shelly's almond shaped eyes flicker over to where Ruth is sitting on the other side of the garden. "Yes, that was very unfortunate."

"Was it?" Beatrice challenges knowingly, waiting for Shelly to look at her. "I mean, rumor has it that what he did to Ruth's daughter was pretty vile, right?"

"Yes, it was," Shelly agrees. "And even though I'm all on board for justice, that whole thing was a little odd to me." She rises to her feet and dusts the dirt off her pants. "I need my lemonade."

Beatrice quickly gets to her feet to follow her to the lemonade table further away from the other ladies. The only thing she's thirsty for is the truth. "Why do you say it was odd?"

Shelly looks confused by the question and then seems to remember what they were talking about. "I don't know, it all seemed so forced." She leans in closer. "Don't tell Ruth I'm saying this, but I never thought that Madeline was telling the truth. There was no evidence of Fred doing such a thing. And I've been to that man's house plenty of times before the whole incident happened and he was so kind and nice. I know that they say people can surprise you and whatnot but there wasn't a bone in my body that believed Fred would have done something like that. He didn't even know the Winthrops."

Beatrice absorbs the information. As much as she wants to hate him for doing what he did to Juniper and Jax, part of her can't. She feels sorry for him. For one reason or another, Madeline did what she did and it costed Fred his entire life.

"God, you probably think I'm a nut job." Shelly puts a hand to her chest as she takes a large gulp of her lemonade. "Defending a man accused of sexual assault."

"No, not at all," Beatrice quickly says. "I was too young to even know any of this was going on. I only spoke to him one time."

Shelly drums her manicured nails against her glass, glancing over at Ruth, cackling with Aunt Edie and another lady about something that probably has nothing to do with gardening. "And then there was *Edie.*"

Beatrice's stomach does a flip. There has to be something in this lemonade because Shelly is looking drunker and drunker the more she sips. Plus, she wouldn't be about to shit-talk Beatrice's aunt if she remembered that Beatrice was the niece. "What do you mean?"

"I mean that she was by Ruth's and Madeline's side during that whole thing," Shelly answers after another drink. "Which makes sense, she and Ruth have always been close. But it was like Madeline was never allowed to be left alone. Wherever she was, Edie was right there with her."

Beatrice glances at her aunt, who is showing off her planted flower, smiling broadly, like digging a hole and dropping a plant inside is something she should be getting a trophy for.

"I'm not saying I wouldn't do the same," Shelly quickly assures, flapping her hand in Beatrice's direction. "All I'm saying is that them babysitting Madeline like they were afraid of her saying something she shouldn't have was just strange."

Beatrice eyes her. "You think they might have put Madeline up to accusing Fred?"

Shelly doesn't say anything. She dodges the question by lifting her glass to her lips again, the ice cubes hitting her upper lip.

"What would they gain from that?" Beatrice ponders, perplexed. More questions swim laps through her head. "Why would they do that?"

Shelly lifts her bony shoulders and then lets them drop. "Why do any of us do the bad things we do?"

Shelly returns to her spot, diving into a new conversation with the other women. Beatrice wanted to join this little garden club meeting so she could get a few answers out of Ruth and Marilyn, maybe even Aunt Edie. But Shelly has given her a huge chunk. If Aunt Edie and Ruth somehow forced Madeline into accusing Fred of something inappropriate, who knows what else they're capable of?

Ashwood. Before.

It snowed the day of Grammy Astrid's funeral as she was laid to rest on December first.

Beatrice stood in her new black funeral dress in between Aunt Marley and her mother, Aunt Edie on the other side, wrapped in one of her expensive fur coats and sniffling into a tissue. Beatrice was too cold to be sad. The dress her mom picked up for her was the last one closest to her size so it was too small and itchy and made her legs freeze, despite the tights she had on underneath. She listened to the man in black recite whatever it was he recited from his book. Beatrice wondered if he was speaking about religion, because they aren't a religious family.

She looked up and Aunt Marley looked exhausted. She had a black hat on with a veil that hung in front of her face, shielding her from the snow and from anyone able to read her expression. Beatrice's mother held on to Beatrice's hand, occasionally giving it three squeezes to tell her that she loves her. Aunt Edie sobbed, shaking her head as she wiped her nose and her eyes with a silk handkerchief.

Once the man in black was finished reading whatever it was that he read for dead people, he said goodbye and began toward the front of the house, his footprints in the thin layer of snow slowly trailing behind him.

"How is this happening?" Beatrice's mom broke the silence between the four of them as they stood in front of Grammy Astrid's open grave, her body covered in a biodegradable sheet next to it. "How does this keep happening?"

"I don't know," Aunt Edie responded when no one else said anything. "It's a shame, though, darling. It really is."

"It's more than a shame, Edie," Aunt Marley barked at her, the whites of her eyes bright from behind the veil. "Shame isn't even the right word to say about this and every other goddamn thing that's happened to this fucked up family."

"Language, Marley." Lena sighed as she squatted down to gently give Grammy a shove into her new grave. "Beatrice is still out here."

"Sorry," Aunt Marley said but she didn't sound like it. Her eyes were glued to Aunt Edie. "How dare you say that this is a shame?"

Aunt Edie looked at her, unsure how to respond. She dotted her cheeks with her handkerchief before speaking. "What am I supposed to say, Marley? I am burying my sister-in-law. I am at a loss for words. The unimaginable happened and I am in shock."

"The unimaginable?" Aunt Marley shot back, putting her hands on her hips. Weren't they both too cold to be fighting out here like this? "How could this surprise you? How could this out of all things surprise you after everything that has happened?"

"What are you talking about?"

Beatrice awkwardly reached for one of the shovels that was used to dig the grave, her mother doing the same as they began to scoop dirt on top of Grammy Astrid's body. In the past, this was done in silence, out of respect for the deceased. But neither Aunt Marley nor Aunt Edie seemed to care this time.

"I'm talking about every single member of this family getting the axe!" Marley raised her voice, flinging her arms around as she spoke. "How does any of this make sense?"

"You're asking me like I know the answers," Aunt Edie fought back but was nowhere near as loud as her niece. "I don't, Marley."

"You know something," she roared.

Beatrice watched her mother's eyes glue to Aunt Edie, almost like she was waiting just as much as Aunt Marley, waiting for her to tell the truth. To finally spill some big piece of news they've been wanting for a long time, now.

"You know something and you're not telling us," Aunt Marley concluded.

Aunt Edie put a hand to her chest and her jaw was clenched so tight that Beatrice didn't look at it, afraid that it might lock into place and she would never be able to open it again.

"On today of all days, you're really accusing me of knowing why things happen the way they do?" Aunt Edie spoke calmly, her voice thick with tears. "How dare you?"

"I'm sorry, but—"

"No!" Aunt Edie cut her off. "You do not get to speak after standing over my brother's wife's grave and claiming that I knew this was going to happen. Why? Why must you girls bring this up again? Why must you run in circles with the same *fucking* questions?"

Beatrice found that last part interesting. Had the three of them had a conversation like this before? Were they arguing just as loud as this one, accusing Aunt Edie of knowing why the luck on their family tree hadn't been the best?

"Because our mother is dead," Beatrice's mom spoke up, sounding desperate. "Our dad, too. Your husband, your sister-in-law, your own parents, your *brothers*. Doesn't any of this mean anything to you?"

"Of course it does."

"Then why aren't you terrified?" Beatrice's mom demanded, pausing from shoving the dirt back into the hole. "Why aren't you wondering like the rest of us why this seems to only happen to the Millstone family? Why deaths like this are *normal* for us?"

It was the first time Beatrice had realized that perhaps these events in families weren't usual, that the Millstones were an exception for uncles falling through stairs and for his ghost to walk the ceilings of Ashwood. Or for her grandmothers to fling themselves out of windows and for grandfathers to not wake one morning because of a snapped neck. It was also the first time that her mother seemed just as lost and confused as she was. Aunt Marley, too.

"I don't know," Aunt Edie cried. "I don't know, I don't know, I don't fucking know! But if I did, don't you think I would be doing something about it? Don't you think I would try stopping it from happening?"

"I don't know," Aunt Marley nearly whispered. "Your claiming that Mom dying is a *shame* speaks volumes in itself."

Beatrice blinked as Aunt Marley started toward the house, hunched over as she tugged her coat tighter around her body, the snow sticking to her. Aunt Edie huffed and followed after a minute, managing to walk all the way to the front of the house to use the front door since Aunt Marley used the one to the mud room. Beatrice looked at her mom—who was watching their path in the snow, snowflakes sticking to her eyelashes.

"Are you okay, Mama?" Beatrice asked her quietly.

"I'm fine, sweetie," she claimed, going back to shoveling the dirt into the hole, quicker this time as the earth was starting to freeze more rapidly. "I'm sorry you had to hear all that. We're adults. We shouldn't be arguing in front of you."

"It's okay."

She stared at her and dropped her shovel. She got to her knees despite wearing a dress in the snow, putting her hands on her shoulders. "If something ever happens to me, you know you're the best thing I've ever done, right?"

"What do you mean?" Beatrice suddenly grew worried, wondering if a year from now she will be standing at this very plot with her aunts instead of her mother. It didn't necessarily seem too shocking, as it seemed like everyone in Beatrice's family were meeting untimely ends far too often.

"I mean, that if you're here without me one day, I want you to know that you are the number one thing I'm proud of." She gently tapped her nose with her finger, a snowflake melting in her eyebrow. "And there is nothing that would ever change that."

"I know."

She stared at her for a long time again and Beatrice usually never minded if her mother looked at her like that. She would eventually say something, and Beatrice knew that. But this time was different and it started to worry Beatrice even more. She swallowed and patiently stared back at her mother, waiting for her to say something else. And she did.

"Honey, I'm going to ask you a question and I don't want you to get scared, okay?"

Beatrice nodded her head.

"You know the House Things, right?" her mother asked. Beatrice could hear her heart pounding. Her lips were chapped from the cold by now and her mother was biting into her bottom one so hard that it split open, a slit of red forming.

"Yes," Beatrice answered her politely, like she did whenever her mother was serious and asked a question.

"Do they... do they say anything to you?"

Beatrice thought about it and shook her head. She'd heard them before but they never said anything *to* her. "No."

"I want you to be honest with me, sweetie," she told her. "It's okay if they do, I just want to know."

Beatrice thought harder this time. The House Things never spoke to her. They stared and lurked and made noises that sounded like animals but nothing was ever spoken in words.

"No, they never did," Beatrice said truthfully.

"Well if they do, you have to tell me, okay?" Her mother stared her dead in the face and when Beatrice nodded, she gave her shoulders a shake. "You have to promise me, Beatrice. That if any of them say anything to you at all, that you tell me."

"Okay, I promise," Beatrice said and then thought about what she was promising to. Why did her mother seem so scared? Why was this so important? "But why?"

"Why what?"

"Why is it a bad thing if they talk to me?"

"Because if they do, we have to leave."

Chapter 20

That evening, Beatrice sits with Aunt Edie in the dining room, rice pilaf and a pork roast sitting in front of them on their plates. Beatrice isn't even that hungry and she usually loves rice pilaf. She pokes around at the food with her fork, her body too busy trying to figure out everything she still doesn't know since being back here. Even sitting across from her aunt is making her antsy. Aunt Edie knows a lot more than she is letting on and Beatrice doesn't know how to move forward.

"You've barely touched your food," Aunt Edie says on the other side of the table after swallowing a mouthful. "I didn't slave over the stove for you to play with it, Beatrice."

"I haven't been very hungry lately." Beatrice gnaws at her pinkie nail, that's barely even there anymore. She switches to the other pinkie, biting down on what's left of that one.

"Is something on your mind?"

What isn't on my mind? Every day I find something new and it leads me closer into thinking that you had something to do with the disappearances and for some reason your friends are involved.

Beatrice barely shrugs, forcing herself to take a bite so she has time to come up with a response. "A lot of things, but nothing you can fix."

"I might not be able to fix them, but I would be more than happy to listen to you rant about a thing or two," Aunt Edie offers, scooping some of the rice onto her own fork. "That's what most people get confused with. They always think that telling someone else their problems is going to burden them. But not me. I enjoy a good old vent every now and again."

"All right." Beatrice sets her fork down on her plate and wipes her mouth with her napkin. "I spoke to Fred the day he died."

Aunt Edie doesn't look alarmed. In fact, she looks way too casual. She shoves more food into her mouth. "And how did that go?"

"I wanted to ask him if he saw anything weird in the woods," Beatrice explains, almost disappointed that her aunt isn't more concerned about her digging for clues. Does she even care that she might know about what happened to the twins? Is she even going to try and lie anymore?

"Anything weird?" Aunt Edie reaches for her glass of wine and laughs. "If I had a dime for every weird thing I saw in my lifetime, I'd be on a yacht being fed grapes by young European men."

"Not just *anything*, I asked him about the girls that lived here before me," Beatrice clarifies, picking her fork back up, now comfortable enough to eat as she is starting to feel like she might have the upper hand. It feels unfamiliar but she's enjoying the power. "You know, all the ones that were never seen again after weeks or months after living here."

"And did he?"

"He saw one of them," Beatrice confirms. "She was wearing a red dress and running through the trees screaming."

"Screaming?" she echoes.

"Yes, screaming," Beatrice confirms again. "Do you know anything about that?"

"Beatrice, I don't want to fight with you again." Aunt Edie looks her in the face for so long that it makes Beatrice uncomfortable. She eats some more. "You've been gone for so long that the last thing I want to do is argue some more about girls you didn't even know."

"But don't you think that it's strange, Aunt Edie?" Beatrice begs her to see things from her perspective.

But that's always been Aunt Edie's problem: she's always seen things from her own point of view. According to her mother, she has never tried stepping into someone else's shoes to gain a different perspective. And judging by how things have been going since Beatrice got here, it doesn't look like that habit is breaking anytime soon.

"Don't you think it's strange that these things happened here?" Beatrice goes on. "You've lived in this house your entire life. It's impossible for it to be a coincidence that it seems to be some sort of black hole, swallowing people up entirely."

"It's not a black hole, Beatrice," Aunt Edie claims. "And yes, I agree that there have been some weird instances here but what am I supposed to do with that information? Call the police? They already know about these missing women. We are located in a very desert area. If someone wanted to kidnap them, this would be the first place to do it."

"But what about all of the members of our family?" Beatrice points out, stabbing her fork through the air.

Aunt Edie sighs, reaching for her drink again. "What about them?"

"Don't you think it's weird that they're all dead?" Beatrice pushes. "My mom should not be dead right now and neither should Aunt Marley or the twins. They should be alive, with us."

"I don't know what you want me to say," Aunt Edie states after a moment of silence. She stares at the wine in her glass, her eyes glossy. "You don't know how long I've tried putting a stop to what has happened in this house."

Now they're getting somewhere.

"What does that mean?" Beatrice pulls the sleeves of her sweater over her knuckles.

"I've tried for so long," Aunt Edie croaks, her eyes still glued to the sparkly glass. "But there are some things in this world that are going to happen no matter how hard you try and stop them."

Beatrice takes a small nibble of the rice, a mushroom slithering down her throat. "So you're saying that no matter what, some things are just… inevitable?"

Aunt Edie looks at her now. "Yes, that's the perfect word for it. Inevitable."

"How did you try stopping all this?" Beatrice wonders aloud, wanting to give her hand at trying to stop it, too. Maybe then Aunt Edie won't die while she's here and neither will Beatrice. They can put an end to whatever curse lingers over Ashwood for good.

Aunt Edie glances at her plate of food. "I see them, too, you know. The House Things."

The words shoot down Beatrice's arms and she swallows the lump forming in her throat. She's always known that the adults saw the House Things just as much as she did growing up. Aunt Edie has lived in Ashwood since the day she was born. She was bound to see one or two of them over the years. But all throughout Beatrice's childhood, the adults rarely ever spoke about their interactions with the House Things. They would tell Beatrice and the twins to pay no mind to them, that this was their house just as much.

But that whole viewpoint changed after Grammy Astrid died. Beatrice doesn't remember full details about the funeral, but she does remember her mom and Aunt Marley arguing with Aunt Edie over Grandma's grave. She remembers them ordering the truth from Aunt Edie, just like how Beatrice has been doing since her return. There is one thing that Beatrice remembers very vividly about that day. She remembers her mother crouching in front of her in the new-fallen snow, telling her that if the House Things ever spoke to her, they would have to leave.

"Do they talk to you?" Beatrice asks quietly.

She shakes her head. "Never. All these years I've spent inside of these walls, none of them ever said a word to me. But they're there. Everywhere. I probably see more than you."

Beatrice blinks. She's only ever saw her dead relatives, and then a stranger she's never seen before every now and again, chalking it up to ancestors she's never met. Like that woman in the mirror. And she once saw a boy lurking in the garden but in the blink of an eye, he was gone. That same boy accompanied a woman in the attic, both of them without eyes. Beatrice's mind flings itself back to seeing a man in a top hat ringing the bell one day when she was little. She opened the front door when no grown-ups were around to get it. The man was so very tall and wearing an outdated top hat that gave Beatrice the creeps. She tried talking to him, and when she did, he didn't respond. He opened his lips to muster something out but the only sound that escaped were these weird grunts that scared Beatrice so much she slammed the door in his face. She never saw him again.

Could there be more of these House Things right under Beatrice's nose that she's never even seen before? If Aunt Edie sees more of them than she does, that definitely means there are some that Beatrice has never seen herself. What if she never left Ashwood? What if she grew up here just like Aunt Edie and when she reached her age, she saw them just the same?

"I used to stay up so late at night, praying that they would go away," Aunt Edie goes on. "I used to beg for them to leave me and everyone else alone. And then I would find myself being woken by someone because I was sleepwalking."

"And they never said anything back?"

She shakes her head. "Not one. Some of them wouldn't even acknowledge that I was there. They would just keep walking. So, I developed a sort of routine. I would get up at night, and walk the house, pleading with them to go away. I tried so hard, but they wouldn't listen. They wouldn't understand what I wanted them to do. The more I told them to leave this house, the more I started sleepwalking. I thought that it was them, you know, putting me into a trance."

"How do you know that it wasn't?"

"They don't have that power," she responds. "If they did, I would have been dead a long time ago."

"Let's just leave." Beatrice reaches across the table to put her hand on her aunt's. She will address the Marilyn and Ruth thing once they're out of here. "We can pack up our stuff tonight and get out of here by the morning."

Her mom appears in her head, seeing her the other night playing through her mind on a loop once again. Beatrice will be sure to visit, but if Aunt Edie is telling the truth and she has spent this much time trying to get rid of the things in this house and they're still here, then there's something bigger happening, something that is out of Beatrice's control.

"We can't do that," Aunt Edie responds. "We have responsibilities here. And I have to put the house on the market."

"I know, but in the meantime, we can sleep somewhere else," Beatrice explains. "We won't have to worry about any of this."

"I think I'm going to take a bath." Aunt Edie rises from her chair without another moment to debate things. "Finish your supper. It's going to get cold."

Aunt Edie glides out of the room and Beatrice is left at the table. She looks around the dining room for any sign of a House Thing she might have not seen before. But that's the hard part about them: they choose when they're able to be seen.

Beatrice awakes that night with an aggressive jerk, sitting up in bed, ripped away from whatever she was dreaming about.

"Sweetie." Her mother sits at the foot of the bed, her legs dangling over the edge and a polite smile playing across her lips.

Beatrice's eyes widen in the darkness, her mother's white shirt lighting up the room. Her mouth feels cotton dry and she finds herself wondering if this is another chapter in her dream. "Mom?"

"You were having a nightmare," she informs her as though Beatrice didn't already know. "You know how much I hate when you have those things."

"What are you doing?" Beatrice demands breathlessly, scooting closer to her on the bed. "Please don't leave as fast as you did last time."

"I don't have much time, honey," she tells her, her words spilling out of her mouth quicker, now. "I have to get back."

"Get back where?" Beatrice orders desperately. She wants to reach out and grab hold of her mom, determined to keep her right here with her. They could spend the entire night talking and her mom can finally tell her what happened the night they tried to leave. "Where can I find you?"

"You can't."

"Why not?"

"Because it's not safe," she snaps at her, her tone growing more and more annoyed. "I told you that you need to get out of here. Why haven't you left yet?"

"Because I can't," Beatrice says. "I can't leave you, not when I've found you again. And I just told Aunt Edie that we can go but she's against it."

"So leave her here." Her voice grows deeper, and an unsettling look crosses her face. She reaches up to touch the spot where the locket used to be, something she used to play with often. But when she realizes it's missing, she drops her hands into her lap.

"I have the locket." Beatrice shows her, keeping it wrapped around her neck but digging it out from under her shirt. "See? Why did Lila have this?"

"She found it," she tells her. "It was left here after I…"

"Tell me what happened," Beatrice pleas, scooting closer to her on the bed. "Please tell me and then I will leave."

Her mom looks at her sadly, the corners of her mouth dipping into a frown. She reaches out to touch her daughter's cheek but her hand hangs in midair and she returns it to her lap again, still never making skin-to-skin contact.

Beatrice frowns. Her mother is so close, yet they can't seem to touch. The grief counseling group floats through her thoughts and she wonders if they've ever discussed this.

She shakes her head, her curls bouncing. "It's not that simple, Bea. There is so much that you don't know about this house, so much I never told you."

"So then tell me now," Beatrice snaps at her. If she wasn't wasting all this time telling Beatrice that she doesn't know a lot, maybe then Beatrice would be well educated on what the hell is going on. "You're here, I'm here, so tell me. I try talking to Aunt Edie about everything but I'm just left as more confused than before."

"I would have to go through the entire family tree for you to understand," she explains. "Or, at least all the way back to Uncle Eli."

"What about him?"

Her mom stares at her for a few long seconds that felt like minutes before she finally speaks. "He saw this man on the ceiling…"

"I made you a cake, Eli," Astrid said happily, carrying a banana cake into the dining area where Eli sat at the table. "And before you go asking if it's moist enough, it most certainly is."

"Uncle Eli is never picky about his food," Marley said sarcastically from next to him, patting her uncle on the shoulder and smiling brightly. Marley's boyfriend, Jesse, sat next to her, smiling a stoned smile.

"Ma, did you even get the lighter?" Pregnant Lena asked, sighing as she braced herself against one of the chairs.

"Oh, shoot." Astrid padded back into the kitchen area, rooting through the drawers to find the lighter.

"You're milking that pregnancy of yours," Edie said from the other side of the dining table next to Hugh. She had a long cigarette pinched between her fingers, her legs spread out in front of her onto an adjacent chair. "You know, when I was pregnant, I barely even gained any weight."

"That is not true, Edie," Astrid scolded when she came back with the grill lighter. "You gained weight."

"Please don't mind my sister, everyone," Edie announced in a voice as smooth as butter. "Her eyesight has never been the best."

Lena looked at her aunt in confusion. "Aunt Edie, you never told us you had any kids."

Edie frowned, her eyes blinking into the very distant past. "They passed away."

A silence so thick filled the room that Eli shifted uncomfortably in his chair. Marley and Jesse exchanged an awkward glance and Hugh pretended to be interested in the grooves of the dining table, not saying a word. Astrid cleared her throat and started lighting the candles.

"Don't forget to make a wish," Jesse told Eli encouragingly. "Mine came true."

Marley blushed as her boyfriend pulled her closer to him and she pecked his cheek.

Eli sat at the table, glancing around at the family surrounding him. He never really made wishes on birthday cake candles. He had always thought that it was completely bogus to wish things on flames that were just going to get burnt out. Something in the mud room caught his eye and when Eli blinked, he could feel his blood run cold.

There, hanging upside down in the mud room was a man wearing a brown trench coat and a polo shirt underneath. He stood on the ceiling as though it was the floor. Eli was confused as his coat was able to still hang to his ankles. He wondered how it wasn't dangling to the floor. He held his breath, watching as the man took several steps forward until he reached the kitchen ceiling, smiling at Uncle Eli as though they knew each other. And then Eli realized, they did. He was Edie's father: Pete.

"Uncle Eli?" Lena broke him from his trance, waving a hand in front of his face. She glanced behind her into the kitchen but then looked back at her uncle in bewilderment. "Are you all right?"

"I'm fine." He blew out the candles.

Uncle Eli mentioned his sighting to Aunt Edie that night, saying that he thought he saw her father walking on the ceiling. Aunt Edie of course told him that he was crazy, like many of us would do later on for small things Uncle Eli would find himself doing. But in fact, he was not as crazy as we all liked to think. Ashwood was.

The following year, Eli buttoned up a flannel shirt one morning and stepped into a pair of jeans, determined to get some yard work done before the rain hit earlier that day. He made himself an omelet and brushed his teeth, spitting into the sink. He glanced at his reflection in the mirror on the wall, yelping when he noticed Pete once again standing on the ceiling behind him.

Eli whirled his body around, bracing himself against the counter and finding his eyes locked with Pete's. "What in the hell are you doing? W-what are you?"

Pete didn't say a word. Eli wasn't even sure if he could. His face was a beaming red color—maybe from all of the blood rushing to his head. Pete was dead. He died falling off the roof years ago, drowning in a pull of blood in the driveway. He couldn't be hanging in front of him now. Similar to the rest of their family members appearing in this house, Pete simply stared, wide-eyed and silent.

"Are you a ghost?" Eli asked him but Pete didn't respond. Instead, he slowly made his way out of the room, his trench coat floating behind him.

Eli would see Pete many times after that. He would see him on Halloween, watching trick-or-treaters from the window. He would see him in the night when he would wake for a cup of water, waiting for him at the end of the hallway. He would

"You see, Eli thought he started to lose his mind. He would see other House Things, but none of them would stalk him like the Man on the Ceiling—which is what he would call him, considering that this thing was no longer Pete, but something else. A creature, if you will.

It wasn't until you were four, Beatrice, that Eli took it upon himself to stop running from the Man on the Ceiling. When he would see him, he would walk toward him instead of running in the other direction. Some might say he was brave for doing this, for no longer being afraid of something that had been following him for so long. But others would claim he was simply mad."

"I want you to leave me alone," Eli told Pete shortly after the twins were born. He stood in the second-floor hallway, glaring at the Man on the Ceiling looming in front of him, his face redder than ever. "You are dead. You can't keep following me anymore."

"Then follow me," the Man on the Ceiling finally spoke.

Goosebumps rose all over Eli's body, as this was the first time he heard him speak. None of the House Things did that. He widened his eyes at the thickness of the man's voice, how foreign it sounded, not like any human voice he heard and certainly not Pete's.

Eli took three steps toward him, Pete taking three steps back. Eli ran a hand over his gut, debating on if he should continue or play it smart and get the hell away from this thing. But maybe the only way to stop seeing him was to follow, was to stalk him back. So, he went forward, getting closer to Pete, while Pete got further away. He slowly made his way to the steps and then stopped in his tracks. He couldn't go down them without looking to see where he was going. But he also didn't want to take his eyes off Pete. Did these things just disappear in midair? Did they vanish like ghosts? Uncle Eli was determined to find out.

Eli couldn't look away from the Man on the Ceiling, even if he tried. Slowly, he started down the steps, opening his mouth to call out for help but no sound came out. He'd had sleep paralysis before and this was exactly what it was like: no control, wandering into oblivion. He tried to stop walking but whatever trance the Man on the Ceiling had him in, there was no way out. And it was terrifying.

"Uncle Eli?" Marley asked from the kitchen as Eli reached the bottom of the steps.

Eli could feel beads of sweat dripping down his forehead as he attempted to stop walking again but he couldn't. His legs kept moving forward, like they were hypnotized. What was happening? Was this what insanity was like? Were all of his family members right in saying that he was just a little bit crazy? If so, they were wrong. He was a *lot* crazy. If he couldn't control his own actions, what else was there that was out of his control?

"Uncle Eli," Aunt Marley said again but Eli couldn't look in her direction. "Are you okay?"

"H-help me," he finally croaked out of desperation, everything around him out of his control. Before he knew it, he was opening the door to the basement without knowing why. Couldn't Marley see him? Couldn't she see Pete standing on the ceiling? Why wasn't she doing anything? Why wasn't she helping?

The Man on the Ceiling beckoned Eli forward and he started down the steps, listening to the sound of the chair legs from Marley screeching against the floor. And before he knew it, his ankle was grabbed from something under the stairs and plunging forward, he sank through them.

Chapter 21

Beatrice blinks into the darkness of the basement shooting down in front of her.

She gasps, grabbing hold of the wooden railing at her side. She whips her head around to find the basement door open behind her, sunlight pouring into the windows of the mudroom. Her breathing grows heavier and her mother's voice floats through her mind. Was that a dream? Or was her mother really in her bed, feeding her Uncle Eli's story?

"Have you been sleepwalking, dear?" Aunt Edie appears behind her, her lips parted to form an O shape and her eyebrows sloped toward one another as though she feels nothing but relatable pity.

Beatrice finds herself nodding her head, too shaken up to respond right away. What in the hell happened? How did her mother do that? She swallows hard, her throat as dry as the desert. She vigorously shakes her head some more, willing herself to come back to reality, to the real world where real things happen and her dead mother doesn't appear in front of her and where she isn't sleepwalking.

"I must have been, yeah," she confirms. "Sorry."

"Nothing to apologize over." Aunt Edie softly smiles. "We know how much I do it, myself. I was just going to make some crepes."

Aunt Edie is padding back into the kitchen and Beatrice remains on the staircase to the basement. She trains her eyes on the wooden stairs beneath her. The fifth one down is the one Uncle Eli fell through, a different kind of wood than the others. She never knew that his ankle was grabbed. Who would have pulled it? Another one of the House—

Beatrice gasps, falling backward onto the steps when she's shocked to find Uncle Eli standing on the ceiling in front of her, hanging upside down with all the blood in his body rushing to his head. Beatrice hears herself scream, scrambling to get the hell back into the mudroom. Her yells are so aggressive that her throat feels scarred. She slams the door behind her, still on the floor, and crawls as quickly as she can to the other side of the room, bruising her knees in the process.

"Bea?" Aunt Edie comes rushing back inside, worried wrinkles lining her face. She's looking all around the mudroom before finding

Beatrice on the floor. "What in the world is going on?"

"Uncle Eli!" Beatrice points to the basement door. "I just saw him! He was on the ceiling!"

Every time she blinks, she sees his body hanging upside down in that foreign way. She thinks about his big brown eyes and the way his chubby cheeks always looked rosy. She shakes him from her memory, her hands trembling before her. She's losing her mind.

"What are you talking about?" Aunt Edie puts her hands on her hips.

She's playing dumb. There is no way Aunt Edie has lived in this house for this long and has never seen her dead husband on the ceiling before. It's embarrassing that she is *still* trying to cover up the truth about the House Things—even after they had that talk at dinner last night about them and how Aunt Edie would try getting them to go away but it never worked.

"I-I saw him," Beatrice stammers, almost wishing Uncle Eli would come out of the basement right now and show himself. But the door remains shut and Aunt Edie remains looking clueless. She runs her fingers through the knots in her hair and clears her throat. "I need a shower."

"Yes, that sounds like a good idea, darling." Aunt Edie helps her to her feet. "Breakfast should be ready by the time you're out."

Beatrice stands under the hot water sputtering out of the showerhead. Little waterfalls cascade down her body and she shuts her eyes, willing herself not to think of Uncle Eli in the basement. This can't be happening. She hasn't seen him as a House Thing for so long. Now, seeing him as the Man on the Ceiling is bringing back feelings that are somewhat familiar to her. When she was a kid, that used to be normal, seeing dead family members in scary positions around the house. But as an adult, she's scared out of her fucking mind.

The story about Aunt Edie's and Grandpa Hugh's father, Pete, being the Man on the Ceiling before Uncle Eli is confusing. Did Pete lead him to those stairs, knowing that something below would grab him? Are the things in this house not as nice as Grammy Astrid once told her they were? Because if not, maybe Beatrice's mom is right. Maybe Ashwood isn't safe to be and it's better for her to get out now before things start getting worse.

But she can't. She needs to find out more. She needs her mom to tell her the rest of what happened because maybe then, she'll finally find out the truth about this place once and for all. She won't need to run around wondering what is going on and she will have clear answers to all of the questions she's been wondering since she was a child.

Beatrice steps out of the shower and dries herself off, pulling herself into some running tights and a zip-up jacket. She doesn't have the energy to wear something less comfortable. Half of her wants to fall back asleep again so that her mom can give her more stories about the dead. She runs a comb through her hair, the shoulders of her jacket are soaked but she doesn't care.

A plate of crepes is waiting for her at kitchen island by the time Beatrice ventures downstairs. Her eyes are still puffy from lack of rest but it's not like she'll be doing much today, anyway. She manages a tentative smile at Aunt Edie when she glances at her over her shoulder.

"How are you feeling now?" Aunt Edie asks, flipping a crepe onto a plate at the stove.

"Better," she lies. In fact, she feels worse. Too many things are being left in the dark and Aunt Edie isn't budging to help her figure out what and why and even *how*. "I haven't slept walk like that in a while."

"Sleepwalking spells can come and go," Aunt Edie says casually, glancing at her again with a knowing look. "Unless there is something someone is trying to tell you."

Beatrice picks up her fork. "What do you mean?"

"There can be a lot communicated over dreams," she explains, not making eye contact with her anymore. "Sometimes they say that when a dead person appears in your dreams, they're trying to tell you something. It's mostly something good, so there isn't a thing to worry about."

Beatrice knows that it wasn't a dream, though. Her mother was really there in her room. She uses the edge of her fork to split open her crepe, filled with apple butter and raspberries. "I don't know. Maybe I just need to start going to sleep earlier."

"Doesn't sound like a bad idea." Aunt Edie spreads Nutella onto a crepe at the counter. "So how did you like garden club yesterday? Sorry you were stuck with Shelly. She can be a little bit of a yapper."

"She was nice."

"What did you two talk about?"

The question is too nosy for it to not have a certain motive. Beatrice stuffs her face to give her time to think about how to respond. She could name a number of things that she and Shelly spoke about: her kids, what it's like to be back in Silver Creek, how long she's been a part of the garden club, or even her sex life with her husband. But

Beatrice is going to take this as an opportunity instead of dancing around the subject.

"Talked about Fred, actually," Beatrice admits once she swallows. "And before you go accusing me of asking your friends things, she's the one that brought it up first."

Yes, it's a lie, but Beatrice kind of wants to prove Aunt Edie wrong. She claims that she used to be a whole lot better at lying, but this will prove otherwise.

"Oh?" Aunt Edie sets her plate down on the other side of the island as she tries reading Beatrice's expression but she's sure not to budge. Aunt Edie looks annoyed. "And what did she have to say?"

"I didn't realize that he was accused of molesting Ruth's daughter," Beatrice tells her bluntly, cutting into her crepe. "It's starting to seem like a whole lot of the truth keeps getting brushed under the rug, huh?"

"I'm sorry, since when is it your business to know about Ruth's family life?" Aunt Edie cuts into her own crepe, stabbing at a strawberry with her fork. "That sort of thing should remain private, within the family, don't you think?"

"If that's the case, then why were you constantly around when the trial was going on?" Beatrice challenges, Shelly's suspicion now becoming her own. "Apparently you might as well been Madline's shadow."

"Because that's what friends do," Aunt Edie says in a clipped tone, chewing her food. "And besides, Fred didn't even get in trouble for anything. The judge claimed that it was a misunderstanding and he got let off free."

Beatrice squints. Does she really think that getting let off free consists of Fred's house burning down? Just because he didn't wind up in jail, doesn't mean he lived his life *free*.

"You do realize that people burned his house down like some mob, right?" Beatrice reminds her. "He was forced to move into some shack in the woods because of Madeline's lie. It ruined his life."

"You don't know that it was a lie."

"And you don't know she was telling the truth," Beatrice shoots back.

Aunt Edie sighs heavily and the two of them continue eating in silence. Beatrice considers saying something else, bringing up the fact that Fred saw Marilyn with the twins in the woods the day they died but she doesn't think that will end on a good note. She needs her mom to tell her a little more before she can walk into another argument blindly and lacking enough ammo to use against her aunt.

"I don't know about you but I'm getting really tired of every conversation we have ending in a confrontation," Aunt Edie finally says. Her eyes are reflective, like they're made of glass. It's what she looks like before she starts to weep into the dramatics. "When you came back, I was so excited, Beatrice. I was over the moon to have you under this roof again. But now it seems like you see me as some monster, someone you don't even know."

Beatrice opens her mouth to tell her that she sees more of what is happening now that she's an adult. There is far more to Ashwood than she ever thought. She's no longer a blind little girl just listening to what her elders were telling her. She can see now, and judging by what she has found out so far, Aunt Edie isn't as glamorous as she once believed her to be.

But, Beatrice needs to stay on her good side for just a little longer. If she keeps pushing her away, it's not going to do her any good. So, she paints a smile over her face. "You're right. I'm sorry. I've just been paranoid and I don't know why."

"Being back in your childhood home can do that to a person," Aunt Edie claims, as though she has experience. She's never left this house, though. Or, Ashwood has never left her. "What do you say that we start over? We wipe the slate clean."

Beatrice nods in agreement just to play along. There is no way in hell she's wiping the slate clean. She and Aunt Edie have had too many arguments about the past and present to pretend like none of it ever happened. But if that's what she wants, then that's what she'll get. "That sounds good to me."

"Okay, good." Aunt Edie exhales and sets her dirty plate in the sink for Beatrice to later clean up. "I'm meeting with Ruth and Marilyn in town. Apparently all of the Halloween store sales are happening and they're wanting to spend a few dollars. Do you care to join?"

"I still have a lot of housework to do," Beatrice responds through a mouthful of crepe. "But maybe I can meet up with you guys later?"

Aunt Edie smiles approvingly. "That sounds pleasant."

Beatrice keeps herself busy by cleaning up the kitchen until Aunt Edie leaves. She waits until she hears the hum of her car pull out of the driveway and lurch toward town. She's been waiting to have the house to herself ever since Xander brought up Aunt Edie's wardrobe and the story of being locked inside. She remembers that Christmas Eve when she saw it for herself, something etched into the door, something she can't even remember. Now that Aunt Edie is out, this is her perfect opportunity to figure out what that is.

Aunt Edie's bedroom door is locked when Beatrice tries opening it and she stares at it hard. Why would Aunt Edie lock her door if Beatrice is the only one home? If that doesn't scream that she's hiding something, Beatrice doesn't know what will. She marches into her room to fetch the keys from the grandfather clock Grandpa Hugh hid years ago. She uses every one, shoving one right after the other into the keyhole until finally, she hears a *click*.

The door eases open with a creak and Beatrice pops her head inside. Her breath nearly escapes her when she finds that the entire room is exactly how she remembers it. A huge round bed is in the corner of the room, angled outward toward the center. Clear drapes blow in the wind, as the window is cracked open just a couple inches. There's a blood red rug draped over the floor and the dresser is cluttered with wrinkle creams, perfumes, and other bottles of expensive product. The mirror above the dresser is still wiped completely clean. Aunt Edie used to claim that a dirty mirror reflects a dirty reflection. Whatever *that* meant. And then, alas, the bulky wardrobe is still pushed up against the wall, the same wardrobe that houses all of Aunt Edie's most expensive fur coats and robes.

Before she can open the wardrobe doors, something on the nightstand catches her eye. It's a photo of Aunt Edie and Uncle Eli on their wedding day. They're cutting the cake together, both of them wearing such young and bright smiles. Beatrice frowns. Uncle Eli was a lot thinner back then and looked a lot saner. She wants to curse at Ashwood for taking that side out of him, for yanking him of his sanity and using it against him until his death. There's another photo that sits behind it and Beatrice reaches for it. They're the only dusty things in this room, everything else seems to be spotless.

The frame on this second photo is a glimmering silver layered with dust. Beatrice uses her thumb to scrape some away off the glass. Aunt Edie is about six or seven in the sepia-toned photo, standing outside of Ashwood with Grandpa Hugh and Lachlan by her side, the three of them squinting in the summer sun. Great Grandpa Pete stands behind them with a hand on Grammy Astrid's shoulder. Great Grandma Dorothy stands next to him with her lips in a straight line. She had short choppy brown hair in thick curls and rounded cheekbones that kind of reminds Beatrice of Santa Claus. She remembers seeing an old picture of Dorothy in one of the photo albums years ago when she was a little girl.

"Who's that?" Beatrice pointed to Great Grandma Dorothy in her wedding gown, smiling at the photo as she stood next to an open window.

"That is Aunt Edie's, Grandpa Hugh's, and Uncle Lachlan's mom," Aunt Marley told her as they sat together on the floor of the study. "She passed away."

"How?"

Aunt Marley grew sad, her finger rubbing the photo of Grandma Dorothy. "She drowned in the bathtub."

This makes Beatrice remember her dream she kept having of being a little girl in the second-floor bathroom and getting shoved underwater, in fear for her life as she kicked and punched the air and water around her to try and stay above the surface.

She sets the photo back down on the nightstand and crosses the room to the wardrobe, where it stands above her, towering over her like a chest of secrets. Beatrice opens the doors, kind of surprised by the aged moan they share as she pushes them aside. And there it is, still etched into the wood after all these years. It's a circle not too round, given it was made by a blade or another sharp object. The circle surrounds a swirl inside of it and Beatrice stares at it for a long time, wondering what it could possibly mean. A jagged triangle is engraved above the circle, their lines meeting. She was hoping for something a little more telling. Maybe a pentagram or a word or something. A swirl inside of a circle doesn't really give her much.

Beatrice takes out her phone and snaps a photo, anyway, shutting the wardrobe back up but pausing when she hears a noise from down the hall. She looks over her shoulder at the door, footsteps getting closer.

"Shit," she curses under her breath, spinning around in circles for somewhere to hide. She knows those footsteps don't belong to one of the House Things.

Beatrice dives under the bed, squeezing beneath it as tight as she can without fail. She pulls herself under it, tucking her legs at an awkward angle just as the door to Aunt Edie's room opens. She puts a hand over her mouth to stop herself from breathing, recognizing Aunt Edie's jumpsuit and heels. The contents under the bed consist of shoe boxes and a heavy scrapbook with pages and stickers popping out of the sides. There is a ripped fur coat and another framed photo but it's too dark for Beatrice to make out what it depicts

"Beatrice?" Aunt Edie calls out to her as she opens the drawer to her nightstand. "I had to come back for my medication. You sure you don't want to come along?"

Beatrice bites down on her lip, wondering if this will prompt Aunt Edie to go searching for her through the house. That would be awkward. She remains as quiet as she can be and listens to the soft rattle of pills in the bottle retrieved from the drawer. She watches as her aunt heads back into the hallway, shutting the door behind her. Beatrice exhales and doesn't move for several minutes, crossing her fingers that the house has now emptied.

When she feels like it's safe, Beatrice emerges from under the bed, crawling to the window to make sure that Aunt Edie has taken off. The driveway is empty. Curiosity screams at her and Beatrice finds herself crawling to the other side of Aunt Edie's bed, pulling out the framed photo she couldn't see clearly from under the bed frame. She frowns, let down by the old photo of Beatrice seated on the porch of the house with a newly carved jack-o-lantern in her lap. She shoves the picture back under the bed, now firmly believing Aunt Edie when she used to tell her that she was her favorite.

The scrapbook catches her attention again and Beatrice tugs at it. The book is covered in dust and age, the plush corners bent and the portrait on the front so worn out that Beatrice has to squint to realize it's a little boy wearing what looks like a sailor outfit. He's staring at the camera in front of a plain white wall, not smiling. Beatrice traces the name written in graffiti beneath the photo: *Benji*.

Who the hell is Benji? The boy looks familiar, though, but Beatrice doesn't know why. She remembers seeing a little boy when she was younger, but she never got a good look at his face. She opens the scrapbook, her eyebrows pulling together as she stares at the first photo of the book. It's of a baby, swaddled in a blanket in Aunt Edie's arms. When Beatrice looks closer, she realizes it's in a hospital, old machines next to the bed. Aunt Edie's hair was frizzy around her face and she flashed the camera a tired smile, holding the child in her arms.

Beatrice sifted through the scrapbook, some pages more stable than most. Stickers line them in no specific ordinance, all over the place and slapped onto the pages just for the colors. A small baggie of teeth is halfway in and the more photos of this Benji boy that keeps popping up, the more Beatrice confirms to herself that this has to be Aunt Edie's son. The story that her mother told her about Uncle Eli last night… Aunt Edie mentioned to them all that she had a child but he had passed away. Why has this never been talked about before? Why was this never mentioned?

Beatrice continues sorting through the scrapbook, carefully turning the crisp pages covered in glue and tape, holding pictures together that show off Benji's life, a life Beatrice never even knew about. From bike rides to home-schooled projects to colored pages from coloring books. The book isn't filled to the end, given the short life Benji lived. It seems like he was only five or six when he passed. That is a handful of years Aunt Edie spent with her child. How come she never spoke about him more?

Beatrice sighs when she reaches the last photo in the book: it's one of Benji's funeral. She remembers hearing the name *Benjamin* before. Or, rather, *seeing* it on one of the gravestones in the family's plot. She never bothered to ask anyone who he was though, just like she never bothered to ask who any of the other graves belonged to in the yard. Beatrice slides the book back under the bed and gets to her feet to leave the room.

Beatrice locks the bedroom door behind her and hurries back to her room, as though Aunt Edie is going to get here again and disrupt her snooping. She collapses onto her bed, putting her hands to her face and squeezing her eyes shut. It's hard to believe that this has become her life: moving back into her childhood home because she's broke and then uncovering past family secrets she never knew about. Beatrice doesn't waste too much time pitying herself over it, though. There are more important things to be doing. She should look into Marilyn's past and find out who she really is. Ruth, too, for that matter.

She snatches up her laptop from under her pillow, opening it up and jabbing at the power button. She impatiently waits for it to load, shooting Clara a text on her phone while she waits. The text takes a few minutes to send, as it seems like the service up here is getting worse and worse by the day. When the screen lights up with life, Beatrice opens up her internet browser, her fingers flying over the keyboard to type: *Marilyn Vance, Silver Creek, Massachusetts.* She clicks the magnifying glass and results pop up about minutes later after a loading screen.

Beatrice's eyes slide down the first few articles available on the web, only the first one catching her eye, as a photo of Marilyn is included. She double taps it, the article leading her to a website called the Silver Gazette, which is named after the town paper. The website looks outdated with poor graphics swirling around at the top and the main photo in question takes forever to load. But when it does, Beatrice leans in closer to the screen. Marilyn stands with a man around her age, his arm around her and his glimmering police badge catching the light. Beatrice recognizes the man, unfortunately. His bald head and saggy gut brings her back to Fred's house. He was the cop on the scene: Hudson.

Beatrice isn't surprised Marilyn and her husband have two different last names, as Beatrice heard Marilyn mention at the pumpkin patch that she was married prior to her current husband. She scrolls down to the caption below the picture, which includes a note about how Hudson was promoted to chief the night of the police gala and his wife came to accompany him. Other images from that night splash across the rest of the page and Beatrice finds herself intently looking at all of them, desperate to find something out of the ordinary but nothing looks out of place. She scrolls back to the top, glaring at Hudson's face on the screen.

This is too much of a coincidence, the fact that Marilyn is married to the chief of police. When Beatrice spoke to him the other day about the missing women, he didn't seem too concerned. In fact, not a lot of the police seemed worried that the counts in missing girls have been rising except for Officer Gomez, it seems. Marilyn played a part in the twins going missing and judging by what Beatrice knows about the past, the police didn't seem all that eager to go out hunting them down. They weren't concerned in the slightest. Aunt Marley was driving herself crazy, throwing herself into the Jungle day after day to search for them, sometimes passing out on trees from sleep deprivation. Could Marilyn have played a part in making sure that they weren't found since she was married to Silver Creek's chief officer?

Beatrice runs her tongue over her teeth, setting her laptop down next to her and getting up out of bed. She picks up the jeans she wore yesterday off the floor, rooting through the pocket for the phone number Officer Gomez gave her in private. Maybe if she sits down with someone that is as confused as she is about all this, she might get some more answers. Beatrice isn't quite sure if she's ready to tell her about what she knows about Jax and Juniper, but she'll decide that when they're able to meet.

Punching the number into her phone, Beatrice paces back and forth at the foot of her bed, listening to the phone ring on the other end until the fourth. She hears a *click*.

"Officer Alejandra Gomez," the cop answers on the other end.

"Officer Gomez, hi," Beatrice says politely. "It's Beatrice Millstone, we met yesterday at the crime scene of Fred…"

Shit. What was his last name?

"Oh, right," Gomez says before Beatrice can think some more. "Of course. How are you?"

I'm going insane and I'm two seconds away from checking myself into a mental hospital but other than that, I'm doing great!

"Doing well, how are you?"

"Not too bad," Gomez responds, the squeaking of a chair peeling off on her end. "I'm guessing you're calling for an important reason, though?"

"I was wondering if you'd be available anytime soon," Beatrice babbles, kind of feeling like she's asking her on a date—which is weird because the only girl she ever asked on a date was her friend JJ in high school when Beatrice thought she was into girls. It didn't end well. "You know, to talk."

"I'm available tomorrow, actually," Gomez offers, following the sound of rustling papers. "If that works for you?"

Beatrice is a little bummed they can't meet today but beggars can't be choosers. "Yep, sounds good."

After making plans to meet at a joint called Penny's Pies, Beatrice and Gomez say goodbye to each other and hang up the phone. Beatrice tosses her phone onto the bed and considers her next move. The last thing on her mind right now is getting the home renovations complete. Sure, she needs the money but all of this other stuff is far more important. She feels like she'd be wasting time sitting around doing pointless shit that doesn't mean anything. But on the other hand, Aunt Edie is expecting her to start getting the house ready. She's already suspicious of her enough. If she comes home to yet more stuff not even done, Beatrice might as well fill her in on everything she's been finding out.

Beatrice spends the remainder of the day learning how to use a hammer on the ancient trim in the upstairs hallway so that the next time Xander comes by, he won't have to deal with taking it off. She has watched countless YouTube videos on how to correctly wrench the trim off the wall and it still managed to splinter uncontrollably. Beatrice stopped caring about the condition halfway through the first wall, pealing it off in chunks and wincing every time she saw more of the wallpaper start to tear in sharp shapes crawling up from the floor. She wipes the sweat off her brow, tossing more of the trim into the pile near the stairs. Putting her hands on her hips, Beatrice stares at the messy hallway in approval, scraps of wallpaper and dust and chunks of wood littering the whole thing by the time she is done.

She isn't sure why, but she feels victorious yet sad, and it's an odd thing to feel after simply taking trim off the walls and tearing some strips of this ugly wallpaper off. She thinks about that message written in her notebook from the attic: *Welcome Home.* She could burn Ashwood to the ground and this would still be considered her home, no matter what. Filled with all of these scary memories and terrible stories she doesn't even know about. Seeing the mess sprawled out in front of her brings her a sense of joy.

Ashwood might control a lot of things, but it's just a thing built out of wood and brick. Beatrice holds the power.

Ashwood. Before.

The day after Beatrice's tenth birthday, she sobbed in her bedroom, holding her elephant to her chest in a tight embrace. She stained her pillow with tears, stuffing her arms underneath and sobbing about what a terrible day she had yesterday. Her little party was sad and only consisted of her mom, her two aunts, and Xander. Xander barely spoke the whole time and was often ignored by the other three when he did. Beatrice wore a mint green dress she had gotten for Christmas, so excited to wear it for the first time on her birthday.

But for some odd reason, Aunt Marley and Beatrice's mom were barely speaking with Aunt Edie and Aunt Edie showed up drunk, refilling glass after glass. She cried over her slice of birthday cake about Uncle Eli not being here and the other two awkwardly comforted her with weird pats on her back and shooting glances at one another that said things Beatrice couldn't even understand. It was just awful. Everyone seemed preoccupied with more important things. Didn't they know that Beatrice reaching double digits was important? Didn't they see how pretty she looked in her dress? Xander was the only one who complimented her and it was the best part of the day.

Now, Beatrice was still wearing the mint green dress, a red ribbon wrapped around the waist as a belt. When she was done feeling sorry for herself, she climbed out of bed and dabbed at her face with a mitten on her dresser. Aunt Edie once told her that she should never wipe at her face when she was crying because it would smear her makeup and tug at her skin. Even though Beatrice never even wore makeup, she was still going to dab at her cheeks for practice.

She left her bedroom, hands tucked behind her back as she headed down the hall toward the study—where her mother was often found these days. She didn't know what she did in there all day or why she liked to put her nose in so many books lately, but it must have been a grownup thing because Aunt Marley would often do the same but lose her patience and march out.

"Hi, Mom," Beatrice greeted her from the doorway, her hands still locked behind her back.

"Hey, there, kiddo." Beatrice's mom looked up from one of the books in her lap. She had stacks of other novels surrounding her, little heaps of stories and words. "You know, just because you're ten now, doesn't mean you have to call me *Mom*."

Beatrice blushed. *Good*, she thought. *I don't like sounding like an adult.*

"What're you doing?" Beatrice approached her, trying to sneak a peek at the pages of the book in her mother's lap.

"I'm doing some reading."

Beatrice plopped down on one of the stacks of books, pulling her knees together. "You're always reading lately."

"Reading is important," her mother told her, running her hands over the two open pages in her lap. "It makes you smarter."

"Depends on what you read," Beatrice joked and then glanced down at all the books around them, some of them bookmarked and others face down on the floor to save certain pages. "What is all this?"

"Research," her mother told her in an uncomfortable voice. She turned down the corner of one of the pages and set the book off to the side. "Random stuff you'd probably find boring."

Beatrice leaned forward, an old brown book cover catching her eye. *Esther Millstone* was at the bottom in gold script. She perked up, realizing it was their last name. She reached for it, holding the book in her rather small hands. "Hey, this is our last name." She squinted at the first name again. "Who is Esther?"

"That is your great, great, great, great grandmother," her mother informed in a matter-of-fact tone. "She was one of the first Millstones."

"And she wrote a book?" Beatrice flipped through the pages, which were covered in tiny words and pictures of old Victorian houses looking similar to Ashwood.

"Kinda," her mom scooted closer, now on her knees to show her some of the pages. "She was an architect—which was a pretty big job for a woman back in the day. But she was the one who actually put this house together. She drew it all up on paper and had it built. Then, she published this book, which is all about houses that look like ours."

"Cool!"

"It is cool, isn't it?" she smiled, and it was the first time Beatrice had seen her *really* smile in a long time. It made her happy. She reached for another book nearby, the drawing of a hairy creature with wings and horns on the front. "This was written by another family member, too."

"It was?" Beatrice set Esther's book down and reached for the other one, her fingers tracing over the engraved photo covering the front. She wondered what the creature was, but she had an overwhelming feeling that it wasn't necessarily a nice one. It wore a scowl and his horns reminded Beatrice of the devil or a demon from one of those supernatural movies Xander would tell her about.

"It was worked on by Grandpa Hugh and Aunt Edie's brother, Lachlan," she told her. "He spent all of his time writing about supernatural creatures, ones that we can't see."

Beatrice flipped through some of the photos, reading about something called *The Noise Behind the Barn*. The photo on the parallel page showed this huge scribble of a shape with two menacing eyeballs. Beatrice wondered if those things were real, as she had heard plenty of times before strange groaning noises from behind the shed. Xander always told her that it was probably a deer.

Another page showed a creature that looked sort of like a corpse crawling out of… a crawl space? Beatrice squinted at the picture, already knowing that she was probably going to have nightmares that night from staring at it for too long. But she couldn't help it. She was still waking up in the night to calls for help from the crawl space in the basement, nails raking against the wood. She blinked at the picture, her eyes widening a bit when she realized that the corpse had such long fingers. Although, they weren't fingers at all. They were curly long nails, sharp enough to break skin if it ever touched.

Another page showed a bunch of hands reaching out from under a flight of stairs.

"Weird." Beatrice shut the book and looked at her mom in confusion. "Why did he write that?"

"It was never published," she said, taking the book from her and setting it back into one of her organized piles. "He went missing before he could do anything with it. And then of course, Aunt Edie found him in the basement."

Beatrice frowned. She wondered if all the noises she heard at night were Grandpa Hugh's and Aunt Edie's brother, begging for someone to let him out, desperate to find a way to escape that dusty old crawl space no one ever used. She fiddled with her hands in her lap, her brain sore from swimming thoughts.

"What's wrong, Bea?"

Beatrice was more scared than ever but she couldn't put her finger on why. Sure, that book Uncle Lachlan wrote was weird and scary and was a little too spot-on to be fiction, but Beatrice had always known there were spooky things in Ashwood. Perhaps realizing that she wasn't the only one who felt that way made her realize that this was a lot more adult than she thought. Being in double digits isn't that fun.

"Weren't able to move again?" Astrid asked when her husband finally sat up in bed, gasping for air. She blinked the sleep from her eyes, rubbing Hugh's back in small circles.

"No." He gasped for air, his fingers numb from him attempting to move them even just an inch for so long.

The thing Hugh hated most about these weird sleep spells was that he wasn't in control of anything. He had spent most of his life controlling things where he saw fit. He would have full access to the reins and wouldn't let up until he decided when. But when he slept, and he found himself unable to move, he was out of his given control. There was nothing he could do to put an end to what was happening. He had to impatiently wait for it to stop and things to go back to normal.

"Maybe we should get you in to see a doctor," Astrid suggested one other morning as they had coffee on the porch of Ashwood. "I don't want things getting worse for you, dear."

"I don't need to see no doctor," Hugh spat stubbornly.

"You sound like every man in America," Astrid mumbled into her coffee before taking a sip. "I think it might be good for you."

But, he never went. He would sleep, deal with his night terrors, and then wake up, wondering what had brought them on in the first place.

After changing into his pinstriped pajamas, Hugh stood in front of the bathroom mirror, holding a little sleeping pill in the palm of his hand. He had been raised to avoid all kinds of pills and medicines that might make something better. His father advised him to take things like a man, while his mother warned him that most medicines have worse side effects than what you were trying to medicate in the first place.

But, Hugh grew tired of these sleep paralysis episodes. He missed his sleep. So, he popped the pill into the back of his throat and swallowed it dry.

Hugh's eyes flashed open that night, his body a lump of coal in front of him, too heavy to budge. His jaw was locked shut and as he laid in the dark bedroom he shared with his wife, he realized something. They were not alone. His teeth grinded together as he attempted to yell for help. He tried moving his left arm to swat at Astrid, who peacefully stirred next to him in her sleep, unbothered by the world outside of her dreams. Hugh blinked over and over again, a figure standing in the doorway with fingernails so long that they might as well be knives.

Hugh knew that he must have been dreaming. There was no way he could see something like *that*. There was no way it even existed. Minutes passed and Hugh grew the strength to move his finger, lifting it an inch above where it lay next to him on the bed. He could only blink and move his eyes, his spine as stable as train tracks.

Blinking in the darkness of the room, Hugh watched as the figure in the doorway witnessed him struggling. What was that thing and why the hell was it in his home? He swallowed the ball in his throat that had swelled so large from trying to scream, he nearly choked. It wasn't until the man in the doorway left that Hugh felt like he could finally breathe. And then, he moved.

Hugh fumbled out of the bed, nearly flinging himself onto the floor from trying to get out of his paralyzed state. He ran for the door, leaving the bedroom and looking up and down the hallway for any sign of the man. But it was empty.

"And this is how Grandpa Hugh lived the remainder of his life. He would wake from his sleep and find himself unable to move. Grammy Astrid would try helping him when she could, doing her best to slowly move his limbs until his body woke up. But with these episodes, came that haunting man in the doorway, masked by a light behind him coming from an unknown source. Each night that man visited his room, he grew one step closer to Hugh's bed."

Hugh tried mumbling out words or a scream when he realized the figure was closer than he had ever been before one night. He was a shadow, lingering in front of him like a bad scent.

"P-please," Hugh was able to make out in a begging tone. It was the first time he was able to speak during one of his episodes. "Leave me alone."

"And the man did. He slowly took his steps back to the door, entered the hallway, and disappeared. But that doesn't mean he stayed away."

Hugh's eyes sprung open very early Christmas morning. He stared up at the ceiling, his body filled with lead. He swallowed a sour taste in his mouth and when he attempted to move his legs, they were too stabilized to budge. His eyes adjusting to the black, he noticed the man standing at the foot of his bed. He had shoulder-length hair, long for a man, but that was how Hugh recognized who the man was. A faded green army jacket and broad shoulders, a wide nose and bushy eyebrows.

It took several minutes for Hugh to open his mouth again to speak, grateful that his jaw wasn't locked like the other times. Perhaps that was an improvement. When he could finally separate his lips, he spoke.

"Lachlan," he said his brother's name, breaking the silence of the Christmas night.

"Hello, brother," Lachlan said, looking exactly the way he did the last time Hugh saw him. "You should start drinking warm milk before bed. It's supposed to help you sleep."

"What are you doing?" Hugh demanded, trying to sit up but his body protested. "What is happening? You're supposed to be dead."

"Lachlan had been missing for years, you see. He moved back into Ashwood shortly after dropping out of college, Hugh and Edie promising him that it would be good for him. He took their word for it."

"And whose fault is that?"

Hugh's brow furrowed, his body on its way to gaining back consciousness, waking from the depths of Hell it finds itself stuck in most nights. "What are you talking about?"

"You locked the doors to the crawl space," Lachlan informed him of something Hugh didn't even do. His voice was low and gravelly and insanely hard to listen to. His gray eyes were bright in the dark and the build of his younger body made Hugh feel way older than he actually was. "You locked me in there and I couldn't get out. Do you know how long I was in there before I died? Thirteen bloody days. I was screaming and kicking at the doors, I was losing my mind. Kicking and screaming, kicking and screaming, kicking and screaming. My mind was lost. Lost. Lost. It was gone. Gone. Gone. Gone." His voice was growing louder, more aggressive. "I was clawing at them, waiting for someone to hear me, waiting for you to come back down and realize what you had done, for you to *find* me. But you never did. No one did. I would spend nights scraping at the doors until each of my fingers had hundreds of splinters. I was so low on energy that I couldn't stay awake for very long. You didn't hear me. You didn't come. If you did hear me, you didn't come. I was kicking and screaming, kicking and screaming. And you didn't come."

"I didn't lock you in there," Hugh assured after bringing himself to speak. He tried shaking his head but he still couldn't bring himself to move. "I swear, I've missed you this whole time you've been gone. I wouldn't have done that to you—"

"Astrid didn't love me," Lachlan cut him off, the words cutting through Hugh like a knife. Words Hugh never thought he would hear. "You painted this picture in your head of the two of us. You were so paranoid, Hugh. Paranoid about something that wasn't ever a thing."

"Hugh was a deer in headlights because his little brother was not wrong, as unfortunate as that is to admit. Lachlan lived life in a way that made his older brother jealous. He was more spontaneous, he had a winning smile and a head of hair women particularly liked. Hugh spent a great deal of time looking in the other direction when it came to his suspicions about his brother and the woman he thought was the love of his life. He turned the other cheek because it was easier to ignore a problem than to solve one. And once that snowball started to roll, there would be no time to stop it. He had no proof that the two of them were madly in love behind his back. He had no evidence that linked them to discussing their futures in front of roaring fires or sneaking away at holiday parties, stealing kisses under the mistletoe. Because it was jealousy and paranoia, battling everything from the inside of his own head. And it only got worse when he began sleeping under the roof of Ashwood."

"And your way of getting back at me…" Lachlan continued, his frame blurring in Hugh's sight as tears flooded both of his eyes. "Was to lock me in that crawl space. Revenge."

Hugh opened his mouth to protest once more, but before he could, a flash of a memory sparked through his thoughts. He saw himself shutting the doors to the crawl space and flipping the lock with the simple movement of a finger. But that wasn't possible. Hugh had no recollection of that. But then why was he remembering a false memory?

"I'm sorry," Hugh croaked, trying to adjust his weight under the blankets but it felt like he was more weighed down than ever before. Maybe it was the guilt. "Lachlan, I'm sorry. I don't remember…"

"But your own blood got the sore end of the stick," Lachlan finished for him. "That seems fair."

Hugh opened his mouth to apologize some more but no sound could come out. His bottom lip quivered, eyes locked with his brother's. He then recalled hearing his brother shouting at him from behind the doors. Hugh ignored them as though he didn't hear them at all, shutting the basement light off at the top of the steps and closing the door.

"Hugh's actions were beyond his control, taken from him by the house. A memory that was stolen and only given back under Ashwood's supervision."

"I would have never done that to you," Lachlan added. "You went insane and I had to pay the price."

Hugh was speechless. He tried with all his might to move, to beg his brother to hear him out, to tell him that he didn't remember any of that. That a House Thing must have urged him to do it or a night of sleepwalking. But he couldn't. His body was useless at this point and there was no way around that. He stared at Lachlan with pleading eyes, regret floating off his entire being.

Lachlan smirked, his head hanging to the side as he stared pityingly at his brother in the bed. "It only seems fair, brother, that insanity between two siblings goes a very long way. What's that vow you made to Astrid?" He put one of his very long fingernails to his chin, pretending to think. "'Til death do you part?"

It was like all of Hugh's strength was thrown back into him. His body had grown into a twisted cramp and when he could finally move after not being able to for so long, his muscles nearly yelped with glee. His limbs flung into action and his neck snapped to the side, a loud *crack* disrupting the peace of early Christmas morning.

Chapter 22

"What are you doing in here?"

Beatrice wakes up, standing in Grandpa Hugh's and Grammy Astrid's bedroom. She hasn't been in here since they sealed it after Grammy's death a year before Beatrice left Ashwood. She let her eyes adjust to the four-poster bed against the wall, the heavy blanket of dust layering the dressers and the nightstands, a lampshade that was once white now yellow from its place in the sun by the window.

The story her mother told her buzzes through her head and Beatrice can't find the words to respond to Aunt Edie, looming behind her in the doorway with a confused expression splashed across her face. Grandpa Hugh was the one who locked Lachlan in the crawl space without remembering it. But how? Was he beginning to sleepwalk just as much as Aunt Edie? Did one of the House Things coax him into it the way Pete had Uncle Eli in a trance? She never pegged Grandpa Hugh as the type to do something so stupid. She never thought that he and Grammy Astrid had any marital issues of sorts, which is why Grandpa Hugh acting on his own accord in that way makes zero sense.

"Sorry," Beatrice finally announces a little too loudly, looking at her aunt. "I was just... I was looking at their furniture. I thought that since the movers will be arriving this weekend, I could take some stuff from the bedrooms."

Aunt Edie looks like she was just smacked across the face. "You're wanting to take the bedroom sets with you as well?"

Beatrice swallows, trying her best to wake up. At least Aunt Edie doesn't know that she was sleepwalking. When did she even fall asleep? Is it morning or did she doze after dismantling the trim off the hallway walls? Her mind tries to get into the swing of things but Aunt Edie's question forces Beatrice to push her thoughts onto the backburner of her brain.

"Maybe," Beatrice answers. "Unless you were hoping to keep them here?"

"I just don't know how much room you have in that tiny shop of yours," Aunt Edie tells her, folding her arms over her frail chest. She wears a long orange cardigan sweater that hangs to her knees, a black gown underneath it with sparkles throughout. "Plus, you're going to have to hire a lot more movers if you want to make that work."

"I'll figure something out," Beatrice assures, rubbing the back of her neck. She feels a knot forming, a stress headache beginning to throb behind her eyes. "But I want to get it cleaned up a bit first."

"Sounds like a good idea." Aunt Edie glides across the room, inspecting a painting hanging on the wall that has hung there ever since Beatrice can remember. It depicts a man's body with a pig's head, chowing down on human organs and guts. "Oh, which reminds me, can you please ask to go into my bedroom before you go in there next time?"

Beatrice's eyes widen a bit and when Aunt Edie turns around to face her, she quickly goes back to her regular face. Her eyebrows pull together to play as dumb as she possibly can. "I don't know what you're talking about."

She laughs like Beatrice is some little girl instead of her niece. "Yes, you do, dear. I always lock my door and when I came back yesterday, it was unlocked. If you're going to be sneaky, at least do it right."

How in the actual *fuck* is Beatrice supposed to respond to that? Admit that she was in there opening her wardrobe to search for whatever weird symbol was carved into the door? Or how she crawled under the bed and found that memorial scrapbook to her dead son? She prompts herself to think fast, to come up with some better excuse than just staring at her like she doesn't speak English.

"Oh, right!" Beatrice plays it off—probably not very good but it's going to have to do. "Yeah, I probably heard something in there."

Aunt Edie squints clearly not convinced. "You heard something?"

"Yep," she lies, scratching at her head. "It was this weird noise and I wanted to make sure everything was okay. It was clear, though. So… it's all good."

Aunt Edie paints one of her fake smiles across her red lips, stepping closer to Beatrice. "Please do not go into my room unless I say otherwise. It's rude and I am your elder. I deserve more respect than that, don't you think?"

Beatrice would like to tell her that respect needs to be earned and since she has been back in this house, Aunt Edie has barely earned a pint of it. Yes, she is very thankful that she has a roof over her head right now and she's getting paid to do some housework, but none of that tops the real issues going on within Ashwood. But she is still trying to remain on Aunt Edie's good side so she nods her head.

"Good," Aunt Edie chirps. "I'm glad to see we're on the same page, darling."

She leaves the room and Beatrice waits several seconds before following suit. She shuts the door behind her and hurries back to her own bedroom, when yesterday finally comes rolling back to her. She ate Spaghetti-o's in her room, filling out informational research for the furniture in the attic. She kept wandering back to the photo of Marilyn and her husband, trying to gain any sort of context clues that could give her more information on if they're responsible for why none of the missing women in Silver Creek are gaining more attention or the mess with Madeline Winthrop.

Beatrice checks the time on her dying phone. She needs to meet Officer Gomez at that pie place in about thirty minutes. So, she throws on a shirt from a pile of questionably clean clothes from the floor and pulls on some jeans. After brushing her teeth and pulling her hair into a greasy ponytail, Beatrice sets off downstairs, an excuse already waiting to be used on the tip of her tongue.

"Can I borrow your car?" Beatrice asks Aunt Edie when she finds her lounging in the parlor with a compress covering her forehead. "Do you feel all right?"

"I was a little restless last night," Aunt Edie admits. "Trying to nap. What do you need my car for?"

"Xander and I need a few things for the new trimming upstairs," Beatrice tells her immediately. "And I'm going to look for a steamer. I figured that taking the wallpaper off will be easier with that."

"Okay." She shuts her eyes and places her hands over her stomach. "My keys are by the door."

Beatrice snatches them on her way out, climbing into the car and pealing out of the driveway. She can't tell Aunt Edie about meeting with an officer, not yet. If Marilyn is married to Hudson, then she might have more power than Beatrice was giving her credit for before. She thought she could talk to her and expose her for playing a part in what happened to the twins. But if the two of them are somehow responsible for what is happening here, then Beatrice isn't as strong as she thought. Turning Marilyn in and giving Gomez this huge chunk of missing information might be a step in the right direction in getting justice for Juniper and Jax.

Penny's Pies is a small joint located on the corner of Portage Road next to a funeral home. Beatrice parks on the street, the sign telling her she has just two hours of free parking. Heading inside, Beatrice glances around the diner, overwhelmed by the banana yellow and lavender purple checkered walls and floors and tables and even chairs. Plastic skeletons hang from the walls and a life-size cutout of Frankenstein's bride stands in the corner. Beatrice glances around the diner for any sign of Gomez but all she sees are older people sharing plates of pies or milkshakes.

Beatrice finds a leather booth in the back, the material groaning under her as she scoots inside and anxiously drums her fingers against the top of the table. She waits for eight minutes, glancing over her shoulder at the door and taking small undesirable bites of the apple pie a waitress brought to her after she ordered. Finally, Alejandra Gomez comes waltzing through the door, wearing an expensive plaid coat over her cop uniform. She makes her way to the booth when Beatrice offers her a small wave.

"Sorry I'm late," Gomez says first, sliding in on the other side of the booth. "I had a lot more paperwork to fill out at the station than I thought."

"You're on time, actually," Beatrice lies, deciding to keep the fact that she thought Gomez was going to flake to herself. She clears her throat and gestures to the other plate next to the pie platter. "I had the waitress bring an extra plate in case you wanted a slice."

"Thank you," she says politely and dishes out a piece onto her plate, reaching for a fork. She's way too pretty to live somewhere like Silver Creek. She reminds Beatrice of some international super model who spends her weekends on private yachts or jets and she eats brunches on rooftops in expensive hot tubs. But here she sits, in a shitty diner wearing a cop uniform. "I'm surprised you called, honestly. I thought that our talk at Fred Macher's house was going to scare you off."

Beatrice wriggles her brow. "Why would you think that?"

"Because I know my partner can be a little intimidating," she mumbles quietly, cutting into her pie. "Officer Hudson is a lot of things. Friendly isn't quite at the top of that list."

"I'm starting to get worried," Beatrice admits in a hushed voice. "There are so many missing girls that have disappeared out of thin air. Hudson nor anyone on the police squad seem to be worried about it."

"Trust me, I've had the same thought." She shoves a forkful of pie into her mouth and generously chews. She swallows and continues. "The police department seemed worried for the girls at first but Hudson took over the cases right away. Obviously, no one thinks anything of it. He's been a cop since forever so everyone looks up to him there."

"Are you saying what I think you're saying?"

Gomez studies her. "I guess that depends on what you think I'm saying."

"That Hudson knows what's going on," Beatrice states. "That he has some weird part in all of this. Every person that goes missing in Silver Creek."

She sighs, glancing at the doors to the kitchen when a clatter of plates pierces the air. She turns back to Beatrice. "I shouldn't be telling you what I'm about to tell you, but I can't quite keep it to myself any longer."

Beatrice leans forward, hoping she doesn't seem more eager for a slice of information than she is over this pie. "I'm listening."

"This stays between us?"

Beatrice nods vigorously.

"Well, you know how I mentioned that the case of the Millstone twins was never closed?"

Beatrice nods again.

"I'm pretty sure Hudson had something to do with that, too," Gomez explains, stabbing at a glazed apple slice with her fork. "There is a huge file at the station filled with cold cases. Sometimes, cops will pick up a case if things are slow. I remember hearing about your cousins' disappearance when I was a kid and the story always stuck with me. Don't ask me why, my mind is weird."

Beatrice can relate. She remembers listening to the news with Grammy Astrid one evening and there was a teen suicide that rocked a town miles away. Months later, the cops discovered that the suicide was actually a murder plotted by a mentally unstable patient from an institution on the outskirts of the county. Beatrice can't remember the details anymore, but she always thought about that story whenever she would see a pretty girl out in public or peer into the Jungle at night, imagining that escaped patient wandering through them and looking for his next victim.

"So, when I started looking through the cases, it was nowhere," Gomez proceeds, pulling Beatrice back into the present. "I asked around but as far as some of the cops knew, the case was still open… until Hudson inserted himself into a conversation and said that it was shut a while ago. But, after more searching, there was never any evidence of what happened to them. There was no trial, no bodies, no proof that they were dead. As far as anyone would guess, the case would have still had to be open."

"Did you ask him more about it?" Beatrice pushes.

The cop shakes her head, dragging her apple around in circles on her plate with her fork. "You don't exactly question the chief of police."

"So, what about these cases for the missing women?" Beatrice wonders aloud. "Are they in this collection of cold cases, too?"

"For now. Until Hudson gets a hold of them, I'm sure. He'll probably remove them in a few years and claim the case was closed with a pretty little bow on top."

Beatrice chews at her fingernails—something she's been doing a lot of lately. This is all too much. Her theories about Hudson were true, though. He's playing a huge part in covering up what is happening to these girls. He's linked to Marilyn, who is linked to Aunt Edie. As Beatrice predicted before, all roads lead back to Ashwood.

"I believe you had some information for me, too." Gomez finally eats the apple she's been playing with.

"The twins died," Beatrice tells her softly and Gomez stops chewing her food. "That's what Fred knew. That's what he told me before he killed himself. He watched Hudson's wife with Juniper and Jax in the woods. Something happened, they collapsed, and Marilyn panicked and left. He buried their bodies."

The officer doesn't say anything for a long time, processing the information. Beatrice takes this time to eat more of her own pie, mostly to keep herself from getting too emotional over the demise of her cousins.

"Wow," she finally says. "I was not expecting you to say that."

"I don't know what to do," Beatrice says honestly. "I don't know if Marilyn was the cause of what happened to them or what, but everything is getting so complicated."

Gomez's perfectly plucked eyebrows pull together. "What else are you finding that's complicated?"

Beatrice opens her mouth to tell her about all of stuff going on at Ashwood but she bites her tongue. If she starts digging into everything that's been happening there, she's going to look as crazy as she did at that group therapy meeting and everything she just told her will lose its credit. She shakes her head and pokes around at the slice of pie on her plate.

"It's nothing," she lies. "I didn't expect everything to be this hard when I came back home."

"Maybe you should've stayed away," Gomez suggests, taking another bite and leaning back in the booth. "Sometimes, it's better to stay far away from where the truth lies."

"You can say that again," Beatrice utters under her breath. "So, now what?"

"What do you mean?"

"Well, I just gave you what you needed to officially close the Millstone twin case," Beatrice states the obvious. "What are you going to do with that information?"

"I'm going to take it to the FBI," she admits casually, as though this is something that is done often in her line of work. She shuffles out of her coat and places her folded hands on the table. "It's kind of what we're told to do when a chief is mistreating his power. But I would be careful, if I were you."

"Careful of what?"

"I've read over the cases of those girls plenty of times," Gomez says. "They had a couple small things in common but the biggest thing they all shared was staying in your house."

"So, you think that part is important?" Beatrice quickly asks, chewing on the inside of her cheek—even though she already knows that that part of this complicated equation is of importance. As far as her knowledge goes, the police force never took the infamous Ashwood curse seriously. They brushed it off, reminding people that a haunted house wasn't proof of anything and could never be used as evidence. "Why do you think that is?"

Gomez sighs and shrugs both of her shoulders helplessly. "I wish I knew. There's a lot of nothing where that house sits. It wouldn't be an uncommon place for predators to wait."

Beatrice thought the same thing when she first discovered the series of disappearances. But judging by Gomez's statement, she must not think much about Ashwood or the people inside. If she grew up in Silver Creek, she can't be blind to the stories that have taken place inside. She has to know more than a thing or two about what has gone on. Everyone and their mothers have to know at this point.

"So, you don't believe that it has anything to do with the house in general?"

Gomez smirks. "Are you asking if I believe that your family and that house are cursed?"

Beatrice nods again, slightly embarrassed.

Gomez thinks about it and picks her fork back up for another bite of pie. "I think that it's not my place to judge. I didn't grow up there. Why should I give my opinion on something I don't even know about? That was your own experience, not mine."

"That doesn't stop other people from having their own."

"I am not other people."

"For that, I am thankful." Beatrice stifles a laugh but she's being truthful. She was almost expecting to come here and not be taken too seriously by someone who knows who she is and her family history.

"Why?" Gomez inquires. "Do *you* know something that I don't about that place?"

Beatrice thinks about the House Things and how Ashwood has a weird way of making one paranoid beyond belief. Grandpa Hugh and Lachlan flash through her thoughts, their tombstones sitting side by side in the backyard. She thinks about the insanity that eats people alive and how when minds get lost, they're never found.

"Oh, who am I kidding?" Gomez proceeds. "Of course you know more than I do. You grew up there. I'm only an outsider looking in."

"It's a special place," Beatrice admits, treading carefully. "But just because something is special, doesn't make it good."

"Do you think that these disappearances have something to do with a certain family member of yours?" Gomez goes on quizzically, squinting her chocolate brown eyes.

Beatrice thinks of Aunt Edie. If she says yes, who knows what would happen? Gomez could run back to the police department and launch a full-blown investigation into her aunt. And what if she is responsible for what happened? What if she is to blame for the twins and the missing women? Is Beatrice ready to see her get hauled off in handcuffs to spend the rest of her life behind bars? Or should she do more digging until she knows for sure that her aunt is either guilty or innocent before she gives Gomez an answer?

Beatrice flips a strand of hair away from her eyes. "Are you kidding? My aunt is old as shit. There's no way she can take on anyone younger than her."

"I thought the same thing when her name kept coming up at the station."

Beatrice straightens her back a little. She remembers Xander telling her that Aunt Edie was investigated after each disappearance, and Aunt Edie herself admitted that, too. It shouldn't be a surprise that her name kept coming up when someone else would vanish.

"Oh?" Beatrice squeaks.

"They're shut down a lot of the time, though," Gomez assures, as though she thought Beatrice was worried… which she kind of was but she can't put a finger on why. "Your aunt had a lot of alibis that checked out. Plus, she wouldn't want anything to do with the women who stayed with her, anyway." She pauses. "Unless, you know something that I don't."

Beatrice shakes her head. "No, of course not. As far as I know, each girl that stayed with Aunt Edie was a stranger before and during their stay at Ashwood."

"And you're sure about that?"

"Yes," she confirms. "I don't have a reason to lie."

"I'm not saying that you do." Gomez wipes her mouth with the square napkin sitting next to her plate. "But I know that I'm not the only one that that thinks it's odd that a lot of those eight girls that stayed there all had similar backgrounds. Not too many friends, not close with their families, usually caught up in risky business. It's a very simple pattern."

"Which means…?"

"Which means one could think that your aunt would target vulnerable ladies like the ones that stayed with her," she clarifies, staring Beatrice hard in the face. "That she would prey on women who were running from something or someone and might not be missed if something happened to them." Gomez leans forward a little. "Your aunt has been very lonely since the last time you were here. She has spent over fifteen years in that house, women coming and going. One might argue that she was trying to find someone that reminded her of you."

Beatrice shifts uncomfortably in the booth. She never thought about that, young girls just like her walking blindly into Ashwood, thinking it was a good place to stay. Could the house have driven Aunt Edie so insane that she has spent all these years hunting down girls that remind her of Beatrice? That seems wild. Too wild. It's reaching for a solution that isn't there.

"Would you say that could be true?" Gomez asks when Beatrice keeps her lips clamped together. "Would you say there's a small chance your aunt might be a little senile and it caused her to harm these ladies?"

Beatrice's eyelid twitches as she studies the woman sitting across from her. These questions are sounding way too serious, now. "I'm sorry, are you interrogating me?"

Gomez straightens her back and blinks three times in a row. "No, I'm not interrogating you. We would have to be at the police station for that and you would have access to a lawyer."

"Then how about the next time you start quizzing me on my aunt's mental health and stability, you wait to do it there?" Beatrice slides out of the booth before Gomez can ask her any other questions.

She doesn't even think about leaving money for the pie as she maneuvers around the tables on her way out of the diner.

Beatrice jerked awake from her slumber one spring night when she heard a very loud and very strange noise coming from outside.

She sat up in her bed, blinking the sleep from her eyes as she let them adjust to the darkness around her. Dim moonlight filtered through the windows and across her floor, beckoning her over to the turret to see outside. The sound was indescribable, but it definitely didn't sound too nice. It was almost like a roar, a very deep roar that sounded like an animal—or something that wasn't human or animal. A creature, maybe, that Jax used to mimic.

Beatrice hurried out of her bed and crept across her room to the window. Aunt Marley was screaming, Beatrice's mother by her side as the two of them tore out of the garden like chickens with their heads chopped off. They were grasping onto each other's limbs like life rafts as they stumbled across the grass and toward the front of the house, their terrified screams echoing through the night.

Beatrice rushed out of her bedroom just as Aunt Edie was coming out of hers, tying a navy blue silk robe around her skinny waist.

"What's going on?" Aunt Edie demanded, as though Beatrice was to blame for all the ruckus. Her white hair was in a dramatic scarf, patterned with Van Gogh's *A Starry Night*.

"I dunno," Beatrice admitted and letting Aunt Edie take the lead toward the steps. "Aunt Marley and Mama are outside. They were in the garden."

Aunt Edie glanced at Beatrice over her shoulder with eyes the size of golf balls. She swallowed a lump in her throat and dashed down the stairs too fast for Beatrice to keep up. She followed to the best of her ability, anyway, her little legs no match for Aunt Edie's stride. Just as they descended the stairs into the foyer, Beatrice's mom and Aunt Marley were slamming the front door behind them, shoving their backs against it, and flipping the lock.

"What on earth is happening?" Aunt Edie ordered, putting a wrinkled hand on her chest. "What are you two doing?"

Aunt Marley was breathing heavily, her face covered in fear.

"There's something in the garden."

"Yes, dear," Aunt Edie agreed gently. "Those are called flowers. It's the first day of spring, they're going to start blooming, whether you suck at gardening or not."

"Something *else*, Edie," Beatrice's mom snapped at her. Her chin was tucked underneath, toward her collarbone and her eyes were dark, filled with anger and fear and some sort of knowledge that Beatrice was out of the loop on. "I thought the House Things were only inside."

Aunt Edie awkwardly glanced down at Beatrice and then looked back at the other two. "Why don't we have this conversation privately? Beatrice needs her sleep."

Beatrice's mother shook her thick brown hair away from her eyes and cupped her daughter's face in her ice-cold hands. "Honey, why don't you go back upstairs? The grownups need to have a talk."

"Okay." Beatrice did as she was told because she never disobeyed her mother. Just because she would wander up the stairs and let the three ladies file into the parlor, didn't mean she was going to *stay* in her room.

Beatrice left her bedroom door open so she could make a quick run back into it when needed. The floors granted her the wish of not creaking too loud as she tiptoed back to the steps, the voices of the remaining ladies in her family floating off from the parlor across the foyer. Beatrice took one step at a time, hanging onto the railing until she could hear just enough but still be tucked away in the shadows.

"You knew about that, didn't you?" Beatrice's mom was saying. "You knew what was in there?"

"There are plenty of things in this house that I know about and plenty of things that I don't," Aunt Edie argued back.

"This is what we're talking about," Aunt Marley hissed. "We have been asking you to be open about things for over a year now and you're still playing dumb."

"I am not playing dumb, Marley," Aunt Edie claimed in a voice that sounded flabbergasted at the thought of keeping secrets from them. "This house is a lot of things. It would be nearly impossible to know them all in one lifetime."

"But you don't even tell us what *you* know."

"My daughter lives in this house," Beatrice's mom reminded her through gritted teeth. "Marley's kids are gone. So help me, if I stay here and something happens to her—"

"Enough!" Aunt Edie roared and Beatrice could hear herself gasp.

"I am so sick of both of you thinking that I had something to do with everything that has happened in this house. I will not stand for it anymore."

"What are we supposed to think?" Aunt Marley asked desperately. "You don't seem concerned about anything. Every single person who has grown up in this family is either dead or missing. And Lena and I are the only two that are starting to wonder why."

Aunt Edie didn't say anything. Beatrice tried craning her neck on the stairs to get a glimpse through the doorway of the parlor but she was too high up in the stairwell to have been able to.

"The house is filled with books and diaries and journals from family members that were here before us," Aunt Marley went on, her tone a lot calmer now. "There are things in them that correspond with certain things that we have seen here. Things that don't make any sense."

"I am terrified, Edie," Beatrice's mother spoke up grimly. "I am scared to continue living here. Not only for myself, but for my daughter. I refuse to keep her in a harmful environment. Especially when I'm not getting the answers I need."

"I don't know them," Aunt Edie croaked. "But this house isn't like other houses, dear. It's different in ways that no one would be able to explain. I wish I could tell you, but I can't. Because not even I have all the answers."

"Well why don't you start by telling us what you *do* know?"

"Because," Aunt Edie responded simply. It made Beatrice confused. "The house likes things the way they are now."

"Grammy Astrid was never too self-involved in how she looked. She knew she was pretty, and she knew that when she was younger, she was often ogled at. But she was never full of herself or boasted about her looks. She was humble."

Astrid pattered around her bedroom, using a toner covered cotton ball to swipe her face with. "Don't forget we have to wake up early for the kids."

"I know," Hugh responded from the bed, sifting through one of the many books he took from the library, some horned creature covering the front but Astrid didn't bother asking him any questions about it.

"It was Christmas Eve night, a night that was stressful for Astrid ever since she became a mother. It wasn't that she didn't enjoy the holidays, in fact she loved them more when she became a mom. But the magic was no longer present and bustling around getting things in order for the children became a top priority."

"You said that last year." Astrid sighed as she walked into their private bathroom, her slippers sinking into the shag pink carpet inside.

"Besides, I'm sure Edie will already be drinking at the crack of dawn."

"Maybe we should do something about that," Hugh grumbled. "She almost fell into the tree last year."

"Maybe I'll water down her wine," Astrid suggested, tossing the cotton ball into the trash next to the toilet. She adjusted her curls wrapped in her head of hair. She studied her reflection, already able to see the glow to her face. "We don't need a repeat of last year. Children see that stuff, you know. It can cause so much traumatic behavior later on in life."

"I don't think Edie being drunk is going to cause too much damage." Hugh put his book on the nightstand and reached over to turn out the lamp. "Are you coming to bed?"

"Yes, I'm coming." Astrid turned on the faucet and washed her hands—a routine she had always done ever since she was little. She found herself gasping when she looked up to see a very familiar woman standing behind her.

Dorothy, Hugh's mother, stood behind her daughter-in-law with a smirk on her face. She was always wearing a smirk, always coming across as a bitch, a word Astrid rarely used but always made an exception for Dorothy. She had jet black hair tied into a low side bun and she wore a polka-dotted red and white dress, the same one she had on when she was found in the bathtub.

"Sweetie, we need to find you something to get rid of those bags under your eyes," Dorothy told her, that pasted smile still playing across her lips like a tune Astrid once grew to despise.

Astrid whipped around to find no one standing behind her. She rapidly blinked, putting her hand to her chest to feel her racing heart. She looked back over her shoulder but her mother-in-law was no longer on the other side of the glass.

The following morning, Astrid slowly brought her husband to sit up in bed, one of his sleep paralysis spells getting the worst of him. She tended to his hands, gently moving each and every one of his fingers until he was able to move them himself. She patiently waited until his jaw became unlocked and he was able to climb out of bed on his own.

"Astrid cared for others in ways most humans didn't. She wasn't going to burden Hugh with how she saw his mother last night in the bathroom mirror. That didn't compare to what he dealt with most nights."

She swung her legs over the edge of the bed, already listening to everyone else slipping out of their bedrooms and wishing each other a Merry Christmas.

The day went by in a blur. Snow clung to every surface outside while Aunt Marley helped the twins tear open their gifts. Beatrice showed her mother what Santa brought her with such great excitement that nothing could have brought her down. Edie and Eli were curled up on a couch together, both holding mugs filled with eggnog. Christmas music floated off the record player in the corner, nearly buried under all the wrapping paper. Astrid sat in her rocking chair, watching the kids' face light up whenever they opened something they wanted or something they didn't ask for but were equally excited.

Her smile slowly faded when she saw Dorothy again, standing directly behind her in the reflection of a ruby red ornament hanging on the tree. Astrid's hands curled up into two fists and she stared hard at the woman who raised her husband, her figure so haunting that it took everything in Astrid not to scream. No one else seemed to notice her presence, though. It was like Dorothy could only be seen by Astrid.

"And that's when it began for Astrid, seeing her dead mother-in-law in reflections everywhere."

Astrid stood in front of one of the glass cupboards in the kitchen, her mother's lurking figure behind her, her face lit up by the afternoon sun pouring through the windows. Astrid dropped her glass.

"Mom?" Aunt Marley gasped from the dining table, where she was feeding the twins. "Are you okay?"

"Yes, I'm fine," Astrid claimed and forced a smile to hide her fear. "You know me, clumsy and all."

"It wasn't like the other members of the Millstone family could never see Dorothy, because we did. She was just another House Thing. But like Pete, she stalked, just like how Pete preyed on Eli. And her daughter-in-law made for the perfect victim."

Astrid wrapped a fluffy pink towel around her when stepping out of the shower, glancing at the mirror to find Dorothy on the other side of the glass, glaring. She quickly looked away, nearly slipping on the water in the tub. She grabbed hold of the wall and her chest, her hair dripping wet.

"Careful, sweetheart." Dorothy broke the silence that filled the bathroom. "Slip too much and you'll die in that very same tub I did."

"You're not here," Astrid croaked.

"But I am." Dorothy's pale white hand pressed against the mirror and her bitchy smirk turned into a tearful greeting. "I'm always here, Astrid."

But she was a liar because she was gone in the blink of an eye.

On a chilly day in November, Astrid carried a basket of laundry up from the basement, nearly knocked over when Marley bustled out the mud room door.

"Where are you going?" Astrid called after her daughter but she ignored her, her head hanging low and trudging through the crunchy leaves toward the woods. She was looking for the twins again.

When Astrid opened the door to the bathroom upstairs, she gasped, Dorothy once again waiting for her in the mirror, greeting her with a polite wave.

"Did you miss me?" Dorothy joked with the tiniest hint of a smirk but it faded quickly into a thick frown. Her big brown eyes looked larger than usual, like she was now a cartoon with a thumping heart and ear-to-ear smiles.

"You're not here," Astrid told her, bustling over to the hamper for the dirty towels. "You have no control."

"We both know that's not true, my precious daughter-in-law," Dorothy corrected her. "Technically, this process is lasting longer than others." She pressed her hand to the glass again. "And I miss seeing your face. I bet you miss it, too."

"I miss nothing," Astrid snapped.

"You miss my son," Dorothy challenged immediately. She giggled, bringing Astrid's stare to her. Did she think it was *funny* Astrid was having a hard time letting Hugh go? "Everyone in this house thinks you're going mad."

"I'm not."

"But you are," she corrected again. "I mean, you're talking to a lady in a mirror. That's grounds for some insanity, don't you think?"

"This is my house now," Astrid reminded her, setting the basket down on the closed toilet seat. "You aren't welcome here."

"I remember hearing you telling Beatrice that the things in his house belong to it just as much as you all." Dorothy's voice was creamy and smooth, luring her daughter-in-law right into a trap Astrid couldn't do anything about. "But you can't see your husband."

"What does Hugh have to do with anything?"

"I often chat to him," Dorothy claimed. "He tells me all of these things about you, things that he would want to say."

"You're lying," Astrid barked. "You're lying, you're lying, you're lying, you're lying!"

"Please don't throw a tantrum," Dorothy growled. "It makes you look like those privileged children in the city."

"You're not here, Dorothy." Astrid's voice shook and she felt like she was going to cry. "You haven't been for a very long time."

"And I love not being there," Dorothy claimed.

Astrid's brow furrowed. "But you killed yourself. How can you say such a thing? You left your whole family behind."

"But don't you see that things are better for me?" She smiled so bright it was nearly blinding. She gestured to behind her at the exact bathroom Astrid was standing in. "I'm safe. I'm all put away now."

"There's nothing good about being… where you are," Astrid said to her breathlessly. She gestured to the round mirror. "You're stuck."

"You're mistaking stuck for being safe." She stared at her long and hard, as though putting Astrid under some sort of spell. "Look at all of the family members before you, Astrid. They were stuck in this house until they were blessed with fate. Now, they're here and they have nothing to worry about. They're no longer stuck, you see. There's safety in knowing that you won't have to go outside. There's a sense of security in not dealing with troubles of the outside world, a very mean and hurtful world outside of this house. Do you understand?"

Astrid shook her head, feeling like a little girl again as her mother tried teaching her a lesson she couldn't process. "No."

Dorothy sighed and looked Astrid carefully in the eyes. "You have no control if you let fate take its course. You don't have the power to make your life what you want. Unless, you become your own fate."

Astrid blinked twice, realizing what she was being told. "You think that offing yourself in the bathtub was your version of creating your own fate?"

She nodded her head, smiling. "And I know you want to do the same. I know you want to see Hugh and Grandma. I know you're tired of feeling unsafe. But you're able to change that, Astrid. You can stay here, with me, with all of us, safe and put away in a world where things don't have to get worse. Where things are always good and happy and we're together."

"So, Astrid thought about it. She thought about all of the family members that had passed prior, all of the funerals she had to attend and assist in digging their graves. She thought about Hugh, how great it would be to see him again. She thought about her mother-in-law and how if everything was happier on that side of the glass, then maybe their rocky relationship would stand a chance. Maybe this dirty world that seems to only get worse by the day wasn't looking too shiny anymore. Perhaps, she could make her own fate and not wind up in an accidental death like most of the other people who had walked Ashwood.

And so, with an encouraging smile from her mother, Astrid did what she was told, and she took her life into her own hands by throwing it out the window."

Chapter 23

Beatrice cries out, feeling her whole body being shaken out of a trance. She jumps, flailing her arms around as she jerks her head from side to side.

"Beatrice!" Aunt Edie yells to calm her down. She's dragging her away from the tall bathroom window, her long nails digging into Beatrice's flesh. "What the hell is wrong with you?"

Beatrice pants. Her entire forehead is covered in slippery sweat, strands of hair sticking to it. She stares at her reflection in the mirror and doesn't recognize herself. She's wearing a shirt that's too small and sweatpants that hang down her bony hips. Has she really let herself go that much since being back here? She uses her wrist to wipe the sweat from her face, the story her mother told her swimming through her thoughts like Michael freaking Phelps.

Grammy Astrid's suicide was hard on Beatrice, as it was for everyone. She kept wondering why someone would do such a thing and she would pray to the universe to show her why. She wanted clarity following another death in the family, this one done on purpose. This whole time Beatrice and everyone else was under the impression that Grandma Astrid just kind of… lost her mind. That Grandpa Hugh's death took such a toll on her that she couldn't live without him for another day. Part of it was tragically romantic but the other part made no sense. Grammy Astrid was never the type to make that decision on her own. Yet, she did anyway, all because of Dorothy.

"You're sleepwalking again," Aunt Edie tells her, her eyebrows pulled together in a thin straight line right over her huge gray eyes. "This is the third night in a row. What is going on?"

Beatrice searches for words, almost forgetting how to speak properly. "I don't know, I guess I'm just not sleeping too well."

Aunt Edie stares at her for a solid beat, as though she wants to ask more questions but is holding her tongue. She pulls her vibrant pink silk robe tighter around herself, securing it in a knot. "I was going to make some French toast. Did you want any?"

Beatrice nods her head and watches her aunt pad out of the bathroom, her footsteps silent against the pink carpet. She glances around at the outdated room. She never even considered what this might look like, as it's always been the most 70's styled room in the whole house. She's going to have to tear this carpet up at some point and probably install a new shower. Mold from water use covers the inside where a rusted drain and faucet is.

Beatrice pinches the bridge of her nose as she makes her way back to her bedroom, her head throbbing. Her mother has visited her every night to walk her through these stories about what happened to Uncle Eli, Grandpa Hugh, and Grammy Astrid. She is almost looking forward to tonight, crossing her fingers that her mom will make her way into her room again to tell her the truth about the last night they spent here and how everything went downhill. She faintly remembers the weeks leading up to that Halloween and how there was so much tension between her mom, Marley, and Aunt Edie. She remembers heated conversations and constant accusations being thrown Aunt Edie's way. Seems like not much has changed.

Beatrice takes a quick shower, scrubbing at her face with an exfoliating face scrub. She dresses herself into ripped jeans and a distressed forest green sweater. She makes her way down to the kitchen, where Aunt Edie is setting a plate of French toast and sausage links down on the dining table.

"Eat up," Aunt Edie directs her. "Maybe you're not sleeping all that well because you have the diet of a seven-year-old."

"I do not have the diet of a child," Beatrice argues, taking her seat at the table. A bird swoops by the turret outside, making her jump.

Aunt Edie is studying her. "You didn't used to sleepwalk when you moved in with Clara, did you?"

Beatrice shakes her head. That same thought has occurred to her, as well. But that's simply because her dead mother wasn't visiting her with nighttime stories about her deceased ancestors. "No."

"Must be a house thing, huh?" It comes off as a joke while Aunt Edie turns back to the griddle to tend to the sizzling French toast. "Any who, darling, I was wondering when you were planning on getting a move on with the house."

Beatrice shoves French toast into her mouth with her hand, syrup dripping down her fingers. She waits to swallow before speaking. "I'm sorry, did the missing trim from the hallway upstairs go unnoticed? And I repainted mom's old room."

"Yes, but you've been here for twelve days now," Aunt Edie points out, flopping a few pieces of French toast onto a plate of her own. She uses tongs to snatch up some sausage links from the skillet. "And quite honestly, I was hoping to be out of here before the holidays."

"Why the rush?" Beatrice asks as Aunt Edie sits down across from her.

"There is no rush." She begins painting butter onto the bread, topping it with cinnamon sugar and syrup.

"It just seems like you're trying to rush me into getting all the work done here," Beatrice speaks her mind. "Sounds like you're trying to get out of here as fast as possible."

Aunt Edie grins, like they're sharing a joke again. "Do you blame me? You and I both know that the things that have happened in this house are a little more than coincidental."

Beatrice studies her aunt, wondering what is bringing all this on. Every time Beatrice brought up her childhood and everything that has gone inside here at Ashwood, Aunt Edie either shuts down or snaps at her to change the conversation after defending it. Now, Aunt Edie is bringing up like the roles have reversed.

"But you've stayed in this house for far too long already," Beatrice reminds her, taking another bite. "Don't you think if something were to happen to you, it would have already happened?"

Aunt Edie picks up her glimmering fork, tilting her head at Beatrice with a furrowed brow. "That's not how it works, Bea."

"Then how does it work?" she challenges, her memories of her aunt and mother floating through her head, their voices hissing at Aunt Edie and demanding answers. "Since I've been back here, I've been thinking a lot about growing up."

Aunt Edie doesn't say anything. She neatly cuts a piece of her French toast off and smoothly steers it into her mouth.

"I remember lots of arguments between my mom, you, and Aunt Marley," Beatrice continues, leaning over her plate a little. "And the more I think about everything, the more I realize that they were just as confused as I am about what happened here."

Aunt Edie chews, her nostrils flaring, like she's about to cry. But that doesn't stop Beatrice from pushing.

"They were trying to figure it out," Beatrice proceeds. "And they kept going to you for answers but you weren't giving them."

Aunt Edie looks pained. She opens her mouth to speak when she dabs it with a napkin. She closes it, thinking, and then opens it once more. "Your mother and Aunt Marley had gotten ill. Not physically, but mentally."

Beatrice stares, bewildered. "What are you talking about?"

Aunt Edie sighs, staring down at her plate. "I really didn't want to have this conversation with you, Beatrice. Truly."

"What conversation?" Beatrice drops the last of her French toast onto her plate, a pit suddenly forming in her stomach and taking away her appetite.

"They were so convinced there was a reason behind all of the deaths that happened here, all of the House Things," Aunt Edie explains to her. "They would spend hours of the night burying themselves in books. Marley would wander the woods, desperate to find the twins…" She stares out the turret window, her eyes glazed over. "My sister-in-law dying was the straw that broke the camel's back. They were determined to find out answers to questions that should have never been asked in the first place, because you cannot answer something that isn't there to begin with."

"The books, you mentioned, they're in the study," Beatrice says, wiping her sticky fingers off in a napkin. "I remember finding mom in there every once and awhile."

Aunt Edie nods. "The Millstone family tree is filled with creativity and ambition. Your ancestors were really good at imagination."

Beatrice tries not to look too unconvinced. She remembers some of those books in there, some of them detailing the Man on the Ceiling and the creature lurking in the crawl space. Those things weren't just ripped from someone's imagination, they were real things that were being witnessed. They were things that were seen and thrown into a book for future generations. Aunt Marley and Beatrice's mom seemed to be the only two that gave a damn about what was in that study to begin with. But, that didn't change anything. They were still taken far too soon.

"I never told you this, but your Grandpa Hugh was a very paranoid man," Aunt Edie goes on. "He was somehow convinced that his brother and Grammy Astrid had some sort of affair with each other. That was never the case, and everyone else knew that but Grandpa."

"So?"

"So, Ashwood has a way of making some people paranoid," she explains softly. "It has a way of feeding you certain things that aren't real. Things that are hard on the mind and make us do things that is out of character. My mother is an example of that. Lena and Marley are, too. They grew paranoid until they lost their minds completely."

Beatrice stares hard at her, angry beyond belief. She is not going to sit here and let Aunt Edie make a spectacle out of her mother. How can she say that? How can she sit in that chair and claim that her mother was crazy? That she and Aunt Marley were just as senile as everyone else here? Beatrice thinks about the family members she knew before they passed and how it *was* true that they seemed a little off before they went. But it never got like that for her mom or Aunt Marley. In fact, Aunt Marley had a reason to go crazy. Her children were missing and probably dead and the cops gave up on her. Beatrice doesn't have kids but she's sure she would be the same way. Any good parent would be.

"I'm sorry." Aunt Edie picks her fork back up when Beatrice remains quiet. "I shouldn't have brought any of this up. It just ruined the meal."

"No, it didn't," Beatrice lies. She now knows that Aunt Edie's lies are so easy to roll off her tongue, that she has no problem doing it if it saves face. Beatrice refuses to believe this about her mom. And the fact Aunt Edie is trying to paint her in that light is making everything a hell of a lot clearer.

After breakfast, Beatrice reminds Aunt Edie that the movers are coming later before brushing her teeth upstairs. She zooms in on the photo she took in Aunt Edie's wardrobe, of the swirl inside of the circle. Tiny wood chippings still cling around the shape, as though it was just made instead of being there for years and years. She's going to lie to Aunt Edie today and head off to the library to do some research. She'll say she's picking up paint for the trim or something stupid. Honestly, the home renovations is the last thing on her mind right now. She needs to figure out what is going on and if she doesn't do it fast, she might have to pay the consequences.

Aunt Edie allows Beatrice to take her car into town without a second's thought. So, Beatrice does, growing used to the humming under the floor. The drive to the library is a little foreign, as Beatrice can't entirely remember the correct route. She never really came here when she was a girl, given they had their own little library back home. The only times they would go was to print off assignments for Beatrice's homeschooling work. Beatrice's car leads her to where the library is located, facing a corner on Carnegie and Firestone. Beatrice pulls into the small parking lot separated from a playground by a chain link fence. Kids chase each other around outside of the brick school building, their squeaks and laughter echoing through the air.

Beatrice makes her way into the building, the automatic doors screeching as they part in her wake. She politely waves to the young guy seated behind the front desk and starts for the aisles of books behind tables of unoccupied computers. She goes straight for the nonfiction section, her eyes browsing history and biographies and cookbooks and then self-help books claiming that *you are a badass*. Beatrice sifts through the books in the next aisle over, finding herself in the spiritual section consisting of books on mythology and paranormal activity and hauntings in Massachusetts. Does she need a book on myths? Maybe something about demons? A thick black book with silver lettering on the spine catches Beatrice's eye right away: *Symbology*.

Snatching it off the shelf, Beatrice sinks to her knees in the aisle, pressing her back up against the shelves and flipping the book open. She tears through the pages, hoping the table of contents might supply her with descriptions of certain symbols that could lead her to a helpful page. But the only things listed in the contents are chapter titles based on certain groups and religions with factoring symbols.

Beatrice turns page after page, her eyes scanning them up and down. The drawings depict things ranging from floral art to circles that remind Beatrice of pizza. There are some in the shapes of hands, others weird combinations of lines and dots. She fans herself as she turns page after page until she finally finds the symbol halfway through the book. She digs through the pocket of her jacket for her phone, pulling up the picture she took in Aunt Edie's wardrobe. Putting it directly next to the symbol in the book with a trembling hand. They are identical. The entire right page goes into detail about how it's a symbol for a journey going from ignorance to divine enlightenment. It explains how this symbol represents a labyrinth, which then represents completion, a journey to ascending into a higher self all the way to the end of a cycle.

Beatrice traces her finger over a word at the bottom of the page, separated from the page number with a thin line. It's under the category of *Witchcraft*. Beatrice freezes, unsure of what to do from here. No. There's no way that Aunt Edie, out of everyone Beatrice knows in her life, practices any sort of *witchcraft*. That's bogus. Beatrice's coworker, Jewel, once admitted that she did a love spell on someone and it completely backfired but Beatrice only pretended to be interested because it was their fourth time working together. That sort of stuff has always freaked Beatrice out. She knows it's real, based on the phenomenon she grew up with. Girls on social media nowadays are making spell jars and hexing enemies as though it's something fun to play with.

Beatrice takes photos of the pages with her phone before rising to her feet, just as a library worker pushes a cart in the next aisle over, glasses perched on the end of her nose. Beatrice leaves the book on the floor, approaching the library worker in a scattered rush.

"Excuse me," Beatrice greets her quietly. "Do you know if you have any books on witchcraft?"

The older lady eyes her up and down, her lazy eye twitching. She has bushy black hair and brown skin. Sighing, she leads Beatrice down the aisle and to the next one. "You kids these days are always trying to mess with things you shouldn't be messing with."

"What?" Beatrice fidgets with the dead skin surrounding her nails.

"Witchcraft isn't a joke," the lady responds, squinting at the books crammed onto the shelves surrounding them. "We're getting more and more kids these days wandering in here looking for books with spells and potions in them. Hollywood has made it trendy." She puts a hand on her hip. "What kind of book are you looking for?"

"I don't know," Beatrice admits. She was kind of hoping just to browse through the titles on her own and go from there, taking anything that reaches out to her. She studies the woman's annoyed expression. "Something tells me you might know about this kind of stuff?"

"I know enough not to fuck with it," she snaps, lips pursed. "If you really don't know what you're doing, you should check out the Dragon's Corner."

Beatrice licks her lips. "What is that?"

"It's a magic shop just a couple blocks over," she responds, heading back to her abandoned cart. "I think you're going to get a lot faster advice from something there than you will here."

Beatrice bites down on her bottom lip. She wasn't trying to go anywhere else today but if heading to this magic shop will give her more answers as to why the hell this symbol might be in Aunt Edie's wardrobe, then so be it. She thanks the lady and doesn't care that she doesn't get a response. She hurries out of the library and climbs into Aunt Edie's car, Clara's name popping up on her screen. She holds her breath before putting the phone to her ear.

"Hey, you," Clara says on the other end. "I have an emergency."

"What is it?" Beatrice quickly asks, worried about the boys. "Are you okay? Are the boys?"

"Yes, it's nothing that serious," Clara assures. "But it's been days since I've seen you and I'm starting to get worried about you."

Beatrice shifts in the seat, watching the kids on the playground chase each other around with innocently bright smiles and not a care in the world. It makes her sad. "I'm fine, really. If I wasn't, you'd be the first to know."

"Why do I get the overwhelming sense that you're lying to me?"

The question rings through Beatrice's ears and she feels caught in a lie. How can she not? She's been bending the truth to Clara since even before she left New York. She fed her all the lies she could to be able to get here and start earning some money. But that plan clearly went out the door faster than she expected it to.

Beatrice sighs heavily, debating on how to go about this. She hates lying to Clara but what else is she supposed to do? Clara is the number one person in the world that would throw a bitch fit if she found out that Beatrice came back here. After leaving Ashwood, Clara was sure to protect Beatrice as best as she could from everything that was being said about her childhood home. She would hide articles and be sure no coverage was being shown on the TV. She would advise Beatrice to ignore kids at school when they realized who she was and where she came from. Clara tried so hard to block out the horror of Ashwood for Beatrice forever. But it clearly wasn't enough if Beatrice was able to return and be thrown into this madness like she never left in the first place.

"I'm not lying," Beatrice promises. "Plus, the movers are coming today so if you want, I can take a picture to prove to you that I'm not in any danger."

Clara is silent for a beat. "Fine. But I expect more than one photo."

Beatrice feels a weight lift off her shoulders. "Deal."

Once she hangs up, Beatrice punches the Dragon's Corner into her Google Maps, running through the directions once before heading on her way. She flies through a yellow light and cuts someone off onto a one-way street before finding the shop on Rosewood. Parking, Beatrice yanks her keys from the ignition and climbs out onto the street, hurrying onto the sidewalk and hesitating in front of the door. This has gotten way too out of control. Just because some weird symbol was etched into Aunt Edie's wardrobe, doesn't mean she's some pagan. There has to be something more behind all of this.

The heavy lime green door creaks as Beatrice pulls it open. A bell above her jingles to signify her presence and her nostrils are assaulted by the strong smell of incense. The store isn't very big, and includes everything that Beatrice has only seen on TV. There are tiny cauldrons on a shelf, bundles of sage hanging above them. There are expensive statues and figurines of different deities and gods, all of them in dominant positions and poses. A glass cabinet holds sharp daggers and crystals hanging from chains. A few Ouija boards sit on high bookshelves, which is crammed with books and tarot card collections. The candle selection is near a wall filled with jarred herbs, their names taped to the front.

"Hi there," a woman in the back of the store, where the checkout counter is, greets. She has thick black glasses, long gray hair, and a deep purple sweater, dark lipstick smeared across her lips. "Is there anything I can help you out with today?"

"Yes, actually." Beatrice starts across the creaky floor, glancing at homemade journals and more books to her left. She pulls her phone out again to bring up the photo she just took at the library. "I was hoping you could tell me what this meant. The woman at the library told me that you might be of some help."

"Sometimes," she answers, leaning over the counter when Beatrice sets her phone down for her to see. "The Spiral."

Beatrice waits for her to go on but when the lady just stares at her, she speaks up. "Okay, and what is that supposed to mean?"

"I suppose it depends on where you saw it." Incense smoke floats through the air in interesting shapes that remind Beatrice of low rain clouds. "Just in that book?"

"No, it was engraved on the inside of my aunt's wardrobe," Beatrice explains to her. "I remember seeing it as a kid but it dawned on me now that it was weird, right?"

The woman studies her closely, her eyebrows slowly pulling together until her expression changes to some sort of realization, puzzle pieces slowly coming together. "You're Beatrice Millstone, aren't you?"

Beatrice winces. She was kind of hoping she could come in here and not be recognized. But who is she kidding with all that hope at this point? "Yeah, that's me."

"That symbol is in *your* house?" she points to the phone and Beatrice nods her head. "Have you ever heard of household deities?"

Beatrice shakes her head and wants to tell the lady that she's never heard of any of this stuff and that she's freaking the fuck out.

"A deity is a god that is worshipped," she explains to her. "Sometimes, usually wiccans and pagans, worship deities and most of them have their own symbols." She points at the phone again. "That symbol belongs to a household deity with the name of Helcatia."

Beatrice watches the woman make her way out from behind the

counter and over to the bookshelves, her fingertips grazing the spines as she reads the titles one by one.

"My name is Winona, by the way," she tells her over her shoulder before selecting a book off the shelf. "Guess it's not fair of me to know your name and you not know mine, right?"

Beatrice forces a smile but doesn't have time for small talk. She gestures to the large book in Winona's hand. "So, this Helcatia… person. I'm guessing if it's a deity, it's good?"

"Oh, no, not at all." Winona sits down at a tiny round table set up for tarot readings, according to a laminated sign on its surface. "Just because something is worshipped, doesn't mean it isn't evil. And, deity might not be the right word. It's not like, a God. Or a person. It's a *thing*."

Beatrice immediately thinks of Satan.

Winona starts flipping through the thick pages of the book that looks older than she is—which is saying something. She dabs her tongue with her finger, aggressively flipping until stopping. She sets the book in between them, turning it around for Beatrice to get a better look at the image. "That's it."

Beatrice flinches. She was expecting the *thing* to look like all of the figures by the door of the shop: broad chests, pointy nipples, muscles the sizes of planets. But Helcatia consists of a dark mass with a haunting face. It looks like a big giant scribble.

"I don't understand," Beatrice confesses. "It looks like a shadow."

"The evil ones often look that way, yes," she confirms, bringing the book back to her side. She scans the words on the page. "Even though most household deities are there to protect those within, most of them can be found outside of the home, still on the lot to secure the exterior. Helcatia seems like one of the deities who is there for the opposite reasons. It sort of gives the house a mind of its own."

Beatrice's heart hammers within her chest and she thinks about the shadow behind the shed in Lila's photo. *The noise behind the barn.* She settles on Aunt Edie. Could she have conjured something up when she was younger? Then what about all of the family members who died before Aunt Edie? Someone else must've owned her wardrobe before her.

"Is this thing summoned?" Beatrice asks Winona.

Winona considers this. "I wouldn't say that summon is the right word. Helcatia feeds off energy, usually during the construction process."

"Construction process?" Beatrice feels more confused than ever. "I'm not following."

"Think of this… deity being created as the house was being created," Winona explains, running her index finger up and down the pages of the book. "For whatever reason, it was created, just like the walls and floors of the house it comes with."

"Well, that can't be right," Beatrice tells her, not accepting something so flippant to be the cause. "Things like this should have to be summoned. It makes zero sense why something as… dark would just be born into any random house."

"I like to remind everyone that everything in life is built around intent," she replies simply. "It's all about energy."

"Why would someone intend for bad things?"

"Well that's an age-long question, isn't it?" Winona challenges, putting a finger to her chin. "Curiosity, boredom, anger, revenge. The list goes on."

"So you're saying this… *thing* is in my house?"

"Not so much *in* your house, but *with* your house." Winona leans back in her chair, her dusty gray eye shadow making her green eyes look dull. "Helcatia feeds off the minds and souls of those inside the structure it was born in. It's how It feeds." She gestures to Beatrice's phone. "That symbol means a labyrinth of sorts. Think of the house it was born into, *your* house, a maze. The more confusion and paranoia those inside experience, the more the house can feed. The more attention given to it, the more energy it is fueled with."

Beatrice is growing anxious. She notices how the symbol sort of looks like a house. The swirl inside of the circle represents a maze within. The triangle over the circle is a roof. She needs to figure something out, something soon. The longer she spends inside of Ashwood, the more likely she's going to wind up like every other apple that has fallen off her family tree. But Aunt Edie has spent her entire life within those walls and she hasn't had a single problem. It's never seemed like she was in any real danger. But why?

"How do I get It out?" Beatrice demands impatiently. "How do I make all of this stop?"

She glances at the bundles of sage on display and wonders if a couple of those will do the trick. She looks at the large jar of white salt, black salt next to it, Himalayan salt on the end. Should she form some kind of protection circle around herself at night? Should she concoct a safety potion? What about making a necklace full of flowers promising to keep her from harm?

"You must stop the feeding," she explains as though Beatrice should already know that. "Make It starve. I'm not saying that that'll work, but it's worth a try."

"I need something that will work," Beatrice barks.

If all of this is true, if what Winona is telling her is actually taking place at her house, then Ashwood has been feeding on people for decades and decades, beginning with the top of the Millstone family tree and ending with random missing girls in Silver Creek.

"Helcatia never goes away," Winona informs, glancing down at the page in front of her. "It can be silenced, but It does not leave." She turns the page and her eyes scan the next page. "Usually It attaches itself onto a single person in the home. Sort of befriends them. That person is safe from the feedings."

Beatrice immediately thinks of Aunt Edie.

"What does someone have to do to become that person?"

"Helcatia chooses," Winona answers, looking up at her. It seems like her mind is on the same track. "You're thinking about your aunt, aren't you?"

Beatrice shifts, swallowing. "Maybe."

"It would make sense," Winona confirms. "Other than you, she's the last one of the Millstone bunch that hasn't been offed in a strange way."

Ashwood's history floats through Beatrice's mind. She thinks of the family members before her meeting untimely ends. She thinks of Ashwood suddenly choosing Aunt Edie to be its right-hand woman. She thinks of Aunt Marley and her mother tearing through the family study in hopes to finally figure out what has been happening to them all. Ashwood targeted each person to step foot in that house and every single person has lost.

"There's a blue moon coming up," Winona says next, looking alarmed.

"What does that mean?" Beatrice orders, trying to get a peek at the book.

"Blue moons occur every two and a half years," Winona tells her, looking at her again and then back down at the book. She stares at it for a long time, sinking her teeth into her bottom lip and nearly ruining her lipstick. "I don't want to scare you. I don't even know you."

"I need help," Beatrice snaps at her. "You don't know how many circles I've been running in since I've come back and this is the first real thing that is giving me a lead."

As much as she has buzzing around in her mind, Beatrice is starting to feel like she finally knows what's going on. It's terrifying, but also freeing.

Winona sighs. "To feed Helcatia correctly, there's one thing that needs done on these moons. If this isn't done, It grows angry and feeds more and more on those within the home—more than it does without the moon. The house is already a labyrinth but it makes it ten times worse when It's hungry."

"What needs to be done?"

Winona stares at her. "A sacrifice."

The answer sends chills up Beatrice's back. She scoots her chair away from the table, suddenly feeling like she might throw up. She puts a hand to her stomach, the pieces of what feels like a never-ending puzzle finally fitting together in her head. This *thing* is responsible for driving the minds inside of Ashwood to insanity. It feeds off them all until there's nothing left. Beatrice thinks about all the missing women that stayed with Aunt Edie when Beatrice left, how their disappearances happened so spaced out from each other. Could it have been every blue moon? Could these girls have been getting sacrificed to some household deity that does anything but protect?

Does Aunt Edie have some sort of deal with Ashwood and that's why she's been alive for this long? And what about the House Things? Are they really just ghosts after all? Ghosts that have been created all because they were fed off of?

"Hey, are you feeling all right?" Winona asks softly.

"No," she admits. "Everything is twisted." She stares at the book in disbelief. "This can't be real."

She knows her childhood home is a twisted place, one that doesn't make sense to the rest of the world. But coming to the confirmation that it truly is an evil place is making the world tilt on its axis.

Winona frowns, pity flooding both of her emerald-green eyes. "Sometimes the realest things are the hardest to believe."

It sounds philosophical but Beatrice has no freaking clue what to do with that statement. But it's also very true. She grew up with something very real living inside of Ashwood, and apparently it wasn't only the House Things. Finally learning the truth doesn't feel as good as Beatrice thought that it would. Maybe because in the back of her mind, she was wishing that Aunt Edie wouldn't be as guilty as she and her mom and Aunt Marley have made her out to be. If this is true, if this is what's going on, Beatrice has to put a stop to it. But she can't run back to Ashwood guns blazing. She needs to devise a plan or else this could all be ruined.

"I have to go." Beatrice abruptly stands up, nearly knocking her chair over behind her.

"What are you going to do?"

"I don't know, but I'll figure something out." Beatrice hurries through the store, almost crashing into a display of tapestries on a rack.

She breathes in the cool fall air outside, using the brick wall of the building to brace herself against. Beatrice squeezes her eyes shut, trying to get herself to calm down but with all of this new information flooding her head, she can't think about anything else other than the fact that there has been some sort of evil god born into Ashwood, hence the reason why her family has been cursed with death in the strangest of ways. Hence the reason Beatrice grew up seeing House Things. Hence the reason Aunt Edie isn't bothered by anything because she was chosen.

The world around Beatrice begins to spin, the image of Helcatia's photo in Winona's book coming back to her. She thinks of Winona telling her about how the deity is usually outside of the home, protecting it from anything going inside. She thinks of the noises from behind the barn, the mysterious thing in the garden. She thinks of all of Aunt Edie's garden club friends smiling and sipping lemonade as they sat among evil.

This morning's French toast appears on the sidewalk when Beatrice pukes. An older couple holding hands stare at her in awe, jumping out of the way and crossing the street as though she's carrying a contagious disease. Beatrice collapses onto the sidewalk and the last thing she feels is her head slamming against the cement.

Chapter 24

Sunlight wakes Beatrice and she finds herself in her bed. Her eyes have never felt heavier, and her mouth has never been drier. She blinks in her surroundings, wondering what time it is and why her head feels like it's on fire. She lazily reaches up to touch it, making sure her hair and skin are still in place. She feels under her jaw for a pulse, just to make sure that her life right now isn't some nightmare. Much to her dismay, she feels the rhythmic beating of her heart.

Aunt Edie comes into view above her with a small smile twisting across her lips. "Excellent. You're awake."

Beatrice sits up, no recollection of falling asleep. The crocheted green elephant is next to her with its trunk aimed toward the ceiling. "What happened?"

"You fell in town," Aunt Edie explains, as though that kind of thing happens often… which it doesn't. "I got a call yesterday saying that you passed out. I brought you home right away and you've been asleep ever since with the occasional tossing and stirring. I also fed you some soup."

Beatrice shifts under the covers as Aunt Edie plants herself down on the edge of the bed. Yesterday comes flooding back to her like a storm. The magic shop, the truth about Helcatia and the origin of Ashwood. She stares hard at her aunt, the secrets between them eating at her like a shark. She wishes they could just be open, that they could tell each other everything they know and Beatrice can leave here with the knowledge of what her childhood was and why. She could pack up her things with the truth about this place once and for all. The thought of it makes her hopeful. But more importantly, she would get to leave here *alive*. Her body feels like it's been drained of her blood and organs. She isn't strong enough to have a conversation like that. Not yet and not until she can gather all the facts. With as much information as she now has, she still feels like she's wandering through the dark, desperate to find a light switch.

"Did you take me to the hospital?" Beatrice questions. "I could have a concussion or something."

293

"According to a few witnesses, you threw up *before* hitting your head." Aunt Edie reaches over to smooth her fingers along the gauze patch on Beatrice's temple. "Do you need anything? Can I get you some more soup?"

"Maybe something a little more solid," Beatrice croaks, finding a glass of water on the nightstand. She reaches over to it and wraps her fingers around the cup. "I don't feel right."

"Well, you've barely done anything for almost twenty-four hours," Aunt Edie claims and rises to her feet. "I'll fix you some lunch. And then, I'm going to run out and pick up some Halloween candy. We don't want the trick-or-treaters tonight leaving empty handed, do we?"

Beatrice blinks. "Today is Halloween?"

Aunt Edie nods on her way to the door. "It sure is. Why, did you have plans?"

She shakes her head, pulling the blankets up to her chest, feeling a draft. "No, of course not."

Aunt Edie leaves and Beatrice listens to her pad down the steps and into the kitchen. She rests her head against the pillow, feeling it throb. She needs a plan, but her mind hurts too much to even attempt to make one. She runs her hands over her face, rolling onto her side and reaching for her phone. She has an email from Declan, asking if the furniture was shipped.

Beatrice darts up in bed, more awake than she was just seconds ago. She throws the blankets off her body and stumbles out into the hallway, not enough strength in herself to keep on her feet.

"Aunt Edie?" Beatrice calls downstairs, grabbing hold of the banister. "Did the movers come?"

"Yes, they took everything you had marked," Aunt Edie calls back in a chipper tone. Footsteps follow. "And I didn't give you a proper thank you. The attic is already looking a lot less cluttered with that stuff out of it."

Beatrice sighs of relief at the sight of Aunt Edie carrying a tray of solid food and the fact that the move went smoothly. She files back into her room and Aunt Edie sets down a tray of sandwiches, chips, and a brownie for dessert at the foot of the bed.

"I'm sorry," Beatrice apologizes to her. "I don't know what got into me yesterday, or else I would have handled everything."

"I'm sure you just had low sugar or something," Aunt Edie responds passively, fiddling with the hefty gold ring on her index finger.

"Well, thanks for handling it."

Aunt Edie adjusts her white and black boa draped around her skinny neck. "I did mean to ask you about that. What were you doing in that part of town? I thought you were going to look at some paint samples for the trim."

Beatrice takes a massive bite out of the peanut butter and butter sandwich. "I was on my way there. I stopped to look at some tapestries for my room."

Aunt Edie isn't buying it and Beatrice can't entirely blame her. The excuse is lame and stupid and Beatrice should have just told her the truth. She could just say that she went there to gather information on the symbol she found in her bedroom wardrobe. She could tell her all about how she knows about Helcatia and the annual sacrifices that need to be made every blue moon. She stares at her aunt, a woman who raised her. Is she capable of all this? Is she really that evil of a person?

"Aunt Edie, is there anything you need to tell me?" Beatrice asks after swallowing, the peanut butter sticking to the roof of her mouth.

"What is it that you mean, dear?"

"I mean, is there anything that you need to come clean about?" Beatrice clarifies. She shouldn't, but she's giving her a window of opportunity to come forward with the truth. To finally tell her what she's been hiding. She wants to give her a chance to come clean about everything she knows and why she did the things that she did.

Aunt Edie shrugs her bony shoulders. "No, of course not. Why would you think there would be?"

Beatrice frowns. Maybe she's too naïve to think that Aunt Edie would choose to do the right thing instead of waiting until she's backed into a corner to reveal the truth. "It's nothing. Thanks for lunch."

"I'll be back soon."

Beatrice eats her lunch in silence while Aunt Edie leaves. She devours the rest of her sandwich, scarfs down the bag of chips, and inhales the brownie so fast she doesn't even have time to enjoy it. She's in mid-chew when she listens to the doorbell ring from downstairs. Xander?

Beatrice hurries out of her room, her body agreeing to the energy she just consumed, and she makes her way down the steps and to the front door. When she opens it, opening her mouth to fill Xander in on everything she learned yesterday, she's too struck by what she sees. Clara stands in front of her on the porch, clutching onto the strap of her purse. She's wearing a baby blue cardigan and a navy blouse underneath. Her pink lips are in a pursed line and her eyes are filled with fury.

"I knew it," Clara says, disrupting the shocked silence hanging between them. "You've been lying to me this whole time."

"Clara—"

"I was suspicious from the beginning but our conversation yesterday was too weird to take seriously," Clara snaps, shaking her head at her. Her strawberry blond hair is tucked behind her ears and Beatrice isn't sure she's ever seen her so disappointed. "Why would you lie?"

"Come in." Beatrice opens the door for her. "I can explain."

"You think I'm going in there?" A horrified look splashes across Clara's face. "Beatrice, you told me that you would never come back here. I told you about this place and how terrible it is—"

"I was desperate," Beatrice cuts her off.

"How many times did I tell you that I would've given you a place?" Clara barks. "That's what I'm here for—"

"Because," Beatrice interrupts. "Maybe a small part of me *wanted* to come back here."

Clara's face goes from disappointed to confused. She's studying her face for answers. "Why would you ever want to come back here?"

"There are so many things I never knew about this place," Beatrice explains. "And being here to figure them out and renovating the house for Aunt Edie and getting all that furniture out of the attic was a perfect opportunity—"

"There is nothing perfect about this place," Clara interrupts her. "And I thought I did a good enough job in making sure you didn't make stupid decisions like this one."

"It wasn't stupid."

"Anything that involves coming to this house voluntarily is stupid," Clara tells her, grabbing hold of her arm. "Come on. We're leaving."

"I am not going anywhere!" Beatrice jerks her arm out of her grasp. "I'm just now figuring out what has been happening here. And I'm not leaving until I do something about it."

"Beatrice, I'm serious." Clara clenches her jaw. "Your mother wouldn't allow this and as her best friend, I am doing what I can to respect what she would want."

"I saw her."

Clara stares at her for a minute, her lips pressed together like it's taking everything in her to not respond. "What do you mean you *saw* her?"

"She's… she's one of the House Things," Beatrice explains in a pleading tone. She just needs Clara to believe her. She doesn't care if everyone else doesn't, just as long as Clara doesn't treat her like a mental patient. "I didn't know until she came to me. She told me all about… everyone. The ones I knew. Uncle Eli, Grandpa Hugh, his brother, Grammy—"

"Stop it," Clara demands impatiently but she still looks hung up on the fact that Beatrice brought up her mother. She adjusts the purse hanging from her shoulder. "This sounds insane."

"I can bring Xander over if you don't believe me," Beatrice offers, glancing down the hill at where Xander's house sits. "He's been here. He's seen just as much stuff as I have. He can make you understand."

Clara looks bewildered. The color drains from her face and she no longer looks upset, but worried. "Xander?"

Beatrice nods her head. "Yeah, he never moved away."

A breeze picks up and golden leaves scatter across the porch, two of them sticking to the pumpkin on the banister. An unknown sense of discomfort moves across Clara's face as she stares at Beatrice, concern bleeding through her expression. Without saying anything, she steps into the foyer and shuts the door behind her.

"Beatrice, please tell me that you're pulling my chain."

Beatrice steps away from her, surprised Clara hasn't said anything yet about her knotted hair or sleep in her eyes or the gash in her head. "I wasn't aware that there was a chain that *could* be pulled."

"Why did you bring up Xander?"

"Because he's been stopping by and helping me." Beatrice's voice is firm. "Why is that weird?"

"Xander isn't… he isn't real." She chooses her words carefully, a hand gently being placed on Beatrice's shoulder. "He was part of your imagination when you were a kid. He was your imaginary friend."

Beatrice has heard a lot of weird things in this house but this has to take the cake… almost. She sputters out a laugh, covering her mouth with a hand. "Okay, and you thought *I* was delusional for coming back here."

"I'm serious," she tells her, looking her straight in the face. "He was never physically here. He was invisible to everyone else but you. Your mom told me about him."

"That can't be true," Beatrice argues. She might *look* like an insane person, but that doesn't mean she *is*. Clara could give her some grace.

"Your mom told me that your imagination was so very strong," she continues. "But I didn't ever think that you would be convinced Xander was an actual living person."

Beatrice's smile begins to fade as memories from her childhood with Xander start to drift through her mind in super-cut fashion. This can't be true. None of this can be. Xander lived just down the hill and would come over all the time to play with her and the twins. Sure, Jax and Juniper might have ignored him a lot of the time… in fact, maybe a lot of Beatrice's family members ignored him a lot of the time. But Beatrice always thought that it was because he was over at the house day after day, that he wouldn't ever just stay home and that maybe the adults were sick of him. She assumed that the twins were just shy when they wouldn't say hello to him. But now she's considering what Clara is telling her, that Xander wasn't ever truly *there*.

Beatrice thinks about the times that Xander would shrug and smile when he was ignored by members of her family, putting on a face that said he didn't mind it. She thinks about all those times when eye contact would only be made with her and never to them both, glossing over Xander. She thinks about her constant mentioning of him when he wasn't around, her guardians just going along with it because he was her friend… but they all knew he was imaginary? They went along with it just because that's what kids do? Make up imaginary friends?

She remembers telling her mother about Xander one rainy morning as they sat on the front porch of the house. Lena had seen Xander plenty of times before, yet she would ask Beatrice all sorts of questions about him. What he looked like, who he lived with, where he came from. Now thinking back, it was kind of like Lena was asking questions about a fictional character, someone made-up. She was simply asking questions to please the imagination of her daughter.

Beatrice thinks about her coming back to Ashwood and mentioning Xander to Aunt Edie and the weird look that flashed across her face, like she was surprised that Beatrice was still seeing him after all these years. But that's the thing, she didn't just stop seeing him because she got old. She stopped seeing him when she left Ashwood.

"Honey, this house isn't good for you." Clara gently squeezes Beatrice's shoulder. "If you honestly thought that Xander was real, then that proves my point. We need to get you out of here, somewhere safe."

Beatrice ignores her and thinks about all the times Xander came over and the two of them played together in the yard. How strange it would have looked, pretending to sword fight with someone who wasn't there. Playing hide and seek by herself. Having conversations with no one while they colored on the floor of her bedroom. Thinking Xander was there when they would rake leaves or have snowball fights in the yard or have pizza roll eating contests. She remembers when Grammy Astrid would quietly sigh when she would have to lay out another plate of food for Xander, putting an extra chair at the kitchen table. She thinks of that huge chunk of her childhood being spent with this person, this person that wasn't ever there at all—according to Clara.

Beatrice's mind ventures to the present, how Xander never spoke with the garden club or Aunt Edie and how he was never home when Aunt Edie was. He would appear when Beatrice needed to speak with him the most, never surprising her off the grounds too far from Ashwood. Doesn't *that* part count for something? Beatrice thinks about him telling her about the symbol inside of Aunt Edie's wardrobe but what if that was her own mind reminding her of seeing it herself on that one Christmas Eve? Is it all really possible? Is Xander truly just a figment of Beatrice's imagination, created during her childhood to... what? Have someone her age to play with since she had no friends outside of the house? To cope with the weird sightings taking place inside?

"Beatrice?" Clara says, wiping a tear rolling down Beatrice's cheek away. "I'm so sorry, sweetie, I didn't know that you were never... aware."

Clara rarely brought up Ashwood when Beatrice left. It was like a chapter of her life closed, never to be reread, only skimmed for important details about Beatrice's mom. Of course Clara would have never brought up Xander. Of course she didn't want to remind Beatrice of this place.

"He felt so real," Beatrice says breathlessly, still a little unconvinced. There's no way Xander is someone she just made up. She can play this part for as long as Clara needs her to but there is more to this and she knows it.

But all of it does make a little sense, even though Beatrice wants to believe otherwise. Looking back on everything now, he does seem like a ghost, someone who was constantly following Beatrice and venturing into the Jungle with her. Fred didn't even acknowledge him the day they visited his shack. But he's more than just some imaginary friend she made up in her head. She refuses to believe that's all Xander is. If he was just this figment of her imagination, she would have leaned on him more than ever after leaving Ashwood. She would have grown out of that phase of having an imaginary friend. If that's all he is, he wouldn't welcome her back home.

"I know," Clara says gently. "Your mother told me that he wasn't real, that you had some imaginary friend named Xander and you said that he lived down the street with his nana. I really thought you'd be at the age to know..."

"I think I'm just exhausted." Beatrice plays it off coolly. "I've been barely getting any sleep lately."

"Yeah, with good reason," Clara says, glancing around as though she's afraid something is going to pop out of the walls and grab her.

Beatrice doesn't respond. Xander is filling her thoughts. She feels a little disoriented, like she's spun around countless times and now everything is upside down.

"Honey, you need out of this house," Clara warns again, just as stern as Beatrice's mother was when she visited her in the parlor... right after that conversation with Xander by the fire. "It is not safe. And you seem to be... scattered."

"You're right," Beatrice lies, running her hands up and down her face. "But I need a shower. And I really need to say goodbye to Aunt Edie. She should be back soon."

Clara's jaw slides to the left. "Well, I am not leaving here without you."

"Check into a hotel," Beatrice instructs. "I've been here for this long and I've been perfectly fine. A few more hours isn't going to hurt. Just send me the address and it'll give me more than enough time to tie up some loose ends here."

"I don't think you're in the right mindset to be by yourself," Clara admits worriedly. She gently puts her fingertips to the wound on Beatrice's head. "And what the hell happened here?"

"I fell coming out of a store," Beatrice answers in a clipped voice.

"Another reason why I shouldn't leave you alone."

Beatrice resists the urge to explode and demand for her to stop treating her like she's some kind of mental patient, because she's not. She's a girl who now knows most of the truth of what happened in her childhood home. She just needs to figure out what to do next to figure out the rest. She's too close to stop now and to prevent anything bad happening again. The truth about everything is right in her reach. She can almost taste it.

"Clara, I promise you, I'm fine." Beatrice looks her in the face as she speaks. "Just get a hotel so I have somewhere to go when I'm done here. Please?"

Clara debates this for a long time, biting the inside of her cheek. "Fine. But I'm coming straight back here if I don't hear from you."

Beatrice ushers her out the door and quickly shuts it. She runs her tongue over her teeth, her eyes sliding up and down the walls around her, fearing that the house itself listened to every piece of that conversation. She would be stupid to think that it didn't. She climbs the stairs to start a shower, needing to gather most of her thoughts before she does what she needs to do. She needs to see Marilyn first. Aunt Edie will be here when she gets back, but she needs to have a conversation with her about what happened to the twins before she goes any further. Then, maybe the police can finally do something useful around here and actually find the bodies belonging to Juniper and Jax so Beatrice can give them proper funerals. With their remains being found, Hudson will have no power against significant evidence and his wife will be held responsible. She will not leave Silver Creek until that happens.

She changes into a black knitted sweater with a lame pumpkin on the front, pulling her legs into a pair of tight jeans and stuffing her feet into her Doc Martens. She lets her hair air dry as she calls a cab and grabs her bag. She waits on the front porch of Ashwood with her phone in her hand, shoving the thoughts about Xander to the back of her mind. She doesn't have the energy to think about that mess right now. She needs to focus on what Marilyn knows and why she did what she did. She needs to also figure out Ruth's story at some point and how that ties in with Fred and Aunt Edie.

"Xander is real," Beatrice chants to herself as she waits for the cab to show up. She rocks back and forth on the steps. "Xander is real, Xander is real, Xander is real…"

Once climbing into the backseat of the dirty yellow cab, Beatrice tells the driver to take her to 763 Rosemont Drive, Marilyn's address. She was able to do some internet stalking while she waited for the cab, coming across Officer Hudson's address from a photo taken for the police department website, him standing proudly in front of it in his uniform with a caption that pretty much screamed *I love abusing power.*

"Ashwood isn't the place to be this time of year," the driver, an Indian man with a thick mustache says from the front. He glances at her in the rearview mirror. "Most people who stay in that home are asking for a death wish."

"What do you know about it?" Beatrice grunts, buckling her seatbelt, mentally telling herself again that Xander is real.

"Enough to stay away," he answers casually, cracking the window. "I've picked up a girl from there before. A week later she ended up on the news."

"Who?"

He shrugs. "I don't know her name. They all kind of blur together at this point."

Beatrice frowns, thinking of the twelve woman who fall under one category and that's it. No one has taken the time of day to read their individual names, they're all just strung together with something in common: they all went missing after staying in Ashwood. She watches Silver Creek distort itself in a blur outside the window as Halloween decorations flash by. Beatrice wonders if she's going to miss it once she leaves today. *If* she leaves today.

Marilyn's home is a perfect white color with a large maple tree in the front yard. The lawn is covered with a sea of orange and yellow leaves. Fake cobwebs decorate the front shrubs and pumpkins line the brick walkway leading from the driveway to the porch. There's an orange and black striped sign propped up against the house outside the front door reading *Happy Halloween!*. Beatrice hands the driver a twenty and walks up the lawn, kicking the leaves in her path. She rings the doorbell two times in a row once she reaches the front door, eyeing the jet-black shutters and the spotless windowpanes, the curtains neatly drawn to the sides.

Xander is real, Xander is real, Xander is real…

Marilyn opens the front door and blinks in surprise when she finds Beatrice on the porch. "Beatrice, what a surprise. And Happy Halloween."

"Hi, Marilyn," Beatrice greets her with the friendliest tone she can muster up to show that she doesn't mean harm. It's the only way she'll be able to get inside. "Do you have a minute to talk?"

"Uh, sure." Marilyn invites her into the foyer, shutting the door behind her. "Come on in, I can get us some tea."

Beatrice looks around at large oily portraits of Marilyn and Officer Hudson strung up onto the white and blue striped walls. She's ushered into the sitting room to the right, where a navy-blue sofa sits with an expensive glass coffee table, classy end tables, and a piano in the corner. Beatrice plops herself down, too afraid to move because if she does, she might knock something out of its perfect position on a perfect piece of perfect furniture. She expected nothing less from this lady.

"I didn't know I was going to have any guests today," Marilyn announces as she returns with a freshly polished silver tray to set on the coffee table, cotton candy pink teacups on top. "Otherwise, I would have cleaned up a bit."

Beatrice glances around again at not a single thing being out of place. She reaches for her tea. "I'm not staying long. In fact, after I leave here, I'm going to head back to Ashwood and then leave Silver Creek."

Marilyn's ocean blue eyes widen as she sits herself down in the leather white chair across from Beatrice, picking up her own teacup. "Oh? Why the sudden rush?"

"There are things I'm figuring out," Beatrice admits bluntly. "Things that aren't making me feel safe here."

Marilyn studies her. "Is that what you wanted to talk about?"

"No," she admits. "I wanted to talk about what you did to my cousins."

The statement fills the room like an aged monster, finally waking from the dead. It's a question no one has probably asked Marilyn in her entire life. It catches her off guard and she clears her throat after taking a sip of tea.

"I don't know what it is you're speaking about—"

"You know exactly what I'm talking about," Beatrice cuts her off gruffly. "Fred Macher saw what happened. He saw you, Juniper, and Jax hurrying through the woods. He saw them fall and you did nothing to help them. You buried them like they were squirrels, not human beings. And then you ran off."

Marilyn stares at her for a long time, her eyes flooded with tears. She removes a piece of jagged white hair from her face and then stares at the thick blue rug under the coffee table. "I've thought about that day for the last sixteen years. And I know people often say things like that when they feel guilty about something, but I'm being honest. I wake up, I think about what I did, I say a prayer for the both of them, and then I start my day. I do the same routine at night."

"Is that supposed to make me feel better?" Beatrice returns the cup to the tray. "You wake and say a prayer and I'm supposed to forgive you?"

"Of course not," Marilyn assures. "I don't ever expect you to forgive me for what I've done." She inches to the edge of the chair. "But there is a lot more to everything than you know, young lady."

"That's why I'm here," Beatrice confesses. "You're lucky I'm even giving you the chance to tell me about this before I go to the police. Because I will if you don't tell me everything I need to know."

"I think you need to talk to your aunt about this."

"My aunt wasn't the one who watched them die."

"But…"

"But what?"

Marilyn stares at her, growing a little antsy, it seems. She puts her own cup back onto the tray and begins rotating her hands around each other, her rings clinking together. "I was trying to help them."

Beatrice deadpans. She didn't come here for Marilyn to feed her a load of bullshit. She can get that at home with Aunt Edie. She came here for answers and if Marilyn doesn't want to give them to her, then the police can handle her. Before she can threaten her, Marilyn goes on.

"I knew what your aunt was planning and I couldn't let it happen," Marilyn goes on, desperation seeping through her hushed voice. "So many people died on those grounds. And I'd heard so many stories about… their ghosts staying there."

"What was Aunt Edie going to do?" Beatrice demands.

A tear rolls down Marilyn's cheek. "It wasn't supposed to be them. It was supposed to be you."

The words cut through Beatrice like a knife the size of Beatrice's arm. She feels like she's sinking into the couch and soon enough, she'll be added to the collection of missing women in Silver Creek.

"What are you talking about?"

"You felt ill that day," Marilyn reminds her. "It was because Aunt Edie made you breakfast."

"I'm going to make you some crepes with apple butter," Aunt Edie told her that morning when Beatrice scampered down to the kitchen. She was already wearing an apron, a scarf holding her hair back. "You deserve it."

"So?" Beatrice says to Marilyn now.

"She put something in the food," Marilyn goes on, her sobbing growing harder. "I don't know what, but… but you weren't supposed to be alive for much longer after eating it."

Beatrice wants to vomit but something tells her to not do it all over Marilyn's perfectly coated home. Another part of her couldn't give a shit less.

"The twins ended up getting into the apple butter." Marilyn reaches for a tissue from the box next to the tea tray. She dots her face, her makeup running. "Edie didn't tell them no. I took them away when I found out what was happening. I overheard Edie and Ruth discussing all of this days prior, how they were planning on feeding you something bad. So, I came by to stop it, to stop *them*. But when I figured out that the twins were the ones who were poisoned, I needed to do something about it. I couldn't just let them die."

But you did, Beatrice wants to say but she's too much on shock right now to open her mouth.

"So when I saw them playing outside, I grabbed them," Marilyn recalls, tears dripping from her eyes and seeping into her corduroy pants. "I knew that if something were to happen to them on the grounds of Ashwood, they wouldn't be able to leave, just like everything else stuck in that house. So, I took them into the woods, trying to get them as far away from that place as possible so if they did pass before I could help, they wouldn't be stuck."

Beatrice's chest heaves in and out. That day she felt sick, she thought it was a simple flu. She ended up vomiting after the twins disappeared with Marilyn into the Jungle. Perhaps that got whatever Aunt Edie gave her out of her system and nothing happened to her. She thinks about Aunt Edie spreading the apple butter into the crepes that morning, topping them off with powder sugar. How could she do this? How could she have been the cause of what happened to Juniper and Jax all this time? She ventured into the woods and town with the rest of the family day after day, hunting for the twins, knowing damn well what she allowed them to consume.

Beatrice thinks about Aunt Marley and how she would be feeling right now if she were here to listen to the truth. What would she do? How would she react? Beatrice shuts her eyes, imagining Aunt Edie and Ruth planning this whole thing. But why? Why were they targeting Beatrice in the first place with this poison? What part does Ruth have to play in all this?

"Why were they doing this?" Beatrice's voice is thick with tears and the crystal room around her is starting to blur from tears of her own. "What were they going to do to me?"

"I shouldn't be telling you any of this," Marilyn hisses, as though Aunt Edie herself can hear her. "It's not right."

"None of this is right," Beatrice roars. "Two kids died because of my aunt. Her own niece and nephew. And she tried killing *me*. What's right doesn't matter anymore. You need to tell me what they were doing."

"I can't tell you that." Marilyn's voice cracks as she shakes her head. "I simply don't know all the answers. I only know what I know. And Edie saved my life, Beatrice. I wouldn't be sitting here right now if it weren't for her. She knew what I did. And she kept my secret for all these years. She and my husband both. Edie didn't blame me for trying to help them, because it wasn't meant to happen the way that it did."

Beatrice wants to claw the loyalty out of this woman. Why is she trying so hard to protect someone that killed her own child family members? Does this mean that Aunt Marley and Beatrice's mother were right all along? That Aunt Edie did play a hand in every little thing that happened in that house? Does this confirm that Aunt Edie is the one who has somehow been feeding Ashwood and that's why she's played it safe all these years? Some deal with the fucking devil?

"Fine." Beatrice gets to her feet. "I'll find out myself. I appreciate the information, but you should know that I'm going to have to speak with the police about this."

Marilyn's expression goes from sorrow to horror. "What? I just told you the truth!"

"And the death of my cousins has gone unjustified for years," Beatrice reminds her. "You and my aunt both have to pay."

"Where are you going?" Marilyn stands up too and follows Beatrice back into the foyer, her wedges clacking against the white hardwood floors.

"Ashwood," Beatrice answers, hurrying ahead, not trusting this lady to be behind her for very long. "Aunt Edie should be back there by now."

"Beatrice, you shouldn't discuss this in that house," Marilyn warns, her proper dialect no longer a thing.

Beatrice turns around to face her when she reaches the front door. "And why is that?"

"Because you'll be outnumbered."

Chapter 25

Beatrice heads to Ashwood anyway after an awkward thirteen minutes of waiting on Marilyn's porch for a cab. She rests her head against the window, shutting her eyes and feeling her head begin to throb. Her conversation with Marilyn flips and whirls inside of her mind. Everyone was right about Aunt Edie this whole time. She's guilty. Sure, she might not be Helcatia or whatever it is that Ashwood *is*, but she's just as evil.

The sun has pretty much loosened its grip on Silver Creek, the tangerine sky fading into a deep blue. Ashwood looks different now, Beatrice notices. There's only a single light on downstairs, but with the windows on the second floor, Beatrice notices they sort of look like eyes, watching her, knowing that she's all caught up on what this house has done, who it took, and why. And most importantly, how Beatrice's great aunt played a part in all of it.

She climbs out of the cab after paying the driver the last of her money. She can't even worry about leaving here without any money to her name. All this madness is far too important to focus on her empty bank account now. She starts up the driveway, a single haunting jack-o-lantern lit on the porch banister. Beatrice ignores it, takes a breath, and steps inside.

"Aunt Edie?" Beatrice calls out, immediately spotting Aunt Edie down the hall in the kitchen. Her heart is picking up the pace, her nerves vibrating around inside her body like sugar-filled children. "We need to talk."

"Please don't tell me you have plans tonight." Aunt Edie frowns, holding a bowl filled to the top with candy. "I was hoping we could find some masks in the basement and scare some of the trick-or-treaters." She's walking out of the kitchen and toward Beatrice, Halloween excitement floating off her frame. "I usually don't do this whole Halloween thing, but I thought it might be fun for the two of us since we started this clean slate thing, you know? I have a pumpkin pie in the oven, too."

"I think there are more important things we should be discussing," Beatrice claims, following her into the parlor. "Things like this house and the twins."

Aunt Edie sets the bowl down on the end table, sighing heavily at the mention of Jax and Juniper. "Now what?" She whips around. "Can't there be one evening in this house when things are normal?"

"Apparently not," Beatrice shoots back. "And you're the reason why."

Aunt Edie looks as if she's just been smacked across the face. Her eyebrows form a V. "I beg your pardon?"

"Well, I—"

"I beg your pardon?" Aunt Edie bellows louder this time, taking a step closer to her. "What did I tell you, Beatrice? I am sick of all these accusations against me—"

"It's all true, though, isn't it?" Beatrice cuts her off in a quiet voice. "Everything that Mom and Aunt Marley thought about you was true."

She glares at her. "I don't know what you're trying to say but—"

"You killed the twins," Beatrice cuts to the chase, a ball swelling up inside of her throat, the same one from Marilyn's has returned. "You meant to poison me, but they got to it instead and you didn't stop them. Were they enough of a sacrifice for you? Was it a blue moon that night?"

She doesn't say anything. She stares at her with eyes as wide as softballs.

"Marilyn told me," Beatrice goes on. "She told me how you kept her secret all this time. How you and Ruth planned the whole thing and she tried putting a stop to it. Fred Macher buried them in the woods when she left them to rot."

"You don't know what you're talking about."

"Then tell me!" Beatrice's scream explodes out of her like a firecracker sizzling to bomb the whole house to the ground. "Don't you have any sense of loyalty to your family? I am your *niece*. We share the same blood. And you walk around here like I'm some stranger. You hide the truth when I have every *fucking* right to know. So you're going to tell me everything. And if you don't, then I am going to the police right now and telling them all about what you did to Juniper and Jax. About how you're responsible for them, and for every other death that happened here. Maybe you and your two little BFF's can share a jail cell."

"Why don't you tell me?" Aunt Edie folds her slender arms in front of her skinny frame. She's challenging her. "If you want to march in here claiming you know this and that, then why don't you enlighten me by filling me in on what I've done?"

"There is something paranormal going on here," Beatrice croaks. "A deity named Helcatia was born into the house when it was built. Call it luck."

Beatrice listens to the house stir and she snaps her head up to look around, wondering if that was real or part of her imagination.

"How did you find out about that?" Aunt Edie nearly whispers.

"You have his symbol on the inside of your wardrobe," Beatrice answers. "I did some digging. Turns out, Helcatia feeds off the energy of those inside wherever It was brought to. And every blue moon, It demands a sacrifice. Either you please It by giving It something to feed on, or It feeds overtime, making the people inside slowly lose their minds. And once their minds emptied, they died. And then they were used to target the next relative. Pete to Uncle Eli, Dorothy to Grammy Astrid. When you ran out of family members to essentially sacrifice, you started recruiting young girls from town. You brought them in long enough for It to feed so by the blue moon, there would be nothing left of them. It would swallow them up whole."

"And that's all you know?" Aunt Edie asks after waiting for Beatrice to go on.

"I'm hoping you can fill in the rest." Beatrice clenches her jaw. "Or this is going to get very ugly."

"Well, I guess that's it, then." She sounds defeated but also maybe relieved.

A long pause hangs between them. It feels like the house stirs again. The grandfather clock in the hall ticks with each passing second. Red leaves blow past the window outside.

"Ashwood is more than just a house," Aunt Edie explains, looking around at the parlor, a sad smile tugging at her lips as her eyes slide across the mounted paintings and the trim lining the room. "Most houses are more than just things that people live in. They have feelings, you see. And Ashwood's feelings are strong. Stronger than most."

Beatrice holds her breath, wondering if Aunt Edie has been driven insane like the rest of her family members. She doesn't say anything, though, letting her continue.

"This house was built with the intention of being something more than just a roof and walls and doors," Aunt Edie goes on, taking a step toward the turret in the corner of the room, where the sun's light has now completely vanished and darkness has draped itself over the room. "Esther built this house with the intention of giving it feeling, supplying it with enough emotion it needs to survive. Like humans."

Beatrice stares at her. "But this house isn't a human. It's a thing."

"With feelings," Aunt Edie corrects, raking her fingertips down the glass window of the turret. "Ashwood is alive, Beatrice. Just as alive as you and I. The pipes are its veins, the windows are its eyes, the walls are its bones." She looks over at Beatrice, sadness still covering her face. "Special structures like this don't just die. They live on, as long as the heart is beating." Aunt Edie pauses, spinning one of her rings around her fingers. "Esther brought a presence here when the house was built, hoping that her vision for this place would come to life. And it did. But not in the way she thought."

"She brought something evil here," Beatrice clarifies. "And it's taken our entire family. It took your husband, your siblings, my mom. Why are you treating this like it's something good?"

"Because this house has done more for me than you know," Aunt Edie explains. "You see, when I was growing up here, I didn't have anyone. I didn't have cousins who hung out with me and my parents weren't very attentive. My brothers had each other. I spent so many days and nights here alone, by myself." She swallows, as though she's about to start crying but Beatrice's sympathy for her is scarce. "I was often ignored, and I was often not given dinner. And when I was bad, my parents would lock me in the basement's crawl space."

Sympathy now tugs at Beatrice and she frowns, but she still remains silent. Yes, people are products of their environments but Beatrice is having a hard time feeling too badly for her.

"The house gave me what I needed," she tells her, staring her in the face. "The house kept me company when everyone else wouldn't. And you must think I sound like a crazy woman right now, but company can come in all different kinds of forms." Aunt Edie sinks onto the sofa, her shoulders slumped, her spine rounded. Beatrice has never seen her look so sloppy. "But this house saved my life by being with me when no one else wanted to be. And I think that's why Esther created it in the first place. So, I had to pay it back. I had to *give* something to it after all that it had done."

Beatrice shakes her head, squeezing her eyes shut for a few seconds. "Wait, so you're telling me that you sacrificed all those women and members of our own family just because you think a house kept you company?"

"You're more understanding of it than you give yourself credit for," Aunt Edie says pointedly. "The house came to me in the form of an imaginary friend."

Beatrice flinches. She's waiting for some cinematic moment when Xander will come through the doorway and reveal himself but everything remains still and quiet. The house softly stirs once again and Beatrice loudly clears her throat.

"Okay?" She plays it off as though the term of an imaginary friend doesn't mean anything to her.

"The house chooses a Keeper." Aunt Edie smiles at the room around them. "It needs a protector of sorts. It came to me when I was a girl, just like it came to you as Xander when you were younger."

Beatrice processes this. If the house wanted her to be a *Keeper*, is that why nothing happened to her? Is that why Aunt Edie's twisted attempt at offing her hadn't worked? Because Beatrice was next in line to be Ashwood's right hand man?

"Xander was never real," Aunt Edie goes on. "Yet at the same time, he was more real than the House Things." She laughs and it sort of hurts Beatrice's feelings. "Think of him as the house taking on human form in order for you to be up for the job. When you first told me about him, I knew the house selected you as its Keeper once my term ended.

"I didn't realize what the house needed all those years before when our family kept dying. I was just as oblivious as everyone else. I stopped seeing my imaginary friend, Maybelle, when I hit puberty. I didn't need to see her anymore because I had gained full trust with the house and the house had gained full trust with me. And then I started sleepwalking and seeing Scarlet."

Beatrice blinks. "Who is Scarlet?"

"My cousin," Aunt Edie answers her. "She died when she was a little girl. Fell down the same stairs Eli died on." There's a pause. "The little twit likes to hide under the steps."

This sounds a little familiar: the sleepwalking and seeing someone that wasn't there. Beatrice thinks about how her mother has been visiting her in her sleep and by the time she wakes up, she finds herself in another room, completely dazed but with a whole new perspective on her dead relatives. It seems as though Aunt Edie was going through the same thing, but this Scarlet girl was the one feeding her the stories.

"She started showing me all these things, leading me onto these… walks." Aunt Edie wrings her hands together in her lap, growing more and more agitated. "They were all so real. And when they ended, I would wake up. But sometimes, I didn't want to go on these walks.

They were horrifying."

"I know a little about that." Beatrice hears herself say. She plants herself into one of the armchairs that is angled away from Aunt Edie. She cranes her neck to look at her. "My mom has been showing me the same things."

Aunt Edie nods but doesn't look surprised. "I had a feeling someone was."

"Why us?" Beatrice asks her. "Why your cousin and my mom?"

She shrugs her bony shoulders. "I suppose they wanted us to see what we couldn't, what we didn't understand. I was at a loss, just like you, when more of our family was dying. I was trying to figure things out. Scarlet helped me see certain things, she helped show me why things happened the way they did."

Beatrice relates, thinking about her mom. "So, you didn't know all of this for as long as you lived here?"

Aunt Edie shakes her head. "I was just as confused as you were, why the house would take who it did. I spent my whole life figuring this stuff out," Aunt Edie explains. "Just like you, about this… thing that makes the house what it is. About why the Millstone family has been targeted for so long. And the house supplied me with the answers I needed. It gave me resources and as everyone else around me was losing their minds, I was gaining a whole new sense of knowledge. But I started to wonder if me knowing about all this was really worth more than my loved ones dying."

"That was something you had to *wonder* about?" Beatrice snaps.

"So, I wanted to give the house someone that wasn't from inside," Aunt Edie goes on, not acknowledging her side comment. "That's where Ruth came in."

Beatrice shifts, preparing for this next part.

"Ruth's daughter had made such a terrible lie about Fred Macher touching her for whatever reason," she explains fast, the words rolling off her tongue so quickly that Beatrice wonders if she's even thinking anymore. It's a good thing, though, and Beatrice doesn't dare to interrupt. "It was such a terrible thing to make up, but she did, and she admitted to it. And I saw the way people in Silver Creek reacted, so I took advantage of it. I blew the whole thing out of proportion and led this hateful march against Fred. Burning his house down would have been so… justified."

Beatrice stares at this woman in horror, a woman that she doesn't even know she can call an aunt anymore. "Justified? He did nothing wrong!"

"I know, but I was so adamant on trading in someone from the outside of Ashwood so no one else would have to be taken from us," Aunt Edie tells her. "I did it for our family. And I figured that bringing someone over that was already dead would feed the house and no one would have to be taken. I was trying to reason with myself, trying to convince myself that he had done this terrible thing so I shouldn't feel badly about feeding him to Ashwood. That it was justified. I could bring an already-dead monster in here and no one would have to be taken. But he got away."

Beatrice's eyes fill with tears but she doesn't know why and she glares at Aunt Edie so hard her eyes almost hurt. "You tried killing me. The day the twins died, that was supposed to be me."

Aunt Edie swallows, making eye contact. She hesitates before speaking. "It wasn't supposed to kill you. It was supposed to make you weak. I realized that Ashwood liked feeding off the weak. It grew stronger the more vulnerable people became, the more insane they went. I found out that usually the house chooses a Keeper every other generation. More people were dying and I feared that I was reaching a point where the house didn't need me anymore. I didn't want to let the house go. I wasn't ready to become like every other Millstone before me."

"How could you do this?" Beatrice cries.

"I'm not the only one to blame," Aunt Edie claims. "Ruth and Marilyn know all about this. Granted, I think they're a little afraid of me. If they do me wrong, they know that Ashwood will protect me."

"So that's why Hudson has been covering up for you," Beatrice states. "So that he and his wife don't... what? Become sacrifices?"

"It keeps us safe." Aunt Edie smiles. "And what more could someone want in a world so filthy?"

"You're a monster," Beatrice croaks, rising from the chair. "You're a murderer and you're a monster."

"Those girls I took weren't very good people, anyway," Aunt Edie quickly claims, also rising to her feet. "They were depressed and lonely and they had made such messes of their lives, that I was bringing them to a place where they could feel safe before they had to go. And when they finally... *went*, they were all tucked away so peacefully."

"So... the House Things," Beatrice says, her voice booming off the walls. "They were ghosts all along?"

"No," Aunt Edie growls. "A ghost is something someone turns into once they die. A House Thing is what you become when you finish the process. You're dead the moment the house begins to feed off you. You're not a ghost. Not if you were completely fed off of until your last breath. You're nothing by the time you reach that stage."

"Why didn't you just leave?" Beatrice demands, desperate for a life that didn't have any of *this*. She thinks about what her mother could have accomplished, what the twins would've done if they got to grow up. She thinks about everyone else who unknowingly spent their whole lives in this house, only to be oblivious that they were its food. "Why did you spend all these years doing this? If you felt that badly about it, then you could have left."

"Because Ashwood is a part of me," she remarks as though Beatrice should already have the answer. "And it has now given me permission to go out into the world, to become who I want to be, to see things I truly want. I dedicated my entire life to this house. And because of that, I can get everything that I've ever wanted and Helcatia is making that happen, Beatrice. You can do the same if you play your cards right."

"I am not going to give *anything* to this place," Beatrice bellows, spit flying out of her mouth. "Not when it has taken everything from me. And the fact that you don't see anything wrong with that, just goes to show how evil of a person you are. You have no love in that cold, dark heart of yours. You're just as evil as this house."

"You ungrateful little girl," Aunt Edie hisses, coming closer to her. Beatrice takes a step back. "Don't you see that I've kept you alive for all these years? I could've easily brought you back here, taken care of you the way I took care of all those other women. But I chose not to. I gave you a chance because that is what Ashwood wanted and because you've always been my favorite. I knew it was wrong. But then when I found out that you were seeing Xander, I knew. I knew that it was time for you to take my place. The house was ready for a new Keeper."

"You're fucking psycho," Beatrice declares through a clenched jaw. She goes to run for the threshold, but she stops in her tracks when she finds Xander standing in the doorway. He's smiling at her, his hands behind his back. The room begins to spin as that cinematic moment she was expecting moments ago has started. "Xander…"

He snorts, covering his mouth with a hand. "Sorry, Beatrice. I still think it's a little funny when you call me that."

Beatrice's blood runs ice cold.

"Xander is here, is he?" Aunt Edie cackles, tossing her head back. "Perfect timing, isn't it, darling?"

"You're not real," Beatrice tells Xander, shaking her head.

The entire room feels like it's vibrating behind her, like it's all sitting on some stereo system at a volume that's way too high. She doesn't want to be sold on Xander not actually being a human. She doesn't want her memories of him spoiled on discovering that he isn't a person, he isn't even a House Thing. He's *the* House Thing.

"I'm as real as ever." Xander takes a step closer to her, the doorbell ringing.

"Trick-or-treat!" kids call out from the other side of the front door.

Xander pays them no attention. His eyes are glued to Beatrice, his cheeks sucked in and his cheekbones prominent. It looks like he hasn't eaten in quite some time. "Some have a different name for me, you see. You might know me as *the Thing in the Garden.*"

Beatrice stumbles backward. She reaches out to catch herself from falling, grabbing hold of the sofa's arm. Winona's big spell book of deities comes flashing back into her mind, her long finger pointing to the photo of a black mass on the page, Helcatia's name written over it. She thinks of Lila's Polaroid photo, captioning it as *the Thing in the Garden.* Both images are identical to each other: messy and unsettling. Xander is no imaginary friend. Beatrice tries pushing all of it out of her head. Xander was the only positive thing to come out of Ashwood, yet it's starting to taint itself into something indescribable. He is the evil spirit that has been feeding on her family, that has been supplying Aunt Edie with the company she desired as a child. He is the heart of Ashwood, and Beatrice shared a childhood with him. It all makes sense yet is tangled together like a web of illusion, a web that has trapped Beatrice so tight she can't move.

"What's wrong, Beatrice?" Aunt Edie looks at her, genuinely concerned as she tries following her gaze but Xander remains invisible to her. "What's going on?"

"Trick-or-treat!" the kids say in unison again but they go ignored once more.

"You can't see him?" She points her finger at Xander but he doesn't look bothered. He seems patient. She wishes she could punch the smirk off his face. "Xander is..." She's breathless, too stunned to finish as her chest heaves in and out, the realization of what she's staring at getting the best of her.

"I don't," Aunt Edie answers. "But I don't need to in order to know what I have to do."

Beatrice shuffles away from her aunt when she finds her lunging at her. "What are you doing?"

"Tonight is the blue moon," Aunt Edie reminds her, grabbing hold of her wrist before she can get away. "Ashwood is hungry, darling."

"I sure am." Xander stares at Beatrice hungrily, his serpent tongue tracing his bottom lip.

Beatrice screams, shoving Aunt Edie away from her with all her might. She watches her crash into the coffee table, shattering the glass structure into little pieces shining in the moonlight from the window. Aunt Edie groans in pain, her eyes bugging out of her head. There are gashes in her arms and she's barely able to move. Xander looks surprised but also impressed. He's oddly satisfied.

"It's about time someone did that," Xander comments casually. "I love her and all, but damn, is she a bitch, or what?"

Beatrice races out of the parlor and covers her mouth with her hands when she finds Aunt Marley blocking the front door. Her jaw is dislocated and she's levitating off the ground, her scream so loud that Beatrice falls to the floor, plugging her ears with her fingers. She listens to her muffled breathing over the violent sound of Aunt Marley's screams. Opening an eye, she notices Uncle Eli standing on the ceiling in the mudroom, his frown rounder than it used to be. A little girl with ruby red hair is peeping out from the basement door. Aunt Marley's eyes roll into the back of her head.

"Aunt Marley saw me the night she got the boot," Xander informs Beatrice over the sound of the screaming. He's still standing in the threshold separating the parlor and the foyer, his arms crossed over his chest as Aunt Edie struggles to get up from behind him. "She and your mother did a little too much research and they reaped the benefits when they tried some ritual to try and get rid of me." He sighs, squatting down next to Beatrice on the floor. "It's sad, isn't it? That most human beings are just so goddamn stupid?"

"Bea." A voice from across the foyer at the foot of the steps catches Beatrice's attention. Her mother is standing there, still in that plain white t-shirt, her curly hair in a wild mane framing her face. "The attic, Beatrice. Go to the attic."

Beatrice uses her foot to kick Xander back several feet into the parlor, shocked that she's able to make contact with him but never did with any of the other House Things. The big bad House Thing can get his ass whooped, then. She gets to her feet again, catching a glimpse at what used to be Aunt Marley, but now is some floating creature with veins bulging out of her neck and bones at angles that have long since been broken. She races up the stairs instead of going out the mudroom door, her mind on two things: her mom and the attic.

"Beatrice, where are you going?" Xander calls from downstairs, laughing. "We aren't finished yet. I haven't eaten you!"

"Get out!" A little girl screams at the top of her lungs down the second-floor hallway. She's wearing a black dress with a white collar, her brown skin glowing in the darkness. Beatrice doesn't recognize her at all. Her feet aren't touching the ground and she's gliding toward her from the end of the hallway as though she's being thrown. Her eyes are beams of red light. "You're going to die, die, die, die…"

She keeps repeating the last word and Beatrice yelps, a ball forming in her throat as she staggers backward against the hallway wall, a painting falling behind her. She tears through the hallway and up the next flight of stairs, knocking a portrait of Grandpa Lachlan down and tripping over a thin table with a floral arrangement on it. Aunt Marley's yelling only grows louder and there are footsteps behind her somewhere. Xander isn't that far behind and he's going to do whatever he can to—

Beatrice screams when her ankle gets yanked from behind. She falls, the edge of one of the steps digging into her kneecap and her chin colliding with the banister before she hits the rest of the stairs. Blood fills her mouth, her jaw throbs with pain, one of her teeth immediately starting to ache.

"Where do you think you're going?" Aunt Edie is behind her, crawling up the stairs like a tarantula—her bony limbs taking the steps one at a time. Fury fills her face, a face that has been tended to for so many years to stay looking young. Now, she looks wrinkled and pasty, something out of a horrific fairytale gone wrong. "I've dedicated every blue moon to Ashwood for over a decade. You are not going to ruin that for me now."

"Get off!" Beatrice tries wrestling her away but Aunt Edie's strength is underestimated. They struggle against each other on the stairs, Xander's howling laugh somewhere down below, in tune with Aunt Marley's terrible screams.

"You're nothing but a little bitch, Beatrice." Aunt Edie wraps her long hands around her niece's neck, her lips pursed in an ugly sneer. Blood from the coffee table glass streams down her bony arms in jagged lines. "I don't know what happened to the young girl that used to live here, but you are not her!"

"Get off!" Beatrice struggles to breathe, all the air pipes in her throat closing in.

"*Get off*," Aunt Edie mocks, raising her upper lip as she digs her thumbs further into Beatrice's throat. "How dare you come into my house and disrupt my peace? Everything was perfect until you showed up. But you just had to go snooping and digging for answers, didn't you? What gave you the right, Beatrice?"

Beatrice grunts, black dots beginning to dance in front of her vision.

"What gave you the right to come in here and screw everything up?" Aunt Edie demands again, yelling now.

Beatrice reaches up for Aunt Edie's neck or face or *anything* but she can't grab hold. The veins in Aunt Edie's arm are getting larger the harder she squeezes. Beatrice's eyes bulge out of her head, jerking her body from side to side to get this bitch off her but her aunt's strength is too strong. She glances to her right, at the flimsy railing Xander mentioned would need replaced. Apparently it's too loose. Without another thought, Beatrice screams, hoisting her left knee up as high as she can to fling Aunt Edie in the opposite direction. She uses every muscle in her body to get rid of her, to save herself from this newfound evil above her.

Aunt Edie cries out as her body falls against the railing, breaking through it and soaring through the air. Her dress flies behind her as she screams on her way down, landing with a solid *thud*. Beatrice gasps for air, wheezing as she looks over the splintered wood. Aunt Edie lies face up, her leg at a broken angle and her arm bent in a position that makes Beatrice wince. She looks like a fractured porcelain doll that had just taken a fall off a very high shelf. All she needs is a few cracks in her face and she'd be set.

Beatrice stares at her dead aunt below. How did that woman go from Beatrice's favorite family member to *this*? Aunt Edie dedicated her life to feeding Ashwood, paying it back for the life it gave her. Ashwood started to prey on Beatrice the same way and Aunt Edie was letting It.

Beatrice coughs as she crawls her way to the top of the stairs, the attic just at the end of the hall. She picks herself back up, refusing to stay down. She ignores Grandpa Hugh standing in the doorway of his mother's bedroom, his neck snapped to the side. She's only ever seen his snapped neck in photos. Another man Beatrice has only seen during her early childhood waits at the end, his face peeled off in thin curls, his eyes scratched at with red nail marks. A woman stands next to him and Beatrice recognizes her as Great Aunt Helen—the same woman Beatrice once saw in the attic during a game of hide and seek. Her mouth is stitched open with thread, forcing a smile over her face.

Beatrice ducks her head, her main focus to breathe and get to that attic, for whatever reason her mother needed her in there for. With a trembling hand, she flips the gold clasp on the double doors and flings herself inside. It hurts to swallow, and she feels like she might pass out at any given moment but she brings the doors shut behind her and braces herself against one of the many wooden rafters. A plastic Santa Claus judges her in the corner, his jolly old smile not so jolly anymore. The furniture is no longer in here, making a little more room for Beatrice to step inside.

"Mom?" Beatrice croaks, her voice hoarse from Aunt Edie's hands. She opens her mouth to plea out to her mother, to tell her what to do, to beg for some sort of direction. But she clamps it shut because a noise catches her attention from outside the attic. She steps away from the rafter, listening to the slow footsteps coming up the stairs. It has to be Xander. There's no way Aunt Edie survived that fall.

Beatrice flies into action, tearing through the attic for any sort of clue or sign from her mom. She finds that scrap of paper she tore out of her notebook after finding what was written on it during her first time back up here: *Welcome Home*. Underneath it sits two dull orange cans of gasoline. And it clicks. She's no longer lost. She holds the can firmly in her grasp and hurries for the doors again, no longer feeling like she's in real time. She feels like she's in one of those awful dreams, when she feels like she's running so fast but she's barely moving at all. The hallway lays out before her and Beatrice braces herself against the wall, weak.

Beatrice isn't sure how, but she seems to be moving at a quicker speed when she realizes Xander isn't up here. But the House Things are. She darts by their quiet figures, ignoring their sad, moon-eyed expressions of loneliness and grief. The gasoline pours fluidly out of the nozzle, splashing across the floor of the hallway and down the steps. Beatrice splashes it over the doors and walls of Ashwood, a hero to those watching around her. Uncle Eli's frown is slowly turning upside down, relief flooding over his face. The red haired girl from the basement stands with Aunt Helen and her husband near the stairs. Beatrice wonders if the little girl is Scarlet, Aunt Edie's cousin.

Beatrice hurries from room to room, finding herself covering every inch she possibly can with the gasoline, knowing she'll run out of the first can soon enough. Beatrice dumps the gasoline all across Grammy Astrid and Grandpa Hugh's pink shag carpet in their bedroom. Grammy Astrid presses her hand against the glass in the bathroom, her mother-in-law standing next to her with a disapproving look on her face. She stops in her tracks when she finds a little boy standing over Aunt Edie's body. Her son. Beatrice listens to Lachlan howl in the basement's crawlspace, so she starts down the steps, throwing the gasoline along the walls in her path and over family portraits and timeless art.

The doors to the crawl space remain shut, doors that have haunted Beatrice for years, doors that were almost never opened in her lifetime. They no longer look scary. Instead, the crawl space feels more like a cage. She pulls them open and Grandpa Hugh's brother emerges from within, bathing in the light now streaming through the dark, damp space he has spent so long in. His nails are as long as yardsticks, curled up and splintering. His hair is matted on his head, a bald spot at the crown. He's gray and he's cowering away from the light but when he sees Beatrice and the gas tank, the corners of his mouth pull up, showing his crooked yellow teeth. The sight is terrifying.

Beatrice continues upstairs, using what's left of the second can of gasoline for the hallway, kitchen, and parlor. She's breathless, but Beatrice has never felt better in her whole life, to know that this place could be going up in flames the way it should have been over a hundred years ago—

"Think you're getting away that easily?" Xander appears in the kitchen, holding a butcher knife. "You aren't that smart, Beatrice. I know you better than you know yourself. I've fed off you for ten years. You're not making it out of here alive."

"Joke's on you," Beatrice barks. "Without anyone else here, you'll starve."

Before letting him speak, she uses the gasoline can to knock him across the face. Xander grunts, reaching out to grab her by the hair. Beatrice fails to think fast. He bashes her head into the china cabinet, glass exploding around her and plates crashing to the floor.

"Then I guess it's time for my last supper."

Beatrice cries, screaming as he bashes her head against the glass again. Blood streaks down her face, blocking her vision. Blindly, she grabs hold of a sharp piece of glass, swinging her arm behind her until she feels it jab into his neck. Xander lets out a yelp that sounds like a wounded animal. Beatrice gasps for air, stumbling forward into the mudroom. She's surprised the glass even went in. Wasting no time, Beatrice grabs the can of gasoline again, charging for the front door.

She limps out onto the front porch, where trick-or-treaters wearing their Halloween costumes are filing up the driveway with pillowcases full of candy. She grabs the lit jack-o-lantern from the banister and carefully takes the tea light out from inside, returning to the foyer.

Before her are the House Things that have roamed Ashwood for years. Her mother stands at the forefront, the missing women from Silver Creek standing behind her in what seems to be a safe cluster, all them tangled together in a big hug.

Beatrice lowers the candle in her hand. "Wait, I can't—"

"Yes, you can," her mother interrupts her, smiling. "You're the only one that will."

"But then I can't see you anymore," Beatrice croaks tiredly, feeling the eyes of everyone else digging into her. Her mouth is filled with blood. She knows they have to be on her side. If they weren't, they would have tried stopping her from torching the place and maybe Ashwood would have fed off her much faster.

"I'm not a House Thing," her mother tells her quietly. "I wasn't fed on long enough to become one."

"Then why are you here?" Beatrice asks desperately, wishing she could take all of them with her.

"We were waiting for you to return. Look around your neck," her mother instructs, gesturing to her own bare neck.

Beatrice does as she's told, finding the locket dangling in front of her chest, the one she took from Lila's box. The squid pendant fits in her palm and when popped open, the photo of Beatrice and her mother is still secured inside.

"You're just as safe as I was," Lena tells her. "Each of these girls wore that when they were sacrificed. A symbol of love."

Beatrice looks at the pendent again, running her hands over the tiny grooves. When she looks up again, the only House Thing that remains is Xander. She grips the locket in one hand and the candle in the other.

"It's never going to work," Xander informs, yanking the glass shard out of his neck. He isn't even bleeding. He isn't human. "You can burn the house, but you can't burn the land. I will forever be here, Beatrice. You can't erase me, just like you can't erase anything that has happened here. It's a part of you."

"You were created on this land," Beatrice reminds him breathlessly. "Created with a house by very lonely people wanting this home to be more than just a house. They wanted it to be a friend. So, then you came along. Embedded in the floors, plastered in the walls, engraved in the brick, stretching from room to room. Watching. Studying. Feeding. You are not what holds this house up. The house is what holds *you* up. Without it, all the House Things are free. But you are not."

Xander's smirk fades when he realizes she's right. He holds his arm out in front of him to stop her from dropping the candle. "Wait! Stop! Think about what you're doing. This is your home, Beatrice. I made this place a home *for* you. Why do you think we've been friends for so long?"

"This isn't a home," she protests. Her head feels like it's on fire from all the glass chunks sticking out of it. She needs to get medical treatment. Fast. "A home is where you feel safe and protected."

"There is protection here," he disputes pleadingly. "Everything I've done for everyone here, they're safe with me, here, in Ashwood. I've taught them what it feels like to no longer fear what could happen to them out there, in the real world, in a place so vile and… sane. Everyone can be together here."

"Don't you hear yourself?" Beatrice can't help but stifle a laugh. She feels like she's going to pass out. "Being driven into these states of paranoia and insanity is not normal. That's not what living is. I would much rather take the unknown world out there than deal with this evil in here. And so would anyone else. The longer Ashwood stands, the longer the people here are stuck. The longer more people will be lured in."

"I'm not ready for that," Xander says sadly. He's suddenly back to being the little boy Beatrice grew up with. The black floppy hair, the wide-set eyes, the straight lines for lips. Beatrice's heart aches seeing this version of him. This short, wildly innocent version. "I've been doing this for so long, I don't want things to change."

"You are the essence of evil," Beatrice declares. "You don't get a say in what happens, just like no one got a say when they crossed your path. Ashwood needs to burn. And you'll burn with it."

Xander continues to beg but it's too late. Beatrice drops the candle and flames shoot out right in front of her just as the boy version of Xander vanishes. The flames follow the gasoline trail up the steps and along the walls, jumping to grab at anything to make itself larger, more dangerous, and more destructive. Beatrice exits Ashwood one last time, her childhood house being swallowed up in flames so hot and big, it's like they all know exactly what their purpose is. The trick-or-treaters stand at the foot of the porch steps, staring up at the house in awe. One is dressed as a ghost, the other as a witch, and a vampire is on the far right.

"What's happening?" the vampire asked through his plastic fangs.

"Shouldn't you be putting that out?" the witch asks next, worriedly.

The ghost remains silent, their eyes wide from the two holes cut into the white sheet draped over their body.

"No," Beatrice answers, turning around to stare up at it with them. She can almost hear the house roaring, and it's not just from the fire. Helcatia is screaming. Ashwood is crying. "This has been a long time coming."

323

———◆———

Chapter 26

"**B**eatrice Millstone, the only living survivor of the Millstone family curse, has validated that the horrors of Ashwood are in fact real," a plastic blond woman on the news announces through a microphone, her cream-colored blazer crisp on screen. "Ms. Millstone not only killed her own aunt out of self-defense, but she burned Ashwood to the ground right after and watched it crumble from the driveway with a few of Silver Creek's residential trick-or-treaters. When questioned by the police, Ms. Millstone claimed that the house was in fact an evil entity. The attending officers asked Ms. Millstone what happened to her aunt and how the house burned down, in which Ms. Millstone confessed to everything. Now, a month later, Beatrice Millstone remains at a psychiatric hospital in New York…."

The patients at Ryde Oaks are technically not supposed to watch the news, but one of the nurses likes Beatrice enough to turn a blind eye in the common room. Beatrice is crumpled up on the sofa, wearing ugly sweatpants and a stained shirt. Her hair is unwashed and she's pretty sure the toothpaste this place supplies her with is either expired or poisoned. She uses the remote to turn the channel to PBS, where a children's show about a girl on a big comfy couch is playing.

Cold rain splatters against the square window to Beatrice's left and she rests her head against the back of the couch. She has thought about her last day at Ashwood every day since being checked in here. She honestly didn't know that people would think she was crazy if she told them the truth about the house and what she discovered leading up to burning it down. But it makes sense. Even Clara was looking at her like her head was on fire when she met her at the police station, embracing her into a squeeze so tight Beatrice nearly suffocated.

Beatrice isn't crazy, and she knows that. But the rest of the world is on cloud nine with another Millstone story to tweet and blog about. The same nurse that has befriended Beatrice let her use a computer last week since she has been showing such good behavior. The first thing she did was pull up all those shitty blogs about Ashwood, where she read thread after thread about theories on what took place in the house before Beatrice lit a match to it. Some people are calling her a hero, while others are calling her insane, claiming that whatever is inside of Ashwood got to Beatrice just like it did with the rest of her family. Artists have even made custom paintings and graphic posters of her standing in front of the burning house like it was all out of some scary movie.

The media has been eating away at Beatrice's mind ever since seeing that. She knows what happened inside that house, both in the past and in the present. She thought informing the police and Clara *and* a reporter that was on the scene would do her some good, that it would put this whole nightmare to rest. But she was wrong, and maybe a little out of her mind with hysterics by the time the police showed up and she realized what she had done. Burning her childhood house down after killing her own aunt and then claiming the house was evil and a hungry God was inside of it is definitely a reason for her to be a patient here. She can't entirely blame them.

Beatrice blacked out at some point during that night. She thinks it was in the back of the squad car, when she was rambling on about how Aunt Edie sacrificed all those women every blue moon and that she could have been the sacrifice for the moon on Halloween. Who knows if Aunt Edie was actually done protecting the house? That seems a little far-fetched that the house would have *allowed* her to just go off and see the world. The cops kept exchanging looks with one another that Beatrice didn't understand so it only made her explain more of what took place in Ashwood, feeding them all the information she could. But it only wound her up enough to get her a room here.

Beatrice knows the only choice she had was to drop that candle on the gasoline covered house, there was no question about it. She thinks about the House Things watching her with such hope as she did, and it only confirmed for her that Ashwood burning to the ground was the only thing that needed to happen for some ounce of justice to be restored. No more Ashwood. No more curses. No more Helcatia.

Beatrice wasn't *entirely* looked at as a crazy person. Officer Gomez backed her up when it came to her knowledge of Jax and Juniper and how Fred Macher buried them when Aunt Edie poisoned them. Gomez spoke up for her and even led the search for the remnants of their skeletons— which were finally found just days ago. Gomez has visited here a few times and promised Beatrice over and over again that she was going to find Juniper and Jax so they could be properly sent off. But even despite being backed up by Officer Gomez, Beatrice knows that she will forever be looked at the last person alive from the Millstone family curse—which hopefully has finally been broken.

"Hey, you," Clara greets her suddenly. She's wearing a tan coat and a matching scarf, an oil-stained white paper bag in her hands. She holds it up, offering a smile. "I come bringing gifts."

Beatrice forces a smile but it doesn't last long. "Powdered doughnuts hardly count as gifts."

"Don't be ungrateful," Clara jokes and settles down next to her on the itchy couch. "It's the only food I'm allowed to bring in."

Clara has visited Beatrice almost every day since she's been in here, even though it's more than forty minutes for her to drive all the way out here. It's nice, having someone to talk to who isn't wearing a white coat and isn't constantly analyzing you with their PhD degrees. But Clara looks at Beatrice like the media would look at her if they could sneak a peek. She can tell she's scared and hesitant to say certain things, walking on eggshells as though something mentioned about Ashwood is going to set her off into a tangent or mental breakdown. Beatrice would be the same way if the roles were reversed.

"So, how are you?" Clara asks her after reaching inside for a doughnut. Most days she brings them, hoping that they will cheer her up as much as they would when Beatrice was in high school.

Beatrice holds one of the doughnuts in her hands, not very hungry but she'll entertain it just for Clara. "Is that a trick question?"

"Maybe, it's one that I already know the answer to," Clara chirps, chewing. "The doctors say that they can't believe how much better you're doing, especially after such a short period of time."

"Well they can fuck off," Beatrice comments dryly, stuffing a piece of the doughnut into her mouth. "Nothing was ever wrong with me to begin with. I shouldn't even be here."

"They just want to see you get better."

"I don't need to get better," Beatrice snaps at her. The anti-anxiety meds they put her on makes her a moody bitch but that's not her problem. She doesn't even have anxiety so why in the hell are they medicating her for it? "I get what happened that night was… wild, but I don't deserve to be in here. I'm not getting better, the doctors are just realizing that there was nothing wrong with me in the first place."

Clara sighs, the powdered sugar falling onto her black slacks. She dusts her hands off and swallows the last bit of her doughnut before looking at Beatrice seriously. "I didn't want to have this conversation with you today, but I think it's about time that we did."

Beatrice takes another bite so she doesn't have to answer.

"You cannot be angry about what people think of you," Clara explains to her. "Like you said, what happened that night was wild, but you talking about it isn't helping anyone see another side of you, the sane side. The side I know."

Beatrice grits her teeth. She's so sick and tired of being stuck within these walls and being told that she's insane. *Ashwood* was insane. The people *there* were losing their minds. She has her mind. It's everyone else around her that is acting crazy. What, she's some lunatic just for calling out the truth? She needs some sort of mental help just because she finally figured out what was going on inside after all these years?

"I'm not saying that I don't believe what happened there—"

"But do you?" she challenges.

It's a question that Beatrice has been too afraid to ask Clara for a month now. Part of her doesn't want to know if Clara thinks she's just as crazy as the world is making her out to be. Part of her feels good not knowing, safe in a bubble that tells her Clara is on her side and she believes every word Beatrice told the police. That she knows Beatrice well enough to believe that she didn't make up a single thing that took place in that house. But Clara has been awfully quiet about the whole subject. Every time she comes to visit her, she either talks about the boys or work or discusses what Beatrice has been up to and promises to check in on Trinkets and Treasures at some point. She dances around the subject like a tango.

Clara sighs again, resting her elbows on her knees as she leans forward, tilting her body toward Beatrice's legs. "I understand that a lot happened to you in that house. But is it easy for me to wrap my head around certain things you described? Hell no."

"Like what?" Beatrice orders. "What part is so hard for you to get?"

"That Esther somehow unknowingly summoned a deity into the house when she built it," she explains. "And that ever since, this spirit has taken shape and fed off the minds of people within it. Beatrice, you have to admit that it sounds pretty bizarre—"

"It's the truth," Beatrice cuts her off, white powder falling from her lips like snow. "I don't know what else to tell you."

Clara checks her watch on her wrist, pursing her lips at how early it is. She's looking for an excuse to leave and Beatrice can't really blame her. "Listen, I have to pick up the boys from basketball. I'll leave the donuts here."

Beatrice allows Clara to kiss her head before padding out of the common room, a nurse ushering her into the hallway. Beatrice shuts her eyes and leans back on the couch. Not one person believes her. Sure, there are freaks on the internet that have made fan pages dedicated to her and whatnot but no one that actually *matters*. She's never been alone so much in her life. She's broke, has nowhere to go once she's released out of this madhouse, and she will be thrown into the public eye once more. Perhaps staying here isn't so bad.

Beatrice tries to sleep that night on her side, facing the wall. The room is nice, despite what most people think about these sorts of facilities. Beatrice pictured a brick cell she'd have to share with someone named Shirley but it kind of reminds her of a college dorm. She has her side, and her roommate, Willow, has the other. It's carpeted in beige and they each have a desk and a dresser. They don't get their own bathroom, they have to share one with the floor, but it could be a lot worse. Beatrice heard that the girls on the fifth floor all have to bathe at the same time like a big shower orgy or something. Since Beatrice's "condition" isn't that severe, her floor consists of a lot of girls with similar situations but Beatrice is sure that theirs is all actually real. Hers is not.

"Can't sleep?" Willow peeks over Beatrice's shoulder.

Beatrice sighs, propping herself up on her elbow. She likes Willow, but it's kind of like sharing a room with a little sister who likes to stay up and talk all night about boys and puppies. She's here at Ryde Oaks for believing that she was used as a sacrifice during a satanic ritual her boyfriend was a part of with a cult. She had a meltdown when she was arrested for "making the whole thing up" but it's hard to see other people in this building as liars when Beatrice has seen things out of this world. Who's to say that Willow isn't telling the truth?

"Not really," Beatrice murmurs, sitting up and leaning against the wall. "I have a hard time shutting my brain off a lot of the time."

"Me too." Willow brings her knees to her chest, perched at the foot of Beatrice's bed like an owl. Her silky Asian hair hangs in front of her shoulders, a pink bunny hat with flappy ears covering her head. "I keep thinking about Rory. Do you think he thinks about me?"

Rory is the ex-boyfriend who she accused of trying to sacrifice her. He has been the topic of their conversations night after night. Beatrice isn't sure if it's healthy for Willow's recovery to constantly be thinking about what he's doing and if he's thinking about her or not but if it wasn't, then the doctors would have probably put Willow in her own room.

"I'm sure he does," Beatrice assures. "But I don't think it's in the way that you think."

"Well what way could it be?" Willows frowns, her eyes growing wide with sadness. "You think he hates me, don't you?"

"I didn't say that." Beatrice shifts in her bed.

She *does* think that Rory hates her. He has a restraining order against her and apparently uses his social media platform to speak out against Willow. He even joined a church to show people that he doesn't worship Satan. But, Willow is like a very fragile flower. If she gets mishandled a certain way, it's all downhill from there.

"I just think that he has a lot of thinking to do," Beatrice tells her gently. "You both do. Why would you want to be with someone who tried to sacrifice you in the first place, you know?"

"I guess," she mumbles into her knees and shakes her thick bangs out of her eyes. "What about you?"

Beatrice eyes her. "What about me?"

"Don't you wonder if Xander ever thinks about you?"

Beatrice winces at the question. She and Willow have gotten to know a lot about why each other are here—it comes with the territory from being roommates in a space this small. Beatrice told her all about Ashwood and her aunt and Helcatia—AKA Xander. Even though Willow made some strange looks and noises throughout Beatrice telling her the story, she's the only person that has taken what Beatrice said seriously. And for that, Beatrice owes her for life for being the only one to make her feel sane after that night.

"I don't even know if he's alive," Beatrice tells her. "Well, I guess technically, he was never alive. But you know what I mean."

"I do," Willow confirms, walking her fingers up and down her leg. "Can I tell you something?"

Beatrice nods, pulling the blanket higher up her waist.

"I listen to you when you sleep," Willow whispers, like she's sharing a secret. "I don't do it on purpose, but sometimes you wake me up."

Beatrice shifts uncomfortably. She didn't even know she still did things in her sleep. She was kind of hoping that now that she's out from under Ashwood's roof, her sleeping habits would return to normal. Apparently not. "Sorry, I didn't realize I did that."

"You get up, too," Willow goes on. "It scares me."

"I get up?" Beatrice echoes. "What do you mean?"

"You get up and walk around," Willow clarifies, her shoulders slouching. "It's like you're looking for something or someone. And you talk to yourself, too. Obviously, I know you're just sleepwalking but it scares me a little. Maybe you should tell one of the psychiatrists. They can give you meds for that."

"What do I say?" Beatrice wonders, curiosity eating away at her like it usually feasts.

Willow's tiny shoulders rise and then fall. "I dunno. You say names. Ellie? Eli? Something like that. And you say *who* a lot, too. And Scarlet. And Benji—which I'm guessing is short for Benjamin."

Beatrice knows that Willow means *Hugh* when she said the *who* thing. Beatrice has woken up here at Ryde Oaks without remembering any of her dreams. She thought that was a telltale sign that she is sleeping better now, that her mother is no longer visiting her in the night to tell her stories about the dead relatives before her.

"You okay?" Willow searches her face. "You look like you've seen a ghost."

"I'm fine," Beatrice answers. "Just suddenly tired, that's all."

"I'll let you go to sleep." Willow scampers to the other side of the room where her own twin bed waits. "If you're right and you say you're going to be leaving here soon, we're going to have to wake up early and make the most out of the days, huh?"

Beatrice smiles in response and rolls back onto her side, her smile quickly fading and replaced with a look of worry.

⬥

Chapter 27

Snow has fallen over New York City and Beatrice sits in the frosted bay window of Clara's apartment, snowflakes sticking to the glass. Technically, it's her apartment now, too, but it doesn't feel that way. Clara's wife, Tonya, has been super welcoming, as have the boys. But Beatrice has been out of Ryde Oaks for a couple weeks now and it doesn't feel real. A small part of her is constantly on edge, worrying about one thing or another. Sometimes she's nervous about nothing at all, and she realizes she only gets this way when she thinks of Ashwood or Aunt Edie.

"Here you go, Beatrice!" One of Clara's sons, Artie, brings her a mug of steaming hot chocolate with reindeer printed on the side.

She smiles warmly at him and takes it. "Thanks, kiddo."

He races off, his brother greeting him near the Christmas tree with his own mug. It's Christmas day, a day that is supposed to be filled with glee and joy and all that other good stuff. But Beatrice is having a hard time painting a smile on her face. Things with Clara are fine, but still not what they used to be. She's convinced that they will never go back to normal but Beatrice doesn't find that as a surprise. If Clara thinks she's just as insane as the rest of the world does, there isn't much she can do to prove to her that she never made any of this up. Beatrice often catches Clara and Tonya whispering and she has no doubt it's about her.

"What are you doing all the way over here?" Clara sinks down next to her on the couch. "I thought we talked about this self-isolation thing."

"I just wanted to watch the snow," Beatrice replies, nodding her head to the window where the snow comes down in sheets. "The weathermen are saying that we'll be snowed in for a few days."

"I'm not complaining," Clara chirps.

"I'm not either." Beatrice looks back out the window and her blood runs cold, even though the thought of being cooped up in a house against her will makes her skin crawl.

Grammy Astrid stares back at her in the glass, Dorothy, over her shoulder as they both offer two small waves. Beatrice jumps up from the couch, spilling her hot chocolate all over her lap. Fumbling over one of the kids' new toys, Beatrice hears herself scream.

"Beatrice?" Clara gasps, leaping to her feet and staring at Beatrice in horror. "What's wrong?"

Her chest heaves in and out and she points a finger at the window, her response about her grandma and great-grandmother on the tip of her tongue but she can't bring herself to actually say the words. Clara is going to look at her like her head has been blown off. She swallows, her thighs burning from the hot chocolate.

"I thought I saw someone out there." She forces a laugh to prove to Clara that she isn't crazy. The boys are watching her, their mouths in the shapes of O's. She gulps down her fear. "Damn, that scared me."

"Tonya, we're going to need another cup of hot chocolate!" Clara calls out to her wife. "Why don't you go upstairs and change, sweetie?"

She does as she's told, locking the bathroom door behind her and splashing cold water onto her face. Her skin is blotchy when she looks at herself in the mirror, her hairline soaked in water. She sees movement behind her, Grammy Astrid's familiar curls. Beatrice quickly ducks her head back down and reaches for the towel slung onto the hook on the back of the door.

"She's not here, she's not here, she's not here," Beatrice chants to herself, her voice muffled by the towel. She hangs it back up, refusing to look in the mirror and slipping out the door.

And that's when it began: Beatrice's downhill spiral into oblivion, a feeling as familiar as Ashwood. She continued living with Clara, her sleepwalking episodes not happening every night, but enough to start concerning Artie and Rico. They would find her swaying at the end of the upstairs hallway, talking to herself. She would snap her head when they would catch her attention and she would beg for them to wake her up. It was Tonya's idea for Beatrice to be put on a sleep pill, which helped a lot. But not for good.

Beatrice could never live on her own, she was too much in debt and Clara worried for her wellbeing. She had her job at Trinkets and Treasures, but even there, in a place she knew so well, she was haunted by the faces of her past. Dusting the store turned into dusting the floor whenever she would find Uncle Eli hanging from the ceiling. Turning corners turned into nearly walking right into Grandpa Hugh, forcing a scream out of her. Beatrice felt like she was going insane, and maybe a small part of her was. Because these faces no longer belonged to her relatives. They were all her own.

The members of her family weren't ever there, not after she burned Ashwood to the ground. But whatever that house did to feed on her during her most recent stay, it did enough damage for something permanent, something horrifyingly permanent. Beatrice kept living her life, finding herself stalked by faces of her own. In mirrors, she stared at herself in another body. In bed, she would find herself standing at the foot, fingernails as long as knives. She would wake to the sound of screaming and soon find herself in the kitchen, levitating off the ground like Aunt Marley. She was officially unstable. Back and forth from the institution she went. She never saw herself in the hallucinations of her mother because Beatrice never found out how she died. She'd like to keep it that way.

"Ashwood," a reporter with the name of Natalia Flora sits in front of Beatrice now, the news cameras aimed right at them with the bright lights of Hollywood above. They're seated on a living room set with plush couches and chairs, a fake fireplace in the background and fake windows on either side.

Beatrice agreed to the interview because it was a paycheck. She's now nearing seventy and she never got another job once Declan fired her. She was spending too much of her time being paranoid, late, and on medication. She folds her aging hands in her lap, the name of her childhood home ringing all sorts of rusted bells inside of her head.

"Why speak about it now?" Natalia asks, folding her legs in front of her. "I mean, don't get me wrong, we're all super glad you agreed to do your first interview about that house, but we're all also wondering why now."

"It's time," Beatrice responds, her mother appearing over the shoulder of the reporter. "I'm going to be checking into Ryde Oaks at the end of the month so it's only fitting for me to speak about this before I leave. And, the money given to me for speaking about this is too generous to turn down."

Natalia laughs and glances at the producer off camera because in Beatrice's contract, it explicitly details to not discuss money deals on camera. "Ryde Oaks is the facility you've been in and out of for a handful of years, correct?"

Beatrice nods. "That's right, dear. But I'm no longer going to be in and out. I'm staying in this time."

"What do you think when you hear the word *Ashwood?*" Natalia asks, leaning forward with anticipation. Her foundation is caked on, eyeliner carefully swept over her false lashes. "What kind of emotions does it bring to you?"

Beatrice considers the question. She hasn't been to the property since she burned it down, but her return is anticipated for tonight. She thinks about the pale-yellow siding, the Victorian turret on the corner, the round driveway, the wooden porch. "Ashwood is a home. And that's a pill that I've had such a hard time swallowing. But with age, you come to appreciate these things more and more."

"How so?"

"Because I used to have this version of a home in my head," Beatrice explains, remembering. She recalls sorting through books with her mother in the study, helping Grammy Astrid bake cinnamon cookies in the kitchen, and racing through the house with the twins. "I used to think that it was a place of safety and protection. A place to go when you ever got scared. But now, I know that those scary things in the world need a home, too. They don't have a place to go to feel safe, so they must create one."

Beatrice finds herself smiling. She can see the headlines now: *Beatrice Millstone Devilishly Smiles During First Interview. Has She Been Possessed?*

"And that's what Ashwood is," Beatrice goes on. "It's not just a house, it's a safety net for the unstable caused by evil. It has a hunger that feeds on what it needs the most, desperate to feel what the people inside of it feel. It tries and tries and tries again until it can feel *something* even remotely close to the joy we feel as good, living humans." She keeps fidgeting with her fingers, staring at the reporter. "Ashwood isn't a scary place. Not anymore. I used to think that it was, even as an adult. But with age comes wisdom. And since when did living in fear get anyone anywhere?"

What's left of Ashwood still sits on the hill that Esther had built it on when Beatrice returns to it that very night once the interview wrapped. She stands in front of it at the very edge of the driveway. The base is still intact where the staircase used to be, the rest of it is splintered and rotting wood, just like the house that Beatrice thought belonged to Xander and his nana. Beatrice takes her first step onto the property since being away all those years ago, her younger self flashing through her mind as she raced through Ashwood, drowning it in gasoline.

Her aging body cracks as she makes her way across the driveway, basking in the moonlight. Her mind buzzes with familiarity, her eyes sliding over to where the garden used to be, and then to the entrance of the Jungle. She stumbles over where the front door once stood, ruined furniture and walls melted around her. Beatrice expects to see her mother or hear Aunt Marley screaming from where the kitchen used to sit, but it seems like everything is empty. No more stirring can be heard. Part of her was afraid to come back, fearing that burning Ashwood down didn't free those who were stuck inside. But it's empty. The only ghosts of Ashwood that remain in the world are the ones inside of her head: herself stalking her every move like a shadow.

Beatrice has lost her mind and she knows it. Clara knew it. The whole world knows it. But she knows what she experienced, no one else can tell her that she's wrong or claim that insanity must be in her genes. Ashwood is the cause of her becoming so unraveled, and that's no secret. Her final days at Ashwood were scattered. It's like she was a loose thread occupying a knitted sweater. With a tiny tug, she unraveled. She refuses to be put back in a place where the doctors will medicate her to shut her up, where other patients bombard her with questions surrounding her childhood. She needs to end things once and for all.

"Beatrice," Xander's voice calls out, echoing through the open house. His child self comes popping out from behind a fallen bookshelf with charred wood and books, everything around him shades of black. He's smiling, ash smeared across his cheeks. "I've been waiting for you."

"We all have." Jax pokes his head up right next to Xander.

"We missed you," Juniper agrees, the corners of her plump mouth tugging up into a bright smile, lighting up the whole night itself.

"I missed you all, too," Beatrice admits happily, hot tears flooding her eyes. She almost forgot what they all looked like. She's been seeing herself through them ever since she left and had never brought herself to look at any photos. The thought itself sparks a tear to roll down her wrinkly cheek.

"What took you so long?" Jax climbs over the bookshelf, his clothes dirty from soot.

"I got a little lost," Beatrice confesses as the three of them casually approach her, staring at her like they've been waiting for an eternity. And perhaps they have. But they're not real. The twins are proof of that because they never became House Things. Helcatia could never properly feed on them. At least Beatrice is sane enough to know they're not actually here. "That's okay, right? That I got a little lost?"

Juniper reaches out and grabs hold of her hand, her tiny one fitting in Beatrice's large one. "We all get lost in the Jungle every once and a while."

"Are you here to stay?" Xander asks hopefully, wrapping his arms around the twins to bring them in closer, a knowing smile spread across his lips.

Beatrice isn't sure what his smirk means, but she finds herself nodding her head to agree, choosing to believe him for who he was when they were kids, not the tarnished image she has of him as an adult. She chooses to believe this figment, this imagined version of him. The evil version of him no longer exists.

"I'm ready to come home."

About the Author

Brandon Kitchen grew up in Akron, Ohio, where he still resides. He often uses his hometown and the surrounding areas as a backdrop for his storytelling. When he isn't writing thrillers and mysteries, he is watching horror films, crocheting, taking pictures, or spending time with his Persian cat, Hala.